Dodging Prayers and Bullets

Karen Beatty

copyright © 2023 by Karen Beatty

All rights reserved.

No part of this book may be reproduced or transmitted in any form or by any means, electronic or mechanical, except for the purpose of review and/or reference, without explicit permission in writing from the publisher.

Cover design copyright © 2023 by Niki Lenhart
nikilen designs.com

Published by Paper Angel Press
paperangelpress.com

ISBN 978-1-957146-54-6 (Trade Paperback)

10 9 8 7 6 5 4 3 2 1

FIRST EDITION

To: my political allies, partners in adventure, and eternal friends, Janice MacKenzie and Helynn Lindsay

There are many truths in this book, though most of them are not real. *Dodging Prayers and Bullets* is a novel, meaning it is fictional—created from my imagination. Of course when you write fiction you must borrow and interpret ideas from people, stories, and life experiences familiar to you; otherwise the novel would not ring true. And to make the various contexts, timelines, and locales show up as real, much of the material in this novel has been researched. I sincerely hope that you enjoy and, better yet, resonate to this work of fiction.

Acknowledgments

WRITING AND PUBLISHING a novel can be as harrowing as it is rewarding. My wondrous daughter, actor/musician Jaime Lyn Beatty, continuously encouraged this project and even created the book cover. My sister, artist Karla Beatty, was my first editorial consultant. She was also with me on a long-ago journey to Kentucky that informed sections of this novel.

Dodging Prayers and Bullets is fictional, but I incorporated actual and imagined parts of many people, including parts of some people it was best to stay away from! Blessings to my mother who birthed eight children and to my father, a Purple Heart Veteran during World War II. I am profoundly grateful to have a large extended family who are more colorful and generous than any character I imagined for my novel.

Brenda Tepper, my kind and wise therapist, sustained me during the many glitches in my life and writing. Cathy Kuttner and Monica Indart are dear friends who continue to swoop or Zoom in to lift me up and carry me forward. Friend and neighbor Sharon Boonshoft literally walked and talked me through the pandemic. And I also want to thank accomplished and prolific author Adriana Trigiani, whom I met in a writing workshop. She buoyed my persistence by assuring me she loved my writing and that numerous rejections are an expected aspect of the publishing process. I am grateful for the psychic and professional boosts I received from early readers, including poet Sandra Storey, friend and sister-in-law Pamela Beatty, educator and returned Peace Corps Volunteer Karline Bird, and peace activist/attorney Alice Slater.

Finally, many thanks to Steven Radecki, the managing editor of publishing at Paper Angel Press. Steven, an author himself, honors and respects his writers, and personally maintains communications. I remain incredibly grateful to Acquisitions Editor Christine Morgan who truly "got" the book, and me. And, of course, much gratitude to all the professionals at Paper Angel Press who contributed to the publication of *Dodging Prayers and Bullets*.

Part One

Kentucky

1

MY EARLIEST MEMORIES go back to 1949, when I was four years old and living in Collier, a tiny mountain town in Eastern Kentucky. Inevitably, when I invite myself to remember, I become Skyla Fay Jenkins again, almost physically present in the moment, with, of course, the benefit and the distortion of an adult perspective.

The sharpest memory is when I'm six years old, the day "the disgrace" happens. That day, I'm not with my cousin and best friend Del Ray Minix, nor am I looking to be rescued. My older brother is at school and, despite Mama's admonitions, little brother Gary is about to follow Del Ray off to the swimming hole again.

To my usual dismay, my beloved playmate Del turns to me and insists, "You cain't go, Skyla Fay. Some of them big boys will be swimmin' bare-ass and they don't want us bringing no girls around." He lowers his head and looks away, so I know he's delivering this more as an apology than a command.

It makes me less inclined to argue; nonetheless I'm miffed. I want to make Del feel guilty, so I mold my face into a pout and indulge in a piteous sulk until the boys are well out of view. Not even six years old,

Dodging Prayers and Bullets

I'm already resenting what I will come to know as gender exclusion.

With Mama at work, I know not to count on anything from Cousin Alma Sue, who is supposed to be watching us, so I scoop up two handfuls of black walnuts from the bushel basket on the porch. Sitting contentedly on the ground near the well, between the back of the Free Will Baptist Church and my house, I'm cracking the walnuts with a rock.

On the embankment above, I see a big truck with an attached trailer pull over to the side of the road. While there are not many vehicles of this size on our back roads in the 1950s, it's not unusual for drivers to pull over to a well to replenish their water. It's the kind of truck my daddy drives, so at first I think maybe he's come back from staying up North with his brother Floyd. But then two strange men drop from the truck and scoot down the embankment. The shorter man is dressed in green work pants and a plaid shirt—the kind that Daddy usually wears—while the taller man has on overalls and an old brown cap.

I'm pretending not to pay the two men much mind, though you bet I have them locked in real tight at the edge of my sight. I tuck the folds of my lop-sided sundress between my legs so my underpants won't show. The men look over at me and the short one grins and calls out, "Howdy, little gal! D'ya mind if we git us some water?"

Startled, my body locks up, while my brain races in review of Mama's endless warnings about talking to strangers. Finally, I simply reply, "OK," as I look toward the men, but not at their faces, then quickly put my head down and go back to the pretense of seriously tending to those walnuts. I'm acting all nonchalant outwardly, but inside I'm a hyper-alert beast, attuned to every move they're making.

At the well, the tall man pumps longer than necessary to clear the initial stream of rusty water. He cups some in his left hand and wipes his face, slapping the leg of his overalls to dry his arm. He is pale-skinned and glummer than the short fellow. The two men appear to be having words—obviously there's a contention between them. The short one keeps peering over at me, but I act like I'm not noticing. The taller man fills his water container, takes a swig, and quickly heads back to the truck without giving me a.glance. The short man lingers a bit, downs some big gulps of water straight from the spigot, peers about, and then saunters in my direction. I look toward the house, hoping Cousin Alma Sue will appear at the door. Inside, I feel like one of Uncle Earl's jittery old mules, but I stay put.

I'm surprised when, in a really sweet voice, the short man inquires, "Do I know you, child? You look mighty familiar." I take a quick peek at him and notice that his hair is slicked back like Daddy's, but some long strands of hair from the top of his head have flopped over his forehead, almost covering one eye. The sharp jagged edge of a black walnut shell pressed hard against my palm rouses me.

I shrug, but then consider: these men probably know Daddy. Mama will surely be mad if I'm not polite to them. "My daddy's Lonnie Lee Jenkins," I offer tentatively. Then, pointing at the rig for authority, I add, "He drives a big truck jist like that one."

Smiling broadly and bobbing his head, the man reaches up and brushes the loose strands of hair away from his face as he responds, "Oh, yeah! My buddy over there knows Lonnie Lee real good. And I heard-tell of him myself. So, you're Lonnie's child! Let's go over there and ask my buddy about yer daddy. What's yer name, honey?"

I hesitate, but then consider: the man is nice, and he knows my daddy. I also think about how happy Mama will be to get word of Daddy, and I will be the one who gets to deliver the news! I smile and announce, "Skyla Fay Jenkins!"

Scampering atop the embankment ahead of the short man, and by now more curious than apprehensive, I cross the forbidden road and approach the truck. From behind, I hear the short man call out to his partner, "This here little girl got a question for ya."

Now, it's hard for me to recollect the details of exactly what happens next. We're deep into May, so the windows of the rig are rolled down and the passenger door, closest to me, is half open. I'm peering up toward the cab of the truck, when, from behind, I get the breath knocked right out of me as I'm hoisted upward by the short man. My left shoulder and right leg bang against hard edges as I'm practically folded up and shoved into the truck. The door slams shut and I'm held down while something like heavy coats or blankets that smell like dirt and oil are piled on top of me. It's near impossible to move or even breathe. I feel like I'm disappearing into a dark tunnel, where I hear gasping and sobs that I recognize, vaguely, as my own.

Someone, probably the short man, pummels the coverings on top of me, and hisses, "You shut up now, or I'll sure enough kill you." Terrified of the man, and of suffocating, I struggle to quiet the heaving of my chest and silence the pounding of my heart.

I'm familiar with my daddy's truck, so I know I'm in the sleeping bunk above and behind the driver's seat. After jolting into motion, the big rig starts speeding and bumping along the curving mountain road.

Concentrating on stifling my sobs and conserving the air under the blankets, I begin praying to God like I've never done before. I want my mama. If only I can get back home again, I won't even consider following Del Ray to the swimming hole. My heart surges in my blood like a timber log jammed in rushing floodwaters, and my entire body begins to tremble as the truck rumbles along, now in a smoother way.

After a while, my insides quiet down, so I try to make myself as small as possible, finally drifting off to sleep. The truck swerves suddenly, comes to a halt, and then starts up again. Luckily the coverings on top of me have shifted to one side and a little more air is circulating. I clap my hand over my mouth to stifle a whimper and paralyze myself in this position so the short man won't notice. In shock and suspended in a dream-like state in the sweltering heat, I pick up some snippets of the conversation between the two men. They seem to be quarreling, like at the well, only even more fervently. I catch the drift, but not nearly enough to understand the intent: "Yer big idee ..." "Crazy bastard ..." "Shut up." "Ain't got the mind for it." "Yer driving" "little late" "... crossing a State line ..." "... penitentiary."

The truck then stops completely and the voices get louder and more contentious. Abruptly, the short man yanks the covers off me and shouts, "Git up, you hear!" He begins yanking me out of the truck, which the driver has pulled off to the side of the roadway.

Now wearing sunglasses and with a cigarette dangling from his mouth, the short man is red-faced, highly agitated and gruff, his head glaring from sweat and heat like the tip of a flare. The other man, the driver, stays in the truck and says nothing; his cap is pulled down and forward. He's facing straight toward the road, like he's intent on keeping his back to me.

Lifting and shoving me forward, the short man has plenty to say. "We didn't do nothin' to you, and you better say as much. You asked for a ride in the truck, and then you made us stop and let you out to pee. Then you run off. You unnerstan?" I can barely breathe, let alone answer. The man shakes me roughly and continues, "If you say anythang different, we're gonna come back and git you and yer mama. I'll run your whole damn family down with this here truck. You unnerstan?"

"OK," I manage to whimper, and then reflexively clutch onto his arm, as I imagine he's about to dump me on the roadway.

He slaps at me and pries my fingers loose, and then pulls me toward some bushes just a short ways off the road, but on the side of the truck where no one can see. Shoving me down onto my back and pressing his left hand hard against my chest and chin, he pins me to the ground and starts tugging at my clothes with his other hand. I'm so scared it feels like I'm not connected to my body, so that's how I come upon the notion of separating myself out. It's like the real-me just up and leaves, so whatever is happening doesn't matter because I'm not there.

Suddenly, like a foghorn sounding from within a murky sea, the air horn blares from the truck. The short man startles, looks toward the road, then down at me, and shouts, "You stay right here, and don't move a-tall if you know what's good for you." He roughly flips me over unto my stomach, yanks at my dress to smooth it in front and back, and then runs for the truck. I hear the door open and slam shut and the truck roaring away.

Feeling like an old rag doll that's been tossed out, I stay put in the stillness for a long, long time until I finally manage to return to my body.

Shivering, I curl up in a ball behind the bushes. I figure I will surely die here or—worse yet—those men will come back to hurt me again, and maybe even put me back in the truck under the stinky blankets. I begin sobbing and gasping like a baby trying to catch its breath after a bad fall. I'm stiff as a two by four, yet my whole body is shaking, almost as if I'm

Dodging Prayers and Bullets

having one of them fits, like Ephraim Whitt takes. A car whizzes past on the nearby road and cool air rushes over me.

I don't know how much time goes by but somehow I manage to roll away from the bushes a bit and raise my arms to bury my head against the ground. I don't even think about standing up or running. I'm not sobbing any more, though—just kind of whimpering like a baby that's giving up on being fed. I know I'm gonna die right here and Mama will never even know.

Then I see what at first I figure is some kind of vision. A dusty green sedan seems to almost drift off the road. It slowly rolls to a stop and a man, then a woman, gets out. The man, dressed in baggy overalls, quickly steps behind a tree, to relieve himself most likely, while the woman wanders about picking wildflowers. She lets out a little yelp when she spots me, then calls out, "Look here what I done found!" She kneels down and touches my shoulder gently. "Are you lost, honey? Or sick or somethin'?"

I'm confused at first, then want to say yes, but I can't find my own voice. I start crying and shaking again.

The man approaches and encircles the woman and me, his eyes inspecting me from head to toe. He proclaims, "Don't see no noticeable injuries. Do ya reckon she run off?" Then he answers himself, "Or, more-'n likely, fell off one of them trucks from up the holler. Them mountain people is always a-loading a slew of kids onto an old pickup and drivin' into town for supplies and treats. She gots to be lost."

The woman replies, "I reckon." Then, giving a little more consideration, she shakes her head. "This one's too little to run away, bless her heart. Her people must be lookin' all over for her." She seeks to catch my eyes. "What's your name child? Kin you tell me?"

The woman is nice; she strokes my head and face and helps me sit up. I can see she has soft white skin, wavy brown hair held in place with clips, and smudges of pink lipstick around her mouth. She's wearing a flowery dress and she smells like coffee and lilacs. I wish I could talk to her—tell her about the meanness of the two men.

I hear the couple speculating about me, until the man determines, "We gots to deliver her to the sheriff. They's surely looking for her."

At that, I recoil from the woman, who is lifting me to my feet. Suddenly I find my body and my voice. "NO!" I protest. "I wanna go home. I want my mama!" The woman holds me close against her soft, flowery dress as I struggle againstin her grasp, screeching, "No po-lice!" Then I begin swallowing great gulps of air and sobbing, "You ... you take me ... on ... home. NOW!"

All the kicking and hollering that I should have mustered when the short man grabbed me are now deployed against the nice lady in the flowery dress who smells like coffee and lilacs. But the lady holds on and talks real soft until I quiet some. The man has the good sense to be still and stand back away. Finally, the woman gets it out of me that I'm Skyla Fay from Collier, which she says is some 15 miles away. They convince me to get in the car and assure me they will drive in that direction. The man tries to engage me further, declaring me "a right feisty young-un." But I just sit stiffly between them and won't say a thing except, "Y'all take me home. I wanna go home."

I'm still wary, but as we leave the straightway and roll along the more familiar winding back roads of the hills, I relax a little and try to describe my house, near the Jackson Bridge, just up behind the Freewill Baptist Church and down the embankment. I tell them Mama's name is Flo-Anna Jenkins but folks call her Flona.

But the man and nice woman are having no part of simply dropping me off. I notice them whispering and exchanging glances, and sure enough the Sheriff's Office at Collier, Kentucky comes into view. I want to protest, but I start crying again as soon as Deputy Sheriff Jeb Bailey steps out and peers into the car.

Jeb was the high school basketball star just a few years back, and he's real handsome. I know he's some kin to me but I don't exactly know how. He calls out to me, "Why, Skyla Fay Jenkins, I declare! What's got into you, chile? I bet you need some pop!" The nice woman starts explaining, but Jeb stops her, helps me out of the car, and carries me into the Sheriff's Office with the woman and man following. He calls to Sheriff Collier, and thumbs toward the couple.

Jeb takes me into the back room, closes the door, and talks to me calmly while the man and nice woman stay up front with Sheriff Collier. At one point the Sheriff ducks his head in and, without glancing at me, inquires of Jeb, "They found her with all her clothes on, but do you reckon we need Doc Wilson?"

I'm embarrassed and most grateful to Jeb, who declines the suggestion with, "No, we're having us a good talk here, and I'm pretty sure ever thing'll be OK."

I finish telling Jeb, and then have to repeat to Sheriff Collier, what little I can recall about the truck and the two men. I feel so tired, and they keep on asking me the same question: Did them fellows do anything else to hurt you?

I can only report in a quivering voice, "They banged my head, and I couldn't hardly breathe underneath them blankets. And that one feller slapped at me, but it didn't hurt, really." I don't tell about the man touching me all over and holding me down or saying he's gonna come back to run over my family. I figure I've caused enough of a ruckus already.

It's odd; I have trouble verbally describing the men and the truck, yet I can picture, so clearly in my mind's eye, the short man whose face transformed from sweet to spiteful. And, lingering in my mind forever, like a faded photograph, is a vague image of the pale man wearing overalls and the old brown cap. Had he deliberately saved me from the other man, or just got scared off? I would never know for certain, but later on I like to imagine that, in the instance when he blew the air horn, there was an essential human goodness that prevailed upon him.

My ordeal, on the day "the disgrace" happens, isn't quite over. Jeb stays with me in the back room of the Sheriff's Office, and I'm pretty much calmed down, drinking a Royal Crown Cola and nibbling on soda crackers, when I hear Mama's voice in with the Sheriff and the nice couple. Mama sounds like she's in a state, half crying and half singing, "Oh, Lord, oh, Lordy, Lordy." I'm a little taken aback, because Mama, a very proud woman, is not one to show that much fervor in public.

As she enters the back room, I see she's got a wild-eyed look. I start to throw myself into her arms and say, "I'm real sorry I caused you all this trouble, Mama." But what happens next hurts me more than being snatched by those ornery truckers. When I jump up and run toward Mama, she reaches out and smacks me hard across the face and head, while she lets loose a diatribe of accusations.

"Ain't you got no sense, chile? Getting into a truck with strangers! And them lowlifes, to boot! Whadda you mean, acting like I ain't taught you no better'n that!" The other adults look away. The nice lady who smells like coffee and lilacs gives out a little gasp and lifts the fingers of one hand to her lips.

The room is awkwardly silent, until Sheriff Collier announces to Mama and me, "I reckon Jeb can take y'all on home for now. The child can use some rest." He nods and whispers to the grownups in that enigmatic way adults have of intimating they know things kids will never, or at least should never, understand. He concludes loudly, "I'll take care of the situation on this end." Turning to Mama he adds, "Don't you fret now, Flona; I'll be in touch."

I can feel my face is red-hot now, and not just from the slap. It's stinging with a sensation previously unknown to me and different from embarrassment: it's shame. Embarrassment is a warm pink liquid that wells up to tinge your face, rendering you all squirmy, self-conscious and vulnerable to others. Shame is more of a piercing shaft, rendering you rigid and blind, completely shutting you down against comfort and reason.

Today I shamed Mama, and now I'm ashamed of myself. I did worse than run off to the creek with Del Ray, and there's no protesting that I didn't have a choice in the matter. It doesn't count that I thought there might be news about Daddy. Theat blow from Mama likewise plunged me to a new depth of rage, an emotion with which I'm generally more acquainted. I'm never going to forgive Mama for this humiliation, even though she is now holding me tight and thanking the Lord for my deliverance. Given the circumstances I know I should lie and say, "I'm sorry, Mama," but I'm barely able to breathe and my throat is a constricted knot, impenetrable to words or sound.

As Deputy Sheriff Jeb Bailey drives us home, Mama is quiet and I pretend to sleep. I'm totally bewildered. What could I have done? Mama is always expecting me to know things that have never been explained.

Jeb carries me into the house, and then he and Mama whisper a bit. (I'm to hear a lot of grown-up whispering around me from now on.) I give rise to the shame again and turn my face away when I hear Jeb repeat, "It's a good sign she had her clothes on."

Dodging Prayers and Bullets

Mama allows the young Deputy Sheriff to put me in the big bed where she herself sleeps. After he leaves, she brings a cool wet rag for my head, which is now feverish. Mama is gentle and easy now, finally enveloping me in her softness. The knot has moved from my throat into my belly, so Mama secures me to the edge of the bed, where I hang my head over and begin gagging and retching violently into the slop jar and even on the floor. "It's all right, baby," Mama consoles, "you jist git it all out now and you'll be all right. You been spared, child. I reckon the Lord has plans for you."

Inhaling Mama's scent from the old feather pillow, I fall into a deep sleep, from that afternoon all through the night, right in Mama's bed. I don't even hear my brothers Gary and Billy Dee come in.

The next day, Mama takes Gary and me to work with her at the County Court House. Everybody is really nice, but nobody talks to me about the low-life truckers or the nice lady who smells like coffee and lilacs.

2

MAMA'S RETICENCE regarding that awful day does not mean that the town hushes up about "the disgrace" that happened to Skyla Fay Jenkins. (Back then, the only secret kept in Collier, a tiny mountain town, is the location of the moonshine stills.)

According to Mama, Deputy Sheriff Jeb Bailey, a second cousin once removed from Daddy, is the grandson of Jebediah Bailey and the son of Joshua Bailey, who married a Jenkins from Stony, about twenty miles outside of Collier. So there's considerable chatter all over Crockett County, though not much in the way of resolution..

Jeb and some of the local fellows were fixing to form a posse, but they soon lose interest, after a few comforting slugs of shine plus the reassurance from Sheriff Collier that, "Them truckers is more 'n' likely from outta state with no res-to-posty, so there ain't much percentage in pursuing the situation." He further assures folks, "Them fellers ain't likely to show they faces 'round these parts again, but if'n they do, we're ready."

That halts any pursuit of the trespassers, but not the speculation over me. I know that I have disgraced Mama, and that she, as much as I, will bear the enduring humiliation.

As time passes, I continue to wince whenever "the disgrace" is referred to, or, worse yet, whispered about. In my presence, people have a way of cutting their eyes and quite obviously switching the conversation. Or, when I look toward them, they suddenly start talking loudly about something completely inane. Of course I notice, and endlessly revisit my shame.

In later years, when Mama takes to obsessing over the past to while away the present, with regard to the sheriff's negligence in authority and morality, she presses the lamentation, "It woulda been different if yer daddy was around."

Besides all that, there must be something about the ordeal of being snatched and dumped on the road that affected my breathing. When I try to fall asleep, I feel like I can't catch my breath. In panic, I sometimes cry out, "I cain't breathe! It feels like I ain't got no breath, Mama." I am also plagued by a recurring nightmare that causes me to sweat and gasp for air: A huge bird hovers above me, casting a dark, menacing shadow. In its sharp beak, the terrifying bird carries a load of hard round marble-like objects that it commences to hurl at me. Some of the marbles become embedded in my skull. I awake from this nightmare sucking desperately for air, my breathing totally out of sync with my body.

After "the disgrace," sleep, even without the frightening dream, is not always a respite. I am mortified that I began to wet the bed at night. It is truly awful when it happens, because at first I feel all warm and relaxed; then, too late, I realize the warmth is wetness. A deep dread sets in, shortly followed by a stringent smell and icy cold sheets. I try wrapping the covers under me, but there is no escaping the odor or the stain left by the permeation of urine unto a mattress. The mattress is stained, and so am I.

There is a slop jar (actually, a chipped old enamel bucket) at my bedside, so Mama complains that it is not like I have to troop to the outhouse in the dark. For some reason, I just can't seem to either hold back my pee or get up to release it. I am as intensely perplexed as

Mama is annoyingly confounded by this shameful development. Since we children all share one bed, Billy Dee, in disgust, takes to sleeping on the floor. Gary, bless him, never complains; the little guy pretends not to notice the wetness to help me avert humiliation. When I get out of bed, I try gamely to hide the wet spot by strategically rearranging the covers. I even attempt to fan away the dampness—of course to no avail. The bed is marked, and so am I.

As time goes by, Mama attributes my bed wetting to laziness, but the whining and gasping, so uncharacteristic of her free-spirited child, worries her. She doesn't, however, figure there is much to be done for me. Mama knows plenty of home remedies (including the multifarious uses for a half pint of whiskey), and she has four ointments for assorted ailments: iodine for punctures; castor oil for bellyaches; Vicks Vapo-Rub salve for colds and coughs, and Witch Hazel for aches and pains. My difficulty with breathing best fits the cold and cough category, so Mama gently rubs the Vicks on my chest and throat, and sometimes brings me into her bed to soothe me, until my breathing eases and I fall off to sleep. Of course, it is the soothing attention, not the Vicks, which actually "cures" me. As I continue to learn over the years, there are many paths to restoration in life.

Though I can't hide the wet clothing and bedding, and I own up to the breathlessness, I never tell Mama about my bad dream of the terrifying bird. Shucks, I figure, Mama's singular cure for non-injury related outbursts is simply a dismissive admonishment to, "Hush that foolishness." So instead, I attempt to counter the disconcerting "bad dream" by repeatedly conjuring up a good dream: *I'm drifting about the heavens amidst puffy white clouds of soft foam. I can jump and soar to my heart's content and never hit any hard edges, and I never have to worry about falling into a well or pit.* The imagery is simple, but deeply comforting.

Cousin Del Ray Minix, almost exactly my age, is the only one who talks straight to me about the confusion (and lingering guilt) of my ordeal with the truckers. Endlessly defending my dignity, he also tries to protect me from the "wagging tongues" and "pointing fingers" of Collier. Del Ray reassures me, "Don't you make no never-mind, Skyla Fay. You didn't do nothin' wrong a-tall. If you ever see them ornery fellers again, you jist holler for me, and I'll take my daddy's shotgun to 'em." That prospect does not afford me particular solace, but at least I feel like Del understands what really happened that day. He persists, "You know I *could* take a shotgun to them fellers."

But I insist I never want to see or hear about those fellows again. Neither do I want to talk more about "the disgrace," nor even think about it. And I don't, for years to come.

3

1983

I'M STRETCHED OUT on one of the blankets we have strategically placed at the far edge of the Washington Mall. The heat is punishing, but we've chosen a spot under the protective shade of a big locust tree, up front enough to hear the speakers and musicians, but peripheral enough for a quick escape from the crowd, or for a cooling dash into the air-conditioned Air and Space Museum.

It's 1983, and science never feels so welcoming as when you need to escape from being scorched, frozen or drenched while demonstrating on the Mall in D.C. For me, and for my friends Caitlyn and Josie, protest rallies in DC are like family reunions—we have gathered in this way since the mid-sixties for anti-war activities and in support of civil rights.

I smile at the wisps of premature gray in Josie's long frizzy hair; my hair is still long, dark and straight, but far too fine to hold a style. Caitlyn, my good-haired friend, frames her face with flowing sand-colored curls. Attired in long skirts, weathered leather sandals and dangling jewelry, our faces barely dabbed with makeup, the three of us maintain that well-preserved hippie look.

Dodging Prayers and Bullets

The "Woodstock Generation" is what we are labeled, but Woodstock was just one small component of what we deem a genuine cultural revolution in the United States. At counterculture gatherings, we understand that the music and camaraderie are tantamount to the political message. Earnest organizers of contemporary rallies sometimes lose sight of that. But not on this day: it's the twentieth anniversary of Martin Luther King's historic march on Washington, so this is an assemblage of uplifting speakers, diversely adorned demonstrators, and damn good music.

Jesse Jackson roused the crowd a few speakers ago, and just after Audre Lorde finishes an inspiring address, the moderator announces a speaker from an organization called the Gay and Lesbian Christian Alliance. Though I'm not paying attention to the exact words, I smile to recognize a tell-tale southern mountain twang in the speaker's delivery. My ear is attuned to that intrusive *r* consonant in words like washed, the dropped *w* in words like flower and the vowel substitution of *i* for *e* in words like get. The dialect reminds me of the speech patterns of my mother, Flo-Anna, who, despite decades of living outside Eastern Kentucky, has never lost her Appalachian verbal lilt, nor her propensity for letter substitutions. "Ya kin take the gal outta the hills, but ya cain't take the hills outta the gal," I chuckle to myself.

Sitting up and stretching forward to get a look at the speaker, I'm stunned that he seems familiar, as in, a face morphed from a long-gone past. The straight reddish hair is longer and receding in the front, but the height, the pale complexion, and the slight build would be about right. The man is attired in belted jeans and a conservative blue dress shirt, open slightly at the collar. A line from Sam Shepard's play *Buried Child* pops into my head: *I thought I saw a face in his face.*

Is it possible? Could Wally 'Preacherboy' Perkins of Collier, Kentucky be here, in this place, thirty years later?

"Sky, hey! Are you OK?" probes Caitlyn, who has noticed me staring at the podium with an odd expression on my face.

She, Josie, and my sister Dory are perched on the adjacent blankets, along with several of Dory's shorthaired women friends who flaunt unshaven armpits in tank tops and loose jeans—emblems of emerging young feminists and activist Lesbians. Caitlyn's husband and son are in the Air and Space Museum.

"Mmm ... not sure," I hesitantly begin. "This sounds crazy, but I think I know that guy, from way back. Anybody have a copy of the program?"

When the speaker was introduced, I did not catch his name, and neither the organization nor the speaker is noted on the flyer Dory passes over. She's convinced his identification and affiliation are omitted from the program because he's gay. "Black Power's not ready to formally acknowledge Gay Power," she concludes, and then relents. "Oh well, at least they let him get up there and speak. Even that surprises me."

"I'll be right back," I announce, standing up and moving toward the elevated speakers' dais. I slither expertly around the bodies packed close together on the Mall and hop over blankets and mounted signs scribbled with messages of hope and denunciation.

Preacherboy Perkins. I grin to myself. Could that little creep have morphed into a partially balding senior leader for gay civil rights? Gay, I believe, but a liberal political activist? Not possible. Anticipating the speaker will exit the platform from the left after the applause, I maneuver through the crowd to intercept him. I want to approach him, but not startle the guy with a shrill accost. That proves ironic, because when I get up close enough to speak, I can barely find my voice. "Preach? Is that you?" I struggle to project.

The man turns toward me, looks straight in my face and bellows, "Why, Skyla Fay Jenkins, I declare!"

We fall into each other's arms, hugging and laughing as we never would have done in Kentucky. Our last encounter, almost 30 years ago, had been at the funeral of Wally's mother, Maudie June Perkins, in the tiny mountain town of Collier.

"It's Sky now," I tell him. "Geez, I haven't been called Skyla Fay for longer than I even dare to recall!"

"Well," counters Wally, "Preacherboy is a handle I sure put to rest more than a couple of decade ago." He smiles. "It's Walter, now."

I blush, put my hand to my mouth, and mumble, "Sorry." I notice him checking out my ring-free left hand. Feeling the need to explain myself, I disclose awkwardly."I'm living with a guy and I'm here for the King commemoration, and for lending support to gay rights of course. Especially for my sister Dory and her friends. You never met Dory; she was born in New Jersey."

Walter smiles and nods kindly. "Right. The last child of Flo-Anna's I recall was your brother Lucas Wesley. But Skyla Fay, I mean, Sky, I'm real sorry about Gary. I actually thought of contacting your family when I heard, but I wasn't sure how you'd all take to hearing from me—you know, after all this time."

"I appreciate that. Mother probably would have loved hearing from you. I don't think she ever recovered from that whole thing; it was pretty much the end of her. Though Dad actually did some healing afterwards. He's not doing so well right now—physically, I mean. But Mother ... I won't say she hadn't slipped before, especially after she left Kentucky, but she never really came back after Gary. It was hard to be around her for years, because he was all she talked about." I think to myself, *it's still hard to be around my mother, but for different reasons,* but I say to Walter, "I bet she'd get a kick out of seeing you. She always defended you, you know. I just couldn't take it when she tried to find God's great purpose in ..." Remembering that Walter is religious, I trail off and tack on, "Sorry, I don't mean to offend you."

Walter shakes his head and waves an uplifted hand. "I guess you don't know me. But then, how could you? I have to admit I was a hideous child." Seeing me shrug, he insists, "No, no, don't deny it. I'm the first to own up to it. I always tell people it took some pretty Amazing Grace to save a wretch like me! However, I do believe I've made up for it. These days, I aim to see that God's great purpose is not distorted to sanction killing and prejudice in this country—or abroad, for that matter. Of course, that's why we're all here today."

"Right," I quickly concur, relieved to get off the topic of Mother and Gary. "This country has a long way to go in civil rights and gay rights, especially homophobia. But I feel like we've come far enough that we're not going to get entangled in another mess like Vietnam, at least not in our life time."

Walter nods in agreement. I wonder if he's as stunned as I that the two of us, after 30 years, are having this conversation. Feeling awkward and non-tethered, I still want to convey enthusiasm, like at a high school reunion when you meet up with someone you used to know but not really.

I lift my arms, palms outstretched toward Walter. "So, like, where are you living?"

"Hold on," he says, reaching for his wallet and taking out a business card, and then awkwardly extricating a pen from his shirt pocket. "I want to give you my home number." He jots the number on the back of the card and hands it over.

I quickly glance at the front of the card: *The Reverend Walter P. Jennings, Executive Director, Gay and Lesbian Christian Alliance.* Jennings? That was not his name in Kentucky. *This is going to be good,* I decide, barely containing a guffaw.

Walter immediately addresses the surprised look on my face. "The name Jennings is a long story. But you might have guessed I'd be gay. And a minister—a preacher if you will, right here in D.C." He grins. "Of course, my politics and beliefs are a little different these days. I hope you can get to meet my partner, Reuben. He works at the National Archives—actually, he's here in the crowd somewhere." Walter momentarily surveys the crowd, and then turns back to me. "Skyla, I surely hope you'll call me. Are you still up there in New Jersey?"

"No, but William—well, you knew him as Billy Dee—and Luke are. They—and their wives, of course—do most of the care taking of Mother and Daddy. I'll have to catch you up on everyone—a few surprises there—though, maybe not—seems like you've lived it all. I'm a college professor, by the way. I live in the City—New York."

"I've heard of it," Walter teases. "So, it seems we've both come a long way from Crockett County, Kentucky!"

I nod and smile in relief. "Are you in touch with any of the folks back home? Maybe y'all heard that my cousin Del Ray Minix is not doin' too well." I give myself a metaphysical slap for continuously slipping into mountain dialect. I hope Walter hasn't noticed, or doesn't think I'm making fun of him.

"Not really," he responds to my inquiry about Del Ray. "Your Aunt Eula is the only one I ever kept up with. I owe my life to her and Earl for getting me out of Collier after Mama died. That's part of the long story, of course. Anyway, she told me your Papaw Reece had died, and then about Gary. And that was just awful about her boy Petey. But I haven't been in touch with Eula for quite a few years now, which I actually feel pretty bad about. You know how it's even harder to pick up the conversation again, when you've let it go so long."

"Yep, I know exactly what you mean," I honestly concur, finally feeling somewhat less like an awkward adolescent having to explain herself. "It seems like we have lots to talk about, Walter. Can you come and meet my sister? She's with some friends over there by the Air and Space Museum."

He shakes his head, seeming genuinely disappointed. "Unfortunately, I've got to run to another engagement, and I'm already late. I hope you'll give me a call, tonight or tomorrow if you can, or as soon as you get back to New York." He pauses and looks me in the eyes. "You know God had a hand in our meeting here!"

Still resisting any possible God ploys, I parlay that remark into something more secular with, "Oh, I'm a believer in destiny! Definitely." I promise to call, adding, "There's so much we have to catch up on, past and present."

I'm simultaneously elated and dazed, like a lottery winner who is yet to turn in the ticket. Drifting somewhat aimlessly in the direction of our blankets, I meander past the spot for a considerable distance before catching myself and turning back. Now it seems fortuitous that I opted to take a hotel room near the train station tonight, rather than to "crash" with Dory and her friends, or take up the offer of a ride back through Baltimore with Caitlyn's family and Josie. My original intent was to use the single room at the hotel for some needed meditation and "down time." I have a new agenda in DC now, because I definitely plan to give Walter P. (for Perkins) Jennings a call.

Realizing that the Reverend will likely be at church on Sunday morning (I intend to pass on that), I force myself to call him from the hotel that very Saturday evening and make arrangements to see him on Sunday afternoon, before I head back to New York. Caitlyn and Josie have departed, and my sister Dory, who is not feeling the urgency of the Kentucky connection, has made Sunday plans with her friends.

So, the Saturday night after the 20th anniversary celebration of Martin Luther King's famous "I Have a Dream" speech, with my adrenaline in over-drive, I lay in a hotel bed in Washington, DC flipping through the back pages of my life. It feels like much of it was spent dodging prayers and bullets. Meeting up with "Preacherboy" Perkins has kicked up a dust storm of memories; I have no choice now but to peer into the obscurity to see what the light turns up and where the dirt settles. I force myself to return to that little child and contemplate the things that happened to me before and beyond "the disgrace."

4

1949

OUR SHACK IN COLLIER is built at the bottom of the embankment beneath Stella Adams' Second Hand Store. The store occupies the top floor of the building, which is situated on top of the embankment, the front porch level with the road. The embankment drops off to the abandoned back lot of the Free Will Baptist Church. The lot and embankment are parallel to Churning River, but because the river bends and widens just after this point, the front of the church also faces a deeper section of the river with more undergrowth.

At the far end of the weed and trash strewn back lot, in the lower level of the building, is where Mama and we three children live. We are just a few yards from the banks of a more shallow section of the capricious Churning River, which is handy for baptisms and summer splashes, but treacherous during periods of heavy rain and flooding. In the middle of the abandoned lot is a working well, which our family shares with the Freewill Baptist Church. Whenever Stella Adams takes a notion to open the store above us, Mama feels a little safer in the shack below, and if Mama is at work at the Court House, she always rests easier knowing Stella can back up our babysitter, the derelict Cousin Alma Sue.

Stella Adams, known as a right-smart God-fearing lady with a happy face, always wears the best of the seconds in Collier. As the proprietor of Stella Adams' Second Hand Store, she gets first pickings on all the clothes left behind by the dearly departed, or those not immediately claimed from the clothing drop at the Freewill Baptist Church.

Since our impoverished little town is Stella's main source for merchandising, she maintains a tiny store with irregular hours. Compared to my mama, Stella Adams is shorter, with a darker complexion and more curves, but the two women dress as fine and proud as anyone in Collier. They are long-time friends and gossip swappers. Unlike Mama, Stella is big-bosomed, so that when she lifts me up or bends down to give me a trifle of some sort, I feel shielded, and I get to handle and admire whichever beautiful brooch adorns her shelf-like chest that day. Even though Mama won't accept charity, from time to time Stella drops off a few special items at our shack, like my favorite off-white sundress.

I live in the shack with Mama and my brothers, Billy Dee and Gary Cooper -- and eventually Luke, who will make his presence known shortly. In the Appalachian Mountains of Eastern Kentucky during the late 1940s, my family doesn't require that much, which is a good thing. There's no kindergarten in Collier, so only Billy Dee is old enough to need school clothes to attend Miss Tackett's class in the one-room school.

If I were to describe my brother Billy Dee (short for William Dean) in simple nautical terms, he would be a rudder. Not a flowing sail or a power-charged motor, but the instrument that guides the craft and keeps it on course. He taught himself to read before he attended a day of school. With close-cropped wren-brown hair, he dresses modestly in muted colors, and his pale freckled face is neither handsome nor odd. Different from most of our cousins and me, Billy Dee insists on wearing shoes and socks. My big brother is taking no chances on stepping on a rusty nail or splinter or incurring a bloody slice on his foot from a sharp piece of glass or stone. Seven years old and tall for his age, Billy Dee is what people call "a team player," meaning reliable, and neither a star nor a bungler.

Of course my mama, Flo-Anna Reece Jenkins, has to have some work dresses that double as Sundy-go-ta-meetin' clothes. She's proud that she was once called "the prettiest girl with the prettiest dress" in Crockett County. But that was before she married Daddy. Nowadays, Daddy is not around, and Mama has seen "a heap o' sorrow." Still, she's proud and won't ever permit one of her own to pose for a photograph without our being dressed in our cleanest and best. In astonishment, I have beheld Mama scrutinizing a family snapshot and altering someone's hair or eyes with a pen. Or, if Mama doesn't in the least like the expression on a particular face, she'll tear the head right off that photo.

I've heard Stella Adams cluck her tongue and whisper to her friend Daisy Howard, "So pitiful; Flona (Mama's nickname) living alone in that shack with all them children—and ya know another on the way—with no electricity or running water." I'm stumped by the child on the way business, but I grin to myself when Stella adds, "But Lawd, Flona don't never complain! And she keeps them young-uns clean!" I know her saying that proves Stella actually likes Mama.

Mama also won't allow any fun poked at us children or at her own self; we all have to be well scrubbed and dressed proper for church as well as photographs. Mama doesn't insist on shoes, though, so I generally don't wear any. On steamy dog-day afternoons my little brother, Gary Cooper, and I often play in nothing but white cotton underpants. Billy Dee is more self conscious, so in addition to shoes he keeps his shirt and pants on.

The Christmas Eve just after Daddy abandoned us to the shack in Collier, Mama is explaining in a dispirited voice that, "Sometimes ole Santa cain't make his way to ever' house, so children got to make do with their stockings." She's trying to sound matter-of-fact, as if this is something ordinary, but I can tell she's as hurt as we are. I don't care so much about Santa not coming, but on Christmas Eve it's awfully hard to bear the burden of Mama's despair.

I can tell Billy Dee is playing along with Mama, trying to be cheerful in the face of our obvious melancholy. Our stocking stuffers typically consist of a bit of fruit, some sweets, including molasses pull

Dodging Prayers and Bullets

candy, and a trinket or two. This year on Christmas morning there are only the sweets. Billy Dee encourages Gary and me to make the best of our meager offerings, attempting to abate our disappointment by handing over to each of us a piece of his candy. I don't want to take it, but I fear he will feel worse if I don't. Forcing smiles, we wish each other Merry Christmas in quavering voices. And give hugs to Mama. Silently, willingly, my family weaves a protective web of pretense around each other.

Spirits are mighty low this morning until we hear a boisterous, "Ho-ho-ho" at the door. Standing there is Stella Adams, with a bundle of the prettiest wrapped packages I've ever seen, plus as good a story as is called for. "Merry Christmas, y'all, and Glory Be!! I reckon old Santa got mixed up and left these here bundles upstairs in my store. Surely they're for y'all!" I wonder if what she is reporting can be true, but Billy Dee is enthusiastically backing the claim, and Gary is genuinely thrilled. I can tell Mama, her face ablaze with humiliation, is holding her tongue.

Stella hands the packages around and urges, "Go on and open 'em now. It's Christmas y'all!"

Gary's gift is a brand new bean shooter, fresh hewn from a forked limb of a laurel tree, the rubber sling made of red inner tubing, and the pouch fashioned from the tongue of a leather shoe. (Stella's brother Doyle, known around the county as a fine woodworker and whittler, was one of Santa's elves that year.) Barely four years old, Gary is too little to use the bean shooter as a toy, much less as a weapon, but he loves holding it, stretching the rubber and smelling the laurel wood where the bark has been shaved.

Billy Dee promises to help Gary learn to use the bean shooter as Mama instructs, "Only outside, away from the house, and don't be pointing that thing in nobody's face." Billy Dee's gift is a beautifully illustrated edition of Treasure Island; the book is secondhand and worn, but splendidly leather-bound with gold leaf around the edge of each page. Billy Dee is proud to own it.

I'm as happy for him and Gary as I am for myself. My gift is a little baby doll that Stella has tucked into a white eyeleted newborn's gown. The gown hangs on the doll like a potato sack, nonetheless rendering me nothing short of enchanted. The doll has one droopy eye, but I don't care a bit and genuinely enthuse, "Look, Mama, it's a-winkin' at me." The body of the doll is stuffed with straw and the hard plastic-molded head has drifted slightly to one side, but the lips and cheekbones are very well defined. A tangled mass of nylon reddish-brown "hair" is lifting slightly along the edges where it has been glued to the doll's head. I pull the baby doll close to my body, support the head, and begin rocking, immediately bonding in protective attachment.

None of us children could have fully rejoiced in that bountiful Christmas morning if Stella had not also brought a gift for Mama. Mama protests her inclusion, but when she opens the box and beholds three little pewter angels, one to represent each of her children, she nods and smiles at Stella. "These here young-uns is my truest gift and blessing," Mama says, allowing her tears to flow freely.

Since we have each received something special, I don't have to be shy about celebrating my good fortune. I truly adore this doll—I sleep with it and gently transport it everywhere. I love to bury my fingers in the matted hair and flip the drooped eyelid up and down by the stiff eyelashes. I call the doll, "Baby."

That's why I really can't tell what got into Mama several mornings later. I'm toting the doll about as usual, when she asks to take a look at it. Mama points out that the matted hair glued to the baby doll's head is peeling further back. "Why, it would look 100 percent better if you was to jist yank that filthy thing off." Appalled and hurt, I will not hear of such a thing. I begin to feel increasingly apprehensive as Mama tugs at the hairline, persisting in convincing me to denude the doll's head.

Later I wonder: Was Mama's pride offended by the grubby look of the hair? Was she jealous of my attachment to the doll? Did she somehow resent Stella's salvaging Christmas when she could not? I never understood what possessed Mama to continue picking at my doll. All I understood at age four and a half was that I was feeling fiercely possessive and protective of "my baby."

I grab the doll out of Mama's hand and scramble under a table against the wall, the doll clutched to my body. A battle of wills ensues, as Mama tries to coax me out from under the table. When I won't give in, she reaches under and snatches the doll away, sending me reeling against the table legs. I begin to wail in utter desolation as she spitefully rips the swatch of hair off the baby doll's head.

"Look, here," she insists, proudly holding the doll up to me, "it looks tidy and pretty now—jist like a newborn baby."

I'm having no part of it. My body is wracked by rage, but my voice is oddly silenced. When Mama shoves the scalped doll back under the table toward me, I take it by the arm and heave it away like it's the hot potato in the game of that name. I turn my face to the wall, curl up in a ball and refuse to come out or talk. Eventually, Gary crawls under the table and snuggles up against me. I remain like that for almost an hour, until there are no more tears or whimpers. At dinner I barely pick at the plate of pinto beans and turnip greens Mama sets before me. I'm obliged to listen while she is in turn defensive, saddened, annoyed by, and finally dismissive of my obstinacy.

Afterwards, I refuse to pick up that doll or accept any other doll. That day I learned the painful truth that it's possible to cold out hate the one you love the most.

The following weekend, the adults are gathered around the oak table in the kitchen at the homeplace, the big house where my granddaddy, Papaw Reece, lives. Del Ray's mama, Clytie, is complaining to Mama and Papaw about "what a trial" her son is. "Why, it's the sins of the father visited upon the children," she proclaims, referencing the biblical Book Of Exodus. Mama then relates the doll incident, and they all commence to laugh.

"That scrawny child got a stubborn streak deep as a well," chuckles Papaw about me.

Meanwhile, Del Ray and I are skulking on the kitchen porch within earshot, as we are frequently given to doing. Seething over what the grownups have said, we vow never to talk about our future children as if they are invisible or don't have a lick of sense.

5

I PICK MY WAY UP the embankment and haul myself into sitting position on the side of the front porch of Stella Adams' Second Hand store. Cautiously, I jiggle my bottom sideways across the worn boards, which are brittle and sharp along the edges like old ragged toenails. Only a threadbare layer of sagging underpants protects my bare butt.

Skinny and small-boned at five-years-old, I don't require much space to situate myself on a smooth section of Stella's porch, where I can dangle my legs and face the road. I take my mighty sweet time in choosing a spot where I can breathe easy, though, because I recollect all too well what it feels like to get pierced by a splinter. Of course, that isn't nearly as awful as stepping on an old rusty nail and having Mama hold you down to yank it out, and then pour iodine on it. Still, it behooves me to be cautious around those old boards.

On this particular day, when I get the idea of sitting on the porch in the hopes of being rescued by a passing motorist, Stella Adams has

Dodging Prayers and Bullets

locked up the secondhand store and gone on home. It's months before "the disgrace" will happen, so I'm relieved that Stella is nowhere to be found. In our shack below the store, Cousin Alma Sue has jammed the door shut against her pesky charges. I know she's in there smoking her Lucky Strikes and keeping secrets with her sometimes boyfriend. The most supervision Alma Sue ever gives us anyway is to moan, "You children oughtn't be doing that."

So, with my brothers and cousin Del Ray out and about, Mama at work, and Stella gone on home, it's an opportune time for my plan. I sit on Stella's porch and wait for a car to come by with a handsome man, or maybe two or three of them. The elastic is loose on the legs of my white cotton underpants, so I hold my knees together and swing my feet as best I can, smiling brazenly so that my rescuers will be sure to notice. They will take me away and keep me as their little girl. They will be so nice: buy me candy and toys, and, best of all, they will sit me on their laps, stroke my long dark hair, and hug and kiss me lots. But they won't touch me "down there," like Daddy's friend, that old red-faced Artie Johnson, keeps trying to do.

My imaginings never go any further, and all too shortly I'm to learn that men who want to take you away are never handsome and gentle, and they don't want to take care of you and let you be their baby girl.

I long to be special, though sometimes I find it rather embarrassing when I am. My most striking feature is the color of my eyes, which changes depending on the light or what I wear. Usually my eyes look grayish blue, like Mama's, but at times they are more of a dusty green, like Daddy's. To compound this oddity, there is an inexplicable brown speck on the cornea of my left eye. "Them's hazel eyes," Mama informs me, about the changing colors.

Gary Cooper, recalling the picture on the Witch Hazel medicine, asks Mama, "Is Skyla Fay a witch?"

"No, baby," Mama reassures the four year old. "Skyla Fay's jist special." Of course, I like hearing that.

On this day, though, I eventually get tired of waiting there on Stella's porch without anybody noticing, so I slide back down the embankment and go to sit on the front steps of the Freewill Baptist

Church across from the Jackson Bridge, that being the outer perimeter of where Gary and I are allowed to play. Crossing the road to the bridge or the road above the embankment is definitely prohibited by Mama. I'm always put out when Del permits only Gary Cooper, a year younger than me, to accompany him to the swimming hole, because it's me (to Mama's eternal chagrin) who is Del's soul companion and running partner. When Del proclaims to Mama his intention to make me his bride in the future, Mama informs him, "Nowadays the government don't allow no first cousins to marry."

"Well, then," counters Del, "I'll jist have to write a letter to the government for special permission." Then he whispers to me, "Cause you 'n' me was made for each other, I know that much."

Thus, being left behind on yet another adventure to the swimming hole, just because the boys are swimming bare-ass, is clearly a gyp. At least I hope that later, when Mama finds out Gary has run off again, she will love me better for staying back.

Not long after, I brace myself against the church steps when I spot Wally Perkins sashaying across the Jackson Bridge toward me. At age eleven, he's six years older than me, but he's known around Collier as a mama's boy. Folks call him Preacherboy, or the Preach for short, because he's forever citing scripture, mainly from the dark side of the Good Book: *Ye serpents, ye generation of vipers, how can ye escape the damnation of Hell?* (Mat. 23:23). Preacherboy also always entreats, "Praise Jesus, are you saved yet, Skyla Fay Jenkins? Have you been washed in the blood of the lamb?"

I can't find it in my heart to love the Preach as the Bible instructs, and the passages he recites from the Bible frighten me. Mama is a comfort when she says, "That Wally Perkins is a big old crybaby, always running his mouth about salvation. He best be lookin' to his own sorry self."

Maudie June, Preacherboy's mother, used to be Mama's friend, and was formerly, by all accounts, "a right pretty, God-fearing young lady." But after giving birth to Wally out of wedlock, Maudie isolated herself, became suspicious of everyone, and simply doted on her baby boy. Eventually, she turned into a regular religious fanatic, as if she aimed to devote her life and the child's to Jesus to make up for the

Dodging Prayers and Bullets

shame of delivering—here, Mama pauses, looks about, and whispers, "A bastard."

Mama once told me that as the years went on, she gave up on Maudie, and had to keep a sharp eye on Wally after he peed in my and Gary's faces when we were "jist little thangs." Truthfully, I have no recollection of that, but I do recall the time the Preach got Gary and Del Ray to play a really mean trick on me. He instructed them to sit together on one end of the teeter-totter and keep me suspended in the air at the other end, where I had to grip the board with both hands to keep from falling. Then Wally put a garter snake down the back of my sundress. Gary didn't know any better, and Del Ray felt real bad about it right away, but Preacherboy giggled insanely and taunted me as I squirmed and screamed until the snake liberated itself from the confines of my dress. Finally Cousin Alma Sue heard the ruckus, deigned to emerge from the shack, and threatened to tell on the Preach.

When Preacherboy's mama came to collect him and heard the story, the Preach started bawling like a big baby and fibbed, "Skyla Fay done blasphemed the name of the Lord. The way of the wicked is an abomination unto the Lord. Jesus told me to bestow an evil upon her from the Garden of Eden. That's why I done it."

Of course, without my mama around, Maudie June was free to take her son's part, and she pointed at me and declared to Cousin Alma Sue, "All I knows is that there Jenkins gal is always a-chatterin' and squirmin' in church when she oughter be a-prayin'."

From that day on, I pretty much figure it's the likes of Maudie and Preacherboy Perkins that I need to be saved from. Still, like Mama, I sometimes feel sorry for the Preach, because he seems so alone and sorrowful in his campaign for righteousness.

Moreover, I once heard Stella Adams snigger that Wally's nickname, Preacherboy, also reflects his heritage: his mama, Maudie June Perkins, had taken up with a rambling preacher man some years back, and Wally was supposedly the fruit of that unholy alliance. The preacher, who had been on loan from the Tabernacle Evangelist Mission of Tennessee to the Born Again Church of Jesus Christ in Sow Holler, Kentucky, never claimed Maudie as his bride. Maudie however, who seemingly lives hand-to-mouth in a house left to her by her deceased parents, appears on a regular basis at the general store with cash in hand. And from time to time Wally acquires something special, like that almost-like-new bicycle, which is the envy of every boy in Collier.

And that isn't all about Wally. There's talk about him. "That Preacherboy is always hanging on his mama and listening to the grownup talk. It ain't natural, him being so prissy." Slightly built, with a freckled face and a crown of red hair, Preacherboy has a mean little mouth and a high pitched, slightly lilting voice that invites mockery. Around the adults, he feigns humility and praises the Lord, but when he's alone with the little kids, and out of sight of his mama, the Preach drops the polite demeanor and assumes the role of God's vindicator. One of his favorite condemnations is from the book of Deuteronomy: *I will heap mischiefs upon them, I will spend mine arrows upon them. They shall be burnt with hunger, and devoured with burning heat, and the bitter destruction. I will also send the teeth of the beasts upon them, with the poison of serpents of the dust* (32:32). Preacherboy is lonely all right, and there is little wonder why.

So, sitting by myself on the steps of the Freewill Baptist, I feel my stomach tighten as Wally Preacherboy Perkins steps off the bridge and glides towards me. "Praise the Lord, Skyla Fay Jenkins!" he calls out, heading up the church steps toward me. Then, crossing his arms in indignation and jabbing a bony finger at me, Preacherboy queries with insinuation, "Why you out here by yerself?"

"I jist felt like it," I halfway mumble.

"You're a-lyin'!" screeches Wally. "Jesus is gonna set the devil after you. You oughta be heedin' the holy Bible: *For the wages of sin is death. And the smoke of their torment ascendeth up forever and ever: and they have no rest day or night*. Eternal burning for you, Miss Skyla Fay." He follows up this infernal future threat with a present one of his own, "I bet Gary run off to the swimmin' hole with Del Ray, and I'm tellin'."

With that, Preacherboy turns abruptly and scurries back across the bridge toward town. I know for certain he will use the information about the missing boys to endear himself to my mama by feigning concern over the whereabouts of Gary.

Well, I'm a little scared of the devil, especially at night, but I'm mostly powerful angry at the Preach, because now I won't get to be the one to tell Mama about Gary following Del Ray off. I scrunch up my face at Wally as ugly as I know how, stick out my tongue, and watch as he crosses back over the Jackson Bridge into town, off limits to me, but where Mama works at the Court House.

I assess that my best option to get back at the Preach now is to ally with Del Ray, who is frequently walloped because of Preacherboy's snitching. And we soon do get even, by stealing the Preach's almost-like-new bicycle and tossing it over an embankment of Churning River near my house where he finds it in less-than-almost-like-new condition.

Delford (*don't y'all be calling me that*) Ray Minix is known around Collier simply as Del. The Delford is after his long departed, little mourned, paternal grandfather and the Ray after his adored maternal grandfather, Lacy Ray Reece. Del was born with curly brown hair that he insisted on shearing as soon as he was old enough to notice it made him look pretty. He has one of those distinguishing upward sweeping lip curls that look cute on little kids and sexy on teenage boys. On him it is more like a grin than a snarl. Del is a lean and supple youth with serious brown eyes that quickly survey and get to the gist of most circumstances. He is good-natured, but wary. The wariness enables him to elude the perils of growing up with an abusive father and a certifiably loony mother. Blessed with raw intelligence, a keen sensitivity to human nature, and an aptitude for art, Del Ray has dreams to counter his mama's deranged visions and talent to counter his daddy's cold brutality. He will almost prevail.

"Good old Del," I sigh to myself.

His daddy is a bootlegger who has little use for the boy, other than as a kicking target during drunken revels. Now, old Rufus Minix always smiles at me and never did any harm to my brothers or me, but everybody knows that man is a trip-wire. When his ire is up and he starts swinging his feet and fists, if his boy Del isn't around for a whupping, any local urchin, or certainly his wife Clytie, will serve just fine.

"A mean drunk is the worst kind of bootlegger," Del Ray informs me. "Pa drinks all the good stuff hisself, and gets all the wrong people plum mad at him. It'll likely all come back on him one-a-these days."

His words will prove prophetic regarding his daddy, and he gets a few other predictions exactly right as well. Del Ray Minix is quick and clever; unfortunately the schemes and dreams, which come to him like so many penny balloons, generally pop right in his face.

Over the years, though, my heart truly aches for Del when, within the confines of Collier, some of his truly fine notions dissipate in that slow, sad manner of a deflating balloon.

6

WHEN DADDY LEFT and my family moved below Stella's store, Mama forbade us to cross the river, but the woods beckoned so relentlessly that she finally acquiesced and simply beseeched us to go in groups or pairs, and to stay away when the water is surging.

And surge, it does! During floods, I watch local fellows don wading boots and head out in rowboats to pull in people and drifting goods. Even when it's not surging, the river can be fraught with danger, especially about a half mile below my house, at the deepest part, where young boys have drowned during trysts of playful abandon. Grownups incessantly warn the enticements of Churning River can be perilous. My cousins and I will eventually learn this the way all before us have—the sorrowful way.

For the most part in the 1950s, however, warnings about such dangers go unheeded, simply because Churning River is one of those essentially adult-free zones of youthful escape and derring-do. In Collier, children do not bond with, communicate earnestly with, or even rely much upon their parents. Children are expected to improvise their own fun and social relationships and not add their neediness to the deficits of the family. Little wonder that the smooth-flowing currents, the rock-strewn solidity, and the leafy hideaways of the river and woods beckon such non-tethered children. Whenever we vandalize or steal something, the river is the ideal place to rendezvous to savor the spoils and avoid scrutiny by anyone in authority. On summer days and after school, with Daddy gone, Mama at work, and Billy Dee perpetually studying or working odd jobs, there is only the lumpen Cousin Alma Sue as our designated caretaker. So Gary and I are essentially free to ramble

I come to appreciate, at a young age, the impermanence of life, the nuances of friendship, the affinity (sometimes inexplicable) for kin and kind. Such tenets should have served as clues, I suppose, about how quickly and dramatically everything in my life could change.

And the changes start one spring afternoon in 1953 when Mama comes home from work early and seems impatient and frenetic. She directs Cousin Alma Sue to fetch her friend Daisy Howard, and sends Billy Dee up the embankment to ask Stella Adams to come down from the store. Stella quickly takes charge and instructs us children, "Y'all go on outside and play now. Your mama will be jist fine, and she's fixing to have a surprise for you."

We obey and head in the direction of Churning River to scour for sour green apples. I bite cautiously around the wormholes and bruised sections of the apples and toss the scraps into the weeds. Frankly, I never understand why folks say you'll get a bellyache from eating crab apples. I can eat green apples and black walnuts all day; sometimes I even do, when Alma Sue doesn't offer Gary and me anything to eat while Mama is at work.

Mama's surprise is taking a considerable while, so Billy Dee corrals Gary and me and we climb down the bank to the edge of Churning River. Gary and I sit on some rocks and watch the dragonflies. Eventually Gary joins Billy Dee in gathering flat stones to skip across the river, but I'm not in a playful mood. I sit in reverie, trying to keep my eyes on the glittery dragonflies and my mind on the gentle flow of the water, rather than thinking about whatever is detaining Mama.

It would be a good day to try a raft, I reflect. Some of Billy Dee's friends have promised to help us construct the next raft. The last one looked pretty good, but it sank as soon as Juddy Jeffers tried to climb up on it. Watching him get drenched was pretty funny, but I'm genuinely disappointed the raft was not buoyant. I dream of lying back on a raft and drifting along toward the mouth of the river, just like boys in story books do.

We hear Daisy calling us and scamper back up the bank of Churning River. My heart starts racing when I see Doc Wilson leaving our house and walking toward the road in front of the Freewill Baptist Church. But then I see Daisy Howard is all smiles. "Y'all got you a new little brother," she announces. "Come on now, and take a look-see for yer self."

Mama appears tired and pale, but she proudly introduces us to our new brother, Lucas Wesley Jenkins. To me he looks rather puny, but I deem it well worth the wait for him when Aunt Eula shows up with some baked ham leftovers and a fresh apple pie.

I can't wait to tell Del Ray about Lucas Wesley, but when I authoritatively inform him Doc Wilson brought the baby to Mama in his black bag, Del just scoffs, "That ain't the truth, Skyla Fay. Babies don't come that way. They's birthed, jist like puppies." That makes more sense to me than what I have been told by the grown-ups about the black bag.

I marvel that Del can figure such things out, but I still have trouble trying to envision Mama actually birthing Luke. It seems to me there should be a big hole in Mama's belly where the baby came out, but when I ask to take a look, she just laughs and tells me, "Quit actin' so simple."

7

A FEW DAYS AFTER I turn seven and "the disgrace" is not the only thing folks consider about me, Del Ray Minix turns up at our shack. He signals me to sneak down the lane with him to hide in the outhouse, where we can talk secrets.

"It's time you and me done our vows, Skyla Fay," Del begins. "Ya know we was made for each other, and that's all there is in this here world. Listen here: Del Ray and Skyla Fay, them names fit just like a poem." I'm smiling and nodding as Del continues, "Married people, they got secret initiations to perform before they make their vows. I reckon it's time for you and me to do such."

I'm beginning to get a little wary, but stay attentive, because I know Del Ray has his ways of finding out about grownups.

I balk, however, when he concludes, "You have to show me what you got, and I show you mine, and that means we is each other's intended."

Now I'm onto him and let him have it. "I know what you got, Delford Ray Minix! I got me some brothers and we take us a bath together ever' Saturday."

And that's the truth. My family has a circular galvanized aluminum tub that Mama fills with hot water on Saturday night. First, Gary and I sit in the tub and then take turns standing while Mama scrubs us down. We only have a single ragged-edged towel, so Gary and I get out one at a time. Billy Dee helps dry us off, while Mama, in order to conserve water, heats up just a little extra hot water to add to the tub for Billy's bath. He gets the recycled water, but he doesn't need any help, so he can stay in the tub as long as he chooses, usually until he shouts, "My butt done froze!" and jumps around the room trying to find a dry spot on the towel previously deployed by Gary and me. On really cold days, we all dash straight from the bath and crawl under the bedding, or we simply beg off the bath.

So, I don't need cousin Del Ray to show me what he has, and ever since "the disgrace" happened to me, I'm even more careful about showing my bottom to anyone. Del's persistence in the matter is matched only by my obstinacy; finally, we agree to touch each other "down there," but only through our clothes, and only with one finger, up to the count of ten.

Del is satisfied for now, so he reaches into his pocket and pulls out the surprise he has brought along to celebrate our bond.

"Cigarettes!" I squeal. "Where'd you git them thangs?"

"I snitched 'em from Alma Sue's purse yesterday up at the homeplace," Del replies with glee, "and I know how to use 'em."

He struggles a bit with the matches, but manages to light one. I'm thrilled to see the smoke curling like ghostly apparitions around the outhouse walls, but when Del passes the cigarette to me, I'm thoroughly chagrined. I blow really hard, but the smoke won't come out the end.

Del laughs and points at me, "Nooo, Skyla Fay, don't blow out on it! Ya gotta suck the smoke in and blow it out yer mouth. Jist don't let it get caught in yer throat."

I suck in, let the smoke puff out my cheeks and then blow it out into the confines of the outhouse. I'm not impressed, and some bits of bitter tobacco cling to my tongue, leaving a nasty taste in my mouth.

"This ain't no fun," I declare. "I was thinking you git to blow smoke rings out the end of this here thing."

Anyway, Del is satisfied that we have completed our initiation and the celebration, so we exit the outhouse to gather green apples down by Churning River.

I try cigarettes more successfully with Del and Gary numerous times after that, and we all get good at pilfering them from Alma Sue and other grown-ups. As time goes on and I'm permitted to take Gary into town, we join Del and other kids in stealing cigarettes and candy from the General Store.

We call a rendezvous the day after Del, Gary, the Jeffers brothers (Juddy and Arlo), and I have built a sturdy new lean-to in the woods across the river. In contrast to our flimsy rafts, the lean-tos we construct by bending and fastening laurel bushes are truly fine. Arlo is a perfectionist when it comes to designing lean-tos. On this day his brother Juddy lets Del know they have pilfered cigarettes, so Del agrees that, with my help, he will supply the candy. This means a trip into town to Clayton Whitt's General Store, where Mama sends me to pick up groceries and the occasional treat.

Holding Gary's hands and chattering on the way, Del and I decide we are natural-born thieves. We figure this is so because we have noticed that, unlike us, Gary and certain other children have to be laboriously trained in the art of thievery, while we, and even Billy Dee, the loner, are good at stealing and not getting caught. Del Ray Minix and I make excellent partners in crime. With his curly hair tamed close to the scalp, those deliberate brown eyes, and that turned up lip, Del is known about town as a little scalawag. In contrast, I have a delicate, innocent look that can fool most anyone. And, of course, my brother Gary is sweet and guileless by nature, so he can always serve as a prop during a heist. Gary is also amenable to any scheme Del or I cook up.

Del and I make a plan to enter Clayton's store separately. Thus, when Gary and I turn up, Del is already inside the store poking around, diverting the shopkeeper's attention. Gary and I get busy stuffing our pockets with loot before I step up to the counter to pay for a small item or two and politely send regards from Mama to Clayton's wife, Mazie. I make a big show of looking up at Clayton Whitt and smiling, and of taking Gary's hand to leave the store. Del hangs back a bit after we leave, and Clayton Whitt continues to keep a sharp eye on him. Finally, whistling nonchalantly, Del Ray leaves the store. Once out of Clayton's sight, he dashes off to meet us at the lean-to.

Our little wayward band of ragtag outlaws mostly steals cigarettes and candy. One day, Del decides to wait across the street for Gary and me, because he has recently had words with Mr. Whitt, who caught him dismantling a carton of cigarettes that, obviously, he did not intend to purchase.

Gary is oblivious when Clayton Whitt motions me to come up to the counter at the general store. To my abject horror he says, "I know y'all are stealing from my store, Skyla Fay, and I surely wish you wouldn't. You ain't got nothin', child, but that ain't the way to git by. Tell ya what, anytime you need that there candy so bad that ya cain't help but steal, you come tell me and I'll jist give it on over to you."

I'm so dumbstruck by this confrontation that I mumble a barely audible, "OK." I can feel the heat light up my face and a dizziness overtake my body, ostensibly over the shame of getting caught, but in truth, more over being branded a charity case than a thief. To aggravate my humiliation, Mr. Whitt pats my head and insists that Gary and I accept a molasses pull candy. Then, as he gently escorts us out the door, he notices Del Ray Minix standing across the street acting all distracted and disinterested. "One more thang, Skyla Fay," adds Clayton Whitt, "y'all stay away from that there Minix boy. He's a bad lot from the git-go. If you stay mixed up with the likes of him, you're borrowing trouble, chile."

I'm stunned and saddened by my encounter with Mr. Whitt. I want to thank him and kill him at the same time. He gave me a reprieve on my thieving, but then tried to rob me of Del Ray, the best friend and ally I have. Of course, I don't tell Del what Clayton Whitt said about him, but I'm condemned to retaining the warning words about Del in my head like a vial of leaky poison.

Also, after this incident I can't quite muster up the same enthusiasm for petty thievery. Not that I don't ply my illicit skills again, but the bravado has vanished, the thrill of the guile has been quelled. Without the associated outlaw gallantry, the material gratification of the haul is considerably diminished.

Del Ray doesn't see it this way. He wants me to use the sympathetic bond between Mr. Whitt and me to enhance our opportunity for acquisition. "Keep on thanking him and git him to give ya free stuff. When ya git a good trust goin', we kin make us a good haul," insists Del.

I balk, and Del sulks. The first serious rift has arisen in our alliance.

8

SOMETIMES IN LIFE, an event pops up to mock you like that bug-eyed clown grinning at you from the Jumping Jack box. That must be how Wally Preacherboy Perkins feels when his mother, Maudie June, just up and dies. Before slumping over in the rocker on her front porch, Maudie had complained of no more than the usual achy bones and indigestion.

When Doc Wilson informs Wally Preacherboy Perkins that his mama has officially passed, the distraught boy falls to the ground and commences a nonstop prayer, "Lord Jesus, I'm a sinner. I believe you paid for my sins with your blood. I believe that Jesus Christ is the Son of the living God. I believe that He died on the cross and shed His precious blood for the forgiveness of all my sins. I believe that God raised Jesus from the dead by the power of the Holy Spirit and that He sits on the right hand of God at this here moment, hearing my confession of sin and this prayer. Please forgive me of my sins. Wash all my filthy sins away in the precious blood that you shed in my place on the cross at Calvary.

Dodging Prayers and Bullets

Your Word says that you will turn no one away, and that includes me, Lord. Please don't take my mama. Please, Lord, I take you alone to be my Savior and take me to Heaven. But spare my mama, dear Lord, spare my mama."

Wally ceases looping these words only after Doc Wilson gives him a good rap on the head; his prayer then dissolves into a woeful maelstrom of wailing and bawling.

Within the hour, Eula and Earl Patrick swoop by the Doc's office to pick up Preacherboy, who, for the first time in his young life, has absolutely nothing to say. The idea that a mama can be taken like that is truly terrifying to me, as well. And, despite our history of innumerable provocations from "the Preach," Del and I commiserate in guilt about the anguish we have possibly, secretly, conjured upon him. What in Heaven's name, we wonder, will happen to Preacherboy now?

We are not to get the answer to that query for a very long time.

The funeral for Maudie June Perkins is held at the Born Again Church of Jesus Christ up in Sow Holler. Stella Adams says, "You gotta hand it to them church ladies—they know how to make a fuss at a funeral for one of they own." Those with nary a decent word for Maudie Perkins prior to her demise praise her righteousness to the high heavens during the funeral lamentations. When it comes time to sing Blessed Be the Tie That Binds, everybody is openly weeping. Apparently, Maudie has lots more friends in death than she ever had in life.

The irony is not lost on "the Preach," who, observing the disingenuous keening of that old mean-spirited busybody Gertie Preston, snaps at her, "All your righteous acts are like filthy rags." I later learn that's a quote from the Bible—Isaiah 64:6—but the remark nonetheless stuns more folks than it tickles.

Unfortunately, Mama makes Gary and me look after baby Luke during Maudie's funeral, so I'm not able to take in the whole shebang. I sort of hoped to get a peek at the dead body, but I never find a gracious opportunity to do so. I do, however, get a good look at Preacherboy, who has never appeared so afflicted and forlorn. He declines the invitation to approach his mama's coffin, and later Billy Dee, who sat beside Wally throughout the service, reports that Wally had confided, "Looks like the Lord has forsaken me." Billy Dee says it was just as well Wally refused to behold his mother in the casket, because Maudie Perkins looked like a waxed dummy. I sure wish I had gotten a look for myself.

Del Ray did not show up for the funeral at all. "Wasn't no how I coulda been there that woulda been right," is what he tells me. Mama thinks Del is rude for not attending, but I understand it's Del's way of being respectful.

I don't know whether Wally "Preacherboy" Perkins had any friends at school, because he didn't attend Miss Tackett's one-room school. Each day Maudie walked her boy to and from a bus stop about a half-mile outside of Collier, where Wally took a bus to a regional high school in Stony. His mysterious benefactor apparently paid for the bus transportation, in addition to his school clothes and supplies.

I always knew Preacherboy was smart, though, because he used big words like lasciviousness, licentious, and harlot. Maudie claimed he could read the Bible before his primer, and he surely memorized a heap of scripture.

Within a day or two after the funeral, and without ceremony, Wally Preacherboy Perkins vanished from Collier. Even Del can't wrangle out of the adults what has happened to Wally. Mama and Aunt Eula only respond to my inquiries with an oblique, "The Lord will provide."

Decades later, Wally Perkins will return to Collier under circumstances that are beyond the sensibilities of anyone in Crockett County Kentucky in the 1950s.

9

BY THE TIME Del Ray Minix and I turn eleven years old, we are not nearly as close as before we started school. Once I learn to enjoy reading and writing, I feel separate from Del, whose main interests are hanging out with his buddies—fishing, gigging (snaring bullfrogs under spotlights with pitchforks), racing go-carts and loafing in front of the Court House.

I am, therefore, somewhat surprised one afternoon when Del, sporting an irrepressible grin, signals me to walk home with him when school lets out.

"I did it with Lulu Baines," he blurts out.

"What?" I respond, genuinely perplexed.

"I fucked her!" Then he quickly adds, "Really. It don't hurt at all. It was easy."

I'm mortified, because I have heard that nasty word before, though without clarity. Del goes on to explain that Lulu Baines, a fourteen-year-old girl known for her bad character and loose ways, was angry at her boyfriend, Butchie Collier. In retaliation, Lulu invited several of the younger boys to enjoy what Butchie considers his "property."

I make Del tell me all the details before I inform him of my unequivocal moral outrage. Of course, Del doesn't let it go at that. "I can show you!" he offers, "It don't hurt, I promise."

Now I'm truly offended, and a little afraid of Del's sexual bravado. Mama is right: boys only want one thing. Del notes my chagrin and looks, mercifully, somewhat ashamed.

"Upon my honor, it won't be like that with you and me," he promises. "I can wait for you, Skyla Fay. You know I been pining for you all my life. You just need to say when."

"Never!" I vow. "I'm going to high school and marry me a rich man, and have a white wedding gown."

Del is obviously wounded by this dismissive remark, but rather than own up to his hurt, he turns away from me and taunts, "You'll jist be an old spinster school teacher, like that Miss Tackett, that's what. 'Sides, I wasn't gonna tell you this, but Petey Ray fucked Lulu Baines, too, and even Gary wanted to."

I walk home feeling very alone in the world. If even perfect little Gary is interested in this sex stuff, there's no hope. Of course, I can't confront Gary or ask Billy Dee about it, and I can never mention it to Mama. Sex is something to be warned about, not inquired about. Between "the disgrace" in the truck, and that old Artie Johnson sniffing around me, I have already accumulated too much shameful familiarity in that area. From now on, my romance will be with books, my love affair with writing.

I never learn how Del Ray and I might have resolved this turn of events, because just a few weeks after the Lulu Baines incident, Mama informs us that Daddy is coming home to move our family to Sunny Vale, New Jersey.

Part Two

NEW JERSEY

10

1957

ONE DAY, Mamaw Jenkins turns up in Collier, ostensibly to visit us grandchildren, but with the predetermined intention of convincing Mama that, if she wants to keep her husband, she'd best prepare to join him in New Jersey.

It's hard to fully know what went into the decision for my family to move north, but I later find out that Effie Clarice Jenkins, my mamaw on Daddy's side, was one of the prime instigators. As Mama has never set foot outside Crockett County in her life, she must have been terrified and angry. It's not until I'm fully grown that I understand what leaving the beloved hills and all her kin on behalf of her children must have meant, emotionally, for Mama.

Besides, Mama never has a good word for the stern-looking Mamaw Jenkins at any time. Daddy, a freewheeling truck driver who was sent to Europe during the war, doesn't understand Mama's reluctance to leave the confines of provincial Kentucky. He also never understands how humiliating his serial abandonment of her is.

I'm guessing that paramount in Flo-Anna Reece Jenkins' ultimate decision to follow her husband north is simply the welfare of us children.

I know Mama is thinking about the "the disgrace" that happened to me, and she understands that I'm coming of age in a risky social environment, and that my brother Billy Dee, a serious student, deserves better educational opportunities than those afforded in Collier. Gary will thrive anywhere, or so Mama imagines, but Luke is already a handful, determined to run wild, with no possibility in Kentucky of starting school for at least another year.

So, most likely to sustain her marriage and safeguard her children, Mama agrees to leave the mountains and the people that comprise the very fabric of her being.

The day of the move, Mama rouses us very early. A seasoned truck driver, Daddy likes to beat the traffic by traveling before daybreak or very late into the night. Mama agrees for a different reason. "Let's git out real early. I don't want the likes of that Del Ray Minix hangin' around beggin' to go north with us. It'd be jist like seein' somebody drownin' and us runnin' off."

Del Ray never even bids me goodbye before we leave Kentucky, but I understand it's his way to disappear when his feelings are hurt or when he's overcome with shame or sorrow. I know he's devastated by the loss of his cousins, especially me, and, unfortunately, this move came up just at the time the Lulu Baines incident deepened the emerging rift between us.

I make a silent vow to stay in touch with Del, and actually will write him a letter shortly after we arrive in New Jersey. Then, life just happens, in ways that separate Del and me irrevocably. I'm to see him again, but never with a light heart.

The physical move to New Jersey is far less complex than the emotional shift. In truth, the only cargo of any value to my parents is their children. The night before the move, Daddy loads Mama's meager belongings unto the flatbed of a battered pickup truck on loan from his friend Artie Johnson. (That guy, again.) In the morning, Daddy tosses the one decent mattress and all the blankets and quilts on top of the household items and ties everything down, so that we children will have a place to sit and sleep in the back of the truck. Mama rides up front with Luke on her lap. The five-year-old squirms and whines in discomfort until Daddy slaps him hard; that quiets Luke, and also Mama, who was already acting cold and unforgiving about the move.

Despite our fear of Daddy's rage, from time to time one of us older children takes a turn riding up front—squeezing between Mama and Daddy and around the gearshift and elbowing Luke out of the way. Because I suffer from motion sickness, the front seat, affording a less bumpy ride and better view, is particularly welcome to me. When I'm stuck on the pile in the back of the truck, I can do little but close my eyes and try to sleep. So as not to provoke Daddy when I'm up front, I sit real still and try to stay awake as we whiz past endless fields of stately rows of corn and huge tobacco leaves flopping like elephant ears. I'm proud that, by this time, I can read and understand the Burma Shave signs.

At mid-day on the way to New Jersey, Daddy pulls over at a truck stop and sleeps a couple of hours while the rest of us take turns gathering wild flowers in the surrounding woods or sit around a picnic table, quietly, impatiently, waiting for him to wake up and continue the journey. Mama never complains, but I can tell it's hard on her. Later I find out that she was four months pregnant at the time.

The full impact of the transition from the rural south to the urban north does not register on my conscious mind until ten years later, in the early 1960s, when I see the film version of John Steinbeck's novel, *The Grapes of Wrath*. Watching the fictional Joad family of migrant workers pile onto the pickup truck with their simple belongings, I choke up and have to run to the restroom to hide my weeping.

While my memories of leaving Collier are jolted by movie imagery, any sense of what it meant for me to arrive in Sunny Vale, New Jersey remains obscure. Though I was twelve when we moved, and I resided in New Jersey the rest of my childhood, I never think of myself as being from there. Sunny Vale, as far as I'm concerned, belies its name. A suburb of Newark, New Jersey that developed around the trucking and manufacturing industries after World War II, Sunny Vale is predominantly populated by Italian and Polish immigrants determined to separate themselves, by more than a neighborhood, from the Black people who had settled decades earlier in Newark.

Daddy's brother Floyd, nicknamed Speed, developed a trucking business in Sunny Vale, where Daddy went to work the first time he abandoned us to the shack in Collier. After an extended stint of driving sporadically for his brother's independent trucking company

Dodging Prayers and Bullets

in Sunny Vale, Daddy had acquired a steady job making long distance hauls between New Jersey and Chicago for the Chicago Express trucking company. On trips between New Jersey and Chicago, before we joined him up north, he sometimes diverted to Collier to see us. I guess Lonnie Lee had good intentions, though, because the regular income from the trucking job enabled him to rent an apartment in a new housing project constructed for working people in Sunny Vale.

At the time, for impoverished Appalachian transplants, the new apartment in Sunny Vale seems palatial: electricity and running water; a full kitchen with a gas stove; a bathroom with a tub and flush toilet, and wood doors separating the individual rooms. Mama warns us children not to waste good water by flushing too often. (She's a precursor of the "if it's yellow, let it mellow, if it's brown flush it down" campaign.) But she promises, "If y'all wants to, once a week you kin take a bath all by yerself!"

The apartment affords Daddy and Mama their own bedroom until Mama gives birth to Dora Lee a few months later. Uncle Speed's wife Thelma sends over a crib so the baby can at least have a separate place to sleep in their bedroom. In the second bedroom, Luke and Gary share bunk beds, while I have a single bed across from them. Billy Dee is content with a fold out bed in the living room, especially since he likes to stay up late to read and study.

In no time, my brothers and I meet friends in the housing project and are looking forward to starting school. In Collier, Billy Dee, Gary and I attended a one-room school; in New Jersey, we are placed in elementary grades on the basis of age. Billy Dee registers for 8th grade, I for 6th grade, Gary for 4th grade, while Luke is placed in first grade, even though he has never gone to kindergarten. During the first week of school, Billie Dee's teacher informs the principal that he is too advanced for the 8th grade curriculum. Though almost a year younger than the other children in Sunny Vale High, Billy Dee is permitted to begin 9th grade.

Not only everything, but everyone in our family changes in New Jersey. If ever there is a time when I'm symbolically "born again," it's just after the move. In fact, most everyone in my family gets a new name, if not a new identity. Mama becomes "Mother" or "Mommy" because nobody in Sunny Vale, New Jersey says "Mama;" Daddy is referred to as "my father." (Even Papaw Reece and Mamaw Jenkins, in absentia, become "Grandpa" and "Grandma.") During the roll call at school Billy Dee is permanently anointed "William," because there are already two Billy's in his class, and I'm introduced as "Sky," because the teacher thinks Skyla is a misspelling of my name. It won't be the last time I hear that up North. (Mama likely just spelled it phonetically, but no one in Kentucky ever questioned it.)

There's a rather amusing and persistent development regarding nomenclature for Gary and Luke in New Jersey. When Gary's fourth grade teacher, a kindly but rather geographically challenged man, notes that Gary is from Kentucky and bears the name Gary Cooper, he announces to the class that a real cowboy has joined their ranks. The children love it and immediately dub Gary "the cowboy." The label doesn't seem like much of a stretch for Gary, who happens to be the handsome, strong, and silent type. Luke, the wild little brother who follows Gary around and adores him, becomes, predictably, "Tonto," a nickname that will come to haunt him.

Mama laughs when she hears that the New Jersey children call Gary "Cowboy." She is, after all, proud of the white fences, rolling hills, exotic blue grass, and thoroughbred horses associated with the running of the famous Kentucky Derby in Lexington. Of course, my family knows that Collier, and most of Eastern Kentucky, is more about mules than horses and more about grit and hollers than stately ranches. Still, it's a relief *not* to be deemed ignorant hillbillies by our northern neighbors.

Unlike in Collier, Mama stays at home in New Jersey; she never learns to drive, so she can't venture out beyond the apartment complex and the nearby supermarket. We children are not used to having Mama at home every day, so we maintain the Kentucky regimen of not relying on her for security, comfort, permission or advice. To Mama's dismay, from day one in New Jersey we spend our time gallivanting. Daddy, who drives long distance and hangs around his brother and friends between runs, is rarely on the premises, but his absence turns out to be a blessing. At best loosely knit in Collier, the marital relationship between Flo-Anna and Lonnie Lee Jenkins completely unravels after the move.

In Collier, Daddy was an intriguing interloper in our family; in New Jersey he's a fearsome despot, always raging, sleeping fitfully, and yelling and cursing at Mama or us kids, usually during supper. I come to associate meal times with terrifying screaming matches between my parents—matches that frequently escalate to where Dad hits either her or one of us, and then stomps out of the house. He returns late at night, sheepish and silent, often complaining of a bad headache; mention is never made of the events that transpired earlier in our household.

As Mother's isolation grows and her unhappiness mounts, she unleashes increasingly furious denunciations of her husband's neglect. She complains incessantly to us kids about her misery. Dad's anger and physical violence increase as he begins throwing things or pouncing upon whoever is within reach. During meals I develop the habit of picking at my food, barely getting anything down before I scoop up Dory from the highchair and hide out in the back bedroom. Both William and I retreat into our schoolwork, while Gary and Luke wolf down their food and race back outside to play sports or hang out with neighborhood pals.

Though we never speak of it, we kids make a pact to stand together in the face of Dad's abusive rage and Mother's hysterical wailing. Whenever Luke and Gary see Daddy's truck pull up, they hide under the beds or dash out of the house. Unfortunately, the streets they take to in New Jersey are a lot more perilous than the fields and hills of Collier, Kentucky.

11

MY RECEPTION AT SCHOOL does not mirror the friendly welcome I received in the housing projects. The first day of school in Sunny Vale Elementary, I know I'm in trouble. Even though Mama orders me shoes and two new dresses from the Sears Roebuck catalog, my clothes appear ill fitted and out of style compared to what most of the girls at school are wearing. In a cruelly misguided attempt to "pinch pennies," Mama always selects clothing several sizes too big for me, so that I can grow into the garments. Of course, I never grow much, especially in width, and even when I do, by then the clothes are worn out. Even the hand-me-downs from Stella Adams' Second Hand Store in Kentucky had fit me better.

In short, Sky Jenkins, the new girl at school, is a fashion disaster. Intensifying the misery of my ostracism on the basis of teen style is my thick-as-molasses mountain accent that unjustly allows the more middle class students, giggling and tittering, to relegate me to immigrant status. Only the girls with Italian or Polish accents smile and talk to the new student with the odd name Sky, and I realize, in abject humiliation, that I *do* seem like an immigrant. I rapidly withdraw from social interactions at school. For almost a year, I don't volunteer answers in class, choosing to retreat to the classroom obscurity of youngsters who are not particularly academically attuned. The only saving grace at school is that I'm dedicated to my studies, so at least I can hold my own with Miss Martin, the sixth grade teacher, who is pleased to have an enthusiastic writer in her class.

My social haplessness, however, is compounded when I observe how readily my brothers assimilate to their new environment. For them, it does not take much cachet—they only have to fashion their hair in the "crew cut" style of the 1950s, wear the same old dungarees and pocket T-shirts each day, and be good at sports. Gary, handsome and athletic, is so popular that he gets invited to parties and within two years is elected president of his class. William is not a lady's man, but he can play basketball well enough, and is able to find smart and respectable friends on and off the court. His ambition to go to college is encouraged at school, and even by Mama at home. Luke is a rough and tumble little boy who simply gets by on energy and enthusiasm.

When Dora Lee is born in New Jersey, I see to it that my baby sister gets plenty of coddling and attention, especially when, six months after her birth, Mother informs me, "Another baby is coming and I cain't take care of two of 'em, so you gotta take this one." When she miscarries mother only says, "Jesus took the baby." No questions fielded or answered. After that, there are no more pregnancies, and not because she and Lonnie Lee employ birth control.

What is understood, however, is that Dora Lee remains my ward. Ever since the time Mama defaced my baby doll, I have not taken up with dolls, but I'm enthusiastic about the notion of nurturing a real baby. Barely thirteen years old, I embrace my baby sister as my own child, and afford mama some unspoken redemption on the doll account. I shelter Dory, carry her about, teach her how to walk and talk, and later to dress appropriately and even to read and write. Most importantly, I encourage Dory to stand up for herself. She sleeps beside me and wets the bed most nights, but I tolerate it. I make a pun about her bed wetting, referring to Dory as "my little Sweet Pea." At night, as Dory snuggles up next to me, I assure my sister that she is as safe as a little pea in a pod. When Dory misbehaves, I affectionately tease that she's "a little pisser." Baby Dora Lee later rewards me and punishes Mother by chanting, "I love Skyla Fay better than Mommy!"

To me, henceforth designated as Sky, adolescence in New Jersey is torture. My clothes never fit right and Mother's (no longer Mama in any sense) attempts at tacky home permanents to make me look "purty" just aggravate my already desperate situation. I'm skinny and flat-chested, when the norm is to be curvaceous and voluptuous, like Marilyn Monroe and Jayne Mansfield, the movie stars in vogue at the time. Similar to my brothers, I'm an excellent athlete and, according to my gym teachers, have great potential as a runner and gymnast. Unfortunately, girls who excel in sports in the 1950s and early 60s are taunted as "tomboys" and are relegated to the fringe of any true feminine or athletic identity.

Also, sports teams for girls sometimes require extra money for equipment and after school time for practice. With limited financial resources, my sister Dory to look after, and Mother in command of my wardrobe, I'm hopelessly banished from middle class sorority and restricted from achievement in athletics. At the same time I don't choose to throw in with the more rowdy, libertine girls from the immigrant and working class families in my housing project. Ironically, in light of my earlier school trauma in Kentucky, the only currency I have in New Jersey is my skill at reading and writing. The social humiliation and personal ridicule I endure at school are rendered tolerable only by my academic prowess.

Sadly, Mother does not encourage my studies; she insists that boys, who are expected to support a family in the future, receive educational priority. According to Mother, I need to concentrate on developing household skills such as cooking and cleaning, in preparation for my future as a wife and mother. In short, advanced education for girls is a frivolity our family can't afford financially or culturally. With regard to Flo-Anna's own domestic deficiencies as wife and mother, such contentions about me seem acutely ironic.

I determine not to be denied or deterred. If I can't shine socially, I intend to glow intellectually. I read voraciously, study incessantly, and write compellingly about issues and ideas. There are teachers who notice and encourage me. I'm tracked for college, though I have no notion of how that could come to pass. My more immediate challenges are prevailing over my diminished social status in Sunny Vale, and surviving the escalating violence in our household.

Soon enough my brothers and I adopt the New Jersey regional dialect, and before long we have little trace of southern accents. Since grade seven is housed at the regional high school, I meet a slew of new students from outreach areas, so I determine to drop the protective mantle of reticence I bore during that first isolating year in 6th grade. The shift to high school enables me to reinvent myself as a New Jersey native. Sadly, I grow ashamed of how ignorant and uneducated my parents sound and appear, compared to my teachers and the parents of the better-heeled students at school. I wince when Mother or Dad say "ain't" or utter any words in a mountain dialect. At first, my brothers and I become essentially bilingual: out of sensitivity to our parents we speak "down home" around the house, while outside in the neighborhood or at school, we use either local slang or "proper" English. Eventually we, and for the most part our father, who is out and about in the world, drop the hillbilly vernacular entirely. Mother, in contrast, never changes her way of talking—or thinking, for that matter.

The move to New Jersey totally shifts my perspective on my mother. In Kentucky she had been proud, vivacious, and in charge of her life—a social contender and staunch defender of her children. In New Jersey, Mother is tentative, self-conscious, and helpless—a social isolate, uneducated, highly anxious, and dependent upon her children. Over the years, lacking strong family and community ties, Mother relinquishes her very identity—and authority—as an adult. She begins to rely upon us children for the simplest social and economic transactions. From Mother's carefully constructed grocery lists, we do the food shopping; we negotiate with the superintendent about repairs in the apartment; we fill out our own school and medical forms. We become contemptuous when Mother is too anxious and distracted to write school notes of permission or excuses for absence or even to sign our report cards. William assumes charge of any family business and school communications; I assume responsibility for Dory and any social obligations required of the family;

Gary and Luke are left to their own devices. I have no privacy or support at home and have to fight for time to read or study, sometimes escaping to the library or staying up into the wee hours in order to accomplish anything.

Determined to have a domain of her own at home, Mother fiercely controls the kitchen and laundry arenas. This, despite the fact that she was never much of a cook or housekeeper in Kentucky, where meals were simple but wholesome: cornbread baked in an iron skillet and crumbled in buttermilk, served with a mess of beans; mashed potatoes with milk gravy and a side of dandelion or collard greens, or maybe a poke sallet cooked in bacon leavings; chicken 'n' dumplings on special Sundays. Sometimes Mother served a bit of bacon or ham from Papaw's smokehouse stock, though she could never abide the bullfrog, possum or squirrel meat occasionally proffered by local marksmen.

In Sunny Vale, Mother has to contend with making choices about packaged food from the supermarket: bottled milk, canned vegetables, boxed cereals and frozen food. In New Jersey, people are keen about ground beef and hot dogs, which the boys take to well enough, but both of which make me gag. I also can't get used to pasteurized milk delivered up in sterilized glass bottles. Dad hands over grocery money haphazardly, so Mother has to make-do with the most basic selections. Whereas in Kentucky, during growing seasons, fruit and vegetables from the gardens and fields were luscious and plentiful, in urban New Jersey, the selections are limited and highly priced. Mother examines a "hothouse" tomato, and suggests to me, "Let's try this here, it's somethin' like a tomata."

The laundry facility for the housing project is located in a special basement area in a separate building. When Mother becomes too intimidated to venture out to the supermarket, or even to church, she limits her ambling outside the apartment to the laundry room, where she will occasionally converse with other women. She is frightened, however, by the strange accents and foreign ways of our immigrant neighbors and warns us kids that such people are dangerous and "downright nasty" in their personal habits.

As we befriend the neighborhood children and get to know their parents, however, it doesn't take long for my brothers and me to conclude that our Mother is the odd one. Since she no longer works outside the home and rarely goes to church, Mother eventually stops tending to herself. She dons only formless, stained, and eventually raggedy housedresses, parsimoniously ordered from the Sears Roebuck or Montgomery Ward catalogs. She gains weight and her belly protrudes, as it never did before, even when she was pregnant. Gradually, we children become Mother's only conduits to the outside world, and she begins to substitute us for friends and neighbors. William and I are, essentially, the adults in the household. Mother, respected and respectable in Kentucky, is a helpless child in New Jersey.

Dad continues to haul long distance for Chicago Express and provides Mother with just enough money for rent and basic food. After she has the miscarriage, he habitually returns home only for a day or so every two weeks. We children get used to ruling the roost in his absence. When Dad comes home, he just sleeps or fights relentlessly with Mother, who, left alone to hone her fears and resentments over abandonment compounded by dislocation, nags him incessantly. Feeling equally frustrated and displaced, Dad resorts to beating up on Mother and us. He's particularly abusive to Luke, who somehow always manages to be in the way. Unconsciously, Luke gets even by throwing up at the dinner table or soiling his pants whenever Dad is at home. Inevitably, during the ensuing chaos, Dad stomps out of the apartment to seek solace with his brother Speed or to play poker with friends at a local garage.

As she becomes increasingly irrelevant to everyone in the household, Flo-Anna Reece Jenkins retreats to recalling memories of Kentucky and nursing illusions about her eventual return there. We roll our eyes as Mother drones on about the old ways, "There was blackberries as big as yer thumb to have for the picking, and Morning Glory blooms to greet ya ever' day." We become inured to her suffering. I later conclude that her afflictions were brought upon by what Kentuckians refer to as "the constant sorrow."

We children all realize that living up north isn't really working for Mother: she never loses her southern accent or Appalachian mindset; she doesn't make any friends in New Jersey, and never comes to accept Lonnie Lee's "lowlife" relatives as part of our family. According to Flo-Anna, children exposed to Daddy's family will be defiled. She warns us about Daddy's trashy (even dangerous) relatives and associates: they lie and gamble and steal things and utter foul words. They leer at little girls and lead little boys astray.

And, like Daddy, the men are dirty—not from the wholesome clean earth of the hollows and fields, but from road and machine dirt ground in by tinkering with old broken-down cars and trucks. Their hands and fingernails are permanently rough and stained black from working in grease and oil. Even after he washes up, Daddy has black outlines along his fingers, like he has just been fingerprinted, and the bathroom sink area looks like it has been splattered in India ink.

I come to see Daddy, his family, and friends as repulsive, especially when I count Artie Johnson among them. I disavow my father, and whenever that nasty perverted Artie comes to New Jersey, I scoop up Dory and beat it. Actually, I develop a kind of phobia about Artie: if he touches a doorknob, or uses a towel, or sits in a particular chair, I consider that object contaminated and avoid all immediate contact with it. Fortunately, Daddy doesn't bring himself or his friends around much, so while my encounters with Artie Johnson are imprinted on my body and soul, they are, for the most part, circumscribed in New Jersey.

12

FACE TURNED TOWARD the wall, I lay in bed sobbing silently, my body clenched in fear and anger. My head pulsates to the rumble of the frightful boiler in the basement directly beneath our apartment in the housing project. I scoff at Mother's obsession that it will one day blow up, but in the wee hours of the night her anxiety seeps into my reason like dirty water staining a good carpet. Sometimes during daylight hours my brothers and I hoist one another up to peer through the window slots of the big iron door that seals off the boiler room from the curiosity and vandalism of the residents of the housing project. We stare at the strange blue flame that keeps the boiler fired up, agreeing the boiler mostly seems like a cumbersome mechanism that the janitor is required to maintain.

At night, however, when I am in my bed, the cacophonic racket of the boiler and my fixation on Mother's warnings combine to make the boiler a monstrous manifestation of the conditions evoking so much vulnerability and uncertainty for my family in our new environment.

Simply put, nothing about New Jersey feels safe.

Contrasting the placidity of my life in Kentucky with the anguish of our lives in New Jersey, my stomach roils with rage, like Churning River after a rainstorm. I plot resolutions: the boiler will blow up, destroy the apartment, and Mother and Dad will both die. I'll dash about saving my brothers and sister, and then a rich smiling family will adopt us all. No, I conclude, that's not realistic. There probably aren't any rich, smiling families with a father who knows best and a mother who goes along with it.

My rescue fantasy is reconfigured to saving the apartment for us kids to live in: Poison gas, particularly lethal to adults, will leak from the stove. Mother and Dad won't recover, and after the funeral, we children will be permitted to stay in the apartment, rent-free and without the cruelty and dissonance perpetuated by adults. Gary can take care of himself, and William and I will watch over Luke and Dory. This can all happen, I assure myself, because the child welfare agency will lose track of our case, but keep paying our bills without sending over any so-called guardians.

Sometimes, if I'm feeling empathy for my mother, I simply plot against the brutal man biology determined is my father: He will die in a horrendous trucking accident, his body burned beyond recognition. Or he will be arrested for some heinous crime and be put to death in the electric chair. Mama will have to go back to work and learn how to be a real person again. I even imagine quitting school to help with my younger siblings—anything to feel safe and at peace, the way I like to recall feeling about my life in Kentucky. Even "the disgrace" that happened to me in Kentucky was an isolated incident, not an ongoing travail like life in New Jersey.

At last, I drift off to sleep, and have the awful dream about the menacing bird spitting marbles at my head. Of course, I no longer go to Mama for comfort; in New Jersey there's no longer a Mama.

13

AS IF TO LAMPOON my nostalgia for my old Kentucky home, the bad news from Collier roils in like sequential squalls. Almost two years after my family left, Del Ray Minix's life, at age 14, changed forever, and all because of his expertise with a shotgun. My cousin could handle a shotgun, even at eight years old. Rufus Minix, his daddy, had no use for Del's brains or ingenuity, but at one time had determined that his fatherly duty was to "make a man outta the boy" by teaching him how to shoot.

Del is a natural athlete who, by the time he was twelve, could hit targets square-on and knock off more tin cans than his daddy. That ended their bonding right then, but for Del Ray Minix, the gun lessons were to launch a life-altering rendezvous with destiny.

Rufus, who had honed his survival instincts as a bootlegger, warned his son Del never to lay hands on the gun again. "I catch you messin' with my shotgun, I'll knock you into next year," is how he put it. From time to time, Del picked up Papaw Reece's 22-caliber rifle and

Dodging Prayers and Bullets

took aim at the English sparrows and squirrels that were pirating Papaw's garden and cornfield; still, like our Papaw, Del didn't really have the heart for hunting.

"Good riddance to them sparrows and squirrels," Papaw instructed. "But don't never shoot them Purple Martins. They's the good birds."

So, while Del did not spend considerable time wielding a gun, apparently shooting is a bit like riding a bike: once you master it, all you do is assume the position, and you're in business again. And a sorry business it was for the Minix family.

Ole man Minix, as the good people of Collier refer to Rufus, was a bad lot from the get-go. He was a bootlegger *and* a drunk, acclaimed foremost for the beatings he administered to his kin, or anyone else within reach. One time Sheriff Collier hauled Rufus in for a couple of days for beating up on Arlo and Juddy, the Jeffers boys. Rufus had caught them vandalizing some of his empty whiskey jugs and fruit jars, so he bloodied the boys up considerably. Their daddy, old Bud Jeffers, couldn't do a thing about it, because he was a big-time moonshine customer of Rufus. But Ida Jeffers, mad as a hornet about her boys taking such a licking over a few empty jugs, marched right into town and cut a shine until the Sheriff visited Rufus and arrested him.

Rufus Minix does not exactly walk in grace around Sow Creek Hollow, particularly in the town of Collier. Still, there are those demanding retribution from Del after what takes place on a cold March night just after Del's 14th birthday. Rather than stay with Papaw at the homeplace, as he usually does, that night Del chooses to sleep on the porch of his family cabin. He is curled up under a pile of burlap sacks and a discarded ragged quilt on the front porch when Rufus comes home, tight as a tick and making a ruckus. Del is sleeping soundly when his mama begins wailing and moaning, trying to get away from Rufus, who, in a drunken rage, is viciously attacking her.

Rufus grabs Clytie, smacks her around and shoves her into a corner like a discarded toy. He staggers to the corner, hovering above her, pounding on her and shouting, "Yer nothin' but a lowdown whoring slut. And I don't claim that bastard son o' yers."

Nowadays people speculate: maybe Del Ray had not gotten over the loss of his Jenkins cousins to New Jersey; maybe, roused abruptly from a deep sleep, he was in some kind of semi-conscious dream state. Or, just maybe, fueled by years of amassed resentment from humiliation endured at the hand of Rufus, Del's own rage could no longer be quelled. Young Del Ray Minix picks up his daddy's shotgun from just inside the door of the cabin, where it was stored for quick access, takes a practiced aim and, with one shot direct to the heart, fells Rufus Minix for eternity.

No one recalls exactly what happened next, but somehow Eula and Earl Patrick arrive at the Minix cabin. Sheriff Collier and Deputy Sheriff Jeb Bailey are already there, along with a passel of curious onlookers. Del Ray is nowhere to be found, and Clytie (who owns up that Del has done the deed in her defense) is in no condition to bear witness. A couple of blockaders, moonshine partners of Rufus, take off to look for Del, but they can't find him, even at the homeplace. Aunt Eula Patrick commences to pray over the inert Rufus, while Uncle Earl assures the sheriff he will take in Clytie for the duration and inform him if Del Ray turns up.

Del doesn't turn up that night, or even for the sparse funeral conducted for Rufus a few days later. (There isn't much to be said for a man as mean-spirited and ornery as Rufus Minix.) Still, from the perspective of some God-fearing residents of Collier, a serious crime incorporating a major sin has been committed, and Del Ray Minix is obliged to answer for it. That is, when they find him.

Three days after the shooting, Sheriff Collier and some of his boys bang on the door to the old Rudd homeplace. Harley Rudd, the kindly, but mentally challenged caretaker who sweeps up around the First Baptist Church, doesn't answer until they threaten to break in. Finally, he comes to the door all stooped over and weeping wretchedly. "It weren't that boy what done it; it were me. I didn't mean it, neither. It was a accident. Y'all leave Del Ray to hisself."

Of course, no one believes that Harley Rudd would have, or even could have, shot Rufus Minix. Harley would gladly have taken the blame and punishment on Del's behalf, though. Calling the gentle giant's bluff, Sheriff Collier bellows, "Well, then, Rudd, look like me and the boys got to take you down to the jailhouse for hanging."

Hearing that, Del Ray climbs out from behind the cupboard. He's crying, too. "It's me y'all are wantin'. Harley ain't done nothin' 'ceptin' feed me." As they haul Del in for questioning, Jeb Bailey reports that Del laments, "I reckon it's the penitentiary for me in this here life and damnation afterwards."

Del Ray might have been sent away to reform school, if Luther Dean Howard, a local attorney Mama sometimes worked for at the Courthouse, had not intervened with pro bono legal counsel. Mr. Howard also brought in a social worker from the county. Del ended up getting probation, under the condition that he live at home and help support his mother with work unrelated to the moonshine trade.

Del doesn't become a blockader (before Rufus' body was cold, his affiliates had dispensed with all traces of the business at the cabin), but within a few short years, he is indulging in drink so heavily that he likely sustains a few blockaders. Though he finds it impossible to live with Clytie, Del does his best to see she is provided for. Unfortunately, and to my enduring sorrow, the opportunities afforded Del Ray around Collier are not usually on the right side of the law. When he finally lands in jail for numerous repeat offenses, including armed robbery and passing bad checks, I'm sickened that Mama claims her misgivings about Del are vindicated.

14

MY BROTHERS AND I need money. I'm fourteen and a half and have been in New Jersey over two years; from time to time, I work as a babysitter to earn a bit of cash. William has a regular paper route and both he and Gary make money helping the superintendent mow the grass around the housing project in the summer and shovel snow in the winter. William and Gary prefer legitimate enterprises, but Luke and I are up for whatever.

Without the conspiratorial sway of Del Ray Minix and the Jeffers boys, however, I'm far less brazen in thievery. The children from the projects routinely lift goodies and cigarettes from the supermarket; they instruct us newcomers in the art of snatching empty soda and beer bottles from behind local taverns or from neighboring hallways to cash in for the deposit money.

It's my own father, however, who finally, shamelessly, arranges for my economic salvation.

Since he still has family and friends in the south, Dad frequently detours there on the hauls he makes to Chicago for the Chicago Express trucking company. On one such trip, on a lark, he brings back two huge boxes of assorted fireworks, a legal purchase in the South, but illegal to transport across State lines to sell in the North. Lonnie Lee reserves the larger explosives for his Fourth of July display, but bestows the smaller, hand-tossed fireworks upon us children. Mother takes a snit, but she's ignored. William defers, but Gary, Luke, and I are thrilled to experiment with the illegal wares. Dad puts me in charge of supervising Gary and Luke with the fireworks, and so it happens that third grader Luke sets the precedent for turning the stock of fireworks into an enterprise. Some fifth graders give him a whole quarter for one of the three packs of firecrackers I've allotted him.

Exhilarated, he dashes home, clutching the quarter, to announce he has referred the fifth graders to me for further transactions. I readily comply, determining the following fee schedule: 5 packs of firecrackers for $1; cherry bombs, 25 cents apiece; ash cans, 50 cents each; and sparklers, 10 cents a box or 12 boxes for a buck. News about where to acquire the coveted items spreads quickly around the projects and at school.

I move my seat to the back of my English class, since I don't have to pay much attention to the teacher to keep up in my best subject. Besides, old Miss Bonner is such a lousy teacher that all the kids despise and make fun of her. Cramming the inner well of my desk with the enticing loot, I establish myself as an official fireworks dealer. Even the kids who are not customers dutifully pass the exchanged money and goods up and down the classroom aisles. It was the late 1950s, so no child would consider telling on others. Clearly, school is jail and the teachers are guards, regardless of what you think of your fellow inmates.

Business is good; Luke and I, and even Gary, who can't resist the immediacy of the cash, each have our loyal customers. Dad is amused and complies by keeping the stock of goods replenished, contributing his typical dubious parental caveat, "Don't get caught, now." Soon my brothers and I are able to pay for our school lunches and buy snacks and cokes after school and movie tickets on the weekend; we can even purchase a few items of clothing. (This seems rather benign, looking back, but consider that in another day and era, our father would no doubt have set us up in the drug trade.)

I know Mother disapproves of the fireworks and the business, so, to make it up to her, I save up enough baby-sitting and fireworks money to buy a nice set of aluminum pots and pans for the family. This is a welcome supplement to the two iron skillets and assorted rusting pots Mother had lugged up from Kentucky. She is so pleased and appreciative of my gesture that next I purchase a set of real glassware to replace the jam jars we've been drinking from. None of this convinces Mother of the virtue of the fireworks trade, nor contributes to any approbation of Dad, but she is genuinely touched that I generously spend much of my accumulated money on items that benefit the family.

Eventually, Dad stops driving for Chicago Express, so the fireworks business folds, and I get a job teaching arts and crafts at the local recreation center. There I come to appreciate earning money legitimately. Each day, I take Dory to work with me, and I'm amazed at how adept the child is at drawing and creative art projects. Of course she is never acknowledged for these talents at school or at home.

15

MORE BAD NEWS from Kentucky. Aunt Eula calls to tell us that Papaw Reece has died in his sleep, of old age aggravated by alcohol. She reports that Del Ray Minix is the one who, late in the afternoon, came upon Papaw lying still in his bed.

I choke up when I think about how awful it must have been for Del to discover Papaw that way. I imagine the old man looked just as he did when we were little kids and found him in one of his drunken stupors; only this time, there would have been no rousing him.

I anticipate Mother will get crazy over Papaw's death, but it's worse than that. She gets terribly sad and quiet—oddly contemplative. My heart aches for my mother over the loss of her beloved father; I can tell William feels the same way I do, but neither of us is able to comfort her or each other. Mother seems so vulnerable and hurt that I don't pay much mind to my own feelings of loss.

It's February, so my parents decide just the two of them will make the long drive to Kentucky for Papaw's funeral. William and I are to stay in Sunny Vale to take care of the three younger kids, so we can all go to school. I feel a little disappointed about not being able to see the Kentucky family, but I like the idea of being in charge of the household without parents for four or five days. Generally, I imagine life would be easier without them anyway.

I have to admit, by the second or third day, I'm surprised at how much I miss my mother. I'm used to daddy being away, but have never been physically separated from mother. Thinking about Mama in Kentucky gets me all choked up. She was such a different person there, a real grown-up person. And to think, Luke and Dory never even knew her as "Mama." I kneel down and kiss Dory on the forehead; hugging my little Sweet Pea tight, I promise, "I'll always be here for you." At the time, I don't know that's a promise I won't keep.

When I contemplate my parents' drive to Kentucky, I can't help wondering, what it was like for them during all those hours alone in the car? Did she talk about Papaw? Did they argue? Did dad attempt to comfort her in any way? Did they remember how it was when they once liked each other? After they return from Papaw's funeral, Mother seems nervous, but she's not particularly forthcoming. A day or so later, she tells me that Del Ray did not turn up for the funeral. Mama's mysterious sister Vertie, however, was escorted from the State hospital to attend the service. "She gits them shock treatments," Mother at last confesses.

"What's wrong with her?" I immediately probe, shamelessly hoping to cull more about the mystery at a time when my mother seems susceptible.

No luck; Mother immediately goes back to relating the story of Papaw's funeral, describing the ceremony with a mix of sorrow and pride. I learn that Papaw Reece, after raising a generation of children, died destitute but not beholden, and his funeral, according to Mother, was a sight for sore eyes. The mourners lined up from dawn to dusk with food and flowers; the eulogies and acknowledgments of gratitude piled up like autumn leaves. The pickup trucks and tractors bound for the service, presided over by Aunt Eula at the Born Again Church of Jesus Christ, were backed clear up into the holler. In honor of Papaw Reece, Sheriff Collier even turned a blind eye to the canebuck flowing as freely as the tides.

Papaw always had a populist aversion to relegating valued land to cemeteries. "I don't believe in burial plots," he protested, "The land should be for the living." The living chose to bury him in a little cemetery on a hillside above Collier, next to his wife Sarah. Ironically, Papaw's wish to preserve the land for the living may have been honored: cemeteries will soon be the only open land in Eastern Kentucky not taken over by large industry and strip mining.

Two weeks after Papaw's funeral, Aunt Vertie sends Mama a rambling sixteen-page, one-paragraph letter filled with non-sequiturs, obscure references and alarming fears and intentions. She's certainly literate, and there's likely some truth in her paranoia, but it's impossible to attach any context to her ramblings. I think because it frightens her, Mama lets me read the letter. Here, without revision, are some of the things Aunt Vertie had to say:

Dear Flona,

It was good to see in Kentucky. Last night I saw a TV show with a woman just like you who died in her sleep. Then Skyla Fay her daughter brought her back to life to try to learn her secret place. I fell asleep on the sofa before it was over. Thinking of my cowardly kin folks. I prepared a letter to Sheriff Sam Wells asking if it was his deputy who forced his way into my private home and arrested me in handcuffs. Eula, bless her good ole heart, is too slow to understand that I <u>cared</u> about being classified that <u>low</u>—being always my heart set on Church and the true values of a Christian. I drove a White Thunderbird that Fanny sold to me for 200 that was dangerous & almost got me killed. I was forced into a shotgun house and innocent. I am the unsuspecting slow fool. At least I paid my own utilities. It was Henry Wendall who undercover sneaked up there and dragged me into an alcohol ward. A woman named Beulah Porter came up here to see me—she'd had breast surgery although she didn't think she deserved it. She brought me a coffee cake that looks like ham. The note said "Love and Prayers on Jesus' Birthday." I've never in my life encountered such a Saintly Hypocrite. And yet because of times past and <u>all our ages</u> I hesitate to go to all out name calling. Makes me look dark like the Burrel daughters—who were criminal, poolroom & whiskey toting prostitutes

Dodging Prayers and Bullets

for many a year. This makes it easy for that strip miner (republican from Tennessee) to do everything they want to, with me out of the running. I was forced into treatment when I did not need that treatment. Also, I had mammography and still don't know if it was a treatment or examination. Usually I don't let people see me because the smell of what they have me on is sickening. At no time in my marriage to Preston Prater or previous was I ever treated for any social disease (if that's what sex is referred to as). Who am I, Flona, What am I? I'm afraid, all alone. No one cares if I agree or disagree. Just as soon as I learn something one way, I have to learn somebody else's way. I learned everything from Preston because we never lived near anybody I knew to talk to. I wonder who from Collier is writing about my life? I guess that a Catholic priest has taken over the town. Collier is full of angels that Billy Graham wrote about that want to control the mind and herd Christians about like sheep. It's a screwed up world—religious wars will take the world under. Nobody (<u>Not even an angel</u>) has the key to the universe. For many years down there they considered me an evangelist missionary for revivals even though I never believed that. I sent $16 to Daniel Paul of MO. who offered to pray for me at the Crucifixion Place in Calvery (Jerusalem). Tell your kids to stick together and get educated or marry money. I think I will go to New York City. I found out I can ride the greyhound roundtrip, but where would I stay? I will go there incognito. Number 1 on my list is Walter Cronkite. But he's married, so my interest in him is purely business not romance. Maybe you can meet me in New York City for the Easter Parade. Of course I will have to wear some old rag, but I can fix it up by adding beads I bought for 10 cents at a yard sale. I bet Skyla Fay is pretty. I haven't seen her since she was a baby. I fixed dinner and ate it with my traditional pickled eggs, and poured myself a wine toddy—of my own recipe—Gatorade (red) with a shot of J.W. Dante (Louisville & Frankfurt) in it. I used to work at Reynolds Tobacco Co. in Louisville. Say hello to Lonnie and the children for me & God willing that in the war, we may be on the same side. Flona I insist on you letting me know if you received this letter, since I am suspecting foul play from Moses Tiller the mail carrier. This makes 16 pages. (Just like the last one.) Vertie

Karen Beatty

Those are just the highlights of Vertie's letter; it really does go on for 16 pages, naming plenty of other people, places, and incidents unfamiliar to me. Mama gets angry that I think the letter is riotously funny. Of course, Vertie is not my mama (or sister), so I can readily indulge in some amusement afforded by psychic distance. I must admit, I'm impressed by Vertie's general knowledge and vocabulary, and by her ability to write script. This is when I first realize that a person can be crazy without being stupid. With regard to my family history, I'm not sure if that is a comforting or disconcerting thought.

16

FOR A SHORT TIME after the funeral, our talk about Papaw and life in Kentucky reduces some of the estrangement between my mother and me. Flo-Anna admits to feeling bad for Del Ray and understanding why he didn't attend the funeral. I know that, compounding Del's pain over the loss of Papaw, is his shame about drinking and his brushes with the law. Of course, now that his waywardness is no longer a present threat to her children, Mama can entertain a modicum of sympathy for Del. "He's a right smart boy, and even got talent in art," she observes. "He jist never had no chance to make somethin' of hisself."

Dad never mentions the funeral, or much of anything these days. I wonder if any renewal has taken place between my parents as a result of the trip to Kentucky. If so, it's not long-lived. Sadder still, Flo-Anna Reece Jenkins seems to have intuited, correctly, that her fantasy of returning to live in the Kentucky of her mind's eye can never happen. Knowing she cannot not return to "what was" and unable to adjust to "what is" gives rise to a kind of desperate melancholy in her, about "what will be." My mother's sadness, however, is soon converted to anger and resentment, specifically directed against my father, the designated malefactor of her denied access to the support of family and friends in Kentucky.

Discontent (displaced by intermittent bouts of rage or regret) reigns in our New Jersey household. Early on a Saturday morning, Mother is dragging the clunky secondhand vacuum about, repeatedly banging the metal extension hose against the bed where Luke is trying to sleep. She is cleaning while delivering a bitter, disjunctive monologue about her wretched life up North and Dad's multiple transgressions.

Finally, Luke gives up on holding the pillow over his head, and shouts at Mother, "I don't give a shit; shut your stupid-ass mouth!"

"Lonnie Lee Jenkins!" Mother screeches back at Luke. "That's who you are. Just like your daddy. Don't appreciate nothin' and don't think about nobody but yourself."

Dad, nursing a migraine and inflamed by the ruckus, jumps out of bed and grabs his belt. His eyes are glazed over, his is hair greasy and disheveled, and his face is reddened by rage. He leaps at Luke like a vicious mongrel unleashed and yanks the covers off him. Shoving him against the back wall abutting the bed, Dad begins whipping Luke with the belt.

Midst the crying and recoiling of all us children, Mother grabs at the belt to try to intervene, so Dad turns from Luke and slaps her a couple of times, then shoves her down on the floor. He then runs back to his bedroom, halfway throws on his clothes, and as he scrambles out of the house, finishes getting dressed. We will not see him again until late evening.

We children surround Mother and Luke, trying to comfort them with our wordless presence. "Get away now," Mother commands. "We're OK, and there ain't nothin' to be done. It's up to Jesus to do His work here." She gets up and retreats to the bathroom, while Luke pulls the pillow over his head and hunkers down on the bed facing the wall, refusing to show anyone his tears. Luke did not try cursing out loud at home again, but I figure that somewhere in the silent reserves of his mind are plenty of evil words for Dad and Mother.

As I grow more independent, I begin to examine my family life more critically, realizing: I have to get out. But how? It's up to William and me to guide the little kids, because after a brief blip of recovery induced by the journey to Kentucky, Mother resumes checking out of adulthood. And how am I to regard my father? Lonnie Lee Jenkins is a violent man who self-medicates, both to stay awake on the road and to fall asleep at home; he can neither stay put nor stay away.

In addition to beating up on Mother and us kids, he does barbarous things like pulling out his own rotting tooth with a pair of pliers and using a hand drill to drain the painful fluid under Luke's thumb when it got smashed in the car trunk. "I cain't afford no fancy doctors," Dad explains, as Mother protests, and I grimace in horror. Later that day, Luke proudly reports that the purple blood under the nail is gone and his thumb feels better. To avoid infection, Mother pours iodine on it, which, Luke complains, hurt worse than the drill.

In New Jersey, high school is no longer a retreat for me. My disaffection over my miserable home life induces in me a general distrust of authority. It's not long before I begin actively rebelling against my teachers. My honors report card (I sign it myself) is chock full of disciplinary comments: disruptive, poor attitude, uncooperative. In a thesaurus, I find the word "cynic" and decide that I am one.

Mostly as a matter of personal pride, and without much effort, I keep up my grades. Getting good grades also serves to frustrate the teachers I seek revenge against for their crimes of disdain, ignorance and harassment regarding youngsters from the projects. As retribution, some teachers choose to block my acceptance in the National Honor Society, even though I have the required grade point average. Outwardly I show pride in the rejection, but inside I'm hurt and embittered. I usually present myself as proud to be "out" because I can never find the way "in" to what I presume is a normal life.

After writing a sardonic essay entitled, "Ain't Life Grand," I have a major confrontation with the social studies teacher, Mr. Weston. The man is a decorated World War II veteran and celebrated alcoholic. During the "duck and cover" air raid drills at school, he "gets off" on donning one of those plastic hard hats with the civil defense insignia and acting all officious and somber. I construct the assigned essay on civil defense from the point of view of an old woman marveling that she has lived long enough after the two World Wars to see her family build a fall-out shelter in the 1950s. The elderly woman in my story debates the efficacy, in the event of a disaster, of shooting her neighbor, who has not been conscientious about preparing for the inevitable mushroom cloud. The storyline is based upon a newspaper article I actually came across.

I got the idea to write satire from reading *A Modest Proposal*, a satiric piece by Jonathan Swift that I had found in the library. Mr. Weston is furious and deeply offended by my essay. He says making fun of national defense directives indicates that I'm not a patriot; he intimates I might even have Communist leanings. This prompts me to go to the library for his social studies reading assignment and take out a book called, *If You Were Born in Russia*. The book has a sympathetic perspective on Russian culture and explains and illustrates life under Communism, rather than outright condemning it. I'm astounded to read that, in Russia, churches are thought of as museums, and that a Russian leader named Karl Marx has described religion as "the opiate of the people." Never would I have dared to entertain such thoughts, but now I'm prompted to contemplate the true nature and purpose of religion, further watering the sprouting seeds of social and religious rebellion in my nature.

When I give an oral report on my book in front of the social studies class, Old Wet Westy, as the kids call Mr. Weston, blows a gasket and tries to have me suspended, even though he's unable to come up with any grounds for suspension other than the charge of "divergent thinking." The Sunny Vale students from the good side of the tracks think I'm "just awful," but my shenanigans make me a bit of an intellectual hero to my friends from the projects. After all, we're the ones who, during air raid drills, typically guffaw and resist when we are supposed to crawl under our desks and practice ducking for cover in case the Commies drop the Big One. We understand who will be left outside the air raid shelters, if it ever comes to that.

Despite my academic ostracism, a couple of the more liberal and empathetic teachers choose to embrace me, and they encourage me to continue writing and stay committed to learning. My junior level English teacher hangs up for display one of my essays describing the beauty of morning glories and moonflowers and the solace I associate with them. Using the flowers as metaphors, I deduce I'm the type of person who only likes beginnings and endings. Eleventh grade in Sunny Vale High School certainly feels like a messy middle part.

17

SHORTLY AFTER my family's arrival in Sunny Vale, New Jersey in 1957, Mother had inquired about the possibilities for worship in our new community ("Lord, Show Me the Way"). Most of our immigrant neighbors are Roman Catholic, a religion my mother considers low class and suspect. She declared, "They worships a man—that old Pope—not even the Lord." She was taken aback to learn that the Baptist and Pentecostal churches are located just outside of Sunny Vale and are exclusively populated by Black people. Flo-Anna had always been told that churches and schools up North are integrated, but, to her relief, that certainly does not seem to be the case in Sunny Vale, where she can choose to be a Methodist, Presbyterian, or Congregationalist without ever encountering a Black face. Still, the segregation of churches by denomination limited her options for worship.

It strikes me as odd that churches, supposedly aiming to promote brotherly love, sort out the brothers by color. Ironically, from what I can gather, services at the segregated Black churches are a lot more like worship in Collier than the services in the white churches. It seems to me that up North, church going is for people to do some thinking, whereas back home in Kentucky, church going is to move the body and the spirit in the presence of the Holy Ghost.

I found going to church in Collier mystifying, while in New Jersey it's primarily boring; it seems like even the music fails to move any souls. With vacant eyes and weak voices, the impeccably dressed congregants in Sunny Vale stiffly prop themselves up in the pews. I keep hoping they will let loose with a hand-clapping, foot-stomping rendition of "Standin' In the Need of Prayer" or "Somebody Touched Me." But no; it's clear that, though I have the spiritual skeptic's lingering desire to be persuaded, I will not have a prayer of finding Jesus in New Jersey.

On the other hand, I will not have to contend with, or answer to, southern religious zealots. I don't even bother to imitate the rigid piety of the white parishioners in New Jersey. Still, in the summer, Mother insists upon signing up William, Gary and me for Vacation Bible School at the Sunny Vale Methodist Church. The main good thing about Vacation Bible School is that they give out grape juice and graham crackers, treats we can't afford at home.

It doesn't take long, however, for us children to balk about attending the Methodist Church, even for the goodies. Mother also stops going, since Dad won't accompany her or even get out of bed to drive her to church, and she has become increasingly frightened of venturing out on her own. She continues to read the family Bible, though, and regularly sets aside small amounts of her household budget to send to the Church, insisting that such tithing assures her a place of righteousness among the congregants, and eventually in heaven.

In light of Mother's loneliness and her alienation from the established church in New Jersey, I find it amusing that she hides from the roving Watch Tower evangelists who set upon our neighborhood. When she spots the Bible ladies, black-skinned or not, knocking on doors in the projects, Mother instructs us, "Jist be real quiet and act like we ain't here." Feeling a little guilty about the deception, she adds, "Now, they's good enough people, them Watch Towers, but ya never know what they believe. Then the next thing ya know, they'll be askin' for money."

Still, a rare Sunday comes to pass without Mother haranguing the family about going to church, and without her bemoaning the invented barriers to her own attendance. William will one day marry a woman whose family are church members, thereby deeply gratifying Mother by their attendance at services and, occasionally, by taking her along; well, that is, when she can overcome her panic about leaving the house.

Despite my agnostic bent, when we moved to New Jersey my personal affiliation with the church was by no means over. Throughout high school, I seek ways to get out of the house and away from the chaos of my family. I'm almost sixteen years old when a friend from school invites me to attend a youth meeting at the local Presbyterian Church. The kids I meet there are nicer than the smart but snooty upscale youngsters I have to interact with at school, and safer than the unruly street kids from my neighborhood. As a social thing, mostly, I join the Sunday evening Presbyterian Youth Fellowship (PYF) and soon start attending regular church services on Sunday mornings. Mother is thrilled.

It's at a Sunday evening PYF meeting that I'm introduced to the new associate pastor, a man in his late twenties, who invites us youngsters to call him "Reverend Dan." Reverend Daniel Hansen is a warm and smiling fellow who is by far more dedicated to working with teens than managing his myriad church-related duties. He has an engaging manner and an open face with grey-blue eyes that, I imagine, peer directly into my soul. It's as if he wants to appreciate and understand everything about me—me and me alone. I'm intrigued and inspired by Reverend Dan. There's nothing pretentious or "holier than thou" about the man. At church youth forums he comes dressed in casual slacks and penny loafers, instead of the traditional suit and laced leather shoes. It's obvious he takes the time to style his dark wavy hair, and he smells wonderful, almost spicy. (I didn't know about cologne for men at the time.)

Even when the Reverend Dan Hansen reads from the Bible or leads young people in prayer, he's different from other adult preachers—he's somehow more attuned, more sensitive and deep. Most captivating about Reverend Dan for me, though, is how smart and well informed he is, especially in the realms of poetry and music. Along with the other PYF teens, I flip when he permits us to sing along to a popular recording of singer Pat Boone crooning "This Little Light of Mine."

Dodging Prayers and Bullets

I'm soon driven to distraction, smitten, by Reverend Dan. The other girls in the youth group -- airheads all, from my perspective -- giggle and flirt with him, but I hold back, assuming a posture of personal disinterest but intellectual absorption. (After all, the man's a minister, and married at that.) It's obvious Reverend Dan is the type of man who frequently has to deflect adolescent crushes. Probably as a result of my reserve and intensity, he takes an immediate interest in me. I also conscientiously do the readings he suggests and come to the PYF meetings prepared to discuss topics like, "Your God Is Too Small."

In addition, I pick up on another, less public, side of the Reverend—his sardonic wit. I usually understand (or certainly dash off to the library to quickly investigate) the literary allusions he makes to the satiric writings of Edwin Arlington Robinson, and my favorite, Jonathan Swift. And he references all the best passages about love and friendship from the Bible, like Corinthians Thirteen: *Now abideth faith, hope, love, these three. But the greatest of these is love.* In honor of the Reverend, I memorize those lines of scripture and several good passages from Kahlil Gibran's *The Prophet*. I proclaim to the other teens and church elders that Reverend Dan makes church a meaningful life experience as well as a religious one. The Reverend notices that I notice, and he's flattered.

One morning after regular church services, Reverend Dan pointedly introduces me to his wife Marsha and their three young children. Marsha Hansen has that "put upon" look: modestly dressed, evasive eyes, tentative in manner and conversation. Worse, permanently engraved upon her "minister's wife" face is a frozen smile that belies a discontented heart. The kids are cute, but cling to their mother in an annoying way. The youngest, a girl about two or three, whines and sucks her thumb, something no self-respecting Appalachian child would do. The girl has one of those permanently tear-stained, moist-eyed faces that bury into the mother and make throaty noises of distress whenever anyone looks in her direction. The boys, aged about seven and eight, seem like crickets trapped in an invisible box: they may have it in them to leap away, but are resigned to the confines of entrapment; in their case, the designation "minister's child." I feign an interest in the children and gush to Marsha about how nice it is to meet her and how important the PYF meetings are to teens in the church.

I can tell, right off, that Marsha doesn't measure up; the Reverend deserves better. No wonder Reverend Dan spends so much time working and studying books in his office or volunteering time to the PYF! He probably has to get away from mousey Marsha and the brat babies. Obviously, I would make a much better wife for Reverend Dan. On my way home from church, I fantasize about Marsha and the kids getting killed in a car crash or electrical fire, and Reverend Dan turning to me for solace and, inevitably, true love.

I find out that Reverend Dan works late on Thursday nights, the night of choir practice at the Presbyterian Church. I'm not much of a singer, and the choir is mainly composed of older adults, but, on impulse, at the regular Sunday church service I sign the sheet circulating to solicit new choir members. At home, I explain to my delighted mother that, from now on, I will have to rush through supper on Thursdays in order to make choir practice.

Reporting for rehearsal the following Thursday evening, I mostly mouth the words to boring songs from a formal hymnal and try to suppress my amusement at some of the elders in the choir who sing in that corny, off-key fashion of faked spiritual passion. Immediately after practice, I race down the back stairs of the choir loft, past the altar area of the stately church and through the sanctuary, toward Reverend Dan's office. His door is, blessedly, open.

"There is a God," I sigh, when I spot him sitting alone listening to music and mulling over some papers on his desk.

Seeming genuinely pleased to see me, the Reverend invites me in to sit and chat. I wonder if he's been waiting for someone to counsel or console, or if he's simply, as I like to imagine, bored and staying late to avoid the home front.

Feeling awkward and guilty, I toss out a conversational thread. "I decided to join the choir, so I came for practice tonight. I've always loved church music." (Well, at least I like southern gospel music, but I don't need to specify that detail.)

Nodding his approval, Reverend Dan enthusiastically responds, "That's terrific, Sky! We need more young people in the choir. And you know how pleased I am with your participation in the youth fellowship."

Dodging Prayers and Bullets

After this exchange, I have no idea what else to talk about. I'm not much of a complainer, and Mother has trained me not to "tell tales out of family," so I'm certainly not prepared to invite examination of my dreadful home life. Thankfully, Reverend Dan accommodates my reserve. Noticing my anxious scanning of his books and diplomas, he rescues me with, "I try to educate myself in different fields. I probably would have studied literature when I was growing up, if I hadn't gone to the seminary. See, I had to make a lot of difficult choices at the time. Marsha and I married young—something I don't recommend—so everything was a struggle." He catches himself and quickly adds, "On the other hand, the ministry is really a two-person job and we were sustained, of course, by our faith."

The conversation is definitely not going according to my fantasy script, so I admire a beautifully bound edition of Walt Whitman's *Song of Myself* on the bookshelf nearest Reverend Dan's desk. That proves an excellent diversion, propelling the Reverend into a lengthy monologue about poetry, music, God, and the common man—a recitation that pleases me far more than talk of his faith and the struggle to maintain his profession in partnership with tacky old Marsha.

I listen attentively for fifteen or twenty minutes, nodding supportively, until I realize this is a school night—I have a long walk home and a pile of homework assignments. I smile broadly and say, "I really love this discussion, but I have to get home now. I'll be up late doing my reading for school tomorrow."

"Of course! I was also losing track of the time," says the Reverend, offering a wink with his smile. We stand up and he drapes his arm around my shoulders and squeezes my arm. Walking me past the offices to a side exit of the main hall of the church, he reassures me before I leave, "I truly enjoy talking with you, Sky. I look forward to continuing our talk at the fellowship meeting on Sunday evening. Maybe we can even discuss some of Walt Whitman's poetry then, if you think the other teens might be interested. At least I know I can count on you!"

I can only smile and nod because I can't find my voice, and I have no control over my physical response. I am electrified; I tingle everywhere Reverend Dan has made contact with my body. Beyond a doubt, I'm madly in love with this man—I come close to fainting right there on the church steps.

The rest of the week I'm simply beside myself until Sunday, when I position myself on Dan's side of the reception line at the end of the morning church service. Since I have to return my choir robe before leaving the church on Sunday morning, it's easy enough to avoid my friends and linger until most of the congregants have departed. Sure enough, when I approach Reverend Dan, his smile broadens, his eyes twinkle, and he presses both my hands in his, thanking me for participating in the choir and acknowledging that he will see me at the youth meeting that evening. His wife Marsha, thankfully, has already left for home, where she belongs.

At the PYF meeting, I play it cool, though I'm all eyes and ears for Reverend Dan. I barely respond to the silly conversation and annoying entreaties of the other teens, and confidently dismiss the vacuous girls who giggle ingratiatingly in Dan's presence or attempt to shift their seats closer to his. Bethany Rogers, an attractive senior, is particularly irritating to me, as she bats her eyes at the minister and brazenly flirts. But I alone understand that the passageway to Reverend Dan's heart is through his mind, and it will have to be Thursday nights after choir practice that I set foot in the portal.

After an interminable choir rehearsal the following Thursday, I deliver my polite and perfunctory goodbyes to the older members and maneuver my way through the church to the office area, catching sight of a teenager I didn't recognize taking leave of Reverend Dan in front of his office. (God on my side again!) I stage a nonchalant wave to the minister. His face promptly lights up, and he motions me toward him. Smiling, he takes my hand and guides me into the office, closing the door behind us. His eyes lock with mine, as he intones, "So nice to see you, Sky."

Terrified and titillated, I can scarcely remember to breathe. Desperately I scan the room for a point of focus, finally settling on an old photo of a young man in a football uniform, obviously the Reverend.

Following my gaze, he explains with a grin, "That was back when I was called Danny. I was quite an athlete before college." (Quite the stud, I silently conclude, managing a smile and nod.)

"What happened?" I intuitively inquire. "It seems like you followed a different path."

This proves to be the perfect segue.

Dodging Prayers and Bullets

Reverend Dan spiritedly prattles on about his good times as a star athlete in high school, while all I have to do is lean forward, nod, or chuckle appropriately to demonstrate my interest. Finally, hesitantly, Reverend Dan intimates, "To tell the truth, growing up in my family in Illinois was rather difficult. There were some serious family problems and I survived it because I got help from the church. That's why I wanted to become a youth minister, to see if I could give something back."

Studying the photo of the handsome and smiling young man, I comment, "I had the feeling something changed for you."

Looking dejected, Reverend Dan confides, "I don't let most people in on this, Sky, but my father was a gambling and drinking man—actually a pretty mean guy. I was close to my mother—she doted on me, in fact. But then, she was no physical, or mental, giant—no match for my father's bad behavior. I had to work to help support the family and finally just gave up on the notion of pursuing sports and an athletic scholarship. But the football coach—he was a parishioner at the local Presbyterian Church—he referred me to this minister, Dr. Oren Dayton. Dr. Dayton thought I had good academic as well as sports potential, so he began serving as both a minister and, I guess you'd say, a father figure to me. I was pretty depressed and messed up at the time, so, you know, I really looked up to Dr. Dayton. Eventually he guided me toward the ministry." (I will later discover that this heartfelt story has been considerably varnished.)

Dan looks away and adds somewhat sheepishly, "I married Marsha to get away from my own family, as much as anything. Of course, when the kids started coming it was pretty tough going …" Obviously seeking to change the somber tone of this present conversation, he stands up and scours his bookshelves. "Take a look at this," he offers, pulling down a high school yearbook and inviting me to sit next to him on the couch to look it over.

I'm thrilled! I can feel Reverend Dan's thigh against mine, and I lean in toward him to look at the photos in the yearbook. He rambles on about this activity and that friend, but I never register a word, and the photos are one big blur. I'm on fire and will gladly remain pressed up against him all night. (Does he sense it?)

Eventually, he notes the time and realizes I should head home. He suggests, "Stop by next week, if you have time, Sky—I really enjoy talking with you."

18

THIS IS ALL way too much. Is Reverend Dan feeling it, too? Is he, like me, lying in bed savoring our present and dreaming of our future?

The following week, after choir practice, I simmer with anticipation. I force myself to walk calmly out of the sanctuary to the offices, only to discover the door to Reverend Dan's office is shut! I stand there in the hall, like a dejected puppy, until Eugene Bennett, the choir director, happens by.

"Are you waiting to see Reverend Hansen?" he inquires, "Just knock on the door and let him know you're here." I would never have done so, but Mr. Bennett stands by to assure that I'm attended to, so, tentatively, I rap at the door. As the door opens, the kindly choir director smiles and departs.

"Sky!" Reverend Dan exclaims. "Can you give me a few minutes?"

"Sure," I answer, thinking, *I'd give you an eternity, if you asked.*

I fidget outside the door praying no one else will come along until, at last, old Mrs. Van Riper waddles out of Reverend Dan's Office, thanking the minister for his kind words of consolation. Smiling at me, she nods toward him and gushes, "This is sure the right person to talk to, honey."

Dan winks at me and guides me into his office, this time straight toward the sofa. "I brought something for you to hear," he enthuses. I'm thrilled he has been anticipating my visit. He closes the door, takes out a record, and actually starts playing an Elvis Presley song on the hi-fi in his office! He explains, "See, people don't know that Elvis started singing in church—he was greatly influenced by gospel and the blues, so he was touched by the Lord in any number of ways. This is one of my favorites."

The song, familiar to me from the radio, is "Are You Lonesome Tonight?" I act like I'm crazy about it, and soon Dan Hansen takes my hand, pulls me to my feet, and begins slow dancing with me. At first, I feel awkward and self-conscious, but finally I just go limp in his arms and allow him to guide me about the office. I can feel his body pressed against me, his breath on my face and neck. Slightly embarrassed, but enraptured, I bury my face against his chest.

Reverend Dan presses in closer and whispers, "It's hard to breathe, isn't it?" When the song ends, he gently rocks me back and forth while the phonograph needle bobbles repeatedly over the empty threads at the end of the record. Backing away but lodging my hand in his, Reverend Dan announces, "You better run along, child, before we both have something to regret."

I silently protest, "NO," but sigh and say nothing.

Dan guides me to the door, and while massaging the back of my neck with his fingers, he proposes, "See you next week, then. Meanwhile, you take care and think of me whenever you're feeling lonesome, OK?"

A minute later, I find myself standing outside the Presbyterian Church in the cool night air, but I can't recall how I've gotten from Reverend Dan's office to the exit. From the time he started rubbing my neck, I began sleepwalking. Shaking myself awake, I practically run home. When Mother inquires, "How did choir practice go?" I almost laugh in her face.

After school the next day, I rush out to buy the Elvis single, "Are You Lonesome Tonight?" Over the protests of Billy Dee, Gary and Luke, I play the 45 repeatedly, secretly obsessing over Reverend Dan and reliving our Thursday night encounter. My fantasizing is slightly blunted when the Reverend seems a little distant after church services the following Sunday and at the Presbyterian Youth Fellowship meeting that evening. I reassure myself that Reverend Dan, after all, has to be even more discreet than I.

Then, on Monday night, comes the wondrous phone call that changes everything. Billy Dee answers and yells for me to take the receiver. I panic momentarily when, handing me the phone, he whispers that the caller has identified herself as Marsha Hansen, the wife of the associate pastor of the Presbyterian Church. My anxiety dissipates quickly, however, when I hear Marsha Hansen's friendly tone on the telephone, "I know it's a school night I'm asking about Sky—is that your real name?—but would you be able to baby-sit on Wednesday, so that my husband and I can attend a church function?"

"It's Skyla," I assure her."

"Well, that's nice," she responds and continues, "If you could come over about 6:30, I'm sure we could get you home by 10:30, if that's OK with your parents."

"Oh, sure, no problem," I enthuse, "just let me check with Mother." I pretend to ask my mother, who is engrossed in the TV show "Your Hit Parade." This 'asking my mother' charade is a pretense I often employ to make it seem like our household is 'normal.'

When I affirm my availability, Mrs. Hansen, concludes with, "We truly appreciate this, Skyla, and Daniel will be sure to drive you home."

Daniel? Skyla? How pretentious, I think. But driving me home—Yes!!

Precisely at the appointed time on Wednesday night, I arrive at the Hansen household, a lovely apartment in the manse behind the church. Marsha invites me in and reintroduces me to the children. (A babysitter's most dreaded moment—the first encounter with the kids in the presence of about-to-depart parents.) Awkwardly, I attempt to interact with the boys, but the whiny girl child clings tenaciously to her mother. I anticipate, correctly, that the kid will give everyone a hard time when her parents try to leave. Meanwhile, I'm relieved the children have eaten and are already dressed for their 8 pm bedtime. That's a hoot for me, since my family never dresses for bed or has a specified sleep time. Orderliness has not taken up residence in the Sunny Vale projects.

Reverend Dan at last emerges from the back bedroom, looking debonair in a tan suit and blue dress shirt, his upper body spiced with that cologne. When he smiles and shakes my hand, I can detect he lingers just long enough to communicate that he, too, is abuzz from our contact.

Critically observing Marsha and Dan interact as they prepare to leave, I determine once again: he definitely deserves better. Marsha is a Nervous Nelly, overwrought about the details of home safety and bedtime rituals, and futilely trying to calm the sniveling little girl to release herself from the kid's clutches. I can tell Reverend Dan is impatient with Marsha; perhaps he's even embarrassed about her vacuity and domestic incompetence. A busy man like him requires an efficient and attentive wife—one who can confidently manage a household and also discuss great books and ideas.

Prattling on obsessively about trivialities, the deficient Marsha almost makes them late, until little Julia, still whimpering, at last accepts the transfer into my arms. Of course, as soon as her mother leaves, the kid stops crying and squirms down to watch TV with her brothers, Jimmy and Johnny, who are content to simply be left alone. Shortly, I win both boys over by inviting them to have some of the candy and chips their parents have left for me.

Once Marsha is out of the way, I note, the kids are pretty nice and probably won't try to take advantage of my unfamiliarity with their household routines. As I'm reading a story to little Julia she falls asleep in my lap and easily transfers to her crib bed. Jimmy and Johnny actually get ready for bed promptly at 8:00 pm, voluntarily brushing their teeth. They're careful not to awaken Julia as they climb into their own beds. Their abject compliancy forces me to contemplate the contrasting chaos in my home—I can't help wondering if orderliness promotes healthy habits but squelches spunky independence in children?

I do homework for about half an hour, until I'm sure the children are sound asleep; then I tiptoe over and close their bedroom door. Now is my opportunity to scope out the Hansen living quarters, starting with the easiest place first, the living room. I peruse the books and records and framed family photos, observing with satisfaction that Marsha and Dan are never looking fondly at each other in any of the pictures. I also note that there is no wedding photo proudly displayed in this public area, a good omen for a potential future for the Reverend Dan Hansen and me.

It's a little after 8:30 pm, and since I had lied to the Hansens about having eaten dinner before I arrived, it's time to check out the refrigerator. Unlike the kitchen at my house, this one is neat and organized and well-stocked. Having babysat for neighbors many times before, I'm practiced at surreptitiously consuming food other than the routinely proffered snacks. If I only pilfer from foodstuffs already open and in ample supply, no one will notice: one slice of bread from the middle of the loaf, a cheese or ham single, a pickle, a couple of olives; small samples of the baking ingredients like chocolate chips and flaked coconut. I detest raisins, so no temptation there. It's not that any of the families I baby-sit for would mind my eating; sometimes they even urge me to help myself. I simply don't want to acknowledge my hunger, or in any way expose the bareness of our family cupboards.

By 9:00 pm, I'm ready to investigate the Hansen bedroom, a move that requires more audacity, since there's no excuse for entering it. I peek in on the children to be sure they're still sound asleep. Then, feeling like a thief in a shameful and thrilling way, I open the alluring bedroom door. I don't have the nerve to look through drawers and closets, at least not this first time, but I do examine everything on the walls and surfaces.

Like most of the homes where I baby-sit, this one has furnishings and art much more expensive and tasteful than anything in my house. Indulging in babysitting domestic forays, while intriguing, forces me to be painfully aware of class disparities. At my home, there are no bookshelves or art, and no one can ever seem to locate even a pencil to take down messages.

In truth, I'm a little disheartened that the Hansen bedroom looks nice— this somehow indicates that Marsha Hansen, at least, values her marriage. Even more dispiriting is a prominent photo of Danny and Marsha in their teens, both smiling and obviously in love. I keep forgetting they were high school sweethearts and were already married by the time he entered the seminary. The smiling and confident girl in the high school photo belies the anxious and timorous woman Marsha has become. Marsha obviously let herself go, I conclude. Poor Dan sure got less than he bargained for. Still, there's something intimidating about the changes in Marsha intimated by the photo. Mildly distressed, I quickly retreat from the master bedroom and return to the living room to complete the homework I've brought along.

When Marsha and Dan return, well before the agreed upon 10:30 pm, they add a tip to the 50 cents per hour I charge, and, as Marsha promised, Dan volunteers to escort me home. At last the evening begins to evolve in a manner that more than gratifies my fantasies.

As we approach the darkened church parking lot, Reverend Dan takes my hand and squeezes it. He opens the passenger door first and guides me to the seat, brushing his hand across my back and shoulders. Then he goes around the car, takes the driver's seat, and pulls the car out of the lot. But instead of turning right toward the main road, Dan heads left along the back streets, choosing a circuitous route to the housing projects where my family lives.

"I don't bite," he teases, reaching across the seat, wrapping his arm around my waist and pulling me closer to him. He steadies the steering wheel with his left hand as he drops his right hand to begin stroking the top, and then the inside, of my left thigh.

He's got nerve, I think, but then I signal my complicity by allowing him to gently nudge my right leg in the opposite direction.

Reverend Dan groans softly and begins to rub between my legs, showing obvious enthusiasm as my breathing deepens, partly due to the stimulation and partly due to terror. He pauses and pulls the car over on a quiet side street, shuts down the headlights, and cuts off the engine. Shifting his body toward me and bringing me in closer with his right arm, he begins kissing me deeply, while his left hand explores my body through my clothes.

This is my first consensual sexual contact, and it's nothing like fighting off old Artie Johnson. Even though my body tingles electric, I've never envisioned anything more than kissing someone with enthusiasm. With Reverend Dan, however, I'm totally enamored and trusting, so I simply allow my body to slump compliantly. Still, this is more than a bit confusing because I can't erase the awareness that he's married and a minister. I'm not at all sure what he intends, or what I should permit. I simply remain mute.

Soon, Dan takes my left hand and places it on the front of his pants. Scared and embarrassed by this maneuver, I stiffen and keep my hand flat and open. Dan cups his hand over mine and moves it around on the outside of his pants. "See what you do to me, Sky?" he whispers.

I never expected or even wanted to go this far with anyone, including my beloved Reverend Dan, but I'm stunned into a submissive compliance. I tug my hand away and drop my head on his shoulder, hoping to communicate that I'm still with him, despite my verbal reserve and physical reluctance. Dan picks up the cue and pulls me close against him, simply rocking and embracing me for several minutes.

"I'd better get you home," he finally sighs, as he grips the steering wheel with both hands, breaking the spell between us.

I shove over toward my side of the car and can't think of a thing to say.

When the car approaches my neighborhood, Reverend Dan reassures me with the inquiry, "Do you want to stop by my office Thursday night after choir practice? I'd like that, Sky."

I nod affirmatively and barely manage to mumble, "Yes, OK."

As I lift the car door handle, Reverend Dan reaches over and squeezes my left knee. I jump out, waving limply and smiling, as he alters the mood by calling out, "Marsha and I appreciate you babysitting on a school night!"

Slowly making my way toward our apartment, I have to admit I'm perplexed. Truthfully, I'm scared and shocked by how far Reverend Dan was willing to go. Other than "the disgrace" that happened to me in Kentucky and the way I've been treated by that nasty Artie Johnson, I've never even had a boyfriend. Yes, this man turns me on, as they say, but I'm not sure what that implies. Maybe, I consider, it would be better to imagine myself as Dan's daughter rather than as his future wife? No, that won't work with Marsha and the kids.

I reassure myself I'm getting carried away, being needlessly fearful. Surely Reverend Dan will never ask me to take off my clothes or to look at his nakedness—or to go all the way? Would he risk getting me pregnant? He is, after all, the youth minister. He'll definitely wait until we figure out what to do about his family, so we can get married.

All week, I perseverate on this. What might Dan Hansen be planning? Might he and I soon declare our love, throw ourselves upon the mercy of the church, and ask for forgiveness? Or might we be required to run away and make a completely new life together? No, he'll probably want to keep the kids and his position in the church. Things could definitely get ugly unless ... Marsha develops some terminal illness! Yes, that's it. I'd be proud to raise (actually improve upon) the children, even if that meant I had to leave high school. Dan and I will stay in Sunny Vale after Marsha's death, so I can still see my siblings and there will be enough money to support everyone. Yes, that's the fantasy that serves my longing.

19

AFTER CHOIR PRACTICE on Thursday night, I'm somewhat reluctant to show up at Reverend Dan's office. I linger in the vicinity until he spots me. He is so obviously pleased to see me that my doubts are assuaged. I decide to give myself over and count on the Reverend's good judgment to counter my confusion.

When he abruptly closes and locks the door behind us, however, my apprehension ascends. I have little time to express any reservations, because he immediately pulls me close to him and intones, "I just love the way you respond—my wife has no passion."

I don't exactly understand what this means, but it impels me toward wanting to please Reverend Dan. I snuggle against his neck as he scoops me up and lifts me onto the sofa. He begins kissing me, then massaging my body, eventually reaching inside my clothes for all the good places. I can't believe this is happening, but I like it in a scary, titillating way. I'm shocked and appalled once again, however, when he opens the front of his pants and presses himself against my inner thigh.

Trying to pull myself up, I gasp nervously, "You wouldn't go all the way, would you?"

"It's OK," the Reverend assures. "Trust me, Sky. I won't make the same mistake again. Let me explain." He sits up and while I look away, adjusts his clothes and then takes my hands in his. "Sky," he confesses, "the reason I gave up football was not to support my mother, but to support my own family." His face tightening, he adds bitterly, "Marsha got herself pregnant." I notice that he reports this as if he's not part of the equation and continues, "See, the football coach knew about it, which is why he took me to talk with Dr. Oren Dayton, the minister at the First Presbyterian Church. Dr. Dayton helped me figure things out, and I got married to Marsha and finished high school. He was the one who made the arrangements with our parents and the school and all, and he gave me an administrative job at the church. He even helped me and Marsha find a cheap place to live. Later on, he guided me through college and the seminary. I was like a son to him, and I still feel that way." Softening, Dan turns toward me, "Believe me, Sky, when I tell you, I'm *not* having any more babies with Marsha or anybody else—so you're safe with me."

This is all way too much information for me, but I feel very sorry for Reverend Dan and want to give him whatever he needs. This time I initiate the resumption of our kissing by gently stroking his face and hair. Soon he's pressing himself against me again, so I close my eyes until he finishes. I see him take out his handkerchief, but I try not to think about what he might be doing.

Over the next few months, Reverend Dan keeps his word and never attempts to go all the way with me. He seems to love getting me all turned on, and then maneuvering our partially clothed bodies into safe, but mutually satisfying, contact. Relishing my newfound sensuality, I decide I'm much better off with Reverend Dan than the silly boys my own age, who are known to kiss and tell. I'm disappointed, however, that the more intense our private intimacy becomes, the less positively Dan responds to me in public. Before our physical contact, Reverend Dan Hansen was attentive and affectionate toward me, particularly at the PYF meetings. Now, when we meet in public, he's reserved or, worse, treats me like one of the troubled teens he works with.

Still, I continue to meet him after choir practice, and we take full advantage of our "car time" whenever Mrs. Hansen calls me to baby-sit.

20

THE FIRST TIME it happens, I'm mortified. It seems like it must be some kind of perverted thing. We're snuggled on the sofa in Reverend Dan's office and he is kissing me and exploring my body in the usual sensual ways, when he slips the tip of his middle finger into my rectum. I twitch and tighten up, assuming he has made an embarrassing mistake.

Instead, Dan grips my shoulder with his other hand, presses me tighter against the back of the sofa, and begins reassuring me, instructing confidently, "Easy, easy just relax. Trust me—I promise I won't hurt you."

I'm not at all sure whether to be offended, ashamed, or honored that Reverend Dan is so uninhibitedly free with my body. I keep reminding myself that this is my future husband, so it's right for him to teach me how to be a good wife. When I nod assent, he begins kissing me again, so I try to relax. It feels nice when he just rubs my behind along the outside, but the insertion of his finger makes me feel awkward and uncomfortable. Why does he like that? What does it mean?

Dodging Prayers and Bullets

The denouement to that foreshadowing comes a few days later. Thinking back on it, Reverend Dan schemed unconscionably for the opportunity. Mother had become accustomed to my baby-sitting on school nights, and Mrs. Hansen has been calling upon my services on a somewhat regular basis. On this particular evening, however, it is the Reverend himself who calls shortly after 8 pm on a Tuesday night. He chats pleasantly with Mother, informing her that he has been called to intervene in a crisis and, unfortunately, Mrs. Hansen is already attending a women's function at the church.

"Would it be possible," he asks my mother, "for Sky to come over to baby-sit for a couple of hours, just until Mrs. Hansen returns?"

Since it's already dark and rather chilly on this late fall evening, my brother William, now almost eighteen and a senior in high school, drops me off at the Hansen residence behind the church. When William had turned seventeen, Dad's friend Artie Johnson—that pervert I loathe and avoid—helped Daddy retrieve, retool, and paint a wrecked car for William. (At least Artie the creep is good for something, I sigh.) I wave goodbye to William and approach the door to the manse of the church.

"Surprise!" Dan Hansen announces, opening the door to his home, "Marsha and the kids are away for a couple of days. You only have to 'baby-sit' me, Sky."

I definitely feel like a bullfrog caught in a flashlight—frozen in fear at the edge of the lily pond. Fortunately, Dan is attuned to my awkwardness as he guides me inside and mitigates by offering me a coke, selecting some Elvis Presley music for the hi-fi, and chatting casually about school and music.

"Hey, here comes our song," he announces, as the prelude to 'Are You Lonesome Tonight?' begins. Taking my hands and pulling me up into a close, romantic slow dance, he whispers the words of the song in my ear as we glide about the living room. Just when I'm dreamily relaxed, fantasizing about our future wedding, Dan navigates me into the master bedroom. He has placed a clean sheet on top of the bedspread and set the pillows on top of the sheet. I balk.

As a wave of panic arises in me, I manage to tell Dan, "This is too fast for me. I'm really scared."

He smiles and reassures me, "Don't worry, baby! You have to trust me—I just want us to be more comfortable, that's all. We're always afraid of somebody walking in on us or interrupting us. This is so much better. Let's take advantage and have some relaxed time together. You'll leave here a virgin, just like I always promise. Trust me ... please?"

"OK," is once again all the response I can muster. I hope I don't look as shaky on the outside as I feel on the inside.

After a considerable period of gentle kissing and snuggling on the bed, it seems like Dan will keep his word. And he does, sort of. I don't want to get undressed, so he just opens my blouse and lifts up my skirt. Eventually, he overcomes my resistance to removing my nylons and underwear, but he continues to be gentle and slow as he kisses and fondles me. I won't look directly at Dan's body, so I'm not sure what he's up to when he reaches across the night table and seems to be rubbing something from a jar on himself. I forget about it in a few minutes, though, when he turns me on my stomach and begins massaging my back in a lovely, sensitive way.

He whispers, "I'm going to write my name on you and it'll stay there forever," as he traces the letters on my back with the tip of his finger, just the way girlfriends do with each other on sleep-over nights.

I'm totally relaxed and comforted, until Dan abruptly rolls over on top of me and presses me against the mattress. I feel like a squashed bug. At my polite "Ow!" he lifts his chest a bit, relieving my breathing, but now he's pressing the lower part of his body against my buttocks. I can feel that he's covered with some kind of lotion or oil.

"I think I better go," I try, as he begins pushing between my buttocks, "I'm scared—Ouch!—that hurts. Please don't, I don't want this."

"I can't stop now," Dan pants. "You got me too excited! C'mon, relax. Haven't you studied anatomy? You can't get pregnant this way." He's pushing and forcing himself inside me.

I start to cry, "Nooo, don't! Please, I ..."

There's no negotiation; it's over before I can formulate any debate or refusal. What he has done to me is downright painful, without even taking into consideration the humiliation.

Dan lets out a deep breath and rolls off me. He pulls me sideways against his chest and keeps repeating, "It's OK, it's OK, don't be upset, calm down." Trying to assuage my sobs, he adds, "It's not really sex.

It's a way for you to satisfy me without getting pregnant. It's normal. All married people do this. It's fine."

I don't feel fine. I'm horrified, ashamed and my bottom feels all greasy and hurt.

Dan Hansen reaches across me for the box of tissues and hands me a wad. "Go on in the bathroom and clean yourself up—you'll feel better." Compounding my shame, he hands over my underwear and nylons as I get up to make my way to the bathroom with the tissues stuffed between my legs.

I stay in the bathroom a long time, cleaning myself with wet toilet paper and running the tap vigorously to splash water on my tear-stained face, trying to stifle my sobs of resentment and, yes, disgrace. Finally, I sit down on the closed toilet seat and just peer around the bathroom. I notice the white bottle of Old Spice cologne, inscribed with red and gray lettering; there's a bottle of yellowy Listerine mouthwash; Ipana toothpaste and two adult toothbrushes and two smaller ones for the older children; a small unopened box of Kleenex. Harbored in the soap dish is a bar of Ivory Soap—the pure white kind that floats. I don't touch it. On the wall toward the shower a blue and white crocheted wall hanging of a country church is inscribed with, "Bring it to the Lord in Prayer." And directly across from the toilet is a framed picture of Jesus with a scattering of children at his feet. The smallest child is handing Jesus a flower as he touches her blond curly-haired head. The caption under the picture reads, "Bless You, Child," and the irony is not lost on me.

I become aware that Dan is knocking repeatedly on the bathroom door, insisting that he needs to get me home. Pressing his body against the door, he attempts to console me, but I'm barely listening. He's so insistent that I have to focus and make sense of the words.

"Don't be like this, Sky," he persists, "You worry too much. Married people do this to stop the babies from coming. You just have to learn about these things. You're still a virgin! Is that what you're upset about? You'll be fine, I promise." Getting no response to that, he takes a different tack, "Truthfully, I'm disappointed; I thought we had something special between us. You have to trust me more. Sky? Please?" When I still don't respond, and go back to contemplating the items in the bathroom, he adds in a more cajoling tone, "C'mon, baby! Didn't I keep my promise that you would stay a virgin? Didn't I?"

"It's OK," I finally utter. I realize that I can't stay in the bathroom forever. I'm too embarrassed to protest that my bottom hurts—it feels pinched, like when you catch your neck in a zipper. Nor do I mention that I found slime and blood on the wet toilet paper.

Without opening the toilet lid again, I flush the shameful waste, and then try to straighten up my hair and clothes. I stuff a wad of toilet paper in my underwear in case there is more dripping. I even look around the bathroom to be sure it's tidy before I open the door. All I want is to go home and for everything, including me, to look normal.

Fortunately, Dan is fully dressed when I come out of the bathroom. Glancing toward the bedroom, I can see that he has restored the bedding. He guides me to the living room sofa, where he has set out a glass of milk and some cookies on the coffee table. I can barely swallow, but manage a few bites of a cookie and a sip of milk, which I hate, but my throat is dry and I don't want to ask for water. I just want to be home.

He gets our coats from the closet. When we reach the church parking lot, he takes my hand, which is hanging limply off my arm like a dead fish. As I stand beside the car shivering from the emotional and physical cold, the Reverend Daniel Hansen leans in and hugs me. I don't feel a thing, and I can tell he's nervous and guilty, as I remain there stiff and vacant.

"Please don't be mad," Dan petitions, holding the car door to let me in on the passenger's side. After he starts the car and pulls out of the church parking lot, he begs, "Come, sit a little closer. I need us to feel OK together."

In a state of rote shock, I move over beside him and try to smile through my muteness.

"Well, here we are!" Dan announces nervously, as we approach the housing projects. "We're still best friends, right?"

"Of course," I lie. "I'm fine."

"You'll come see me after choir practice, right?" he urges. "I promise we'll only talk, or do what *you* want, OK? I never want to lose our friendship, Sky."

"OK," I respond, like an automaton.

I reach for the car door and Dan touches my arm. "Oh, wait, hold on a minute." He pulls a five-dollar bill and a one-dollar bill from his wallet and hands the money over to me. "For the baby-sitting," he laughs, definitely with more anxiety than amusement. At my baby-sitting rate of 50 cents an hour, six dollars is triple what I usually get, but the whole transaction only makes me feel worse. As I'm departing, Reverend Dan calls out, "I really care for you, Sky."

I hoist my dead arm up and quickly drop it, forcing a smile. But I'm not really buying it, and never will again.

Luckily, Dora Lee is asleep and Mother and the boys are glued to the TV set when I come into the house. That means I'm not required to engage in small talk, so I'm able to dash upstairs to the bathroom to inspect myself with the sink mirror and a hand mirror. My face looks as ugly as my bottom. I'm glad the light in the hallway is out when I quickly slip from the bathroom into my bedroom.

A short while later, little Dory, who shares my bed, wakes up when she hears me crying. I tell her I have a bad headache, and she snuggles up next to me. I vow to watch over her always, even though I know vows by grown-ups don't do much of anything to safeguard children.

21

THOUGH IT'S CERTAINLY the end of my naïve romantic illusions, that awful night of fake baby-sitting, sadly, is not the end of my relationship with Reverend Dan. There is no one I can ask about the propriety of what happened, so I'm left gasping for breath in the noxious vapors of guilt and angst.

Is it possible that sperm can drift from my butt to my womb and get me pregnant? Is there such a thing as rectal virginity? Is Dan Hansen a pervert, or is it true married people usually do this thing? Maybe it's an indication he plans to marry me? (Do I even want to marry him?)

At the town library, I surreptitiously peruse the biology and anatomy books, but there's nothing that describes what Dan did. The part of me that's angry aches to ask the Reverend what Jesus would make of our activities, but the scared debased part shuts me down.

I skip that week's choir practice and the PYF meeting. After the regular Sunday church service the following week, Reverend Dan maneuvers his way in my direction and presses me to come to see him the forthcoming Thursday. "Just to talk things over," he insists.

Good shepherd that I am, I dutifully show up in his office, feigning an enthusiastic greeting. I'm glad Dan seems nervous when he talks about how much he cares for me and misses me. He tells me he wants me to be happy, and eventually works his way into hugging me, in an awkward fatherly fashion. He does not attempt to take off any of my clothes, and I can tell he wants me to forgive and forget. How ironic that I had seen him as my (blessed) shelter from the storm!

I can't even think about talking to anyone else about what happened, so I continue to seek solace from Dan on Thursday nights. But it's never the same. He's always gentle and discreet, almost apologetic in his affection; for my part, I simply leave my body to him, shutting down my mind and emotions. It takes three regular menstrual periods in a row to convince me I'm not pregnant.

The next time I baby-sit for the Hansens (at the request of Mrs. Hansen, of course), I experience the relationship between Dan and Marsha in a new light. There's obviously no love lost, or found, between the couple. He seems rather cold and self-absorbed, and I feel some empathy toward the formerly vivacious Marsha's pathetic attempts to please her important husband while she manages the children and household—alone and in the background. Though I don't know it at the time, I'm nurturing the first seed of what is to become my far off bloom of feminist consciousness.

Though constantly chastening myself for doing so, I still sometimes justify my liaison with Dan Hansen by imagining that we will one day marry and sanctify everything. Especially now that we've established some sexual boundaries, I am more relaxed about our post-choir-practice rendezvous. I'm asked to baby-sit less frequently for the Hansens, however, and whenever Dan drives me home, he simply kisses me goodnight in a very sweet way. Our secret, illicit passion in the office of his ministry is thrilling in a perverse way, and, of course, serves to sustain my increasing cynicism toward religion and the church.

Had Dan in general adhered to a little more personal restraint, I might have eventually accorded further sexual experimentation, or even initiated it. My fantasies of mutual devotion between us are abruptly dashed, however, when I decide to drop by his office for a surprise visit after an early Tuesday evening of research at the town library. Reverend Hansen's door is closed when I approach, so, recalling the previous prod by the choir director, I knock gently. Dan opens the door a crack and quickly steps out closing it behind him.

Nervously and formally, he addresses me, "Good evening, Sky. I'm so sorry; I have appointments tonight, but I'll definitely see you, as usual, on Thursday."

"Oh, sorry," I mumble.

But, upon his retreat into the office, I catch a glimpse of Bethany Rogers seated on the sofa with Dan's high school yearbook in her lap. At the Presbyterian Youth Fellowship, I had been noticing beautiful dumb Bethany, a senior at Sunny Vale High, developing a mad crush on Dan Hansen.

And there she is, sitting where I once sat, performing the yearbook ritual. It's déjà vu gone bad.

Stunned and dejected, I slowly head home, everything suddenly, crushingly, illuminated. I recall how, after school one day last week, I had noticed Bethany walking Jimmy and Johnny Hansen home. At the time, I was vaguely bothered that Bethany was now also baby-sitting for the Hansens, but I had not considered I was about to endure yet another indignity in the service of the Reverend.

I arrive at home, somehow get past Mother, lock myself in the bathroom and sob piteously. Once again I examine my red and swollen face in the mirror, wondering if this will forever be my life. I shake my head in self-loathing and disgust, and douse myself with cold water. Then, I begin laughing, genuinely insanely, because I have been such a naïve, stupid fool. Luke is banging on the bathroom door, so I walk out with a towel pressed against my face, pretending to be drying myself off. I lie down on the bed, where five-year-old Dory, sensing my distress, tries to comfort me. Telling Dory that I don't feel well, I curl up under the covers and silently review my predicament.

Miraculously, I conclude that, despite my bitter and thorough humiliation with regard to Bethany, in a weirdly ironic way, I'm now in charge of my relationship with the Reverend Dan Hansen. He knows that I know. Of course, if I tell on him, he can always claim I'm a troubled teen who made up our physical relationship. Someone once told me a story about a guy who was charged with rape and got off because he had several other fellows testify that the girl was also having sex with them. Even if I were to get the sympathy (and there's certainly no guarantee of that), the last thing I want is a public spectacle, a sexual scandal in the bosom of the church. No, I assure myself, any shame inherent in exposure will inevitably, primarily, be mine.

So I determine that my best recourse is to silently punish Dan—to keep him guessing by simply hanging around Bethany Rogers in his presence, and becoming very friendly and attentive toward his wife, Marsha. In truth, I never plan to tell anyone about our relationship, but Danny can sweat that out. I know Bethany is too dumb to figure out anything, and Marsha's sense of self was decimated long ago.

That leaves *me*, the keeper of the secrets, with the upper hand. Hallelujah, and God Damn!

22

JARED STANTON, a young man I know from the Sunday evening Presbyterian Youth Fellowship, finally helps me disengage emotionally from the ever-so-Reverend Daniel Hansen.

Despite my determined bravado, I find I can't bear to be in the same room with Bethany and Reverend Dan, so I skip several successive meetings of the PYF. One evening, Jared, who attends a local private school, calls me at home, begging me to return to the group. The "Golden Boy" of the youth fellowship, with blonde hair and sparkling blue eyes, Jared is very sweet. Actually, he's beautiful to behold. Though he's not really my type—I'm attracted to the swarthy, intense, unavailable types—Jared's attention definitely mitigates the bizarre turn in my relationship with Dan Hansen.

Jared makes a point of sitting next to me at the next PYF meeting, and then begins phoning me at home during the week to talk about school and friends. He tells me how much he admires Reverend Dan, and confesses he has even consulted him about "some things."

Dodging Prayers and Bullets

I can't imagine what kind of concerns someone like Jared, from a perfect, wealthy family, could possibly have, but I'm no more inclined to discuss my personal problems with Jared than he is to share his with me. I can tell, however, that Jared is genuinely interested in me; he invites me to the movies, buys a soda for us to share, and walks me part of the way home, even though he lives at the opposite end of Sunny Vale. He seems to appreciate my humor, intelligence and sense of adventure ... qualities most boys his age find irrelevant, if not downright daunting, in girls.

Conducting this flirtation with Jared under Reverend Dan's nose, I feel as if I've saved a bit of face. Unfortunately, since Jared is physically rather shy and reserved—more a boyfriend for "show" than romance—I soon miss the physical contact and sexual energy I can work up and release with Dan.

Without any illusions, I drop by the Reverend's office on the occasional Thursday night; neither of us ever mentions Jared or Bethany. Still, Reverend Dan's audacity continues to astound me, and I perpetually have to hold the line since I don't trust him to toe the line regarding how far we will go. There will certainly be no more "home visits" on my part. I make sure to restrict our alone time to the more public venue of his office. Pathetic, yes, but also true.

It's the spring of my junior year of high school, and since there's no way I will be asked by anyone else, I'm relieved to invite Jared Stanton to be my date for the dreaded Sunny Vale Regional High School Junior Prom. Sadly, I'm not sexually attracted to Jared, but, in appearance and manner, he makes for a princely prom date.

Looking back on all this, it's now rather obvious neither Jared Stanton nor I understood what Reverend Hansen surely knew: beautiful, beatific Jared Stanton was gay. In 1962, in Sunny Vale, New Jersey, homosexuality was so far removed from the realm of alternate realities that it was not even on the register of possibilities. The only one who likely had a clue was Dan Hansen. I later discover that Jared, like me, was getting a lot more than spiritual guidance from the Reverend.

Still, I might have benefited from the genuine friendship I was developing with Jared, if his mother had not gotten a load of my family.

Eleanor Stanton is somewhat of a celebrity in Sunny Vale and the surrounding New Jersey towns. Wealthy and educated at Vassar, she's the "society" editor for the *Weekly Chronicle*, a newspaper that covers local news, sports, and gossip in Sunny Vale, and also reviews art and social events in nearby Newark, New Jersey. Having visited England more than once in her youth, Eleanor has contrived a vaguely British accent and, for good measure, married Dr. Edgar Stanton, a cardiologist by profession, who serves on the Board of Deacons of the Presbyterian Church. Gripping a well-stoked pipe as a perpetual prop, Dr. Stanton is the type of man who wears slippers and lounges about the house in a smoking jacket, priding himself on social restraint and brevity of articulation. On the Board of Deacons, Dr. Stanton restricts himself to esoteric comments and erudite nods. Upstanding and righteous, he's the epitome of white Anglo-Saxon Protestant values.

Jared rarely speaks of his father; on the other hand, he adores his mother, the elegant and eloquent Eleanor Stanton, who is also President of the Ladies of Letters, the book study club of the Presbyterian Church. Mrs. Stanton is impressed that I'm familiar with several books on the club's recommended reading list. She might have condoned Jared's friendship with me for an extended period, if fortune had enabled Jared to be just a few months older.

Alas, it happens that Jared is four months short of his 17th birthday on the evening of the Junior Prom. Since he does not yet have a driver's license, Mrs. Stanton graciously volunteers to chauffeur us. Unfortunately, out of curiosity about the family of her beloved son's prom date, she also elects to accompany Jared to the door when he picks me up at our apartment in the projects. The meeting could only have been more disastrous if Dad had walked in raging.

My enchantment over the beautiful corsage Jared presents me at the door quickly dissipates to dread when I see his mother, bedecked in finery, climb out of her car and head toward our door. I have no choice but to invite them both in. My mother knows that Eleanor Stanton is a writer for the Weekly Chronicle and an "educated lady." Mother is so intimidated by Mrs. Stanton's formidable presence that she compensates by talking nonstop nonsense and scurrying about the apartment bewailing "the state of things." The TV is blasting, and clothes and bedding are strewn about the unmade sofa bed in the living room; there's barely a place for anyone to sit. Luke and Dory, sensing Mother's discomfort and Mrs. Stanton's contempt, put on what could best be described as a "Wild West Show." They start whooping, jumping about, and tossing projectiles—to distract, no doubt from the awkward emotional tension in the room. My face turns bright red when I notice the appalled look on Mrs. Stanton's face as she regards our unkempt household and the histrionics of my brother and sister. My mother's feeble, "Y'all hush that racket" does nothing to quell the chaos.

Straining a smile, Jared tactfully suggests we promptly depart for the prom—just in case any extra help is needed with the set up. In the car on the way, he, Mrs. Stanton and I conduct a polite, constrained conversation, and, somehow, I get through the night, managing a feckless apology to Jared about the reception at my home. He is kind but, as I correctly assess, I will no longer be on Mrs. Stanton's list of approved social contacts for her Jared.

In a way this rejection is more emotionally devastating than my discovery of Dan's duplicity. I'm ashamed of my family, but at the same time bitterly resentful of Eleanor Stanton's arrogant judgment, which is based primarily on our less fortunate circumstances. I mentally dismiss Jared as a mama's boy and a coward. Though I repress the affront during my remaining high school days, within the recesses of my emerging consciousness, outrage is festering about the injustices of class and economic inequities.

Fortunately, the summer before my senior year is just a few weeks after the prom. To make some money and distract myself from the loss of both Jared and my fantasies about a future with Reverend Dan, I take on two temporary jobs. Mother repeatedly expresses disappointment that I have dropped out of the PYF and the church choir, but by then Mother is used to fielding disappointments from life and family.

23

SENIOR YEAR IS REPUTED to be the best of high school, since everyone supposedly lets go of petty grievances, suspends the social competition, and prepares to move on and away from home and childhood. It seemed to go that way for William, who is now a junior in college enrolled in a pre-law curriculum on full scholarship at Rutgers University. Mother is proud of him, and William has certainly earned the accolades and the opportunity.

For me, senior year at Sunny Vale High School is a horror. I have no plans for college, no ideas about my future, and no boyfriend prospects. Harboring the secret of my relationship with Dan Hansen, I find it impossible to connect authentically with any of my peers, male or female. Also, the boys at school seem extremely immature, and I certainly don't want to risk another rejection from the likes of Jared Stanton. In contrast, the boys from my neighborhood are more physically developed, but they're also rough and ready, with no qualms about demanding sexual accommodations from their girlfriends. I'm aware that once such boys are finished with the girls—many poor immigrants—they make fun of them and label them "sluts" or "cows."

Wanting no part of that adolescent caste system, I find myself essentially alone, an economic and social isolate with no vision of the future. My only personal determination is to protect my younger siblings from our increasingly violent and chaotic home life. I might as well have wished for world peace.

Perhaps there is some divine, or at least moral, justice that the Reverend Daniel Hansen ultimately emerges as my savior—of sorts. When Dan realizes I'm at a loss regarding my future and have not applied to any colleges, he gets on the phone, just the way Dr. Oren Dayton had done for him many years ago. Reverend Dan arranges a belated interview for me at North Essex State Teacher's College in New Jersey. Since I have no interest in becoming a teacher, I'm reluctant to follow through, but Dan personally hands me the college application and guides me in filling it out and mailing it.

A few weeks later, the college requests an interview, and Dan insists on driving me to the campus. His wife Marsha opts to join us in the car, bringing along the Hansens' little girl, Julia. (Marsha assures me that Bethany Rogers will pick up their sons, Johnny and Jimmy, after school …)

I'm in total dread of this trip. *Just great,* I think, *Bethany gets more entrenched, and I get to play pathetic foster child with Dan and Marsha.*

Actually, things work out far better than I anticipate. Little Julia, probably sensing my discomfort, asks to sit and snuggle with me in the back seat of the car, enabling Dan and Marsha to position themselves up front. I feign sleep with Julia to avoid chattering with Marsha. Sadly, I overhear Marsha expressing to Dan her personal disappointment about never attending college. An unsympathetic Dan treats Marsha's wistfulness as a criticism of him. He cracks, "I don't recall you expressing any such interests in high school and you've never mentioned it since."

She counters, "I never had the time to think about such things. It was your future we were always concerned about. But I'm interested in the world and I like to read, too, you know."

Dan snorts. "Come on, the *Betty Crocker Cookbook* and the *Ladies Home Journal* don't exactly count as college textbooks."

Marsha looks back to assure I'm sleeping (ha!) and whispers a defense of some sort. I can't catch their next exchange, but the tension and resentment between them is palpable. The ensuing silence reconfirms for me a life maxim that I already understand from growing up with my parents: there are, at minimum, two sides to every horrid relationship.

My interview at North Essex State College goes well, and I'm easily admitted on the basis of my academic record. When the bills for tuition and the dormitory arrive, however, I apologetically inform Dan Hansen I can't really afford to go. Dan contacts my mother, who confirms our family has no resources for a girl to attend college, and that I'm needed at home to help out with Dory.

I'm disheartened, but, to his credit, Reverend Hansen is not to be deterred; he brings me a State Scholarship Application, and assures me that I will receive an honorarium from the Presbyterian Church to cover books and supplies. William helps me fill out the forms and, when the State Scholarship comes through, I also learn I can earn extra money through a work-study program on campus.

Shockingly, in early September, Dan goes to the garage where my daddy, Lonnie Lee, hangs out and gets him to agree to drive me to my dormitory. Whether Dan Hansen does all this out of kindness, guilt or self-protection ultimately doesn't matter.

The paradoxical culmination is, he who stole my adolescence delivered me to a tenuous adulthood. Amen.

24

SO IT IS THAT in September 1963, I pack my few belongings in a laundry bag and a cardboard box, and climb into Dad's reconditioned 1959 Chevy for the trip to college.

Little Dory, unable to verbally express her despair over my leaving, leans into the car window and tugs on my neck and shoulder. My three brothers are at school, so, thankfully, I had mentally taken leave of them the night before. Dad invited Mother to come along on the trip to Montclair, but Flo-Anna, by then an entrenched agoraphobic, makes the usual excuses about being too busy with the house and feeling light-headed, meaning set upon by one of her "dizzy spells." I can tell she is deeply distressed over my leaving, but I'm still appalled that, in her best hillbilly vernacular, she responds to my 'see ya soon' with, "God willin' and the creek don't rise."

Torn between the prospect of emancipation and the terror of separation, I choke up as I wave goodbye to a sobbing Dory and a teary Mother. "I won't be away long," I assure Dory. That was a patent untruth, though I really didn't understand how much so at the time.

Dodging Prayers and Bullets

Although my father seems to get it that college is a means of escape for me, he's likely perplexed by his own role in the accumulated family anguish necessitating this escape. About twenty minutes into the drive, he breaks the sorrow-infused silence in the car by commenting, to no one in particular, "I wish I coulda gone to college."

"Yeah," is all I choke out, muted by the sickening awareness that, though they are both smart, neither of my parents will ever have the opportunity to fulfill their latent potential. Nothing more is said between us on the drive. Dad turns on the radio, and I pretend to sleep.

In truth, I'm reviewing my life, from its rural simplicity in Collier to the complex agonies of Sunny Vale, New Jersey. I detest that my empathy for my parents' pain makes me feel like a traitor—distancing myself from their sorrows and abandoning Gary, Luke and Dory. To compound these sentiments, William is not around these days to mitigate on behalf of the younger kids. Committed to his high school sweetheart, he's struggling to support himself through college in preparation for law school. William has always understood that our family is trapped in a cycle of poverty, a culture of failure, and he's determined to break it. Me? I just want to get out, to save myself.

I mull over the prospects of my younger siblings: though lacking direction, Gary, the cowboy, is popular and does fine in school; he will make his way in life. Luke, now twelve years old, is more worrisome. He still adores Gary and is protected by him at school, but he's too young to be part of his older brother's world. Luke seems increasingly inclined to live up to the "alienated Indian" side of Tonto, his designated namesake. For a school project, he does research on American Indians and discovers that the Lone Ranger's Tonto is not exactly a role model for real Native Americans. On the other hand, Luke is thrilled to learn from me that our great grandmother, Sarah Lovely Reece, was part Cherokee. He identifies with the idea that Indians are rather enigmatic and exist on the fringe of modern American society. Luke occasionally gets into scraps with boys who taunt him with the name Tonto, and he once had a confrontation with his social studies teacher, who said something demeaning about native people in America. As it will turn out, I'm rightfully concerned about the direction Luke's anger and disaffection are taking him.

And little Dory! I smile to myself. Dora Lee Jenkins is loving, artistic, smart, funny. I sure hope she will continue to thrive without her big sister to encourage and console her. Away at college, I will miss most my affectionate relationship with Dory, my little Sweet Pea.

Dad is good with directions, so he easily finds the North Essex campus and helps me locate my assigned dormitory, but then says he prefers to wait in the car while I check in. Eventually, he has to come in to sign something, though, and I'm suddenly aware he's dressed in dirty work clothes. With his head down and both hands clutching his cap over his groin, in the manner of the shamed men depicted in bread lines during the Great Depression, Dad is subdued and uncomfortable in the college milieu.

It is, indeed, a humbling epiphany for me to see my father, to me a frighteningly formidable man, so obviously cowed. He tells the suited and over-solicitous dormitory official that he has no questions and is given permission to help carry my belongings to my room on the top floor of the new dorm. I have been informed my assigned roommate is named Susan Duncan. Luckily, this Susan has already dropped off her suitcases and gone off somewhere with her parents. By placing belongings around, Susan has claimed the bed by the window and one of the desks. Frankly, I'm relieved not to have to make any choices. The metal-framed beds have crisp blue chenille spreads that match the curtains. Since I've never even had my own bed before, much less a desk, all of this to me is a world of untold luxury.

Dad perks up looking out the window at the trees and the distant view of the New York City skyline. "That there's the Empire State Building," he informs me. Dad, who is far less intimidated by roads than institutions, once drove us kids into New York to look across the Hudson River at the Statue of Liberty. That day, he also cruised us through Times Square, and downtown to the Bowery, where we observed drunken bums and prostitutes languishing in a destitution that made us kids feel privileged to have a place called "home."

Since neither Dad nor I know what else to say to each other there in the dormitory room, he finally mumbles that the place is "real nice" and he has to get going. "I don't know what else to tell you," he apologizes. "Here's a couple o' dollars. I ain't got no more."

Dodging Prayers and Bullets

"It's OK," I manage, fighting back tears. "I'll be fine. Thanks for driving me."

"Bye," says Dad. "You take care and call if you need something."

I wave at his back and close the door behind him. Sobbing wretchedly, I throw myself on the mattress of the unclaimed bed.

Why, oh, why, am I crying? I hate my parents, but somehow, just now, it seems like it isn't their fault. What am I doing at this school, anyway?

"Oh, shit," I mouth, recovering my composure and sitting bolt upright on the bed. This Susan Duncan could show up at any minute.

Luckily, we are in the new dorm that has suites with adjoining bathrooms, rather than the shared communal bathroom at the end of the hall. I quickly jump into the bathroom and lock the doors on both sides. The bathroom suite consists of a shower stall and a cabinet with shelves for four girls. The college has even supplied a bathmat, towels and washcloths—luxury items to me. I select a towel from the four on the rack, wash my face, and pull myself together just in time to hear Susan Duncan and her family enter the dormitory room. I'm careful to unlock both doors of the bathroom suite, and emerge, smiling, to a formal greeting from Susan's mother, Louise Duncan.

"You must be Skyla Jenkins, Susan's roommate!" Mrs. Duncan chirps, extending her hand. Clutching a small navy handbag, she is tall, well coiffed, and dressed in a white blouse beneath a pale blue jacket with coordinated skirt and pumps matching the handbag. Placing her hand on the shoulder of the girl neatly attired in pink slacks and new white sneakers, she continues, "This is Susan, and my husband, Paul. I hope you don't mind that we chose a bed and desk for Susan? They always say, first come first served!" She actually chortles while delivering this line.

"Oh, not at all," I truthfully assure them. "It's nice to meet you," I begin, and then deploy a fib, "My family had to head on back home already. They send regards."

"What's your major?" Susan blurts out, while enthusiastically moving toward me. "I'm an English major and I think we have to read about twelve books for one class!"

"Actually, I didn't choose a major," I confess. "I'm not sure yet."

"Really?" interjects Mrs. Duncan, exchanging glances with Mr. Duncan and surveying the room to see if I have any real luggage other than the laundry bag and cardboard box. I despise the woman already. She knits her eyebrows and muses aloud, "I didn't think it was an option not to have a major."

There is an awkward pause; Mr. Duncan looks uncomfortable and mumbles, "I'm sure it's OK."

I blush, shrug, and look down.

Mrs. Duncan looks at me piteously, forces a smile and continues, "Oh, well, dear, I'm sure you'll figure it out soon. By the way, what kind of name is Skyla?"

"It's just a name my mother liked," I offer. "I go by the short name, Sky."

She doesn't seem very satisfied with my explanation. "Well, we expect to see Susan's name on the Dean's list, so she better get cracking on those twelve books tonight."

To her credit, Susan is embarrassed by her mother and, graciously, manages to steer the conversation in a different direction. "Don't you just hate these bed spreads?" she moans. "Mother thinks we should invest in some soft, fluffy ones—you know, that still match and all."

I smile weakly and mumble, "Blue's not my favorite, but I guess they're all right for now."

Finally, the Duncans launch their formal goodbyes, with Mrs. Duncan cataloging a variety of issues Susan should remember to be concerned about, the most important, of course, being to get good grades.

As he's leaving, Mr. Duncan slips Susan a twenty-dollar bill and urges her to keep good account of it, warning, "There are those who will happily relieve you of it." He winks at me to act as if he doesn't mean me, but I know, of course, he does mean me. The man's very demeanor makes me feel like stealing the money, but I have vowed to give up thievery. I decide that Mr. Duncan, in his dull gray suit, with trim short hair and clean fingernails, is likely an insurance salesman and a Republican.

"Are you a Protestant?" is the first question Susan posits to me after her parents have departed.

"My mother's a Methodist," I say, already anticipating another lachrymose trip to the bathroom.

"Great!" exclaims Susan. "We just found a Methodist Church only a couple of blocks from here. We can go together. My family is Episcopal, but any Protestant church within walking distance will do."

Dodging Prayers and Bullets

Feigning a weak smile of enthusiasm, I nod. "Sure." I figure I might as well throw in with Susan Duncan and the Methodists. At least I won't be alone, and it could all be a distraction from the question of what on Earth I, secretly Skyla Fay Jenkins from Collier, Kentucky, am doing at North Essex State Teacher's College.

25

AT NORTH ESSEX STATE, I learn there's a kind of playful college hazing in which incoming freshmen have to walk around during orientation week wearing red beanies and large cardboard placards designating their majors. Upperclassmen who detect incoming students not displaying their beanies and placards are permitted to take their names and later confront those freshmen publicly in a mock trial called "Rat Court".

Not wanting to be a teacher and having no specific academic interests, I have not chosen a major. I'm mortified, however, at the prospect of Rat Court, so I beg the academic advisor to give me a placard with a designated major. Chuckling, he renders me a sign that reads, in bold letters, "Uncommitted."

For the duration of orientation, I'm thereby condemned to meander about campus publicly displaying my irresolution. The placard is humiliating and soon leads to some mild but embarrassing taunting from a group of Junior frat boys. They threaten to send me to

Dodging Prayers and Bullets

Rat Court on the technicality of my displaying no major. Noting I'm terrified and holding back tears, one of the boys, whom they call Ryan, takes pity on me and insists the others back off. I appreciate Ryan's compassion and understand he's taking a risk for me in front of his peers. (In the near future, I'm ashamed to admit, I will not respond to him in kind.)

There are several other students, and even a few faculty members, who are intrigued, if not charmed, by my unusual placard; some even remember my name because of it. By the end of freshman hazing week, I decide the designation "uncommitted" is a kind of existential omen for my life.

On the final day of freshman registration, I resign myself to majoring in English. Replicating Susan Duncan's schedule seems sensible, since she already has the books and has figured out, in her inimitable, compulsive, Republican manner, the names of all her professors and where their classrooms are located. I have already determined that the best thing about Susan as a roommate is that she studies all the time and never asks any probing personal questions. After learning my family is Protestant and that my father works in the transportation business, Susan simply chirps, "Oh, great! My father's a businessman, too."

Three days after classes begin, while Susan stays up reviewing what we have already over-studied, I roll over toward the wall adjacent to my bed and muffle my sobs in secret shame. There is no way I belong at North Essex State Teacher's College. I desperately miss the camaraderie of my brothers, the affection of my sister Dory, and even my convoluted dalliance with Reverend Dan Hansen. I feel like I have exchanged house arrest in Sunny Vale for solitary confinement at North Essex State.

After three consecutive Sundays of accompanying Susan to tedious services at the North Essex Methodist Church, I begin obsessively consulting the calendar to determine when I can return home without losing face. Dispiritedly, I fantasize about quitting college and even taking up with Dan Hansen again. At least in Sunny Vale my misery was familiar and usually predictable.

All such thinking and intent changes when Caitlyn McClary befriends me. I first noticed Caitlyn in my American Lit class, because Caitlyn, unlike docile Susan, challenges the assumptions and values put forth by the professor. It's the sort of thing I did regularly in my latter years of high school, but am too intimidated to attempt in college. One morning, just before class, Caitlyn hands Susan and me a flyer advertising an event sponsored by the Christian Union, an ecumenical religious association on campus. ("C.U. There!" is the corny punned slogan.) "The advisor is a cool Jesuit priest," Caitlyn assures us, "Check it out."

Why not? I think. It might provide an excuse to beg off the Methodists, who are gearing up for their annual campus crusade with the rival Newman House Catholics.

Despite my upbringing and the studies I have begun about world religions, there is something about being a religious person I can never quite get the hang of. I wonder if there is such a thing as the God gene, and I'm possibly deficient? Then again, maybe it's just the dissonance I observe between the words and actions of many who espouse religious beliefs. It seems to me, the more religion people aspire to, the more mean-spirited and narrow-minded they become. To the "true believers" in Kentucky, one is either a follower of Jesus the Savior, or a heathen banned from Glory Land. Always assuming I simply didn't get the calling, I never considered there might be alternate paths to the Lord or salvation.

I am, therefore, truly amazed when I learn at college that a person can choose religion rather than the other way around. Some of my new friends make a big show of declaring themselves atheists, but I don't see the point—it seems like a lot of effort expended on proving what you're not. Also, surmising that something mighty expansive is required to cover a concept as awesome as God, I find myself drawn toward what I discover is called pantheism. Still, I don't catch on to idea of talking to God in prayer, and I scoff at the notion of Jesus as the immaculately conceived child of God. In my class about comparative religions, I'm learning that religion is a universal construct. I thus resolve to give this so-called eclectic Christian Union a try.

Though my roommate Susan is reluctant, I convince her to sleep in on Sunday, skip the Methodists, and instead attend the Sunday evening service of the Christian Union. The service is indeed ecumenical, primarily based on song and social commentary, with silent prayer or meditation time. Serving as a musical accompanist on guitar, Caitlyn picks away at "Michael Row the Boat Ashore" and "He's Got the Whole World in His

Hands." Afterwards, she introduces Susan and me to Father James Toland, a lifelong Jesuit priest who held posts in South America and Africa before accepting, in his latter years, a more mundane role in a campus ministry. Beloved and admired by students and numerous faculty members who attend his services, Father Toland has dark, compassionate eyes and hair like strands of white silver. He's short and slight in physical stature, but out of respect and affection, both of which the priest effortlessly and humbly commands, the students have dubbed him "Lord Jim."

After the Christian Union service, Caitlyn walks back to the dorm with Susan and me. She's pleased I'm animated and enthusiastic about the service. In contrast, Susan, who is unnerved by the less rigid and narrow approach to worship espoused by Father Toland, is rather subdued. Later, Susan confides to me that even attending the Methodist Church is a compromise for Episcopalians; worshipping with Roman Catholics and assorted others, guided by a Jesuit (Susan wrinkles her nose and says the word as if it meant something foul-smelling and suspect) could qualify as heresy. I think that's hilarious, since my mother has always contended Episcopalians are just Catholics with money.

For my part, I'm captivated as much by Caitlyn and Lord Jim as the nontraditional service. After that Sunday, I regularly choose a seat next to Caitlyn in American Lit, her proximity soon empowering me to speak up in class and express more divergent points of view. To my astonishment, many college professors appreciate oppositional digression. Caitlyn, who is not a great writer, sometimes even talks her grades up. The two of us are soon known as the intellectual dynamic duo of the English department. The obsessively conscientious and ingratiating Susan Duncan is nonplussed by Caitlyn's behavior and perplexed by my adulation of it.

One of the more staid professors confronts Caitlyn about why she writes her name "Caitlyn" though it is spelled "Caitlin" on her permanent record. She cleverly responds, "Poetic license, my good man." Not only does Caitlyn McClary verbally seduce the faculty, she's also a boy magnet, readily connecting with upperclassmen as well as the freshmen guys. I conclude that Caitlyn is somewhat like Del Ray Minix: one of those people way ahead of their time. (Sadly, I wonder what Del might achieve if he were offered any kind of opportunity. I never mention his name to anyone, though, and I try to repress painful and guilty thoughts of him.)

Karen Beatty

Caitlyn seems to be on a tear to date even more boys than Anna Marie Donaluna, the amply (though not intellectually) endowed, campus femme fatale. I wish I were as attractive as Caitlyn, but at least she has chosen me to be the moon to her sun. From time to time, Caitlyn offers to "fix me up" with a guy, but I demur. Maturity-wise, college boys don't measure up to the most Reverend (ha!) Dan Hansen.

As I get to know Caitlyn better, she informs me that her family used to live in New York, in the Bronx, before they moved to South Jersey. They had moved after her oldest brother completed his jail time for something called "criminally negligent homicide." That sounds pretty awful, but Caitlyn assures me it means he only accidentally killed someone during a robbery and stolen car heist with some other teens. "Kiddie jail didn't exactly improve upon his personality," she confides. Caitlyn also has an older sister who died, and another older brother who is a mentally unstable alcoholic. That brother was eventually hospitalized and diagnosed as schizophrenic, finally becoming a ward of the State. Caitlyn's three younger siblings also seem to be suspended in various states of academic and social arrest.

I'm surprised at how unabashedly she describes her rather degenerate family. Her daddy, like mine, beats up on her mother and the kids. Unlike Lonnie Lee, however, Owen McClary is a drunk, and the family subsists on Welfare. "I'm the sole survivor," Caitlyn proudly announces.

Susan Duncan is horrified by this information, but it only serves to endear Caitlyn to me. I consider Caitlyn a "soul" survivor, and am relieved to hear someone so special can come from a family that seems more "whacked out" than mine. I am emboldened to admit that my father is a truck driver and my mother behaves, at times, "a little strangely." I quickly add that I adore my brothers and sisters, and, of course, do not make any reference to my life in Kentucky, or the "disgrace," or to my liaison with Reverend Dan.

It turns out Caitlyn never felt close to any of her siblings and lives pretty independently of her family. She visits her mother out of what she calls "social compulsion, false hope, and sociological curiosity." Also, for mail and residency purposes, she lists her address as her mother's home in South Jersey. Caitlyn explains her enrollment at North Essex State, "I got a Rehab scholarship from the State of New Jersey, and this college was 15 miles from New York City and 120 miles from my family. I simply did the math. And, NO! I don't want to become a teacher."

I'm also relieved to know I'm not the only student at North Essex State with no intention of becoming a dreaded high school teacher, and I rejoice incessantly that Caitlyn McClary resonates to the same bell, marches to the same drum, and chants the same mantra as me at "No Sex" State Teacher's College. A few weeks later, lounging on Susan's bed while Susan sits at the desk obsessing over the forthcoming midterm exams, Caitlyn announces, "OK, I figured out where to get the bus from this morgue to New York City, so who's up for a movie?"

"I'm in!" I immediately volunteer, shifting toward Caitlyn from where I'm slouched on a chair.

Appalled, Susan warns, "Are you guys forgetting that we're in midterms?" Then, grimacing, "Besides, going into New York City? Ugh! It's dangerous. Who wants to see all that dirt and all those grubby people?"

Waving my hand vigorously I shout, "I do, I do!" To Susan's chagrin, Caitlyn and I fall out laughing.

After our first successful jaunt to Times Square, we return to New York repeatedly to see movies, shows, and museums. Sure, I consider, there are scary characters in New York, but even Collier and Sunny Vale have their quota of crazies, some of them even in the ministry!

It happens that Caitlyn McClary is one of two freshmen students who were assigned a private room in the dormitory. She shares the bathroom of a single's suite with Patsy Enders, a depressed and overweight young woman who is not doing at all well at North Essex State. Patsy is a whiner with minimal social skills and an unusual body odor, which means she garners little sympathy and much aversion. Some students begin referring to her as "Fatsy" behind her back. I feel sorry for her and try to be kind, but Caitlyn has no patience for Patsy's wallowing in self-pity. (Nor, for that matter, does she tolerate Susan Duncan's multiple anxieties.) When Caitlyn learns Patsy is leaving school, she determines to make me her new suite mate. I can't imagine how it'd be possible, since it's the rehab scholarship that entitled Caitlyn (as well as Patsy) to first dibs on a single room.

Caitlyn begins probing, "So, Sky, how bad is your family situation—really?"

"Crazy," I respond, honestly.

"Excellent!" retorts Caitlyn. "Tell me more."

"We moved up here from Appalachia—Kentucky, actually," I confess. "But it's like my mother never left that place. I mean, my family has *no* money. My father, he drives a truck and spends every penny he gets on cars and cards. We barely get by on the rent and food money he turns over to my mother. Besides that, it's like re-enacting the Civil War whenever he comes home. We don't see him that much, thank God. My mother's the opposite—she goes on about church and God all the time, but she never leaves the house. It's like she's scared of everything and everybody."

"Agoraphobia," Caitlyn gleefully proclaims. "It's a mental illness."

Wincing, I continue, "The worst part is, when they fight, my father usually ends up punching out my mother. He gets crazy mad, and sometimes just starts slapping whoever's around. It's like he gets these bad headaches and gets furious over my mother's nagging and just loses it. Usually he goes after her, and I try to stay out of his way, and so do my brothers. Once, when he tried to kick my brother Luke, he missed and his foot went right though the wall. My little sister is terrified of him. But we all are."

Caitlyn shakes her head and then grins. "A Rage Disorder—it's a diagnosis. All we gotta do is write this up and you'll definitely qualify for a single. Fatsy Enders is out and you're in."

It isn't quite that easy. To maintain her rehab scholarship, Caitlyn, who comes from an impoverished family with seven children (including an imprisoned homicidal brother and an alcoholic father) is required to meet weekly with Dr. Elton Davis, a staff psychologist at the college. Dr. Davis is a sweet man, so when Caitlyn tells him about me, he agrees to help me apply for the single room across from her.

First, he informs me, I have to consult with Dr. Martin Gross, the head of North Essex State College's Psychological Services. The aptly named Dr. Gross is gruff and disgruntled, a man who is obviously a "lifer" in a cushy academic setting he considers beneath his intellect and never-to-be-attained professional potential. I've seen him around campus and am actually afraid of him. As I tentatively knock at his door, Caitlyn waits in the hallway, around the corner and out of view.

"Open the door, come in, come in ... What?" Dr. Gross snaps as I step in and approach his desk. Enmeshed in paperwork, he's distracted and irritable.

"Dr. Davis said I should talk to you," I try.

"Well," responds Dr. Gross impatiently, "speak up. Is it an emergency?"

Not knowing what, exactly, constitutes an emergency, I hesitate. "I'm not sure."

"You don't know?" Dr. Gross blusters. "Well," he continues, now in a belittling tone, "are you considering suicide or anything?"

That's quite enough of Dr. Martin Gross for me: I've survived more formidable assaults than this. Confronting his arrogance, I shoot back, "Are you offering it up as a suggestion?"

I've already bolted for the hallway when he shouts, "Get out of my office until you learn some respect, young lady."

I'm laughing and crying simultaneously as Caitlyn and I beat it out of the building.

After hearing the story and applauding me, Caitlyn determines, "We're gonna report that S.O.B. to the Dean."

As it turns out, that was the perfect maneuver. Dean Marshall Horton is an effete and ineffective administrator who has repeatedly been belittled at academic meetings by the notorious Professor Martin Gross. Hearing the details of my encounter with the head psychologist, and learning of my family background, the Dean readily over-rides the required consultation with Dr. Gross and assigns me, for mental health reasons, to the single room opposite Caitlyn McClary. I will be allowed to have the required counseling consultations with the kindly Dr. Elton Davis. Furthermore, while Dean Horton regrets that I may not, retroactively, apply for a rehab scholarship, he wants me to see the Financial Aid Officer about a new federal program I might qualify for, under the auspices of the Economic Opportunity Act. If eligible, I will receive a substantial monthly stipend to help me afford my undergraduate studies.

I'm stunned and enormously grateful to the Dean, and, of course, to the loyal Caitlyn McClary. I now have my own room in the dormitory, opposite my new best friend. Caitlyn helps me move my stuff over and deal with Susan Duncan's resentful pout over my desertion. Sure enough, as Caitlyn predicts, though Susan is considerably put out by my departure, she's not very good at having fun on her own. Soon after acquiring a boring new roommate, Susan falls back in with Caitlyn and me, and we are joined by two other girls who adhere to the philosophy, "Never let your studies interfere with your college education."

Susan doesn't quite fit the profile, and she especially gets on Caitlyn's nerves, but I'm OK about her hanging around, because never again will I need to make excuses to Mrs. Duncan about our not purchasing fluffy matching bedspreads. No longer will I need to deflect Mr. Duncan's inquiries about what, exactly, my father does in the transportation business. In the solitude of my new abode, I can laugh or cry in privacy, seek out Caitlyn whenever I want a tête-à-tête, and choose whether to join in the general revelries of the dormitory or to hit the books. For long periods, I write in my journal or sit alone, sometimes in meditative gratitude for my spacious single room. Savoring the magnificent view of the New York City skyline afforded by the window over my desk, I could never even imagine that I will one day call the bedazzling lights and magnificent spires "home."

26

SHORTLY AFTER I MOVE into the singles suite, I become one of the first North Essex State College students accepted as a "hardship case" in the new Economic Opportunity Act program. The State Scholarship continues to cover my tuition, so that the E.O.A. funds can be allocated for dormitory and meal fees and books and for a glorious category labeled "general expenses." It seems incredibly bizarre to me that the poverty, abuse, and deprivation I've endured throughout my life qualifies me for something positive.

Now I have the residual funds for those trips to Mecca (New York City), for purchasing holiday gifts for friends and family, and even for the special snacks (pizza, submarine sandwiches, etc.) the dormitory students frequently order up for evening "pig-outs." Beginning to feel like a member of a real community, I finally release the breath I've been holding since my father dropped me off at North Essex State College in early September 1963.

It's only a few weeks later, on November 22, 1963, that President John F. Kennedy is shot, and I become friends with Ryan Janssen, the young man who rescued me from his fraternity brothers during freshmen orientation. Hearing about the shooting in Dallas, my Theater Arts professor, a man with a heavy southern drawl who frequently brags about his home state of Texas, dismisses the class, announcing that on this day he is ashamed of Texas. Students begin gathering in the student lounge to listen to the radio updates on the loudspeaker; I go there to look for my friends and happen into a conversation with Ryan. When Caitlyn notices us engrossed in a dialogue about the political implications of the attack on President Kennedy, she maneuvers Susan out of the vicinity. Ryan doesn't seem to recall me from our encounter during orientation, but he's imprinted on my memory, and I've always kept an eye out for him on campus. Overjoyed to have at last caught his attention while I'm not wearing the stupid freshman beanie and 'uncommitted' placard, I spend the afternoon commiserating with him over the shooting. We arrange to meet in the cafeteria for lunch the next day.

Everyone is in a state of shock over the assassination. Amid a swirl of speculation and debate over who has done the deed and why, a pall envelops the campus. Some people argue that Kennedy is not really dead—that he's being treated for massive brain injuries—or, that he's alive and safely secluded while awaiting the full official investigation. Such heightened sentiments and prevailing uncertainty spawn rapid and spontaneous bonding amongst the students and faculty at North Essex State. Despite the unseemly circumstances, I'm thrilled Ryan has been delivered to me.

Sadly, over the next few weeks, it rather quickly develops that the more interest Ryan Janssen expresses in getting to know me, the more I pull away. Drawn to the notion of having a real boyfriend, but still contaminated by Reverend Dan, I can't seem to work up any physical attraction or deep emotion for Ryan. He persists, and we date, even doubling a couple of times with Caitlyn and her selected date de jour. Luckily, since Caitlyn is so free-wheeling about dating, I don't feel the need to explain why I'm keeping Ryan Janssen at a safe distance. In truth, I'm not sure why myself.

Meanwhile, I have to survive the Thanksgiving holiday at home in Sunny Vale.

27

DESPITE RUMORS to the contrary, President Kennedy is dead. At North Essex State, Thanksgiving break is upon us, and I remind myself I certainly have enough to be thankful for. The Economic Opportunity Act funds will enable me to continue my college studies; I have a boyfriend prospect, several new friends, and at least I have both parents to go home to. I can't help wondering how the Kennedy family will handle this holiday. At college, I miss my brothers and sister terribly, but I have to admit that the notion of returning home to my family in the projects for the long Thanksgiving weekend is more daunting than pleasing.

Like many misguided students in freshman literature class, my imagination has been captured by the title of Thomas Wolfe's book, *You Can't Go Home Again*. Upon my return to the family, the words prove sadly prophetic. William picks me up at school and, on the drive back home, catches me up on his plans for law school and his intent to marry Mary Lou Ross after graduation. Though I understand his need for a little personal dignity, I've never fully gotten used to thinking of my brother as

Dodging Prayers and Bullets

"William" instead of "Billy Dee." Once William had left for college, he never moved back home. Now working as an aide in a law office, he's somehow managing to support himself and keep his grades up at Rutgers University. "Dad actually tried to hit me up for some bucks!" William reports, shaking his head and releasing a puff of air.

I nod and my stomach contracts as William goes on to warn that, since early September when I left for college, the flames of discord between our parents have ignited on numerous occasions. I understand, without his saying so that, like me, he feels guilty about abandoning the little kids to the volatility of our parents. William then comments that he's particularly worried about our youngest brother, who is going on 13 years old, "Luke is carrying this identification with the Indians thing way too far. Wait 'til you see how long his hair is, and he still wears that stupid headband."

Apparently, school is not going well for Luke, and he's taken to hanging out with a couple of older, like-minded buddies. Though none of them are old enough to drive, the boys sometimes hitchhike to places where they can fish, camp out in the woods, and commiserate over their disaffections.

Regarding little Dory, William remarks, "She seems quiet, and she really misses you." I smile to myself, savoring the mother-link to my little sister.

On the good news front, William is excited to report that Gary, who made the Varsity football team in his sophomore year of high school, now, as a junior, will be the starting quarterback at the big football rivalry on Thanksgiving Day. Even Dad is going to the game.

As we approach the housing projects, William announces, "I'll drop you off here and see you tomorrow." Then he cautions, "Expect the worst from Mother."

Entering the apartment on the eve of Thanksgiving, I can see my mother is agitated; I dread that the next day will be another "hollerday," the term we kids use to describe celebrations at home with our parents. Still, I'm happy to see Dory, Luke and Gary, so I choose to ignore Mother's background harangues about "not enough Jesus and too much rock'n'roll" and "the poor people who got nothing while the rest waste food," and how "money couldn't save that President Kennedy, more'n likely killed by them Republicans." She talks incessantly and compulsively, and so much so that we've all learned to shut her out in order to survive in the cramped apartment. It's more of a challenge for me to do so now that I'm getting used to the more managed, if not always sedate, living environment of the college dormitory.

Although Mother wants nothing so much as to gather the family at home for a blessed Thanksgiving, her psychic quandaries always intensify on holidays. Despite her best intentions, she can neither manage the preparation and presentation of a major meal, nor measure up to her self-decreed role as spiritual guardian of the family. And whenever Dad's at home (briefly between long distance runs with the truck, or on holidays), he and Mother just can't seem to adjust to being in each other's company again.

This Thanksgiving, Mother is forced to make excuses about why she can't go to Gary's game or even stop by next door to say hello to the neighbors. Usually, she claims to be having a "dizzy spell" or a sick headache, or insists she's the only one who can handle the numerous things that need tending in the household. At the same time, she's furious at being left out of any family configurations, especially if Dad is home to drive us kids somewhere. During religious holidays, like Christmas and Easter, Mother's distress presents as more manic, because, in addition to explaining away inadequate meals, she has to make excuses about not going to church while dutifully prodding the rest of us to do so.

I know that my mother suffers, but there never seems to be a way to unburden her. At times she feels like a black hole of despondency, and the best I can do is navigate away from the abyss. Had I not been living away from home and gotten out of practice shutting down emotionally and verbally, I might have quietly, if resentfully, finessed Thanksgiving. It was not to be.

On holidays in our household, the boys routinely stay outside, away from the house, while Daddy, whenever he is there, sits rigid as a stone sculpture in front of the TV until he drops off to sleep on the living room sofa. When we get back from an exciting football game this Thanksgiving, Dad quickly assumes his place on the sofa. As always, when dinner is ready, Mother assigns us the scary task of shaking Dad awake to join the family for dinner. Since I feel guilty about being away at college, I volunteer for the awakening, and Dory agrees to back me up. Anxiously approaching Dad, where he's laid out on the sofa with the TV blaring, I shake his shoulder, while Dory petitions, "Mommy said it's time to eat." Dad groans and turns away, so I announce firmly, "You gotta get up. It's time for Thanksgiving dinner."

He groans more and tosses about like a fish on some rocks, but soon gets up, lumbers toward the table and slowly drops into his designated chair. In rumpled clothing and looking removed and sullen, he assumes a pained expression, turning his mouth down like a method actor preparing for the tragic part of a script. Not daring to keep Dad waiting, the rest of us scurry to our places around the table.

Even though (or perhaps because) Gary's football team has won handily that morning, with Gary garnering the MVP trophy and Dad and the rest of us (except for Mother) in attendance, Mother uses the Thanksgiving table to unleash a diatribe. Refusing to sit down to eat, she aimlessly circles the table, cataloging her fears and complaints:

Here it is Thanksgiving and there's poor people ain't got nothing. We ought to be thankful, rather than concentrating on them old sports all the time. Them Republican snakes is a-hoardin' all the money; why, they's the ones killed President Kennedy. And that old Pope, misleading the true believers. But I reckon I'm raisin' heathens myself. It's no wonder. Spawned from that low-down, foul-mouthed Jenkins family out of Harlan. The sins of the fathers, the sins of the fathers. (She begins to talk about our father as if he is not right there.) And yer daddy— my so-called husband—he's the prime example. He only cares about sports. Sports and them old cars. The Bible don't say nothin' about cars or sports.

Flo-Anna pauses, but noting the dearth of gustatory, as well as spiritual, enthusiasm at the dinner table, she starts up again.

Y'all better be eatin' now. This family cain't afford to waste good food.

She throws up her hands in resignation.

Aehhh, it don't seem like Thanksgiving no how. And here I am stuck around next-door neighbors from ... who knows where? Filthy in mind and body alike. Catholics, too. And my own family don't appreciate nothin'.

Mother then begins singing about the crucifixion, "On a hill far away, stood the old rugged cross, the emblem of suffering and shame" and bemoaning that her suffering is akin to that of Jesus. Then she resorts to a familiar, sorrowful refrain, "I reckon I'll jist have to wait for my rewards in Heaven. Amen. I won't live long enough to see Luke and Dory grow up."

The part about dying always makes Dory and I well up, but Gary and Luke sneak glances at each other and make faces of bemused contempt. They smother their over-cooked string beans, packaged stuffing, and dry turkey meat in gravy. William assumes a vacant expression and eats with rote motions. Dad, shaking his head, looks down with a grimace and rapidly consumes his portions. Feeling as if I can't swallow, I nibble at the stuffing on my plate, and cut up small bits of meat to offer Dory. I try to peer into the living room and focus my attention on the news about the Kennedy family in mourning: the compelling, blurred images are repeatedly scrolled on the black and white TV that perpetually sounds in our living room, even when it's vacated.

At Mother's insistence, I manage to ingest a couple of bites of mashed potatoes and turkey, while my parents' repetitive cycle of violence plays itself out like a phonograph needle clinging to the grooves of a familiar old record. After first ignoring Mother's harangue, and then shaking his head at several more of her accusatory verbal assaults, Dad grows red in the face and shouts, "You shut that mouth o' yours right now, before I'm the one that shuts it for you!"

Of course, that confirms Mother's contentions about her husband. She positions herself opposite him on the far side of the table and taunts him further with, "Now yer showing us what a real Jenkins is like. I shoulda known you was jist like the worst o' them—yer old man included."

Since his father had died in jail after recurrent episodes of debauchery, Dad is particularly vulnerable to that invective. "Goddam you, woman!" he shouts, heaving his plate of food against the wall nearest Mother. Taking stock of the hand he has cocked to slap her, he quickly looks around at us children, takes a deep breath, and lowers it. He stands up, glares at Mother, curls his fingers into a fist and punches his palm twice. Cursing under his breath and turning away, he goes to the closet to grab his hat and jacket. Slamming the apartment door hard on his way out, he heads for his car. We children are actually relieved that today's confrontation has gone no further. (Something to be thankful for on this holiday of gratitude.)

Mother isn't finished of course. "See," she hisses, lifting her head in the direction of the door. "See how a Jenkins behaves!" She turns and surveys the kitchen area. "Look here at this mess. It's a disgrace to decent people." Mother resumes her pacing and gospel singing, urging us to keep eating and not waste the food she has slaved to prepare.

Fighting off a rush of tears, I pick up Dory, my distraught little Sweet Pea, and carry her into the back bedroom. A minute after Dad pulls away in the car, Luke, looking pale and shaken, dashes out the door with Gary in pursuit; William stands up and awkwardly announces that he will spend the remainder of Thanksgiving day with the family of his fiancée, Mary Lou.

Mother begins to cry and sing about Jesus, and, left alone, cleans up the Thanksgiving dinner and the odious mess left on the wall and floor from the smashed plate of food. Later in the day, at her behest, we go to the refrigerator and pick at some leftovers.

Dad comes home after dark, and no reference is made to the earlier events of the day. Mother serves him pumpkin pie and coffee, and we all gather in the living room to watch, in silence, the Ed Sullivan Thanksgiving Special and a continuous loop of news about the Kennedy assassination, including profiles of Lee Harvey Oswald and Jack Ruby.

Nobody, except for Mother during her harangues, expresses an opinion on the events. I can't help wondering once again what Thanksgiving is like for the Kennedy family. I lament silently, *Even without the President, likely better than mine.* I go to the bedroom to hide out and read a book in bed. Dory follows, resting her head on my lap, behind the book.

On Friday and Saturday, my family maintains our emotional distance, doing our best imitation, I imagine, of Jackie Kennedy "keeping a lid on it." By Sunday afternoon, however, the accumulated heat of resentment and the suppressed steam of rage pop the lid. When Dad comes home from his buddy's garage to drive me back to college, Mother must be jealous that he can do something for me; perhaps she resents my leaving, even my ability to leave. Furthermore, William, who has called to say goodbye to me, does not ask to speak to Mother.

As I sit reading a book on the sofa, ignoring the background static of the TV and the bluish glare from the screen, Mother looks out from the kitchen and begins a discourse on the frivolity of girls attending college. "I ain't never understood why a girl's got to go to college. It's the boy's got to work and support a family. Poor people can't be getting uppity jist for its own sake." Nobody responds to the lob, so Mother winds up and directs a hard, fastball, "Miss Skyla Fay Jenkins don't lift a finger around this here house—always got her nose stuck in a book. It ain't right."

"Isn't," I correct, barely looking up from the book. Luke sniggers behind a comic book.

"What?" says Mother, suspiciously perplexed.

"It *isn't* right," I look up and challenge. "Ain't isn't proper English."

"Hush up," warns Dad, shooting a dirty look at me from the kitchen table, where he's sipping coffee. But it's too late.

"My own chillern turnin' against me," Mother begins to wail. "I sacrifice, and I pray, and I work my fingers to the bone, and it ain't never appreciated."

"Don't do it!" I retort, shoving the book into my handbag. "I don't ask you to. I never ask you for a penny."

"Who's talking about money—the root of all evil?" Mother counters, charging out of the kitchen and wagging an accusatory finger at me.

Of course, I can't resist the temptation to correct the Biblical misquote, so I mouth, "It's FOR THE LOVE of money."

Her face distorted in spite, Mother's voice pitches high. "All the book learning in the world don't get you no common sense, child. You ain't never had no common sense—getting in that truck with them lowdown fellers like you did."

This gratuitous reference to "the disgrace" that happened to me in Kentucky sets my face ablaze with shame and fury; my head begins throbbing.

"You crazy old bitch!" I scream at Mother.

It's the first time I've ever used such a word in front of my parents, let alone directed it *at* my mother. Even the boys have learned not to use "blasphemy" at home—that's Dad's bailiwick. I shudder, in fact, recalling the time when Luke had let go with a few expletives. That's the scene catapulting through my mind immediately after I scream the curse on the Sunday afternoon of Thanksgiving weekend.

Dodging Prayers and Bullets

Dad's head snaps in my direction. He springs up from the table where he's seated, spills his coffee, and knocks over the chair as he lunges forward. I throw my hands over my face and head for protection, then gasp in relief—and horror—as Dad begins slapping and pummeling Mother.

"Oh, Lord, oh, Lordy," Mother whimpers, bent over and cowering in a corner of the living room.

"Stop it right now!" yells Gary, as he and Luke jump up from the floor where they're watching TV and run to pull Dad away from Mother. She manages to get up and run, and, once again, lock herself in the bathroom.

"Goddam, woman!" shouts Dad. Seizing his jacket, he turns to me and snaps, "I'll be back to drive ya to that there college in one hour. You jist be ready." He stomps out of the apartment, slamming the door. I hear the tires screech as he pulls away, and I run sobbing to the bedroom with Dory at my heels—this time the child is attempting to comfort me. Luke and Gary bang on the bathroom door, assuring Mother that Dad is gone.

After about fifteen minutes, Mother comes out of the bathroom with a huge bruise on her left cheek. She busies herself in the kitchen, while the boys hover behind comic books with the TV on extra loud in the living room. They're afraid to leave Mother alone, but neither do they want to see her bruised face nor hear her whimpers.

As he has promised, Dad returns an hour later, shamefully looking downward, cap in hand, to take me back to college. The family lulls about, outwardly presenting with blank stares and restrained voices, while beneath those demeanors are the roiling pits of rage, shame and despair. Mother busies herself in the kitchen, keeping her back to Dad.

Midst the muzzled silence and despite the throbbing in my head, I have somehow managed to gather my books and personal items and stuff them into a shopping bag. As Dad and I move toward the door for the return trip to North Essex State College, Mother emerges from the kitchen to foist upon me some dried out, unappealing Thanksgiving leftovers that she has packed up in greasy, recycled tin foil.

"There mighn't be no food when you get back to that there dormitory," Mother observes, in a wavering voice.

I accept the packet because it's easier to do so than not, and, holding back tears, mumble, "Thanks," as I hurry out of the apartment toward the car.

Mother steps outside the door and calls after me, "Skyla Fay, you come on back when you can, now; this here's your home." I nod, trying to smile and swallow despite the thickened lump closing off my throat. I wave toward my sister Dory, who blinks back tears.

In the car, I lodge the shopping bag and food between my father and me, and shift my body as far as possible toward the car door. Feigning sleep most of the way back to the college, I avoid looking directly at Dad, whose rigid face and sad eyes are locked in the reverie of a very private pain.

After an achingly long and silent car trip, as we pull up in front of the dormitory, Dad shrugs and tries, as a goodbye, "I don't know what to tell you."

"It's OK," I respond, quickly opening the car door and grabbing for my shopping bag suitcase. I inadvertently knock the foil-wrapped leftovers to the ground beside the car, where I ignore them. "Thanks for bringing me back," is all I can muster.

"Hold on just a minute," he calls out, before I can shut the car door and turn away. Taking out his wallet, he reaches toward me with a five-dollar bill. "I want you take this here."

The money feels like an embarrassing bribe—a gesture inhabiting a murky area somewhere between acknowledged guilt and deficient restitution. I don't really want to take it, first because I do not intend to forgive either of my parents, ever, and second because I know that Dad can't afford the money. But, doubting my ability to continue to dam my tears there in front of the dorm, and determining that Dad's departure, and my discomfort, will be prolonged if I try to refuse or explain, I accept the bill, and mumble, "Thanks, I can use it." As my father turns the key in the ignition, I add, "Be careful driving home."

"Bye," Dad calls after me, slightly lifting his right hand as I turn away.

His gesture seems so pitiful that, when I'm sure he won't notice, I look back to watch the car disappear. I try to imagine the sadness and confusion in his mind, but soon have to run around the side of the dormitory building to avoid meeting up with other returning students,

Dodging Prayers and Bullets

especially since I fear I may throw up. Braced against the cold wall, the stones fashioned to look like bricks, I manage to get my sobbing and nausea under control, so I can return to complete the first semester of my freshman year of college.

28

I'M TOTALLY GRATEFUL to have my own room in the dormitory, but returning from a brutal Thanksgiving weekend at home, I don't want to be alone with my ruminations. I can hear Caitlyn McClary strumming the guitar on her side of the suite, so I take a deep breath, bang on Caitlyn's door, and mock the inanely popular Mickey Mouse Club TV show by shouting, "Roll call, Mousekateers!"

"Hey," Caitlyn cheerily responds. "Come in and tell all. But first, you gotta hear this song I picked up over the weekend."

"Cool," I enthuse. There's nothing I enjoy more than listening to Caitlyn play, and I'm relieved to have a diversion. The song is "Now That The Buffalo Have Gone," a lament about the contemporary plight of the Indians, written by a Native American singer called Buffy Sainte-Marie. *Luke will love this one*, I think, attempting to memorize the words of the chorus the second time around. It's one of many protest songs that I pathetically attempt to harmonize on with Caitlyn. When I hear the closing words to the Buffy Saint Marie song -- *And what will you do for these ones?* -- I'm choking back tears.

"Whoa," says Caitlyn, throwing her head back in questioning surprise. "I didn't know you had such a thing for Indians."

"Oh, no," I quickly protest, "I was thinking about my brother, Luke. You know, how he always identifies with the Indians—excuse me—with Native Americans, and how my father always beats up on him."

"And how was *your* Thanksgiving weekend?" Caitlyn chimes sardonically, "No doubt in the great American tradition of pumpkin pie and father knows best."

"It was bad," I confess, and proceed to tell Caitlyn the details of the fight between my parents, leaving out, of course, Mother's reference to "the disgrace" that had happened to me in Kentucky.

I feel blessed to have a friend like Caitlyn—someone who can empathize about the afflictions of a crazy family and the distress it can inflict, even during a short time period. In fact, with her violent alcoholic father and a brother who has "done time," Caitlyn is the one person I've met at college whose family seems worse off than mine. I have to admit there's some perverse comfort in knowing that someone you like and admire is prevailing over more dire circumstances than you. For the first time since I left Kentucky, I'm able to acknowledge how completely wretched my family life is.

"Tell 'em to fuck off!" exhorts Caitlyn, putting the guitar down and tossing her right arm in a dismissive gesture. "That's what I do with my family."

I'm a little put off by Caitlyn's casual deployment of the "f" word and by the hardened contempt with which she references her kin. (It was still the early 60s, so I was not very liberated in word or deed.)

Noticing my raised eyebrows and slight shift away, Caitlyn softens her demeanor. "Look, I figured out a long time ago that it was me or them. And I'm not gonna let it be me. It's that simple. And you shouldn't be the one to go down, either. Do me a favor, go and talk to Elton Davis about this—for a shrink, he's a pretty good guy. He's nothing like that big shit, Doctor Martin Gross. Even if talking to Elton is a bust for you, it'll mean you stay on the college's list of 'mentals' and you'll get to keep your single room across from me. See, we gotta have both these rooms because of our band."

"Our band?" I inquire, confused but relieved to change the subject.

"Seventh Heaven, of course," announces Caitlyn, shoving her pillow against the wall and leaning back with her legs crossed and her shoes right up on the covers. Pointing at me, she continues, "You're on tambourine and me and Josie play guitar. We'll try something out at the Christian Union and see how it goes from there."

I "get" the name Seventh Heaven right away. Caitlyn and I, along with Josie Schumacher, who's part of Susan Duncan's suite, all live on the seventh—top—floor of the new dormitory. Instead of studying, we frequently sit around with other girls on the floor, singing folk songs like "This Land Is My Land" and "Four Strong Winds." Activities of our assemblage also include the boisterous telling of dirty jokes and the occasional food fight.

Obviously, Susan Duncan is not a "regular" at these festivities, and she complains about the racket when we gather in Josie's room for raucous jamming and hamming it up. Worse, girls from other floors in the dormitory taunt us, declaring that the oxygen must be a little thin at the top of the building. Proud to be a seventh floor "outlaw," I conclude in 1963 that not that many females have a sardonic sense of humor.

Though enticed by Caitlyn's proposal to form a band, I protest, "I can't really sing."

"Well then, stick a kazoo in your mouth and a tambourine in your hand and just come in on the choruses," Caitlyn coaches. "You're in and so is Josie." She ponders. "Maybe we'll ask Elaine Agnewski to sing with us. She's a voice major and not that much of a pain in the butt, as long as she doesn't get all maudlin or try to upstage us."

It's settled. Putting the five bucks Dad had reached across to me to good use, I go into New York with Caitlyn and purchase a beautiful tambourine with a dark wood frame; the owner of the music store throws in a kazoo for an extra 50 cents. The following Sunday evening, our band Seventh Heaven makes its debut at the Christian Union. We play "Rock-a My Soul" and "Where Have All the Flowers Gone?" A few weeks later a faculty member who heard us play at the C.U. service invites Caitlyn and "the band" to join with some other campus groups to lead the songs at a hootenanny scheduled for January, after the Christmas holidays. I'm really nervous about that, but Caitlyn is, as always, gung-ho and raring to go. She gives me one of her old guitars and teaches me to pick a few chords so I can have a prop to hide behind on stage.

Needing to practice for the Hootenanny and definitely not intending to go home for the long winter break from school, Caitlyn and I petition the psychologist Elton Davis and Lord Jim of the C.U. to make arrangements with the Dean and the Dormitory Director for us to remain in the dorm, except, of course, on Christmas and New Year's days. To justify using the campus living facilities, and for the much-needed extra cash, I take a job working in the Admissions Office, and Caitlyn gets herself hired by the Audio-Visual Aids Department.

Over the winter break, I love being among a handful students ensconced, with special permission, in the tranquility of a subdued dormitory and deserted campus. On most nights, Caitlyn and I work on songs, think up ways to spook one another out, or sit around compiling a list of "converse platitudes," which we intend to publish as an expose of the contradictory aphorisms imposed upon young people at home and school. One of us recites, for example, "Look before you leap" and the other responds with "But he who hesitates is lost." Or "A bird in the hand is worth two in the bush" with someone appending the quick rejoinder, "But nothing ventured, nothing gained." We come up with almost a hundred such contradictory directives.

"No wonder the youth of America are so screwed up," Caitlyn groans. "We're paralyzed in irresolution."

The college administration sends around a notice reminding the two of us that we must vacate the dorm on Christmas day, so, with trepidation, I invite Caitlyn home with me. I think maybe her presence will mitigate my parent's hostility toward each other. Surely Flo-Anna and Lonnie Lee can control their animosity for one day, especially since Mother doesn't believe in "letting on" to problems in front of strangers.

The folks do manage to keep their bad behavior in check during the few hours Caitlyn visits, mainly by anchoring themselves to the TV screen. (Later Caitlyn and I chuckle about the "mystery meat" Mother served.) To my siblings, Caitlyn is an oasis of sanity on Christmas day. Singing and plucking away on her guitar, she seduces the kids away from the TV, even getting my mother's attention when she offers up a gospel spiritual.

Still concerned about Luke, I hope to interest him in the guitar, especially when I ask Caitlyn to play the Buffy Saint Marie song about Native Americans. All Luke wants to talk about, however, is his "inside information" that President Kennedy is not dead, but was critically wounded by the CIA and has been squired away by the Kennedy family to an obscure island, where he lingers on, brain-damaged and paralyzed from the neck down. Sure, I suspect that the facts behind the Kennedy assassination have not been fully disclosed, and though I admire Luke for questioning the government and news media, I remain concerned about his paranoid comrades and the dubious sources of their information. Gary and William are, predictably, as turned off by Luke's pronouncements as they are by my civil rights rants. William lets me have it with, "Sky, you better stop talking against this country. It just encourages Luke to act crazy. You're not the one who's gonna have to deal with him."

Although Luke shows only passing interest in Caitlyn's music and no interest in the guitar, little Dora Lee is enraptured by the singing and excited about the instrument. Months later, when I give up learning to play with any semblance of dignity, I pass the guitar on to Dory, who makes good use of it. The next time I'm around my family, I try not to defend Luke or myself, but neither do I apologize for, or desist from, talking politics. Of course I worry about Luke as much as William does, but I figure, at least, the kid will talk to me.

It will turn out that neither William nor I was much of a surrogate for the parenting Luke desperately needed.

29

BACK AT "No Sex State College" one evening between Christmas and New Year's, Caitlyn and I take the bus into New York City. This time we figure out how to ride the subway, specifically the A train, downtown from Port Authority to Greenwich Village. We have heard that a place called Gerde's Folk City on 3rd Street has regularly scheduled hootenannies on Monday nights, but this is a Friday, so we're hoping some bigger names might be performing.

First, we roam MacDougal and Bleecker Streets in the Village, enthralled by the shops and colorful street life. We nudge each other and gawk at the colorful characters exiting the Gaslight Café, the Bitter End and Caffé Reggio. Many of the men, including the young ones, have beards, and both the men and women have long hair; some are wearing sun glasses—even in the winter—while others are dressed in high boots and long, loose coats that look as if they've been culled from Salvation Army bins.

Over our first taste of espresso and Italian pastry at Caffé Dante on MacDougal Street, Caitlyn peers about and quips, "I don't think these people are going to apply for admission to North Essex State Teacher's College!"

Later that evening we barely gain entrance into Gerde's, which is smoke-filled, reeking of booze, and packed wall to wall with enthusiastic fans, many of them musicians themselves. The patrons, however, are friendly and accommodating, cheerfully squishing together to make room for everyone. The featured performer is a funky blues singer named John Lee Hooker, who alternately bites into his pipe and takes swigs from a whiskey bottle as he performs. Caitlyn and I join the audience in nodding and swaying or stomping to the music, and shouting "Boom, boom, boom!" along with John Lee. Elated, we keep nudging each other to acknowledge that we have finally found "our scene."

At the conclusion of John Lee's first set, the emcee announces that there will be a surprise set from a musician named Bob Dylan. The guy steps up to the stage with his guitar and some kind of metal rack fixed around his neck for positioning a harmonica. There's a great deal of hoopla from the audience—applause, cheering, whistling; apparently many people recognize this musician with the dark feathered curls and sideburns. Slight of build, his face pale and delicate, he's definitely attractive in an aberrant kind of way. Bob Dylan smiles shyly, tuning his guitar and adjusting the harmonica contraption. He makes no eye contact with the audience; it's almost as if he's taking cover behind the instruments and the cigarette dangling from his lips. He fidgets and seems embarrassed to honor the crowd's vociferous request for him to sing, "Blowin' in the Wind." Neither the singer nor the song is familiar to Caitlyn or me, so we're stunned when Dylan tosses the cigarette and begins delivering his poetic message in such an unusual voice. As he performs, people hang on every word, mouthing the lyrics or joining the refrain. Enthralled and teary-eyed by the end of "Blowin' in the Wind" Caitlyn and I add to the clamorous applause.

Unfortunately, we can't stay to hear more from Bob Dylan that night, as we have to dash for the subway to reach Port Authority in time to catch the last bus back to North Essex. Still awe-struck, however, we both intuit that what just came out of Bob Dylan is not simply folk music, but an invitation to anchor in a new milieu. No more mid-town for us, no more dodging creeps in Times Square. From that night forward, our forays into

Karen Beatty

New York City will be to coffee houses, theaters, and poetry readings in Greenwich Village. North Essex State College quickly begins to feel like a suburban wasteland where everyone is trapped in the somnolent 1950s.

Bob Dylan, of course, quickly moves on from basket clubs (venues where a basket is passed around for donations to the performers) and village coffee houses. Upon hearing his song "The Times They Are A-Changin'" on the radio in the spring of 1964, Caitlyn and I understand that our lives, and America, will never be the same. Hootenannies are passé, as is our silly band, Seventh Heaven.

It's right around this time that Lord Jim (Father Toland) takes out a map at a Christian Union meeting and shows the North Essex State students and faculty members in attendance the location of Vietnam. The Jesuit priest has frequently talked about meeting Martin Luther King and participating in Civil Rights walks and demonstrations, but this Vietnam issue is new to the college community. Lord Jim contends that the fighting in that country constitutes a civil war, and sending American troops and resources to the South Vietnamese to safeguard U.S. policies and interests is strategically and morally wrong.

Provoked by the points made by the priest, I rush over to the library to look up some articles about the history of Vietnam. I expect to discover at least some justification for the U.S. involvement in the war. Instead, I'm stunned to learn that the majority of the popular assumptions about this war are based entirely on political lies and half-truths. Agitated and appalled, I share my discoveries with Caitlyn, who "gets it" immediately. Several other students whom I talk to about the situation in Vietnam are intrigued and want to mull over both sides of the issues. Sadly, most of the North Essex State future teachers of America dismiss my assertions with patriotic contempt. In particular, Susan Duncan has a nervous premonition that I have lifted the lid and am poised to stir a toxic stew.

She petitions, "I think we should leave foreign policy to the officials who are paid to see 'the big picture' and make the decisions. You seem to be forgetting that we elected them. It's called democracy."

"More like demon-crazy," I retort, and Caitlyn starts taunting Susan with lyrics from "The Times They Are A-Changin'."

But Susan Duncan is having no part of defection from the Red, White, and Blue. At least not during the spring of 1964.

30

AT THE END of our freshman year, both Caitlyn and I sign up for summer school and obtain permission to retain our work-study jobs, so that, as during the winter break, we can stay in the dorm and not return to our homes. The income I will receive from the job, and the summer school class I enroll for, easily justify to my family my choosing to stay at the college. Likely they feel hurt and rejected but they don't bring it up.

In truth, I've determined never again to spend more than a few hours at a time in our apartment in the projects, in the hope that my parents might control themselves during my abbreviated visits. William reports that nowadays our father is absent more than ever, which seems to work just fine in maintaining some semblance of equilibrium in the household. Mother complains about Dad's absence, of course, but is far less distressed when he's away. With Dad frequently out of the picture, she expresses more sadness than anger. Sometimes, when she laughs or sings mountain songs, I catch glimpses of the Mama I used to have in

Dodging Prayers and Bullets

Kentucky. Still, there's no way to help her feel content in New Jersey. Even I can't tolerate too many thoughts of Kentucky; they're all mired in loss and guilt, especially regarding my cousin Del Ray.

By summer's end, Caitlyn has somehow managed to scrape together enough money to buy a used Volkswagen. To the chagrin of the North Essex State community, she paints flowers all over the car and draws a huge peace symbol across the humped back of the VW. With few exceptions (those in the Father Toland camp) most of New Jersey is in no way ready for flower power or any semblance of the peace movement. As we drive around in Caitlyn's car, we're often given the finger by other students, as well as by the local residents of North Essex, New Jersey. Once, when Caitlyn parked the car off campus, someone smeared dog shit on the peace symbol.

And it's not just the car that generates hostility. Near the beginning of our sophomore year, on a beautiful day in late September 1964, Caitlyn, Josie and I are sitting with our musical instruments on the green outside the dormitory. While leading a small group of students in relatively innocuous songs about love and peace, we're taunted and pelted with eggs by students in the dorm rooms above. Even the politically conservative Susan Duncan is appalled at the wrath our gentle music incites.

The hostility on the North Essex campus and in the uptight surrounding community only serves to strengthen my resolve. I let my hair grow long and straight, in emulation of folk singers I admire, like Joan Baez, Joni Mitchell, and Buffy Sainte-Marie. Undertaking a guileless and oddly prescient endeavor, I do a report for my biology class on the hallucinatory drug lysergic acid diethylamide tartrate (acronym, LSD). I discover that Professor Timothy Leary and his colleague Richard Alpert are conducting LSD research on hospitalized Veterans and graduate students at Harvard University. I'm disappointed none of my North Essex State professors in the sciences or psychology take an interest in the research, which, to me, seems promising in the area of human consciousness.

Fortunately, though, under the helm of the Christian Union and Lord Jim, a few professors have become involved in the controversy over the war in Vietnam. President Kennedy's successor, Lyndon B.

Johnson, vows, "We are not about to send American boys nine or ten thousand miles away from home to fight a war …" Yet, that's exactly what he's doing, and the ante, in lives and resources, continues to go up, while the efficacy of the war is never discussed on my New Jersey campus or even much in the national media. The moral issues seem quite clear to me, but, other than discussions at the C.U. with a few like-minded friends and professors, I have no venue for connecting with others who resonate to my views.

On a brief visit home to Sunny Vale, I make the huge mistake of sincerely trying to convey my perspective on the war to my family. Mother is frightened and offended by my blatant criticism of the United States government; furthermore, Lyndon Johnson is a southern Christian, so she has total faith in his leadership and intent. William, the Republican with no love for President Johnson, informs me that my way of thinking is wrong-headed from a patriotic point of view and dangerous from a legal one. Though I applaud Luke, now in junior high school, for growing his hair long in contrast to the buzz cuts so popular in New Jersey, I remain uneasy about his affiliation with some people calling themselves Survivalists. The group seems to be against state-sanctioned violence, yet not against individuals arming themselves. Luke spouts things like, "Kill 'em all and let God sort 'em out!" He applies this parroted slogan to U.S. citizens as well as the Vietnamese. I try in vain to explain to him that such thinking is counter-productive to the peace movement. Gary, not one to enter a controversial fray, says little, but is visibly disturbed by Luke's posturing and my politics.

Dad is not home the weekend of my notorious rant against the Vietnam War—a blessing. Not that he ever talks about it, but he was a World War II Veteran—infantry and tanks—and the recipient of a Purple Heart. Feeling ever more estranged from my family that day, within a few hours of my visit I take a bus back to North Essex and choose not to go home for Thanksgiving. I don't even go home when my mother calls to report that my cousin Petey Ray Patrick, Aunt Eula's son, has drowned in a canoeing accident on Churning River. During a telephone call to me, Mother pines, "It's a downright shame about Petey. I feel so sorry for Eula and Earl. Losin' a child is worse than losin' a parent. It ain't the natural order of things."

Dodging Prayers and Bullets

Little does she know that she's right in synch with Simon and Garfunkel who are singing that "the words of the prophet are written on the tenement walls." I feel bad about Petey Ray and know the loss must be hard on Del Ray Minix. Still, I determine to be finished with Kentucky, and with my family's compliance in the unholy alliance between God and country. Selecting a specifically non-religious sympathy card that was a challenge to find, I force myself to write a brief note of condolence to Aunt Eula and Uncle Earl.

31

OSTENSIBLY, RYAN JANSSEN is a good match for me, but I can feel nothing (other than friendship) toward him. Since I myself don't really understand why, it's becoming increasingly difficult to explain to Ryan that I don't want to "make out" or become more "involved" with him. It's particularly awkward that he believes I'm just modest or reserved. Finally, during the winter of 1965, the second semester of my sophomore year at North Essex State, I resolve to break things off.

I rely on my participation in anti-war activities to shut him out, lamely explaining that he, a senior who wants to be a social studies teacher, will be shunned by any school system that associates him with campus radicals. Ryan, who doesn't take politics all that seriously, at first laughs and mocks my contention, but then turns bitterly resentful when I won't budge regarding my decision to stop seeing him.

Eventually, he resigns himself and retreats, turning, for solace, to a rather quiet sorority girl, a future teacher of America no doubt. I'm mildly jealous when they get engaged, but mostly I'm released from the guilt of rejecting a truly "nice" guy. Ironically, the guy I can't help thinking about is the Reverend Dan Hansen. I should feel nothing but shame and anger toward the man, yet fantasizing about him is the only thing that turns me on.

Surprisingly, Caitlyn is overjoyed I'm disentangled from Ryan, because now she feels she can trust me to hear about the guy with whom she has been carrying on a surreptitious rendezvous. The mystery man turns out to be Tony Medina, our poetry professor, whom we first met at the Christian Union. Tony, well into his thirties, has a wife and two children, but Caitlyn assures me the wife in no way appreciates his increasingly radical politics, and that Tony is in the process of separating from his family.

I'm more shocked to learn Caitlyn is not a virgin than to learn she's dating a married professor. "What's the big deal?" challenges Caitlyn. "It's better to make love than war. I assumed you knew."

I can't help blurting out, "So Tony isn't the first?"

"Duh?!" Caitlyn responds, shrugging her shoulders and cocking her head while extending her palms.

"It's cool," I nervously assure her. "I just never thought about it."

Caitlyn rationalizes, "Hey, the revolution is as much about sex as politics. It's about breaking the bonds of oppression personally, as well as well as politically. Virginity is no big deal. When it comes right down to it, chastity is its own punishment. Anyway, it's your *choice*, that's what it's all about, right? Of course you don't let some creep talk you into giving it up, but with the right guy ..."

"I totally agree," I utter. "It's just that there hasn't been a 'right guy' for me—even on our side of the revolution." Shrugging dismissively, I continue, "Certainly it's not Ryan Jannsen, BMOC." Of course, I don't bring up my relationship with Dan Hansen. Caitlyn would insist that I blow the whistle on Reverend Dan, and I'm not ready for that—yet.

"OK, then," Caitlyn nods, speaking in a more relaxed tone. "So now that you don't have to drag Ryan along, Tony can hang out with us sometimes. I know you can keep your mouth shut. You know, I liked Ryan and all, but Tony can't have people gossiping about me and him getting it on. Especially in the English Department—and at least until his separation from the wife is official."

After my tryst with Reverend Dan, I have my doubts about Tony Medina's intentions regarding Caitlyn, but I honor her request to keep her secret liaison to myself, especially since she is not soliciting opinions on the matter and seems to be having a fantastic time. And Tony Medina is definitely attractive and fun. I like the idea of hanging out with a professor, even clandestinely, and, since Caitlyn and I are both excellent students, we don't feel compromised by the automatic A's we will receive in Tony's poetry class.

Caitlyn starts seeing more and more of Tony, and I'm not always up for providing cover. I'm envious that she's "getting it on" with him in his office, and even back stage in the auditorium after the theater building is shut down at night. Caitlyn jokes that she and Tony are rehearsing for "living theater."

Since I'm no longer with Ryan, I find myself alone more and more. Though I sometimes feel isolated and sorry for myself, I prefer reading and listening to music in my room to making small talk with Susan or even Josie. I listen to Dylan and Phil Ochs, but my current favorite song is Simon and Garfunkel's "*I Am a Rock*." Along with the popular duo, I mouth, *And a rock feels no pain and an island never cries*. That song is for deep personal pain. For general malaise, I prefer "Sounds of Silence." When I'm in a good mood, I can get into the Beatles, but in 1965 Caitlyn makes fun of them. "So what if they have good hair," she cajoles. "C'mon, Sky—love, love, love and holding hands? No relevant message! Stick to the Beach Boys if you want to be frivolous."

In addition to growing his hair long and sporting a beard, Professor Anthony Medina is certainly doing his part to uphold the cultural defections of the 1960s, especially in his poetry class, Introduction to the Moderns. From Caitlyn via Bob Dylan, I'm already familiar with the poetic ruminations of Keats and Rimbaud, and now Tony introduces us to the contemporary works of LeRoi Jones, Allen Ginsberg, Gregory Corso, and Laurence Ferlinghetti. He also suggests, as an extra credit assignment, that we read the William S. Burroughs novel, *Naked Lunch*. When the word *fuck* turns up in some of the assigned work, a debate is sparked in class about what constitutes literature. It's not much of a debate—more like an orchestrated rebuke of the minority of conservative students (including Susan Duncan) who dare challenge the evolving perspectives of counterculture intellectuals. To me, it's definitely exciting to be on the side of a rebel professor *and* freedom of speech. This is when Tony Medina first institutes what will become known, traditionally and notoriously, as the "Fuck You lecture" at North Essex State College.

Determined to heal the uptight reactionaries in the class, Professor Medina assigns each student to bring in two index cards for the next lecture: one card must contain a quote or passage from traditional or contemporary literature that uses profanity, obscenity, or "dirty" language; on the second card, each student is to write down a word or phrase that he or she has (or at one time had) hesitancy in saying, especially in public. Caitlyn and I love the assignment and even Susan Duncan gets into it. The next day in class, the Professor has everyone read their literature cards first. Then he begins inviting the students to introduce their personal forbidden words and phrases. Some students blush and can barely whisper words like *fuck*, *asshole*, and *cunt*, while others say the words while laughing hysterically. When anyone balks, Professor Medina has the entire class shout out the word or phrase in unison until the individual can say the words assertively, without blanching. The purpose of this assignment, Professor Medina explains, is to desensitize us to the specific words, so we can focus on the structure and nuances of the language.

Unfortunately, after a rousing "Fuck you, America!" resounds throughout the hallway, Professor Lucinda Gunther, Chair of the Foreign Language Department, comes whipping into our classroom, her face pinched and contorted. Assuming her best authoritarian mien, Dr. Gunther insists (in her German accent) that "Professor Medina" step outside the room, where the two of them engage in a heated exchange. Holding our collective breath, our classmates exchange glances in mute in trepidation. Tony comes back into the classroom to announce defiantly, "Despite my esteemed colleague's arrogant attempt at censorship, *in America*, no less, we shall continue our lesson." This whips us into a frenzy of raucous enthusiasm, especially since Professor Lucinda Gunther is rigid, unpopular, and withholding in grades as well as praise. Even Susan Duncan, at last aligned with the rest of us, is laughing as she plunges, unabashedly, into the permissive rebelliousness of it all.

Unfortunately, Professor Anthony Medina, one of the most popular professors among the students, is not in good stead with his own Department. Shortly after class, Tony is confronted by the Chair of the English Department, Dr. Nabonier (No Boner, as the students refer to him), who, with the backing of Dr. Gunther, is determined to have Tony censored at the next faculty meeting. This incident, and the subsequent debate it sparks regarding academic freedom, is what incites the faculty, administration and students of North Essex State College to at last begin to determine which side they are on. To Dr. Nabonier, condoning vulgarity in the classroom, even as an academic exercise, represents the end of civilized discourse in America. He's right, of course, but for all the wrong reasons.

One thing leads to another, until, incredibly, "No Boner" and the President of North Essex State College, a doddering and ineffectual figurehead who has way over-stayed his form as well as function, both resign! Free speech has carried the day, and professor Anthony Medina's "Fuck You lecture" will become an institution for many semesters, until the shift in American popular culture inspired by the latter 1960s makes the use of street language and profanity in literature a moot point.

Bob Dylan is singing, "The lines they are drawn, the curse it is cast," and I think it is more than ironic that our small band of campus "radicals" can't stir up any discussion, let alone action, regarding the issue of sending American boys to serve as killing machines and/or fodder for the people of Vietnam. Yet, "No Sex State College" is thrown into bureaucratic chaos over the use of words. Lenny Bruce had it right.

With regard to the consequences of the first "Fuck You lecture" at North Essex State, a peripheral outcome will one day prove momentous in the lives of my friends. During the class debate about profanity and literature, before Professor Gunther intruded and galvanized the class toward liberalism, the conservative students were united in resistance. On that day, one of the students who supported Susan Duncan's traditional view of language was Anatoly (Tolya) Karpov, a strikingly proud and handsome young man of Russian descent. Tolya was actually better acquainted with Caitlyn and me than Susan, but we considered him intellectually arrogant and a bit of a narcissist. Tolya had told us that his family had immigrated to the United States from Russia when he was in grammar school. He's proud of his Russian accent and likes to comport himself as an intellectual in the revered Russian literary tradition.

When Tolya sided with Susan in the debate about language, and then walked her back to the dorm after class, she was smitten. Tolya, basking in Susan's admiration, returned the affection. A strange and wondrous romance ensued. Caitlyn likes to quip, "The bumps in his head fit the holes in hers."

None of us could imagine, at the time, the tragic cultural destiny in store for the budding liaison of Susan and Tolya.

32

OH, SHIT, I'm thinking, I forgot to remember to worry about Gary. My older brother William and I always assume that the popular and athletic Gary will follow our leads and figure out a way to go to college—maybe even on an athletic scholarship. When he and his two best friends from high school don't apply to any colleges, I figure he just needs more time, or maybe he even feels the need to stay at home to protect Mother. (Better him than me.) Gary, after all, is Flo-Anna's favorite son—the one she named after Gary Cooper, her Hollywood cowboy crush.

Shortly after graduation, Gary takes a job at the Sunny Vale Recreation Center and also volunteers as a Little League coach. During the fall, he enjoys great popularity serving as a coach for the Pop Warner Football League. I figure, someone in our family has to do the Norman Rockwell thing.

Now it's January 1966, the second semester of my junior year of college, and my brother William calls to report that Gary has been

Dodging Prayers and Bullets

drafted. Immediately I consult Father Toland, ask Caitlyn to cover for me in classes, and throw some things together to enable me to stay in Sunny Vale for several days. My mission is to prevail upon Gary to become a draft resister. Only denial born of desperation enables me to even contemplate such an option could be in the realm of possibility for my brother, who has never even spoken out against the war.

I'm beside myself as I prod him to get out of the draft by any means possible. See a psychiatrist! (Forget it, Sky.) Fake an injury! (Lie?) Injure yourself for real! (Get outta here!) I tell him I know how to get in touch with people who can help him apply to be a conscientious objector, even escape to Canada. Anything!!!

My petitions fall upon the deaf ears of Gary, and upon the rigid, resentful mindset of the rest of the family ... except, of course, for Luke, who's against anything associated with the government. I still continue to beseech, "Explain why, Gary? PLEASE. Why would you agree to go over there to shoot people, and maybe even get killed yourself? This Vietnam crap is not heroic. It's madness, stupidity. Immoral, even."

Gary shrugs. "I won't necessarily end up in Vietnam. Besides, I have to do something. I'm tired of school, and I don't have any other plans. I can't just hang around the family and play sports the rest of my life. YOU didn't! Look, I wouldn't have volunteered for the military, but my number came up. There's nothing wrong with me, and lots of other guys are going, so why not me? Besides, I think it's my duty."

To the chagrin of Mother and Dad, the embarrassment of William, and the bewilderment of young Dory, I simply won't let up; even sanguine Gary is beginning to lose it listening to my diatribes against the war, against America. He challenges me with, "I suppose you'd be happy if I went back to Kentucky and hid out in the holler." For an insane few seconds, I mull over that alternative. Noting my distraction, Gary shakes his head and grimaces. "Then what? Mother and Dad both sacrificed too much to get us out of that place. We're not going back, Sky. I'm going to basic training to be the best damn soldier I can. Even if I have to go to Vietnam, I'll talk to the other guys and figure out why so many have signed up—you know, why my President—who knows more about this stuff than the rest of us, by the way—wants us to go." Then he grins and tips an imaginary hat, "Besides, it'll take a lot more than the army to break the Cowboy!"

For Gary's sake and for the sake of peace in the family, I relent and attempt to be supportive of his decision—at least as far as my conscience and good sense will allow. I understand it's bad enough the family has to contend with my running around Sunny Vale in brightly colored tunics, moccasins, and bellbottoms—my hair flowing long, and, of course, the peace symbol dangling from my neck.

Worse, Mother and William partly blame Luke's erratic behavior on my bad example. Besides, even without my provocation, Mother is a mess about Gary going into the army; she's weeping and praying incessantly that he will not be sent to Vietnam. Like most parents faced with the prospect of a child entering the military, she believes the war is necessary and honorable; she just doesn't want her kid to go.

After two days, I leave Sunny Vale pretending that I've come to terms with Gary's decision to comply with the draft, and promising my mother that I will pray, in her words, *ever' day that Gary don't get taken in Vietnam, that God-forsaken place.* If God has a stockpile of prayers waiting to be addressed, Flo-Anna Reece Jenkins is certainly making a mountain of the molehill of such petitions.

Gary will ship out to basic training in South Carolina within two weeks. Since our last interaction had been so contentious, I don't honestly know how he feels about his accepted mission. Is he scared? resigned? proud? Is he feeling patriotic or just trapped? Fighting back tears and my own anger but feigning my support, I call to wish him well, but I can't bring myself to go to Sunny Vale to see him off.

33

IT'S A FORTUITOUS TURN of fate that Dad is at home and all the kids are at school when the government-issued sedan pulls up to the projects.

Dad and some of the neighbors know exactly what's coming the instant they spot the officers in the car with the military insignia. (A few months before one of our hometown boys was killed in Vietnam as a result of friendly fire, the most mockingly cruel of military euphemisms.) When the vehicle pulls directly in front of our block of apartments, Mother remains clueless, or at least in denial, half-expecting Gary to pop out. Instead, three officers in crisp dress uniforms, one obviously a chaplain, emerge from the car and come to the door.

Mother has gotten her prayers answered in that bitterly ironic way people have of getting what they ask for but not what they intend. Gary was not slaughtered like a lamb in the allegedly unholy land of Vietnam, where, in truth, the people are as gentle and unassuming as he. The three Casualty Assistance Officers, as the trio of messengers refer to themselves, report to Flo-Anna and Lonnie Lee that their son, Gary Cooper Jenkins, was killed in a basic training mishap at Fort Bragg, outside Fayetteville, North Carolina. The officers cannot, or will not, provide any detail. Later, we learn Gary died in a routine convoy accident, a fluke event involving a horrible crash and intense flames.

It's odd about my mother: at the times I expect her to become most unhinged, she reaches down for some deep reserve of mettle and clarity. Upon receiving the news of Gary's death, Flo-Anna Reece Jenkins simply says, "Oh, Lord," and sits quietly with her hands folded. Daddy, stunned into a stony silence, accepts all the papers from the casualty team without looking them over or asking any questions. He tells the officers, "My eldest boy, he's in law school. I reckon I'll have him look this over." The chaplain offers a prayer, which my docile parents accept, and the three officers take their leave while neighbors throughout the projects peek out, aghast.

I can't even begin to imagine what those few minutes must have been like for my parents. "You better come on over here, it's about Gary," Dad tells William on the phone. As the eldest son and a prospective lawyer, William is designated to manage family business and dispense bad news—an entitlement he would gladly have forfeited.

When Dad tells him what has happened, William chokes up but then shifts into administrative mode and immediately calls me, whose family role is to handle the younger kids and anything emotional related to our mother.

In my state of self-imposed exile from the family, I feel guilty as well as horrified about Gary's death. For me, this is the worst possible denouement of a seemingly inevitable tragedy. Over the holidays, I had not spent much time with Gary, and then I had returned home in early January specifically to make a scene over his complying with the draft. AND I DIDN'T GO BACK TO SEND HIM OFF. Between my guilt over harassing Gary about a choice that was his to make, and my anger at the government and military for claiming him, I feel as if my soul has been ripped asunder.

I recall that, about a week after Gary left for Fort Bragg, North Carolina, Mother had received a brief note from him, reassuring her things were fine. At the time she was pleased he was assigned to training in a Southern state. William says the army confirmed that Gary was killed in a training accident, but he can't get more than the rudimentary details about how or why it happened. Apparently, this kind of information is "classified."

Our family does receive, however, reams of paper work and baffling assurances that Gary Cooper Jenkins has made the ultimate sacrifice—died a hero in the service of his country. President Lyndon Johnson also sends my parents a personalized letter of gratitude and condolence. Mother informs me that the visiting chaplain was a very nice young man and that all three Casualty Assistance Officers expressed great sympathy over our loss.

Afterwards, when Mother inevitably falls apart, she obsesses repeatedly over Lonnie Lee's remission in not turning the TV off while the Casualty Officers were there, and her own negligence in not offering the officers something to eat and drink. She talks as if there is some kind of protocol she and Dad were responsible for maintaining while being informed that their nineteen-year-old son has been inadvertently massacred.

The news of Gary's death stuns and devastates our family, and the subsequent funeral proceedings will torment me for the rest of my life. For reasons no one in the family wants to speculate about at the time, the army prescribes a closed casket for Gary, and delivers his "remains" to Blanton Brothers, the Protestant funeral home in Sunny Vale. Both the evening before and the morning prior to the church service, my family gathers for a "viewing" in the parlor of the funeral home. Noting the colorful blooms with attached notes of condolence adorning the room, I'm not at all required to wonder, "Where have all the flowers gone?" I have to will myself to look in the direction of the beautifully honed casket draped in an American flag with a photo of Gary in army dress uniform at the head. (I think bitterly, at what is presumably the head.) In stark contrast to his typical aura of good-natured self-confidence, Gary looks serious and vulnerable in the formal photo of him in uniform. I keep thinking about how handsome and confident my father appears in his World War II photo, one of the only photos of Lonnie Lee that Mother displays proudly. You can bet this army portrait of Gary is not going to be prominently displayed.

I find myself wondering if Christians believe they can post prayers after the fact, so to speak, to change reality in some way. Since Mother's multitude of prayers didn't manage to save Gary, my forlorn and minimalist post-prayer would be that he had not seen it coming—that Gary died quickly and obliviously. I never discover if that prayer was answered.

My entire family is in shock. Watching my parents prepare for the funeral, I can tell they are in no way a comfort to each other. Flo-Anna is extremely self-conscious and taking forever to get dressed; though not a word is uttered regarding her delay, she accuses us all of rushing her. Worse, she keeps justifying Gary's loss, casting him as some kind of martyred Christ figure, singing hymns, and, in a quavering voice, reciting her interpretation of passages from the Bible: *No greater love can a man give than to lay down his life for others.* Of course I understand my mother *has* to believe that, but having it hammered at me incessantly is more than a trial. Finally, I just hold on tight to Dory and, with clenched teeth and empty stares, hover near my distraught mother.

In an ill-fitted suit, Lonnie Lee looks dumbfounded and displaced amongst the mourners. Obviously, he's not at all convinced this is his son's finest hour. My father received a Purple Heart for his injuries in World War II, but the army will not be awarding Gary a Purple Heart. William was able to determine that the medal is reserved for those wounded or killed while engaged in actual combat with the enemy. Purple Hearts are about who gets at you, not how you serve or even whether you die. My father had it about right when he once said of life, "Jist when ya get to thinkin' it's a warm puppy, it turns around and bites ya on the ass."

Naturally, the minister and the fine Christian patriots of Sunny Vale, New Jersey give the Lord and America the beautiful a "pass" on their making Gary expendable for the greater good of all. With my personal grief undercut by outrage, guilt and bitterness, I struggle to hold my tongue, especially just before my family leaves for the funeral home when Mother hisses at me, "Don't you go to makin' a spectacle outta this." I'm one deep breath away from shouting, "Tell that to the United States Army! That's who made a spectacle of Gary, not me." But I behave.

Luke, on the other hand, in no way behaves. William prods him to change out of the army surplus togs he typically wears, so Luke dons one of Gary's white dress shirts that is way too big for him. On the shirt pocket he pins a small button that reads, "Live Free." At the viewing he keeps giggling inappropriately, and later ravenously attacks the buffet table the neighbors have set up for the mourners. William and I decide Luke is definitely *on* something, and it isn't anything from the local pharmacy. We assume it's alcohol, though we can't smell it on him. I know Luke is sneaking off for cigarettes, but it will be another five or six months before I readily recognize the scent and effects of marijuana.

The minister and guests at the funeral service steer clear of Lucas Wesley Jenkins, chalking up his bad behavior to the shock of losing a brother and the presumed guilt he feels for being too young to serve his country. The ultimate rebuff, I think: they simply neglect to acknowledge Luke's grief or political message.

It is, in fact, not Luke but William who is likely suffering from any free-floating guilt associated with the sacrifice of a brother. Had he not been self-supporting and enrolled in law school, William understands he could easily have been the one taken. And as a Republican, patriot, and Christian (at least in the trappings), William doesn't have the entitlement I have to sulk in righteous indignation. Besides, he has political as well as legal aspirations on the horizon, and his marriage to Mary Ann is already in the works. William is required to be the good shepherd who stays with the flock, regardless of any doubts, regrets or lost sheep.

Being around my family at the viewing and funeral is horrendous, but I refuse to let any friends, including Caitlyn, attend the services. "It's a small family funeral, and private," I lie. As usual, I'm just too emotionally wracked over how to conduct myself to entertain the sympathy of friends. To appease the family, I dress "normal," in a plain black dress. In that much sorrow there's little room for the politics of provocation. For now, my intent is to put myself aside to protect my parents and Dory, to defend Luke, to empathize with William, and at the same time to honor Gary. I will turn to my friends at another time.

For appearances' sake, I go through the motions of mourning—masking my bitterness with tears, stifling my outrage with quiet sobs, covering my guilt with weak smiles and nods. Our good and patriotic neighbors hug me and whisper condolences, while, as in my childhood, I mentally plot my escape from the narrow, suffocating confines of

Sunny Vale, from the shell of a woman who used to be my mother, and from my capriciously raging father, who is momentarily cowed by abject grief. At the funeral parlor I briefly excuse myself for a trip to the "powder room"—a stupid thing to call a toilet—lock myself inside and throw up. Returning to sustain myself through the rest of the viewing is the hardest act of civility I will ever have to perform.

The religious service is held at the Sunny Vale Methodist Church, where Daddy, William, Luke, and three of Gary's loyal friends act as pallbearers. The best part for me is that I don't have to talk to anyone during the proceedings. Not even pretending to pray, I sit there reveling in the satisfaction of my status as a "died again Christian." Two representatives from the U.S. Army, including one of the "nice" messengers of morbidity who originally came to the house, attend the funeral to present the family with a folded flag and a brass grave marker. (The souvenirs a family gets when its child makes the ultimate sacrifice.) The army officers salute Gary's casket and also thank Dad for his service in World War II. It happens to be true that Gary was honorable, but I know he, like most of the others sacrificed for this war, died not as a hero but simply because he couldn't help it. At the time of Gary Cooper Jenkins' personal High Noon, the Cowboy simply wasn't able to dodge the bullet.

Gary's death certainly puts the lie to the great American myth that cowboys, at least the ones in the white hats, always win. I may have been plunged into deep despair, but Gary's loss is the end of Mother. She's never "right" again, and her moaning and wailing, and, worse yet, attempts to justify what happened in the name of sacrifice to God and country, causes an irreparable rent in the already weakened fabric of our family. During one of her more unhinged rants, Mother blames me for putting a curse on Gary. She quickly thinks better of it and in tears recants the accusation with, "Now ya know I don't mean that. I jist cain't make no sense out of this no how." But I'm in no mood to forgive my mother or America, and, obviously, God and prayers are not part of this equation.

William, who has been called upon to handle the funeral arrangements, also does the administrative work for the life insurance benefits—specifically the "death gratuity," a few thousand dollars allotted by the government for the family to deploy at their own discretion. For my family, it is a lot of money. Dad is inclined to buy a truck and go into business for himself, but William prevails upon him to use the money as a down payment on a house, at last transitioning our family from the projects. In a bizarre and woeful sense, Gary managed to take care of them. Dory and Luke each now have their own room, and Mother creates a garden in the back yard, taking some comfort from working the earth with her hands. Luke even gains a measure of redemption by helping with the digging and maintenance of the garden. Eventually they harvest a considerable selection of vegetables and flowers. The garden serves, I suppose, as the last vestige of Mother's former life in Kentucky.

As Gary's casket was lowered into the ground in Sunny Vale, New Jersey, I understood that my mother's remaining ties to Kentucky were buried along with him. Flo-Anna Reece Jenkins will never leave the final resting place of her second son, named after her favorite cowboy.

34

I'M GRATEFUL TO HAVE college as an excuse to leave Sunny Vale a day after the funeral, but back at North Essex State, I can tell the professors and friends who know me feel awkward around me, especially since they know my position regarding the war. I'm like a wounded animal that they want to approach, but are afraid to because they might jostle me in the wrong way and do more damage or even provoke an attack.

Good, I think, because I don't want to talk about what has happened to my brother.

As far as everyone can surmise, I simply came back and lost myself in academics. On my door in the dorm, I post a quote from a Shakespearean villain: *If one good deed in all my life I did, I do repent it from my very soul.* Later I will reflect upon this time as my bitter blue period.

Thankfully, Dr. Elton Davis, the college psychologist, is not the probing type; he is content to allow me the space to handle my grief in my own way. He continues to support my need for a private room, and I'm grateful for that. And, though Caitlyn is obviously hurt because I won't lean on her more, she blessedly does not allow me to languish in lament or dissipate in discord. She remains loyal without discussing things, allows for my distance, and sometimes even insists that I join in the dormitory revelry. Caitlyn is more available these days, because, predictably, her tryst with Professor Tony Medina ended abruptly when his wife became suspicious and Tony chose to renew his commitment to his family.

Though I continue to attend the Christian Union meetings, where the war is discussed, I don't talk personally about it, nor what Gary's loss means to me. Privately, I allow myself to break down in front of Father Toland, seeking something akin to spiritual comfort. I'm grateful he does not try to justify or attack the war in any kind of Jesus or religious terms, and, at the same time, he doesn't use Gary's death to grind a political ax. Thoroughly embittered and grieving deeply, I understand that it's necessary for me to take some action on my own behalf. To save myself, I determine to put more distance between me and all the elements of my New Jersey life, especially my family. If I stay in New Jersey or even move to New York City, I will feel obligated to make frequent phone calls and visits to Sunny Vale to comfort my parents, visit Gary's gravesite, and, in general, explain myself; those tasks are just too daunting. All I am hearing in my head is that tune by the Animals, *"We Gotta Get Out of This Place."*

With some investigation, I find out I can apply my Economic Opportunity Act scholarship toward tuition and fees at any college in the United States. YES!! Dr. Davis and the Dean of Students strongly advise against my transferring out of North Essex State, especially at this time. But I've been avidly following the events transpiring at the University of California at Berkeley. I decide it's there, a good 3,000 miles from New Jersey, where I will find the social and political milieu I desperately crave. I take it as sign that Lord Jim (Father Toland) has an administrative contact on the Berkeley campus; with the support of the priest and a couple of strong references from my English professors, I fill out a transfer application.

By early April, I'm accepted at Berkeley for the fall 1966 semester, in a special program of the English Department called Literary Studies. I'm able to transfer all my North Essex State credits, and discover that if I establish residency in California, my out-of-state fees will eventually be reduced. At most, I might need to complete an extra semester in order to graduate. I intend to do that. Never again will I use Sunny Vale, New Jersey as a mailing address, a determination that carries practical as well as psychic import.

Caitlyn, of course, is devastated that I'm leaving North Essex State and abandoning our alliance. I urge her to try to transfer, too, but her grades have been slipping, and, on some level, I think she doesn't believe I will actually make this move. When she can no longer deny my intentions, some atypically awkward tension arises between us. In truth, I have shut her out, but I can't help it.

One day in mid May, unable to suppress a grin, Caitlyn, along with Josie Schumacher, appears in my dorm room singing *California Dreamin'*. After a few bars, Caitlyn proclaims, "We're *all* off to Berkeley at the end of the semester." Totally flummoxed, I scrunch up my face and turn my head from Josie to Caitlyn.

"For real!" Josie chimes in. "My father's lending me the station wagon for a cross-country trip to stay with my Aunt in Sacramento. I'm gonna work in her flower shop this summer."

"We're all hitting the road together," Caitlyn adds. "You can't escape me!"

"It's true!" Josie continues. "Caitlyn's going to hang with you in Berkeley to get you settled, and she can drive back to New Jersey with me at the end of August."

Listening in flummoxed disbelief, all I can do is flop down, take a deep breath, and finally blurt, "Far fucking out!" (These days, expletives roll trippingly off my tongue.) Then, I jump up and reach out for both of them. Laughing and crying at the same time, I spurt, "I love you guys. I've been obsessing over how to get out to California, and now I can't believe it's with my best friends."

The next day, I contact the UC Berkeley housing office, but they inform me I can't be assured dormitory space until fall. It doesn't matter; I'm going to Berkeley in June with Caitlyn, and we'll find a place to stay until I start school in September.

Part Three

Berkeley, California

35

JOSIE SCHUMACHER'S FATHER is a strikingly handsome retired Navy Captain whom Caitlyn dubs "the Admiral." He assembles Josie, Caitlyn and me for our "behaving responsibly under my watch" lecture. It is mainly about driving safely and not comporting ourselves like crazed hippies while we traverse the country. Painting flowers or a peace symbol on the station wagon, as Caitlyn had done on her VW, is definitely proscribed by the Admiral.

He isn't a bad guy, though—really. He informs us that, while he doesn't approve of desecrating the flag or burning draft cards, he's not entirely convinced this "Vietnam business" is necessary, or that a proper war is being conducted there. In addition to the loan of the car, he gives Josie a credit card, "strictly for emergency purposes." The Admiral's only other request is that, each day as we make our way across the country, we stop for a good night's sleep and never attempt to drive straight through the night.

Thanking him profusely, we enthusiastically agree to his provisos and hit the road early the next morning. At our first rest stop, without even a proprietary discussion, we plaster "Stop the War Now," "Flower Power" and "Draft Beer Not Students" bumper stickers on the car, and drive all day and straight through the night, to get well past Ohio. So much for parental caveats and intergenerational contracts.

Seeing a great swath of the country on a road trip with friends is the ideal way to minister to my disaffection with America. "America the Beautiful" should definitely be our national anthem. The trip also serves as a spiritual balm for the void I'm experiencing after the senseless loss of my brother. Convinced Gary died, under dubious circumstances no less, FOR NOTHING, I'm struggling to find meaning in something. I find myself awed by the "big sky" of Wyoming; enamored of the New Mexico desert; inspired by the rivers and boulders of Utah.

Josie, Caitlyn and I conclude that this country is far too magnificent to turn over to the petty bureaucrats and warmongers currently in power. Just as Mario Savio urged from the steps of Sproul Hall at the University of California at Berkeley, we will join in the fight for the true principles of freedom and democracy. Armed with our wits, two guitars, a kazoo and a tambourine, we sing, debate, and commune our way across the country. In, for her, a rare acknowledgment of the Beatles, Caitlyn finds the chords to "Ticket to Ride" and we belt that out, along with Woody Guthrie's standby, "This Land Is My Land."

When we stop at gas stations or diners, or at small eating establishments along the way, the locals gaze at us with suspicion, sometimes hostility; at times they insult us and even threaten to do us harm. More than once, because of our long hair and colorful attire and the bumper stickers on the car, drivers with faces contorted in anger and contempt pull alongside our vehicle and give us the finger or shout, "Hippie scum!" On a few glorious occasions, however, people applaud us, or other "freaks" driving along raise up the two finger peace sign to us, or call out, in unity, "Hell, NO, we won't go!"

But the children are the best! Across the United States, in diners or from the back seat of the family car (when their parents aren't looking) the children raise their right arms and flash the two-fingered peace symbol. Apparently, there is hope for America's future.

"Yes!" I exclaim, thinking of Dylan's salient lyrics: *Your sons and your daughters are beyond your command.* At such times, I know the so-called "counterculture" will prevail, simply because it's so evident to the youth of America that aspiring to be a hippie is a far more thrilling prospect than anything being "straight" has to offer.

By the time we pull into San Francisco, my friends and I are primed to rock. And the Golden Gate Bridge signals the gateway to Mecca for American youth. Never mind that the bridge turns out to be orange—named for an era rather than a color—and that it is not, in fact, the passageway to Berkeley. And never mind that we're shocked by how cold San Francisco is with the fog rolling off the bay: the Haight-Ashbury district totally delivers!

During the summer of 1966, in both dress and attitude, the advocates of anarchy hold sway in the streets of San Francisco. The concordance is: if you've got it, flaunt it! Every street corner sports an array of performers rendering vibrant art, music, dance and poetry. On the streets of the Haight, Josie's car is just one of many touting anti-war and anti-establishment slogans. Even old guys have long hair and are flamboyantly adorned; numerous people greet us with smiles and flowers, imparting to us the sentiments and convictions of this colorfully pulsating assemblage. Lawlessness rather than political persuasion seems to fuel the frenzy, with numerous individuals distributing flyers touting lofty notions and/or drugs. I purchase a button that reads, "Support Your Local Anarchist." It's a heady time, both literally and figuratively.

I have to admit, however, that I'm somewhat unnerved by the scattered clusters of Hell's Angels tempering the general elation with elements of danger and ambiguity. At least the Vietnam Veterans Against the War have a poignant and relevant message—one that is particularly sad and compelling to me, though it's impossible to separate the politics from my personal loss. I wonder what Gary, had he survived and served in Vietnam, would have made of the Vets against the war. Might he, too, have become disenchanted with the carnage, and turned woeful and resentful of his country's involvement? Or would he have grown rigid, conflicted and vacant-eyed, like so many of the returning Vets who have lost their moorings and can neither be proud of their service nor against the war? I pick up some literature and make a donation to the Vietnam Vets, but I can't yet bring myself to talk with them. I can tell Caitlyn and Josie are keeping an eye on me, but fortunately neither is so crass as to make a comment.

Dodging Prayers and Bullets

Next ,we come across some lively musicians and performers who describe themselves as guerrilla street artists. They enact short skits poking fun at the Johnson administration and bemoaning the war in Vietnam. Caitlyn and I are enthralled by the pure electricity generated in the Haight-Asbury district of San Francisco, but Josie is becoming somewhat intimidated. She insists we move the car to a more secure area. Returning to the car and driving into downtown San Francisco, we're astounded by the stark contrast of a clean and efficient-looking business district, seemingly impassive to the uncomely youth culture ensconced around it. Secure! Uptight! Boring! So, we study our map and drive toward the waterfront, deciding to check into a cheap hotel (with parking) a bit inland from the water.

We agree to stay over just that one night in San Francisco, since Caitlyn and I are anxious to get to Berkeley, and Josie still has ahead of her a long, lonely drive to Sacramento. With parking and accommodations secured, we're thrilled to jump aboard a streetcar heading to the San Francisco Bay. Near the waterfront, I stare at a young sailor who looks like a reincarnation of my brother Gary. I say nothing about it to my friends, but the delusional sighting of my brother is a phenomenon I soon get used to. Sometimes, at the most unlikely place or time, I will see a young man's profile, hear the turn of a phrase, or even detect a particular scent, and Gary's presence is there. I might then catch myself resting my head on my forefingers, as if in prayer. Caitlyn tells me my eyes glaze over at such times, and she understands not to inquire about my mental absence; she simply hovers nearby and waits to gently shift my focus. She is a forever friend.

I'm enticed by happenings in the Haight, but at the same time soulfully captivated by the waterfront, the San Francisco of tunes and postcards. Of course, the three of us indulge in a seafood dinner, and, in homage to our poetry professor, Tony Medina, we stop by Lawrence Ferlinghetti's City Lights Book Store. Caitlyn shrugs off Tony's split with her as "his loss." I buy a signed copy of Ferlinghetti's poetry book, *A Coney Island of the Mind*. I love that he resonates to New York as well as to California.

Early the next morning, we check out of the hotel and cross the Bay Bridge (not the Golden Gate) into Berkeley. We're already enthralled by the hills and greenery of Orange County, but when we reach the vicinity of the University of California, I'm simply awed. I understand full well that the Berkeley campus is the epicenter of our national student unrest, especially for the Students for a Democratic Society (SDS), but the place is also sunny and bountiful: flowers and eucalyptus trees are everywhere, and there are even banyan trees that, when pruned, look like a hand with too many fingers splayed upward.

In contrast to the streets of the Haight, Berkeley streets are dominated by student types—mostly longhaired youth sporting peace symbols and buttons with positive messages about peace and love. Though I desperately want to enter the campus grounds and check out the University, Caitlyn and I know the first priority is finding temporary housing. I can figure out something more permanent in the fall, when the university housing office has promised to help me get situated. From a newsstand, we buy a copy of the *Berkeley Daily Gazette*, and also pick up a small, politically oriented paper called the *Berkeley Barb*. The latter, purporting to represent the voice of the people, looks more interesting, but the former has the listings for housing.

To sit and mull over possibilities, Josie suggests we try a Mexican restaurant, a cuisine commonplace in California, but not at all familiar to us east coast transplants in 1966. The waiter, a university dropout, obligingly looks over the newspaper ads for housing and advises us on locales accessible to campus. Munching on chicken flautas and guacamole in a cafe blasting Jefferson Airplane music and jammed with long-haired freaks debating politics, I know I have, at last, alighted upon a milieu congruent with my values.

After lunch, Josie drops Caitlyn and me off on University Avenue, where we intend to take a look at the Earl House, a place advertising available rooms for students. It's almost 2 pm and Josie has to hit the road for Sacramento, so, in youthful exuberance, we wave goodbye to her from the sidewalk, and Caitlyn and I drag our luggage into the lobby of the guesthouse.

Uh-oh! Inside, the Earl House looks like every mother's nightmare of where her daughter, the runaway, would end up. It's dingy, cluttered with antiquated furnishings, and smells of stale smoke, mildew, caustic fluids (medicinal or cleaning?), and decaying lives, if not bodies. All manner of characters, not just hippie freaks, are lounging about the lobby: an odd little man quietly dispensing paranoid proclamations; a middle-aged woman mumbling to herself, a younger man whose face is marred by a reddish birthmark snaking from beneath his left eye to under his chin, and, without doubt, an aging prostitute. Leaning against the railing on the second floor, a shockingly obese man in a suit and tie lurks and leers at the congregated anomalies below.

Moving toward the front desk my eyes immediately lock on the cream-colored plastic statuette of Jesus attached to the register. Perfect dissonance. I nudge Caitlyn and roll my eyes. She starts humming the tune to, "I don't care if it rains or freezes, long as I have my plastic Jesus."

A smiling desk clerk of Asian descent nods and greets us enthusiastically, "Welcome! My name is Chung-Hee Kim. OK, you can call me Charlie. I'm so happy to meet you." Charlie delivers the equivocating news that there is "room at the inn."

Had Josie not already departed, I would have split from the Earl House in a nanosecond. Instead, Caitlyn and I step aside, huddle, and agree that we have to stay this one night so we can look around for a better place baggage-free.

When we ask the desk clerk for one night, he protests, "No, that's not so good. You're students. It's better if you stay longer. You can talk to the owner tomorrow morning, Miss Price." Apparently, as Chung-Hee Kim, aka Charlie, insistently explains, transients are relegated to the (seedy) annex of the guesthouse instead of to the better student quarters.

"We might go stay with a friend," Caitlyn lies, "so we only want tonight."

There is single room only occupancy in the transient annex, so we're forced to rent two separate spaces, not even on the same floor. Room keys in hand and unescorted by the desk clerk, we wander down a long unkempt hallway to the to the back annex of the building. I find it truly intimidating, like the setting for a cheap horror movie, or worse, porno film. Caitlyn tries to assure me that the residents are more horrifying than dangerous, but her assigned room is on the second floor, closer to the stairs than my third floor assignment near an unsecured rear exit. We both decide to leave our stuff in Caitlyn's room. Making sure the door lock clicks into place, we grab the *Berkeley Daily Gazette* and immediately beat it out of the Earl House to look for better quarters for tomorrow.

We have no idea how Berkeley is laid out, so, relying on the lunch waiter's advice and a bus map, we explore rather aimlessly on foot. We come upon an entrance to the University just a block and a half from the Earl House, but, feeling the need to secure a safer place to live, we once more resist the urge to start exploring the campus. Everything listed in the paper is either too expensive, has a "no transients" clause, or seems to require a car or long bus ride to reach even the vicinity of the campus.

Sitting on a bench peering through the ads, we are approached by a thin and smiling young freak with dilated pupils who asks if we want to score some dope. As he addresses us, his whole body gyrates in a gentle sway, and he phrases every sentence very slowly, as if struggling to connect his brain to his mouth. He remains amiable even when we decline to purchase, and then, noticing that our newspaper is open to the housing ads, he posits, "Are—you ladies—by—any chance—looking—for—a crib?" When we acknowledge that we are, indeed, seeking a place to crash, he introduces himself as "Acid Rain"—Sid, for short—and says he knows a place that might be available.

We follow Sid some distance from campus, where he bangs on the door of a dilapidated house. A gruff and disheveled guy of indeterminate age opens the door and escorts us inside. Indicating the two of us, Sid informs the guy, "They're—cool." Then to us, "This—is Puck—he—runs—the place."

The older guy looks us over, shrugs and nods his head, then points and responds gruffly, "Take a look at that room over there. You get to clean it up and I always want my money up front—for the crib and any business we do." The part about business is rather cryptic, and nothing about this guy seems appealing or trustworthy.

Like the rest of the house, the windowless room is a filthy mess, reeking of a strange sweet smoke. Aged and torn psychedelic posters and anti-war flyers are taped haphazardly to the walls, probably to cover up broken plaster and mold. Discarded food wrappers and beer bottles litter the floor. The lighting consists of one bare bulb and several drip candles stuffed in wine bottles. The room is furnished with a stripped double bed mattress (full of cigarette burns) on the floor and a warped dresser missing the second from the bottom drawer, making it look like a mouth agape. There's not even a lock on the battered door.

I'm terrified and dumbstruck, especially when old Puck tosses out, "Are you dyke chicks, or what?"

Fortunately, Caitlyn gets a grip and snaps back, "Not your business, Bro. We got a couple of other pads to check out, so we'll have to let you know." Turning to me, she points toward the door with her head, "OK, let's split."

"It's cool," says Puck, suddenly becoming a tad more solicitous, "Dykes, whores, fag hags, I don't give a shit. You want a place to crash, right? If you don't take it, there's plenty that will." He motions at Sid with a flip of his hand, "Later."

Struggling to keep things mellow, I thank the guy and lamely repeat that we'll let him know, as he continues to assure us that this is the best deal around. Exiting the house quickly, with Sid in tow, Caitlyn and I begin laughing semi-hysterically and head back toward campus.

"Hey, Bro," Caitlyn gently explains to Acid Rain, "We gotta do our own thing now. We'll let you know about the place later." I feel sorry for the kid, who is only trying to help us out, but I'm immensely grateful Caitlyn can assert herself.

Sid, who seems accustomed to being dismissed, smiles and responds, "I'm cool—with—that. Peace—out. Look—for me—on Telegraph. If you—need—shit—or whatever."

With Sid on his way, Caitlyn and I immediately begin extolling the relative safety and amenities of the Earl House. After the junkie haven we have just surveyed, the Earl House seems benign and particularly well located. We agree to spend the night in the annex there and will talk to the owner, this Miss Price, the next day. We'll at least check out the main part of the complex, supposedly for students. Until then, we can relax and look around the University, where I will enroll come September, with the promised housing assistance.

Finally, it's time to explore the enticing campus! Caitlyn and I promptly fall in love with the University of California at Berkeley. Compared to North Essex State, it's huge, stately, and abloom with flowers and trees. And, of course, it is already storied as well as history-laden. Passing through Sather Gate, we come upon throngs of hippies and anti-war activists, students and non-students, sprawled around the square, spontaneously singing, chanting, and engrossed in vibrant political discourse in front of a building called Sproul Hall. There are tables piled high with free activist literature and, for sale, posters of abstract florals and buttons with clever proclamations. Caitlyn and I stand about reading and nudging each other over the various messages on the buttons. Finally, to complement the button I had picked up in San Francisco, I buy a colorful button decorated with flowers that states, "War Is Unhealthy for Children and Other Living Things." Thus commences what is to become my extensive collection of revolution-inspiring buttons.

Meandering off campus through an exit unto Telegraph Avenue (the place Sid had referenced) my mind is blown. This is a less raw, more student-dominated Haight-Ashbury with a true political edge—a three-block-long strip of stores and street vendors catering to counterculture tastes in music, politics, art, jewelry, clothing and drug paraphernalia. In Berkeley, Telegraph Avenue is the place to see and be seen, and, in 1966, definitely the place to be heard, especially for those pesky individuals the University of California disdainfully labels "off-campus agitators." Caitlyn and I are thrilled to find a place that seems like the vortex of political and flower power. We gather a ton of literature announcing political rallies, happenings, and music events and decide to return to the Earl House to sort through it. I linger momentarily by another button vendor and buy a cream-colored one that states simply, "Question Authority."

On the way back to the Earl House, we pick up some food to eat in our room, because it's getting dark and, at the sinister Earl House Annex, we prefer to be in our room with the door locked well before the witching hour. As we enter the lobby, Charlie, who is about to turn the desk job over to the night clerk, greets us like we're returning dignitaries. Even the plastic Jesus seems welcoming.

"We might decide to stay on," I tell Charlie, who introduces us to Byron, the balding night clerk, "but we can't let you know until tomorrow."

Byron is one of those people who assume a permanent bored expression and wear it like a waxen mask. I chuckle to myself that he is a living testimony to every mother's adage, "Be careful or your face will freeze like that." Considering us laconically, he informs us, "You don't get to decide that. Tomorrow Miss Price will say if you can move into the main house. That is, of course, if you're not Lesbians."

The audacity! I think, cutting my eyes toward Caitlyn.

Charlie waves Byron off. "No problem! They're nice girls." He smiles toward us and inquires, "Are you Christian?"

I don't wait for Caitlyn to rescue me on this one. "Buddhists!" I declare.

"No problem," Charlie repeats, obviously disappointed, but still rooting for us. "You're nice. You can talk to Miss Price tomorrow. You'll stay here a long time, just wait."

As Chung-Hee Kim (aka Charlie) departs and Byron continues to ignore us, we gaze about the lobby of the Earl House. Fortunately, it does not seem quite so intimidating as earlier in the day. Some of the odder-looking people have retreated to their rooms—in the Annex, no doubt. We think a few people coming and going might actually be students, or at least not just human detritus. Perhaps they are returning from work. Still, to be on the safe side, Caitlyn and I both sleep in the one double bed in Caitlyn's room, the irony of the "dyke" accusations not lost on us.

We survive the night and report to the front desk to meet the illustrious Dorothea Price the next morning. As we anticipated, the proprietor of the Earl House is a character. Quick to inform us that she is a retired actress, Miss Price, who must be in her sixties, addresses us in an obvious "stagy" nonspecific European accent. Her hair, dyed flaming red, easily trumps her scarlet lipstick and nail polish.

"Now, darlings," she wishes to assure us, "I understand that you're students, so I want you to know that I insist on running an upright establishment. No way will junkies, prostitutes, and rabble-rousers be tolerated on my premises. After all, I want your parents to rest easy when you stay here. They're backing you financially, correct?"

Of course, Caitlyn and I assure Miss Price, trying not to look at each other and burst into laughter. She tours us around the guesthouse, which seems fairly deserted in the mid-morning hours. The double rooms in the main house have twin beds with matching chenille bedspreads (shades of North Essex State) and two combination wardrobe/dressers, plus a desk and lamp for each student. The bonus item for our particular room, located on the second floor, will be a small refrigerator—if we promise not to bring in a hotplate or electric frying pan. The room is plain but, thankfully, clean and spacious. Outside a gated window is a fire escape that leads down to a courtyard overrun with weeds and litter or, alternately and creepily, across the back of the building to the notorious Annex.

The Earl House is definitely convenient to campus and, assuming Caitlyn and I can both find summer jobs, reasonably priced. We go back downstairs with Miss Price and sign a year's lease, falsely affirming that we're both students who will stay on in the fall while attending the University. Miss Price reminds us again that the use of drugs and soliciting for prostitution are prohibited at the Earl House. *How upstanding,* I muse.

When we move our stuff from the Annex into our new room, Caitlyn snaps up the key to the window gate and unlatches the window to check out the fire escape. She hauls in a small brown paper bag containing a rubber tube, a lighter and a bent spoon, obviously the drug "works" of the former tenant. I immediately toss the bag and its contents unto the rubble in the courtyard below. We make sure the metal grate over the window is secured, pull the shade down, and hide the key out of reach of the window. We remain creeped out by the Earl House, but still, it's a sanctuary compared to Puck the Fuck's decadent pad.

Toward noon, on our way out, we are detained in the lobby by Miss Price and obliged to listen to way too much information about her life in the theater in the good old days. This was followed by her downfall after the war, and her blessed recovery in the hotel business, which she has inherited from her dearly departed father. Miss Price, who has our names down, introduces us to several non-student residents, now seated in the lobby. They appear to be on Welfare or have been remanded to the Earl House from institutions of one sort or another. They seem harmless enough in the daylight, but they all want to tell us their life stories or their present predicaments, so I pretend I have an appointment on campus.

Hitting the streets again at last, Caitlyn and I purchase muffins from a corner bakery and begin exploring the stores and restaurants around the periphery of the campus, soon lured, of course, by the inexorable magnetism of Telegraph Avenue. On a street corner just below Telegraph, we hear music and see a band surrounded by a crowd of people who are dancing and waving their arms in the air, some with their eyes closed. We rush to join the festivities and are informed that the band is called Quicksilver Messenger Service. People are passing around flyers about an upcoming benefit concert for the San Francisco

Mime Company. QMS is the first of many bands we will enjoy for free on the streets of Berkeley—that is, shortly before all the musicians get co-opted and sign restrictive recording contracts.

When we reach Telegraph, it's not long before we run across Sid. We hug and greet each other like old pals, even though we once again decline his offer of scoring some "grass," which is apparently what pot is called on the west coast.

"Hey," says Caitlyn, "Tell your friend Punk or Puck, or whatever the fuck his name is, that we don't want to stay at his place. Actually, we found something a little more upscale."

"Way—cool," nods Sid, genuinely happy for us. "His name is—Puck—like in—Shakespeare—dig? He's—my—main man."

Yeah, Puck, I think, *the one who goes around collecting drugs and laying them on the unsuspecting. A regular literary aficionado.* But I will wait until later to share this metaphorical association with Caitlyn. Instead, I inquire of the young man, "So, should we call you Sid, or do you prefer the longer handle, Acid Rain?"

"Sid—is cool. My—real name—is—dig this—Ashton Raines—the Third. But—now it's—Sid. You know—like in—Aaee-CID. And, and—Ashton Raines—Acid Rain. Like—itza hard—rain—a-gonna fall—'n' shit. It—like—came to me—when I—was—tripping."

"Yeah—Dylan—and shit." I can't resist emulating the kid's spaced-out speech pattern.

His face is angelic, but he's terribly thin and his long locks are greasy and unkempt; plus, his eyes are glazed and weird. He seems like he might clean up nice, but that's unlikely to happen. We tell him our names are Caitlyn and Sky, but don't offer any surnames. Sid goes on to tell us that he's from Virginia, a state he describes as a bastion of phony southern gentility with capitalist bourgeois values. His family disinherited him, but that's a tribute, he assures us. I don't mention that I was born in Kentucky, but I authoritatively report that New Jersey has no gentility at all and, as far as I can tell, no values.

"Gotta split," Caitlyn determines. "We gotta find a way to make some bread to pay for our fancy crib."

"That's—cool. If you—wanna—play it—straight," Sid suggests, correctly surmising that the two of us are not yet fully invested in the revolution, "check it—out—they might be—hiring—at—Cody's Bookstore." He points down the block a ways. "That—place—rocks. It's—like the—Grand fuckin'—Central—of the underground."

"Where do you crash, Sid?" I'm suddenly curious, since it didn't seem like he lived at Puck's place.

"Oh," responds the kid. "Like—here—and there."

I don't know why, but I hug him as we leave. Caitlyn is a bit nonplussed by my gesture, but there's something compellingly endearing about Sid, something that, in a vaguely disturbing way, reminds me of my brother Luke. Sid is messed up, but unlike Luke, he's not at all angry or mean-spirited.

On the way back to the Earl House, I buy a button that says, "May the Baby Jesus Shut Your Mouth and Open Your Mind."

36

BERNARD (DEFINITELY NOT BERNIE) Dressler, the manager of Cody's Bookstore on Telegraph Avenue, is at first reluctant to consider hiring what he calls "a dyad" to work at the bookstore. But after he determines Caitlyn and I are not dykes (that again), and not dummies or druggies, he relents. He's impressed with our familiarity with traditional and contemporary literature and poetry, and we both assure him that we're not students and have no intention of leaving or quitting our jobs come September. (Right ...) Of course, it's also obvious he's attracted to Caitlyn, which is probably all that really mattered in his decision to hire us.

In a synthesis of physical and metaphorical perfection for a bookstore manager, our new employer, Bernard Dressler, resembles nothing so much as an owl. Atop a rounded face with a beak-like nose, his longish brown hair is prematurely flecked with white, and he reflexively blinks his small round eyes in a rapidly disconcerting tic-like manner. And, as if to obstinately reinforce his owlish persona,

Bernard affixes round, horn-rimmed glasses to his face, and wears dark, drab clothing—in stark contrast to the vibrant multitudes assembled around him in the Bay area in the mid 1960s.

Jesus, I think, this must be a California thing. Everybody out here actually fits that Central Casting joke. I'm grateful that Caitlyn, who is used to managing the yearnings of men, is the object of Bernard's affection and not me.

Working in Cody's Bookstore on Telegraph Avenue is, in the vernacular of the day, a trip. Everyone eventually drops in—from Allen Ginsberg checking out the titles on mysticism, to CIA operatives checking out Allen Ginsberg. Alerted by a street activist that you can spot a government spook or undercover cop by his shoes, I regularly check out the footwear of our customers. Police agents will don love beads, colorful clothing with bell bottom jeans or overalls, BUT, since sandals, moccasins, or biker boots are not part of their everyday attire, they tend to stick with their silly-looking bureaucratic wingtips or some standard issue cop shoe. When I suspect a particular guy is snooping rather than browsing, I take out and prominently display a button I once purchased on the way to work that reads: "Even Paranoids Have Real Enemies." They ignore me, of course, but it's fun to imagine I'm harassing them back.

Within two weeks of settling in at the Earl House and Cody's Bookstore, Caitlyn acquires a boyfriend. He's a doctoral program dropout, now a freelance writer and aspiring guru, named Harvey Rosenblum. The guy is way too chunky, hairy, stoned and self-absorbed for my taste. (Studying him, I figure that somewhere, back in New York, Harvey's parents are looking at a Bar Mitzvah photo and weeping.)

But Caitlyn doesn't seem to mind. "He's brilliant, and good in bed," she explains, providing me with far too much information.

Harvey makes a respectable living by selling articles about politics and "contemporary culture" to the *Berkeley Barb* and to Paul Krassner's *Realist*, and, through the Associated Press, he has placed pieces in the *San Francisco Examiner* and the *East Village Other* in New York. Describing himself as a gonzo journalist in the spirit of his idol, Hunter Thompson, Harvey is a (spouting) font of practical information about the who, what, and where of the counterculture in the Bay area.

On their second date, Harvey takes Caitlyn to a bar on San Pablo called *The Steppenwolf*. She returns to the Earl House that evening and reports that she tried smoking grass with Harvey.

"No way!" I scream, at once threatened and envious. "You have to tell me everything. Are you, like, stoned right now?"

"Probably," reports Caitlyn. "It's not such a big deal, like I thought it would be. But I only took a couple of tokes, because I had a beer first. I felt a little light-headed. Then we were starving, so we just went to this Mexican place and pigged out."

"I have to try it," I insist, not even attempting to assuage my envy. To myself I lament: *Hey, I'm the one "into" the altered consciousness thing and here is Caitlyn getting the jump on me.* Then I clutch and add, "But not with Harvey." Not to offend Caitlyn, I append, "I'm, like, scared something about Gary might come up. But with just you, I'd do it; I wouldn't be afraid."

Caitlyn considers. "Well, if I ask Harvey for a joint for you, he will want to act as your guide and shit. Why don't you just get it from our new best friend, Mr. Acid Rain?"

When I find Sid on Telegraph, he is more than happy to accommodate. He teases, "You—are about—to be—SKY HIGH!" He only charges me three bucks for what he calls a nickel bag that normally goes for five bucks. He laughs when I shrug that I have no idea how to roll a joint. He walks me to a head shop where I purchase E-Z Wider rolling papers and something called a roach clip. "You—don't—want—to miss out—on the— really—good shit—in—the last—few tokes," he instructs.

We sit down at the curb on a side street just off Telegraph, and Sid demonstrates the art of rolling your own. I have to admit I'm a little grossed out over the part where he swipes the rolled joint between his lips to tamp it down, but, within a few minutes, Sid has expertly produced five neat and tightly wound "smokes."

After he hands me the goods, there's no need for me to make an excuse to split, because diagonally across the street on Telegraph, a striking-looking couple is signaling to Sid. The man sports a dashiki and a humungous Afro and the woman, laden with exotic beads, displays several layers of colorful clothing. I'm certain they could appear on the cover of *Life Magazine* as fashion icons.

Dodging Prayers and Bullets

Sid crosses over toward them, and I head home, surreptitiously examining my joints along the way. I'm thrilled and enthralled: romantically besotted with the notion of getting high. Grinning dopily (while loving the pun), I chide myself for unconsciously humming, from the musical West Side Story, "Tonight, tonight, won't be just any night."

With income from our jobs at the bookstore, Caitlyn and I, over the past couple of weeks, have fixed up our room at the Earl House. We taped up colorful music posters—a red and blue one with roses and a skeleton that advertises a concert by the Grateful Dead, and another, in florid dayglow swirls, promoting an emerging Latino group, called Santana. To show that we love our country but intend to change some of its policies, we turn the American flag upside down and fasten it to the wall. We string a bead curtain from the inside door frame, partly for effect and partly to obscure a direct view into our room when the door is open; then, for no particular reason, we hang from the ceiling a gas mask purchased at an Army-Navy store. We also make curtains from an Indian cotton bedspread and set up speakers for our stereo, to groove out on our considerable collection of albums. I hammer a piece of orange fabric from an anti-war banner to the wall to display my button collection. Fixing up our room at the Earl House in Berkeley sure beats the prospect of selecting fluffy matching bedspreads with Susan Duncan back at No Sex State College!

On the appointed night of my initiation into the drug culture, Caitlyn returns from her work stint at Cody's at about 10 pm. I have already lit candles around the room and selected my music: I definitely want something upbeat, so that means the Beatles. In this new context, the Beatles tune "Ticket to Ride" from Revolver resonates nicely.

The idea is for me to smoke the joint, holding the smoke in as Sid instructed, and for Caitlyn to just hang out to make sure I don't get all paranoid or *weirded* out. I've heard so much about the joys of getting high; I really hope this whole thing won't be a big bust like that time I tried cigarettes with Del Ray Minix when we were little kids.

After awkwardly inhaling and holding in the first two puffs, I cough a lot and take stock of myself. Nothing. Another long puff produces a little light-headedness, but, I wonder, is it from my unaccustomed inhalation of smoke or from the grass? Caitlyn just sits across from me on the opposite bed, grinning.

"This—is sooo—stupid!" I announce, as I ever-so-slowly tip sideways, giggling. "Nothing's—happening," I protest and start laughing harder.

"Right," says Caitlyn. "That's why you're already talking like that kid, Sid."

The "kid Sid" rhyme strikes me as extremely funny, and I yell out, "I'm already—Sky High!" and I start singing, off-key, between giggle fits, *itza harrrd rain—zahhhgonna fall.*

Then suddenly, "Ohhh—wow! I—get it. This room—is—a womb." I slowly shake my head and elevate my right hand, pointing with my index finger. "Not—a tomb. Don't go—there. A womb—a safe—place—yeah. Caitlyn—my friend. It's all—good. This—is exactly—where—I'm supposed—to be. This is—my destiny. And—it's—sooo—good. This room—is—amazing. Look—at that—candle—that, that flicker. It's—definitely—trying to—say something. Something—like—YES!"

Caitlyn is cracking up listening to me, but she remains a true friend and guardian, so resists the urge to join me in this, my first smoke. (Later we'll do the remaining joints together, of course.) For now, she simply humors and anchors me while I'm having a phenomenal time philosophizing, bestowing personalities on the furnishings, and entertaining myself with stupid witticisms that seem, at the time, ever so clever and insightful.

After about 45 minutes, which I believe has been three hours, I begin to level off, and announce, "Eats—I need—food. I'm fuckin'—starving!"

Caitlyn says she will go out for something, but I begin to panic at the thought of her leaving. Luckily we have a stash of junk food—some chips and a candy bar and a coke in the refrigerator. After wolfing down the eats, I decide not to finish the joint I have started and just go to bed to sleep off the effects. Caitlyn carefully wraps the remainder of the joint, still attached to the roach clip, and makes me promise that, on the weekend, we'll finish this one and do the next joint together. No problem agreeing to that.

I'm amazed I got wasted on my first try, without even finishing one joint. "You're a cheap high, Sky," Caitlyn teases the next day.

Still feeling a little shadowy from the experience, I head for the Berkeley Public Library to surreptitiously scan a medical reference book regarding the long and short-term effects of marijuana use. Satisfied that getting high is worth any of the possible risks, I eagerly anticipate the next try. And the next ...

When I tell Sid of my experience, he beams like a proud father observing his baby's first steps. He also gives me a little bonus—a tab of LSD, the hallucinogen I had researched back at North Essex State. I'm particularly thrilled, because recently I've been further intrigued by reading in the *San Francisco Oracle* (an underground newspaper) about the "acid tests" that transpire at periodic gatherings of musicians and hippies. Apparently, at these events LSD is distributed in paper tabs or sugar cubes (or even in food or drinks) to a throng of people who will trip the light fantastic, so to speak, as one.

"I copped—that shit—straight from—Bear," Sid assures me, as I gratefully and carefully tuck the acid tab in my pocket. "You—know. Owsley—the acid man—himself."

Passing a street vendor on the way home, I mull for a minute and purchase a green button that petitions, "Keep California Green—Stay On The Grass." Back at the Earl House, I stash the tab of acid in an envelope in my underwear drawer. I'll get to it soon enough.

37

BY EARLY AUGUST it's obvious Caitlyn is not going back to North Essex State. She's getting stoned almost every night, if not with me then with Harvey. Getting back into a "New Jersey head" is simply a psychic infeasibility for Caitlyn.

She decides to continue working at Cody's, and I agree to forego campus housing to remain at the Earl House with her, even after my classes start. We figure, if I'm a campus radical and Caitlyn is an off-campus agitator, we can pretty much cover all the revolutionary bases. Stopping by our favorite button vendor, I select one with a mocking picture of Lyndon Johnson that reads, "Kill for Peace."

During the third week of August, I get a letter from Susan Duncan. Lord Jim has helped Susan and Tolya get summer jobs at a camp for inner city kids in the Catskills: an eye-opening, mind-expanding endeavor for Susan, the entrenched suburbanite who has never been exposed to poverty, let alone to minorities. In the letter, after her typical chatty digressions, Susan drops the Big One. She and Tolya are "getting it on," and plan to marry after their graduation the following year.

As I read the letter aloud, Caitlyn lets out a whoop. She's imagining the jolt to the priggish bourgeois lives of Susan's parents, Paul and Louise Duncan, when their errant daughter informs them she has lived and worked with poor Black people all summer and intends to marry a mad Russian.

Dropping my head on one hand, I contribute, "Her parents probably blame me. They were on to me from that first day of college, when they got a load of the laundry bag I was using for luggage!"

"A tell-tale sign of a bag-lady-in-training!" chortles Caitlyn.

Sure, I'm laughing along with Caitlyn, but I also find the sexual intimacy between Susan and Tolya rather disconcerting. Here I am in Berkeley, California, the free love capital of the world, getting nothing, while up-tight Susan Duncan is making it with one of the New Jersey locals.

It isn't that I can't find a guy in Berkeley; I just don't feel attracted to any of them, maybe don't trust them, whatever. Surveying the offerings at a button vendor's table on Telegraph the next day, I purchase one displaying the face of a fierce looking suffragist that proclaims, "All Men Are Beasts" and another that chides, "Chastity Is Its Own Punishment."

That night, Caitlyn takes out her guitar and strums a special song that represents my sentiments. The song begins, "Oh, he wears love beads, but fuckin's on his mind …" Caitlyn always gets it just right, especially when it comes to the musical interlude.

38

INFURIATED. THAT'S HOW I truly feel toward Caitlyn, just days before I'm to start my classes at Berkeley.

This guy named Larry Douglas comes into Cody's laden with buttons and posters plastered with his own image. He's all up on running for mayor of Berkeley. His message is: *Larry Douglas for a new community: withdraw from Vietnam, end police harassment, eliminate poverty.* Though that seems like an inflated platform for a prospective local mayor, I do have to admire the unbridled optimism.

Unfortunately, during a friendly political exchange with the guy, in what I deem a capriciously thoughtless act of betrayal, Caitlyn blabs to Larry about Gary getting drafted and bizarrely killed during basic training. Larry Douglas is now badgering me to stand beside him and tell Gary's story at an upcoming rally sponsored by the Vietnam Day Committee, an anti-war activist group.

"No way I'm doing that!" I insist. Caitlyn should have known better. Just recently at a street rally, I had momentarily "lost it" when trying to join in with protestors chanting, "Hey, hey, LBJ, how many kids did you kill today?"

The loss of Gary is way too present and painful. I'm adamant: neither I, nor the memory of Gary, will be exploited by Larry Douglas, who's so full of himself that he actually thinks he can change my mind through flirtatious entreat.

Besides, I already had old Larry on my radar from hearing him speak at a prior rally. He's too narcissistic and ego-driven—about as opposite of someone like my brother Gary as it's possible to be. No way am I supporting Larry Douglas' self-promoting agenda.

I'm already increasingly irked that it's always the guys who lead the protest events and make all the proclamations. On the political stage of the 1960s, women play, at best, supporting roles, while Lesbians are viewed as downright dangerous. I know that if I'm ever to talk about what happened to Gary, it will be at a venue of my choosing—not in the service of Mr. Larry Douglas.

On the other hand, I have more respect for Larry's cohort, the activist leader Ben Levin. More than once I've heard Ben speak out eloquently against the war, and I've conversed with him a few times in the bookstore, learning he has a Master's Degree. I appreciate Ben's intellect and outrageous humor; he seems genuinely committed to working for change in social and economic inequities, and, unlike Larry Douglas, Ben Levin never takes himself too seriously. Still, I would never offer up Gary's demise as a prop for promoting an ideological platform. Gary Cooper Jenkins is one of many human casualties and political miscalculations belying the war in Vietnam. He's also my little brother.

On our walk back from Telegraph Avenue to the Earl House, I accept Caitlyn's proffered words of sincere contrition regarding her disclosure about Gary to Larry Douglas. I'm confident that it was out of character for Caitlyn to, in any way, exploit my private sorrow, and, certainly, I believe her that nothing like this will ever contaminate our friendship again.

Just as we round the street corner at Shattuck, we come upon a band assembling their instruments. Some bystanders tell us the group is called Country Joe and the Fish. We wait around to listen, chatting with the musicians and the crowd. The band is great: electric country rock with an incisive political twist. Spaced-out hillbilly activism, I think, the perfect balm for transitioning out of my funk.

39

AS SEPTEMBER APPROACHES, I'm terrified about starting classes. What if, despite my making the Dean's List at diminutive North Essex State in New Jersey, I'm sorely unprepared for the academic challenges of the University of California at Berkeley?

I decide to sign up for an anthropology elective, in lieu of one of my required literature courses, just in case I can't handle the reading and research papers required of English majors at Berkeley. As it turned out, I had nothing to worry about. I'm perfectly prepared and competitive in all my classes; I just have to curtail my drug intake enough to enable myself to concentrate. That proves the real challenge.

At Berkeley, my North Essex State bitter blue period has dissolved in a purple haze. On and off campus, marijuana is practically doled out like Halloween candy, while everything from LSD to smack is readily available for the asking, at negotiable prices.

For more exotic indulging, Caitlyn and I need look no further than her boyfriend, Harvey Rosenblum, who is intent on fashioning himself as some kind of plebeian Tim Leary, pioneering the hallucinogenic fringe. Harvey is forever looking to guide Caitlyn and me on one of his experimental "extensions of the blown mind" trips, many of which he has read or even written about in the underground press, or has simply gleaned from talk on the street. Mostly, the experiments are harmlessly amusing games, like getting high on grass and taking the Binaca Blast (a popular strong breath spray laced with alcohol and peppermint oil) or, in an altered state, dragging our feet along a carpet in a dark room to exchange simultaneous static electricity sparks. At Harvey's behest, Caitlyn and I gamely chew Teaberry Gum that has been wrapped in a banana peel for two weeks, ingest nasty Morning Glory seeds, and drink nutmeg stirred into sugar water. (Harvey read that Eldridge Cleaver, the Black Panther who did jail time as a young man, got high on nutmeg in prison.) Midst one of Harvey's extension experiments, I can never quite discern whether I'm reacting to a newfound high or just recoiling from a major gross-out.

At other times, however, Harvey gets truly carried away, especially when he makes up his own variations on formula highs. Once, Harvey told us he read in the *San Francisco Oracle* that if you get high on Queen Anne's Lace, you can see through walls. Since there are no specifics in the article about how to prepare the flowering weed, Harvey just makes something up.

First, he convinces Caitlyn to help him scour the open fields of the Berkeley Hills to accumulate a carload of Queen Anne's Lace plants. (I wouldn't be surprised if Queen Anne's Lace became extinct in Berkeley after that article appeared.)

Laying the plants out on a sunny section of the fire escape above his apartment, Harvey observes them for two days, and then gets impatient with the natural drying process. He bakes some of the plants in his home oven and adds the dried material to a regular joint. Not satisfied that this has released the full potency of the Queen Anne's Lace, Harvey soaks the remaining plants in water and boils them down to a vial of foul-smelling black liquid. Both Caitlyn and I decline a sample. We should have known, however, that Harvey's experimental tenacity was not so readily quelled.

A couple of weeks later, Harvey invites Caitlyn and me over to his basement apartment to try a potent new brand of grass, which he calls "Wonder Weed." Soon the three of us, nudged along by Harvey, are feeling no pain. At the peak of our high, susceptible to suggestion and hungry, Caitlyn and I gratefully accept Harvey's offer to prepare us a special treat. He disappears into the kitchen and returns with two tall glasses of chocolate milk.

As we marvel over the drink, Harvey coaches, "Can't you feel the chocolate? You've never had chocolate milk taste this great, right?" Caitlyn and I concede that this chocolate milk is the most incredibly luscious drink ever. Harvey keeps up the banter. "You've never been high like this before, right?" We graciously agree, half believing it.

Soon, however, we begin to get suspicious, because Harvey keeps asking us to describe the special nature of this high, suggesting, indeed, that the quality of this high is enhanced, even beyond the Wonder Weed that's supposedly making us "feel" the chocolate milk.

He keeps at us with, "Tell me if you have ever had a better high than this! This is as far out as you've ever been, right?"

Suddenly converting the mood, Caitlyn demands, "Why do you keep laying that on us?"

"Yeeeah?" I immediately chime in, struggling to connect my body to my elusive mind.

Harvey evades the question at first, but soon, almost proudly, he confesses, "OK, I stirred the Queen Anne's Lace extract into the chocolate milk!"

Caitlyn runs to the bathroom and barfs. Too bad I couldn't do the same. Until the marijuana effects wear off, I'm stranded somewhere between indignant resentment and morbid paranoia.

That's the last of my experiments in extensions of the blown mind with Harvey Rosenblum. Caitlyn and Harvey later make up though. He denied putting the Queen Anne's Lace in the chocolate milk, but I never doubt that he had, and I never fully trust him again, regarding drugs or relationships.

Once I start classes, I'm grateful for the nights Harvey entices Caitlyn to stay over at his place. I want to do well academically, but find I'm getting migraines and having difficulty focusing after smoking a lot of grass. It's likely the smoke irritating my sinuses and lungs, but I still associate it with the grass itself. Caitlyn, ever faithful to our friendship, understands my commitment to school, and waits for me to initiate our drug indulgences, which I restrict to weekends and holidays.

I like all my literature classes at Berkeley, but regret signing up for the anthropology elective. The erudite but rather dry professor is primarily intent on enlisting his class to sort through data he has collected for various research projects, obviously in the service of his own career advancement. I had not deemed it possible to make a topic like anthropology such an insipid drag.

From a personal perspective, however, I've often noted that the seeds of either my demise or my elevation are planted just beneath my consciousness, well in advance of their actual fruition. Fortunately, signing up for that anthropology course falls into the uplifting category.

During the third week of the course, the professor announces that his request for a graduate teaching assistant has been granted. He can, therefore, take more release time for writing and research, while the TA manages the class, under his supervision. (Meaning, according to long established academic artifice, the professor does nothing while the assistant takes over everything.) Before taking his leave, the elderly professor jokes that the females, in particular, should rejoice at this new arrangement, because the graduate assistant is single and available. *Oh, yeah, right,* I think.

Mercifully, my cynicism is misplaced! The first time Gabriel Cooper walks in and introduces himself to the class, I gasp and struggle to maintain my composure. Right off, the resonance of the name: Gabriel, meaning angel, *and* Cooper, referencing my brother, Gary Cooper. I'm not religious, but I'm certainly spiritual enough to recognize a godsend!

Later, I learn that on his father's side, Gabriel traces his ancestry back to the writer, James Fenimore Cooper. Clean-shaven, but casually dressed in jeans and an Indian cotton shirt, Gabriel Cooper has wavy walnut brown hair that falls just below his ears. Practically qualifying as an "older man" at age 28, he's also a flirt: the engaging smile and those riveting deep blue eyes! Plus, this TA substituting for the professor is informed and witty, ardently describing his adventures, and misadventures, on a recent trip to India.

I figure I don't stand a chance with him. Wrong again. Gabriel Cooper is not just a detached academic—he views the classroom as a laboratory, and his students an endless source of data for understanding cultural influences on the human condition. He is genuinely intrigued by diversity in people and is keenly interested in their personal backgrounds and family traditions. I don't say much about myself in class, but in the first written assignment, I describe, at length, my birthplace in Kentucky and the transition my family made to New Jersey. By the time he learns about the circumstances of my brother Gary's death, Gabriel Cooper is enthralled. He walks me home after class, and, later that week, invites me to a folk club called The Jabberwock to hear the guitarist John Fahey.

I think Gabriel Cooper is the most gorgeous and fascinating man on earth, and I'm astounded the attraction seems mutual. Sharing a joint with him at his apartment on our third date, I no longer have to feel like the only flower child not reaping the personal benefits of peace and love. That week I buy a button that at last reflects the veracity of my proclamation: *"Make Love, Not War."*

During the next month, in the company of Caitlyn and Harvey, Gabriel and I crowd into a small basement reception hall in Berkeley to hear Janis Joplin perform with Big Brother and the Holding Company. (Chugging Southern Comfort, chain-smoking, and casually bantering with the audience in a husky voice, Janis simply blows us away with her rendition of "Ball and Chain".) Then, Harvey gets the four of us complementary seats for a double-billed Blues Project/ Charlatans concert at the Fillmore, and Gabriel treats me to a Doors concert that opens with the Paul Butterfield Blues Band at the Avalon Ball Room, where we dance in the aisles and on the seats.

It's 1966, so everyone dances in groups, whether they showed up alone or with a partner. Tossing my long straight hair, I can gyrate with abandon by myself, but I always feel a little awkward and graceless trying to follow someone else's moves. Not so with Gabe. I lean into him and just go with the flow of the music and the mutual rhythm of our incredible physical and emotional nexus—I'm galvanized. When Gabriel touches my face or takes my hand, even without the aid of a joint, I literally vibrate. The sensations are best captured, I believe, by Walt Whitman's line, "I sing the body electric."

Caitlyn is pleased and bemused at how madly in love I am with Gabriel Cooper. "And you know that can't be bad ..." she borrows from the Beatles as she strums the guitar. Caitlyn has come around on the Beatles, especially after the Revolver album was released. She proclaims their now astonishing relevancy as "delayed development."

Unfortunately, it soon becomes obvious that Harvey and Gabe don't really hit it off. Harvey thinks Gabriel, who intends to pursue a Ph.D. in anthropology from Stanford after his near-completed Masters at Berkeley, is selling out to academia. Harvey tells Caitlyn, "The guy is a pretty boy, and clueless." He also keeps calling him Gabey, a nickname Gabriel despises only slightly less than Gabby.

Gabriel views Harvey as a pretender, one of those hangers-on who dally in the naiveté of counterculture pseudo-revolution. Gabe insists, "Rosenblum's so-called journalism pieces in the underground presses pander to the lowest common denominator of intellectual curiosity."

In defense of Harvey, I try lamely, "But I like reading his articles. Besides, Harvey always knows where it's at. You've attended plenty of events he recommended."

Gabe raises his eyebrows and rolls his eyes. "Fine, we'll make him Social Chairman. Just don't call it journalism."

Lifting my hands and shrugging my shoulders, I signal surrender. I figure there can be only one rooster in the hen house, so it's best Gabriel and I don't mix it up too often with Caitlyn and Harvey. That's a bit disappointing, but I determine not to let this compromise my friendship with Caitlyn.

In contrast to Harvey, the residents of the Earl House adore Gabriel. They refer to him as their angel. He listens attentively to the demented ones and tolerates the shameless flirtation of the elderly women. Miss Price, the owner, practically courts him, and, around Gabe, even grumpy Byron, the late night desk clerk, deigns to adjust his expression in the direction of a smile. Gabriel develops a special affection for a young gay male resident of the Earl House named Kip, who came to the United States from Amsterdam. Kip works the streets of San Francisco in drag, as a prostitute. Harvey is chagrined at Gabriel's connection to Kip, because Kip has refused to allow Harvey to do a (confidential) story on him that Harvey is convinced he can place in the *East Village Other* back in New York.

With an androgynous body, blue eyes with long natural lashes, and blonde curly hair of an ambiguous length and style, Kip is beautiful to behold as a man or woman. He's 23 years old, but he can pass for 15. Kip invites Gabe and me to his room at the Earl House to watch him do a male to female transformation. I have to admit I'm a bit discomfited watching Kip fasten his genitals discreetly out of sight in a pair of women's fancy red underpants.

Unfortunately, Kip is addicted to living dangerously, both on the street and through his drugs of choice. One of his modus operands is to hook a john, get the money up front, and then excuse himself to the "Ladies" to freshen up, while the john waits for him at the bar or by the outside door of the establishment. In the women's bathroom, Kip, who carries a reversible, collapsible handbag, changes back to his guy persona and slips away under the john's nose. If that ploy isn't workable and he ends up in a hotel room with a john, Kip explains that the guy is usually so drunk or wasted, he never realizes he has picked up a man.

"Honey, they're just looking for a hole," Kip tells the bemused Gabriel. "When they're finished, they always pass out. I take my tip from their wallets—sometimes I 'accidentally' pick up a credit card along with the cash, of course. I also figure, this guy don't need to get any more wasted on his supply of coke or speed, so I remove the source of his temptation!"

Gabe chortles along with Kip and begs for more anecdotes. While I find Kip's exploits fascinating, they also seem rather appalling. I express my fears to Gabe, and he agrees to try to influence Kip to be more careful.

Sadly, Kip is not open to behavior modification, so soon enough the sadly inevitable will transpire.

40

GABRIEL IS A POLITICAL LEFTIST (he invited all his anthropology classes to join him on the SDS-sponsored Black Power Day), but he's no militant. While he likes smoking weed from time to time, he's not perpetually stoned like Harvey, and he's definitely not into the psychedelics. He is also uneasy about the rhetoric and tactics of some leaders of the Black Panther Party.

Thus, in early November, when Caitlyn, Harvey, and I leaflet Oakland with the Panthers and other activists from the Peace Brigade, Gabe declines to participate. And while he supports Caesar Chavez and the grape boycott, Gabe scoffs at some of the more outrageous political actions that I am enthusiastically embracing. To me, sardonic antics are fun—even significant—in their own way. OK, so what if it was a bit inefficacious for Caitlyn and I to (meticulously) punch out the God's eyes on the pyramids pictured on the back of one dollar bills? (Our intent was to symbolically separate spirituality from materialism.) But joining the Bay Area Peace Coordinating Committee to boycott Dow Chemical (the people who bring us Saran Wrap for birth control and Napalm for splattering Vietnamese civilians) carries immense import. And, in solidarity with those against Ma Bell's monopoly on telephone communications, I join with people who refuse to put stamps on their payment envelopes, obliging the conglomerate to shell out for the postage.

Now, maybe there's a bit of gratuity in the Barf on Johnson Campaign, wherein the government eventually threatened the instigators with conspiracy charges. (The FBI actually explained that if enough people barfed on Johnson, he would die.) Still, I applaud the terrific scatological symbolism of the Give a Shit for America action (I call it the Bowel Movement), in which the U.S. mail is enlisted to deliver the slogan's manifestation to the State Department in DC.

And, in the planning stage is the East Coast effort to encircle the Pentagon and attain a powerful state of altered consciousness with the goal of levitating it. I keep trying to explain to Gabriel that these seemingly insane activities represent an "in kind" response to the state-sanctioned violence and paranoia of a United States administration and military out of control. He's not particularly moved or amused.

Inevitably, I'm occasionally irked that Gabriel, unlike Caitlyn and Harvey, will not lighten up enough to appreciate the socio-political significance of guerrilla theatrics. Yet I intuit that the "straight" side of Gabriel is part of his appeal to me—frankly, I need an anchor, an incentive to adopt a modicum of restraint.

It's obvious to me, however, that Gabriel will not be the best person to enjoin for my experiment with the tab of acid I have squirreled away in my underwear drawer. In early October, when I hear the possession of LSD has been outlawed and there will now be a crackdown on public consumption (Who knew that dropping acid was ever legal to begin with?), my urgency about giving it a try escalates.

The opportunity presents itself in November, when Gabriel travels to Chicago for a conference during the same weekend Harvey goes back to New York to visit his ailing grandmother. Left to our own devices, Caitlyn and I intend to carpe diem on the acid trip. I ask her, and a laid-back acidhead named Richie, whom we know from the Earl House, to join me in dropping the tab. I feel safe with Caitlyn, and I figure Richie will know what to do if either of us starts bumming.

Richie's girlfriend is a pale and delicate-featured university dropout who calls herself Crystal Dew. She has wealthy, deluded parents who keep supplying her with money for school, even though she has long since blown off her enrollment. Crystal, an experienced tripper like Richie, wants to join in the acid revelries, so they invite us to their pad in the Earl House.

Richie and Crystal have created the ultimate in tripping venues: framed psychedelic posters and Kama Sutra prints on the wall; Turkish carpets beneath mattresses bedecked with colorful silken bedspreads; drip candles in recycled wine bottles, oils of incense, and even a lava light. They have all the right music, food, and vibes, plus the bonus of a refrigerator stocked with food and a supply of acid, booze, cocaine and speed. For our first acid experience, Caitlyn and I insist on the "never mix, never worry" rule, and Richie and Crystal agree to be "down with that."

My adrenaline is surging as I drop my Owsley Special, while Richie and Crystal share some of their own acid stash with Caitlyn. Not much time elapses before we're feeling "at one" with each other and the universe.

I savor each salient detail of the experience: time slows to the point of near suspension. The colors and textures in the room take on a rich and startling vibrancy. I am adrift outside my body, observing, for the first time, objects in the room and a Being I call "self." Studying the intriguing somatic extensions that are my hands and fingers, I raise my arms and sense that my body gives off a glowing aura of iridescent color, some kind of heat or magnetism that extends beyond the outlines of my flesh. Richie holds his hands congruent to mine, and it is obvious that, without actually touching, we make physical contact. I experience an awesome clarity about the inter-connective energy between all living beings.

"Ohhh, wow!" the Being that is me exclaims, "It's all—about—the molecules. And— neurons. They keep it—going. And—they know—they show us—the way. It's like—like the whole—God idea—no—it *is* God."

"Oh, yeah—*yes*," adds Caitlyn, "And—they're moving. The molecules. They are—for us. Or—with us. No, no—of us. And, and—the energy—and—they see—wait—they *know*—everything. And so—do we!"

Richie and Crystal are nodding, smiling and embracing one another. "And—it's all—good," he affirms. "You only—have to—breathe."

We all do so, consciously; our collective breath permeates the room with harmonizing energy. Who speaks next is irrelevant. We are in sublime synchronicity, enmeshed in dancing atoms and omniscient molecules beyond any definable dimensions of space and time. We are awestruck by the sacred alliance engendered—we give ourselves over to oneness, the god-fullness, to unabashed love.

Eventually, I locate my individual self and contribute, "It's like—it all—matters. Yet—doesn't matter. It's—it's all—matter. About life—or death. And—Buddha. And—even Jesus. It's all—about—love—and—connectedness. And it's—just right—perfect. And, and—it's—OK. It's OK—about Gary—and— Papaw—and—everyone. They're—with us—always." There are tears in my eyes, but not of sadness or anger.

The four of us hold each other and sway from side to side. For a long time we just stay like that, immersed in the music, the lights, the unity. In a gentle and positive manner, Richie eventually talks us all back. He assures us we have visited the macro world and now it's OK, even important, to live in the micro one. We have seen more in the eye than out. Nothing has changed, but we will never be the same.

Afterwards, I will come to think of my LSD enlightenment as visiting the realm of Knowing, meaning there is never again the place of Notknowing. Certainly I will experience anger, pain, and fear again, but part of me will retain at least the shadow of an awareness that those states are ultimately trivial, meaningless, temporary; that the essential goodness—the love—in the Now is all that matters.

Richie regals us with food and drink before we fall asleep in a heap on the mattresses. The next morning, Crystal passes around a chalice of chamomile tea as a libation, and we recount our visions and insights. I now understand that, to make my separate peace with life, I have only to finish a chapter, not close the book, on Gary and my family. I determine to reconcile with them, in New Jersey and in Kentucky.

My LSD experience was one of mind-bending perfection. The next button I add to my collection reads: *"Turn on, Tune in, Drop out."*

41

WHEN GABRIEL RETURNS from Chicago, I'm excited to tell him about my experience on acid. Predictably, he's intellectually put off, but jealous in an abstract way, giving rise to the first serious rift in our relationship.

Gabe typically deals with conflict by barraging the opposition with facts and caveats. With respect to the argument regarding the efficacy of the use of hallucinogens, I'm now clearly his adversary. Even though I understand he's hurt I experimented behind his back, I just know that, had Gabe been there, he would have talked me out of it, or certainly tried to. I can't, in good conscience, assure him I regret the circumstances under which I dropped the acid.

When logic gets him nowhere with me, Gabriel posits, defensively, "Maybe I would have done it with you guys."

That comment irks me because he continues to focus on his exclusion rather than my experience. "C'mon," I protest. "You're much more about guilt-tripping than acid tripping."

"Fuck you!" he shouts. "As soon as I'm out of sight you team up with your little acid-head freak friends. Maybe I would have tried it with you—if you showed me any trust."

This is a new low in our communications. I challenge him with, "OK, then let's drop some acid together—with or without Richie. I can pick up some tabs anytime you're ready." His bluff called, Gabriel shakes his head, turns away and resorts to a sulk. I take some deep breaths, and try again. "Look, I don't need all this negative energy. I'm not gonna start following the Grateful Dead around. The truth is, I probably won't drop acid with you, and I don't have plans to do so with anyone else."

I don't say this just to appease Gabriel; it's also because there's a part of my acid trip I haven't shared with Gabe or with my cabal of visionary friends. During my state of heightened (altered, I'm satisfied, is the wrong word) consciousness, I learned that the ultimate trip is death: the reason even non-addicted druggies keep going after more is simply that death is, so to speak, the final frontier. And death is not a bad state at all; it's simply an irrevocable one. I'm not ready to make that choice, so I'm finished with acid and hard drugs. I even secretly vow to moderate my use of marijuana. Adventurous, I am; suicidal, I'm not. I don't want to make a big deal about this awareness, especially with Gabe, or even with Caitlyn. But, from now on, for me, smoking grass will be a party or social indulgence, not a daily or even weekend regimen. I consider this a personal, not a health or moral, decision.

After a while, Gabriel gets over my dallying with LSD during his absence. Well, we stop talking about it, at least. I frequently reflect inwardly on the experience, however. Dropping acid, I discover, has enabled me to respond more expansively to the occasional joint. I tell Caitlyn, but not Gabriel, that more than once I have experienced what is called an acid flashback—a sudden heightening of the senses and a vivid recall of what I refer to as my acid journey (in contrast to trip).

The flashbacks happen at odd, unpredictable times. Once, in Golden Gate Park, when I lifted up from a gulp of water at a fountain, I momentarily floated above myself, adrift with the dancing molecules. A bit of a panic attack accompanied this vision, so I rushed off to the library again to see if it—if I—am normal. (I'm satisfied that it is/I am.) These flashbacks continue to frighten me for a while, but then I begin to just sit back, relax, and enjoy the show. One time, when I'm studying with the electric music of Country Joe and the Fish in the background (probably the trigger), I find myself gazing at multi-colored layers interfacing my body and space.

Caitlyn is jealous. After that first time with me, she has tripped several times with Harvey, and she never gets anything resembling a flashback. "Hey, Sky-High, I told you, you're a cheap high," she teases.

My last unintentional flashback from the Owsley special besets me in March 1967, the first time I hear the quintessential tripping anthem "White Rabbit" from the Jefferson Airplane album Surrealistic Pillow. Afterwards, I condition myself to induce a trance-like, semi-altered state of consciousness whenever I hear the song. Decades later, I will still be able to attain that state—at the right time, in the right place, with the right people.

Caitlyn is always taunting me at awkward moments by singing lyrics from "White Rabbit": *When men on the chess board get up and tell you where to go, and you've just had some kind of mushroom, and your mind is moving low ...* "Damn, girl," she admonishes. "I gotta keep a' eye on you. I'm into smoking and tripping, but I manage to stay on earth afterwards."

42

HAVING LINKED the synapses of life, death, love and God during my acid trip, I feel the need for some significant contact with my family, especially my mother and Luke. I write a long loving letter to the entire family, telling them about Gabriel and the University of California, the only parts of my current life they could handle hearing about. I include separate notes for Luke and Dory. I'm a bit cagey about what I write to Luke, as I know that Mother does not respect boundaries and will open and read any mail addressed to anyone in the household.

By now, it's totally obvious to me that Luke had been smoking marijuana at Gary's funeral. I want to caution him about getting further involved in the drug culture. The prospect of losing another brother seems beyond my earthly capacity. Still, I don't dare consult William, who would freak out if he knew Luke (let alone I) was doing drugs. *Something is happening here, but you don't know what it is, do you, Mr. Jones?* (Bob Dylan, "Ballad of a Thin Man.")

Dodging Prayers and Bullets

I'm pleasantly surprised when my mother writes a sad, but sensible (and not grammatically bad) response to my letter:

Dear Skyla,

We all surely miss you. It don't seem like family with you away and Gary gone. Your Daddy don't drive long distance much these days, but he's working regular. We been able to keep up the mortgage on the house, a blessing. Its a gift from Gary, whose in Gods House now. I know what happened was Gods will, but it has been a trial for us all. I go to the garden each day and talk to him and <u>HIM</u>. Some day we'll all gather in the garden of Heaven, but we won't be the ones to decide when. Age don't matter. I saw where you wrote to Luke and Dory. They miss you, especially Dory, the child seems lost without you here. Luke can't seem to ease his mind these days. I wish he would try harder at school. He's smart enough. I guess there's not much here to interest you. We all understand you want to better yourself, and that's good. And we're all doing just fine, when it comes right down to it. But if you get tired of that place, I hope you know where your home is. Theres no place like home, like they say. I don't want to say much about it, but expect a surprise announcement from William soon! Stay in touch, and I'll try to.

Love, Flo-Anna (Mother)

I can picture my mother laying out notebook paper on the kitchen table and carefully forming the individual alphabet letters with the stub of an old pencil. How can she seem so lucid on paper and so off-the-wall in person? I chuckle, because, since my acid trip, the stuff she wrote about uniting with God is not the irksome stretch for me it once was!

The next night I go to a pay phone with a supply of coins and call William. He's excited to hear from me. "Sky," he says, "It's so great you called. Mary Ann and I have some great news. We're getting married the last weekend in August!"

"Congratulations!" I respond, genuinely pleased for him and relieved to start our conversation off on a positive for a change.

He adds, "Now, we want you to be here for the wedding. You can be in it if you want to. We'd like that. Mary Ann would have to fill you in on the details, of course. I'll send money to help you get home, if you need me to. We just want you to be here."

"Don't worry about it," I assure William. "by August I'll definitely be due for a visit home, so we can work all that out. I even thought about trying to come home for Christmas, but I can't really manage that. What else is going on there? I got a letter from Mother and she sounds pretty good."

It turns out the wedding is the only happy news in the rest of our exchange. William reports, "Well, things here aren't quite as rosy as Mother paints them. Daddy's working, but he seems depressed or something. He hardly even watches TV—just sleeps or complains of headaches when he's home. Maybe he's sick, but I don't know. In some ways, he takes Gary's passing worse than Mother. And the two of them still go at each other. She says he threatened her with a knife, but I never saw it. As for Dory, she's pretty withdrawn. She seems to miss you more than anyone. Luke, I never understand. He declared himself a vegetarian, so Mother gets crazy when he won't eat her food. They argue about it all the time. He's even more taken with the Indian stuff these days, but, thank God, he seems less involved with those Survivalists, whatever they are."

Even worse, William furthermore confides, "Sometimes Mother gets obsessed over never seeing Gary's body. She believes he might still be alive—maybe he was sent to Vietnam by an oversight; you know, maybe he got captured and can't get a message through or something. You know, stuff like that, over and over again."

My conversation with William leaves me overwrought with guilt and despair, but, frankly, I'm relieved to be 3,000 miles away from the emotional morass engulfing my family in New Jersey. When December rolls around, I don't even consider a trip home for Christmas, so I carefully select and mail out gifts for the family and agree to be there at end of summer, 1967, for William and Mary Ann's wedding. I let Mary Ann know, "I'm honored, but since I'm not even sure when I'll be back, it's just too hard for me to be a bridesmaid. But I'll be at your wedding, and my boyfriend (I'm never comfortable with that word, but it facilitates communication with traditional people) Gabriel will definitely be there with me."

43

WITH REGARD TO my typical family "hollerdays," having it not really feel like Christmas in California is a good thing; in general, however, on the West Coast the season seems oddly devoid of sentiment. The December weather is neither here nor there: the afternoons are warm and sunny, but a damp chill is in the air most mornings and evenings. I pick up a winter jacket at a thrift store and wear it to classes in the morning; by afternoon I'm sweating and lugging it around on my arm.

A few days before Christmas, I run into Sid on Telegraph Avenue. He's slumped on a bench, huddled in an oversized jacket, so I don't recognize him at first. He looks like someone off skid row—emaciated and pale, coughing, his nose all runny.

He tells me he got the floppy jacket from a guy called "Street Buddha" who is one of the Diggers, a commune whose members frequently sweep the streets of San Francisco and Berkeley in search of those in need. The Digger tried to convince Sid to go to a shelter and get cleaned up, but Sid declined, needing to sustain his "business" in order to maintain his habit.

I'm not looking to buy drugs, but I insist that Sid join me for a bite to eat. As I snuggle up next to him in a booth at a cheap eatery frequented by Hell's Angels, he remarks, "Sky—you're the—only—one—NOT—looking for—either—my soul—or my goods."

"I care about you and I love you," I reply. "You were my first friend here. Hey, you rolled my first joint for me!" I desperately want to lift his spirits and get him on some kind of path to healing. I try a personal tack. "Sid, I feel like such a different person than when I first came here. And it's all good. Hey, I've been in touch with my family back home in—New Fucking Jersey. I was wondering if you ever think about your family?"

Sid perks up a bit. "Oh, yeah! I—got this—far out—letter. From—Charlotte. My Moms. I'll—show you. It's—like—how much—she—misses me—and—God—forgives you—and shit. I—could tell—she was—like—crying and shit. The truth—is—I was—her favorite. But he—he didn't—like that. My—old man. Ashton Raines—the fuckin'—Second. He's—like—a fuckin'—capitalist pig. Told me—like—'don't—ever—darken—my doorstep—again'—and shit. He's like—Mr. Fuckin'—N-R-A. It's like—he fought—fuckin'—World War Two—to make—the world—safe from—dopers—and fags. And, and—I'm like—both, man."

There's a painful interval where I sit in silence with my hand on his back while Sid snivels and coughs.

I hand him some napkins, as he tries again. "I gotta—throw off—this fuckin'—cold. Get my—shit together. Yeah. I, I—thought about—going back—home. I—wonder if—there is—an Ashton Raines—the Third—like—the 3rd degree. More—or less. I mean—anymore."

He's totally wasted. I beseech him to come with me to the Berkeley Free Clinic for some medical help. He won't budge just then, but promises he will go later. When I hug him goodbye and head for my Contemporary World Literature class, there's no button for sale on Telegraph Avenue that reflects anything I'm feeling.

44

MORE THAN CHRISTMAS and New Years, my friends in the Bay Area have been anticipating the massive "Gathering of the Tribes," a powwow of Berkeley activists and San Francisco "heads" planned for the Polo Field in Golden Gate Park in mid January. Called the first Human Be-In, this event signifies a long over-due synthesis of people power and flower power, incidentally promising to deliver the FREE party of the century.

On this glorious day, the Merry Pranksters are in synch with the San Francisco Mime Company, and spiritualist Tim Leary and activist Abby Hoffman are on the same page. Of course, the music is also far-out fine for dancing and grooving: Quicksilver, Moby Grape, the Airplane, the Dead, Big Brother, and Sopwith Camel. Jazz great Dizzy Gillespie is here, his horn an appendage to his mouth and his cheeks puffed out like a humongous blowfish. Richard Alpert (who will eventually morph into Ram Dass) is holding court. I even spot Dick Gregory, all emaciated from a hunger strike. Allen Ginsberg beats a drum and chants, while Lawrence Ferlinghetti, Lenore Kandel and Gary Snyder read their poetry. Ben

Dodging Prayers and Bullets

Levin is one of the speakers. I even note that Larry Douglas, who has lost the election for Mayor of Berkeley, is there lobbying for a platform of unity between hippies and activists; he likely envisions a Utopian love nation with himself as the head guru.

I shake off Larry Douglas, determined to contain, at least at this event, any residual remorse over Gary—basically to eschew all negative energy today. At the Be-In, food, drink, joints, cocaine, and tabs of acid are flowing freely, all in the spirit of actualizing positive transformation on a foundation of peace and love. This is a drug fest par excellence! It's rumored that even the free turkey sandwiches distributed by the Diggers are laced with acid.

In the company of Gabriel Cooper, I decline the White Lightning, the latest Acid concoction of Augustus Owsley Stanley III, but Caitlyn and Harvey certainly don't abstain. Just to tweak Gabriel, Harvey invites me to snort a little coke; it's not my first time. On this day Gabriel doesn't even care; everyone is minimally on a contact high and most people are completely stoned; plus, the vibes are far more uplifting than at a tent revival meeting. For a brief interlude, during and shortly after the Be-In, I fantasize Harvey and Gabriel might become friends: that me and Caitlyn and the guys will move into a house and raise kids in a harmonious communion of love, music, and activist politics.

It was that kind of day in Golden Gate Park.

Then, just a few months later, in the spring of 1967, almost as quickly as it gelled in Golden Gate Park on that stupendous January day, it all comes crashing down. Caitlyn, Harvey and I had spent a long and terrifying day on the coast, confronting the military police at a civil disobedience vigil at the Naval Weapons Station (Port Chicago, where the napalm is shipped from California to Southeast Asia). Filthy and exhausted when we get back to the Earl House, Caitlyn and I are accosted by that nasty shit Byron at the front desk.

"Your little drug dealer was here asking for you."

At first, I have no idea what Byron is talking about, since I almost never have to buy drugs these days. (In Berkeley grass, coke, hash and acid are as ubiquitously free and plentiful as antiwar flyers. Unless you're insatiable or into the hard stuff, you just get high on whatever free shit people are passing around.)

Noting I look confused, Byron appends, "That skinny little freak kid. He said to tell you he was going to look for Ashley or somebody like that. That was it; he barely got it out. He just left."

Oh, he's talking about Sid, I realize. *Sid might have come to let me know he's contacting his family, maybe going back to visit them to get his shit together, or something.* I pick up bad vibes, but figure they are emanating from Byron, not from the message. Since the beginning of the year, Sid has actually gotten some help from the Berkeley Free Clinic and has cleaned up his act a bit. He recently joked with me that he went to the clinic to get antibiotics to clear up the cough wondering if his body could handle "that kind" of drug.

The next morning, as usual, I get up early for classes in my shared room with Caitlyn at the Earl House. To awaken only myself, I leave my clock radio set quietly to a local station. Each morning, I typically listen to a couple of songs and a bit of news to rouse myself to a semi-waking consciousness. On this particular morning, while still in the drowsy state, I hear the following:

The University of California at Berkeley has now identified the body of the person who jumped from the sixth floor of the campus library late last evening as that of Mr. Ashton Raines. It is not immediately clear whether Raines is enrolled at the University. A wallet and some personal items belonging to Raines, including his shoes, were left on a table near the rear of the library. Though the police investigation is ongoing, the incident appears to have been a suicide. The Raines family, in Virginia, has been notified.

I'm freaking as I shake Caitlyn awake. We turn up the radio and sit listening for almost a half hour until the news segment finally comes on again. Desperately holding back an avalanche of dread and guilt for not looking for him last night, I keep hoping I have misheard the news report. No such luck.

Shortly after Caitlyn and I both hear the confirmation, Harvey bangs on our door to make sure we've gotten the news. I get dressed and go to find Gabriel, who has just heard about a jumper, but has not realized it's Sid. As a teaching assistant at the University, Gabe is able to make some inquiries. There's nothing more any of the rest of us can do.

Gabriel ascertains that the police investigation has turned up nothing, and, apparently, there was no note, though the circumstances indeed indicate a suicide. The body will be returned to Virginia, along with a letter from Charlotte Raines, found among Sid's belongings. Somehow, Gabriel is able to get me the address of Sid's—that is, Ashton's—family in Virginia; I'm grateful.

Later in the day, Caitlyn and I hike up into the Berkeley Hills. While sharing a joint we tearfully sing, "It's a Hard Rain A-Gonna Fall," the best we can do to say goodbye to our first friend in Berkeley. There's simply nothing else we can say or do. We don't even know where Sid had been living.

A few days later, I sit down and start composing a handwritten note that begins,

Dear Mrs. Raines.

I rip it up and start over:

Dear Charlotte,
I was a friend of your son Ashton in Berkeley. I'm sure his loss under such terrible circumstance must be very hard on you. I want you to know that Ashton was a wonderful person. He was my first and kindest friend here in Berkeley.

Then, for some reason, I append "the Big Lie":

I thought you should know that Ashton had recently talked to me about you. He said you were a good mother and that he loved you very much. Despite the problems with his father, he was making plans to visit you. I'm sorry things didn't turn out that way. I will remember him as a good friend. I hope you will remember him as a loving son.

I sign it simply:

Sincerely, Sky.

No last name and no return address on the envelope. It's a small eulogy for Sid and a tiny gesture toward a post-mortem reconciliation, limited to him and his mother. Sometimes I like to imagine that the letter served as an incentive for Charlotte to leave old Ashton Raines the Second. Likely, NOT.

45

SID'S SUICIDE is just the first of an ominous string of Berkeley bummers unleashed at the beginning of spring, 1967. Within the following two weeks, the buzz around the Earl House is that Kip Von Riel, our resident young gay male, is missing. A few days later, he turns up as a floater in San Francisco Bay. "Foul play is suspected," according to the police report. I'm not at all surprised, but it's still depressing as hell, especially so soon after we lost Sid.

Next, Caitlyn delivers some personal bad news. She and Harvey have been at odds, especially since Caitlyn has long passed being impressed by Harvey's press credentials and counterculture database. Fearing she was pregnant, however, she and Harvey secretly went to the Berkeley Free Clinic where the pregnancy was confirmed. (DAMN!) When the two began discussing the situation, Harvey behaved badly, expressing more anxiety about the news leaking to his family in New York than any concern for Caitlyn. He insisted she should have an abortion, which he would pay for. No, no, of course not at the Free Clinic, he assured. You see, Harvey, the self-anointed mensch, will arrange for Caitlyn to see a private doctor to be sure she gets the abortion he wants.

Caitlyn is pissed as well as hurt. Not because she actually wants to have the baby, but because Harvey is moving ahead with the abortion plans and making decisions as if he's the one carrying the baby, as if it's all about HIM. I have to step up to help Caitlyn explore her various options, exactly as I think a friend, or any decent boyfriend, should do. According to Caitlyn, "Harvey, that shit, never even offered to marry me! Not that I would marry the fucker. I can't think of a lousier father. But you can bet he's damn well paying for whatever I decide to do. After that, he's history."

After some soul searching and research, Caitlyn chooses abortion. Gabe talks to Harvey, who is more than willing to pursue the abortion angle. Unfortunately, since abortion is illegal in 1967, it isn't that simple, especially when a private doctor is involved. The male gynecologist Harvey finds in the phone book insists that Caitlyn first have a consultation with a psychiatrist, and then have the abortion at a hospital.

The doctor also gives Caitlyn, but not Harvey, a nasty Christian-based lecture on mending her loose morals and wayward behavior. When Caitlyn, seething and mortified, inquires about the possibility of a prescription for birth control, the doctor responds, "No, I will not prescribe birth control pills. You shouldn't even be thinking about sex in your condition. However, I don't particularly think you should be a mother. That's my reason for agreeing to the abortion. But legally, that won't fly. So I'm referring you to this psychiatrist." He hands her a card, adding, "There's a provision for legal abortion if the mother's life is in danger. Don't mention the boyfriend is still involved. I suggest you explain to this psychiatrist that you are so ashamed about the pregnancy you are considering suicide. That will serve as the legal justification. He'll then make a recommendation for the abortion, and I can schedule you for the procedure. I suggest you talk to the psychiatrist in a convincing way about this suicide thing. I think you will only have to see him that once. Have him call me after you've seen him. Bring your payment, by the way; he won't agree to billing you."

Caitlyn feels like she has been knocked up by Harvey and mind fucked by the gynecologist.

The psychiatrist, gratefully, is more sympathetic than the gynecologist, but Caitlyn has a hard time convincing him not to contact her family in New Jersey. He wants her to get their support, an almost laughable proposition. She practically has to actually attempt suicide to make the psychiatrist relate to her as an independent person.

Ultimately, Caitlyn gets her abortion in the hospital, without parental notification, and Harvey pays. I go to the procedure with her in lieu of Harvey. For Caitlyn, of course, the entire ordeal is humiliating and infuriating. And this is certainly the end of any relationship she, or I, will ever have with Harvey Rosenblum.

Caitlyn's abortion and Harvey's response set off an emotional avalanche in me. I start to have my doubts about Gabriel's intentions. First, I'm a little put out that he, like Harvey, was gung-ho the abortion alternative. Caitlyn furthermore points out that, while I know that Gabe is making plans to attend Stanford for his Ph.D. in the fall, he has never brought up whether I will join him there, or even how we might maintain contact.

I start making my own plans. With all my Essex State transfer credits, if I take on a heavy course load this spring and get special permission to take three summer classes, I should be able to graduate by summer's end, 1967. Of course, I will miss the formal graduation ceremony in June, but these days nobody takes such ceremonies seriously.

Although: graduation venues do afford good theater when students act out against the war or "stick it to" the establishment during the event. Ronald Reagan, notorious for the proclamation, If you've seen one giant Redwood, you've seen them all, is governor of California. Particularly chagrined at the faculty and student body of the University of California at Berkeley, Reagan and the Board of Trustees of the University are threatening to remove Dr. Clark Kerr, the president. In fact, though there have been numerous vitriolic confrontations between Berkeley students and the administration of Clark Kerr, we students are fond of wearing a button that reads <u>F</u>reedom <u>U</u>nder <u>C</u>lark <u>K</u>err.

So, though graduation could make a handy staging arena for a political action, I'll forgo it.

Without the official ceremony, I'm poised to graduate after the summer session, but whenever the topic of future aspirations arises, I come up empty. Gabriel, meanwhile, enthuses about his prospective doctoral program at Stanford (he will reside in graduate student housing, as he does at Berkeley), and gushes about a promising fellowship application he has made to join a research expedition in the Himalayan Mountains of Nepal.

Great, I think, *he plans to leave me for the Abominable Snowman.* And he actually does.

46

WHEN GABRIEL gets the invitation to join the Nepal expedition, with funding, he blows off graduate school at Stanford. He also blows me off, never raising the possibility of my meeting him in Nepal or awaiting his return.

In a cavalier gesture, however, he does promise to travel via New York on his way to Nepal, in order to meet my family in New Jersey and attend William's wedding as my escort. I'm stupid enough to be grateful he will toss me this scrap, because it feels like it will be less humiliating than turning up in Sunny Vale alone. (Hah!)

I comfort myself by rationalizing that the Nepal expedition will be all male, and Gabriel's departure will give me the space to figure out some kind of obligatory education or employment move for myself. Even though his posting is, ostensibly, temporary (just for a year), in truth, I'm left crushed and floundering by Gabriel Cooper's impending departure for Nepal. Meanwhile, Caitlyn is doing a far better job of moving on from Harvey Rosenblum. Ironically, while she was in the hospital having the abortion, she got to know an orderly named Gene Daniels. Originally from New York, Gene graduated from Berkeley a semester or two ago. Congruent with his moral and religious convictions regarding the war, he applied for Conscientious Objector status from the Selective Service. Turned down on the presumptive grounds that a practicing Catholic is ineligible to qualify as a conscientious objector, Gene acquired the backing of the ACLU to become a test case in the courts.

Since Gene's family and permanent address is in New York, where the case will be adjudicated, he recently accepted admission to a doctoral program at the University of Buffalo. Conveniently situated a few miles from the Canadian border, Buffalo, New York is a safe haven for many draft resisters whose digits have not yet been called in the notorious draft lottery. Buffalo is infinitely more appealing than scenic Saigon.

My favorite new button, a harbinger of the times, reads, "What If They Gave a War and Nobody Came?"

47

FOR THE SAKE of my academics, it's just as well Gene is a diversion for Caitlyn and the romantic intensity between Gabriel and me is on the wane. I'm determined to finish my graduation requirements during summer school, so I can turn up for William's wedding in New Jersey with a degree and a boyfriend in hand, even if that boyfriend is on his way to, of all places, Nepal.

I honestly don't know how I will get through the spring and summer terms at UC/Berkeley. I had transferred almost all my credits from North Essex State, but my excellent grade point average there was not factored in. My grades are now slipping at Berkeley, of course, but I don't much care, since I have no further academic goals.

My state of mind, as well as the state of the nation, renders grades a trivial pursuit. The social and political milieu in the Bay area is getting hairier, both literally and figuratively. Even Gabe has grown a mustache. (It makes him look more dashing than radical, but that suits him well enough.) Most of the guys, including Gene Daniels, have unkempt beards and shoulder-length hair. The ambiance in San Francisco and Berkeley is definitely shifting from lava lamps to strobe lights, from making love to "getting it on," from sharing acid to hoarding amphetamines.

At a social gathering, I indulge in a couple of snorts of coke that turn out to be laced with quinine and heroin. The bitter, burning sensation at the back of my throat quickly gives way to a wave of nausea. That incident alerts me to how readily innocence and good intentions can become contaminated in a drug-ugly atmosphere.

An increasingly militant Black Panther Party sees to it that Oakland and Berkeley maintain their political edge, but by Spring 1967, San Francisco is a quagmire of religious cults and mystical weirdness. Many musicians have hit the Hippie Highway for LA, and social activists are retreating to communes in the countryside. The Gray Line Bus Company is actually conducting tours of the Haight-Ashbury District for tourists to San Francisco who want to observe hippies in their natural habitat. (On a lark, Caitlyn and I go to the Haight to join some street activists in holding up a mirror and running alongside a tour bus so the passengers have to gawk at their own bizarre selves.)

Like everything else that's out of control, the drug culture gets intensified and hardened by the widespread distribution of STP, crystal meth and smack. This automatically puts more desperate people on the street, many dealing and hustling to support their habits. People like our friends Richie and Crystal Dew go way over the top in their indulgence, eventually even depleting the funds unwittingly supplied by Crystal's family. (Richie and Crystal moved out of the Earl House into a commune; I never learned what happened to them.)

Hepatitis and gonorrhea are rampant in Berkeley, setting off an emergency education and free treatment campaign in the schools and streets. Not even the music scene is spared. Just a few months ago we had all been participants in a communal celebration; now we are an audience targeted for financial exploitation. Caitlyn and I refuse to attend concerts with inflated admission fees and crowd control driving the events. Many musicians seem to be replacing acid trips with power trips; playing real good for free becomes playing for a fee, and a steep one at that.

In the Haight-Ashbury District, petty crime and hate crimes are as commonplace as headbands. People who once hailed each other

"Brother" now instead substitute the term "Dude." The Weathermen faction of SDS holds sway over the goals and strategies of the organization. Activists who don't support the aggressive "actions" promoted by the more militant groups are bullied and harangued. Instead of "Support Your Local Hippie" popular new buttons urge, "Kill the Pig" or "Up Against the Wall, Motherfucker."

Unlike the Panthers, who mostly operate under an organized socio-political manifesto, numerous so-called "political actions" are undertaken by enraged, sometimes deranged, individuals with dubious personal agendas, or even by loose-knit grudge groups, some paramilitary in nature. A popular "people's" slogan is, "An armed man is a free man." When I read those words, I hope my brother Luke stays put in our small town on the East Coast.

I'm pained to see the underground newspapers mourning the death of flower power and the hippies; yet, it can't be disputed that, while white youth in San Francisco blithely dance in the streets, black youth in Newark and Detroit are being gunned down in their streets.

Sadly, the social and political messages are becoming increasingly dissonant and distorted. I pick up a button with a picture of Muhammad Ali that reads, "The Vietcong Never Called Me a Nigger." It turns out that when the former Cassius Clay refused military service, his actual comment was, "I ain't got no quarrel with the Vietcong." Like a poker game gone rampant, the counterculture ante is being upped with every hand.

By the summer of 1967, the California Dreaming theme is devolving into a nightmarish, "If you're not part of the solution, then you're part of the problem," meaning that if you don't "get with" the espoused program, you are fair game for attack, robbery or various forms of abuse. Testosterone, of course, rules the roost and the discourse; free love has become synonymous with rape and escape. For vulnerable young women, especially, the ground is fertile for sprouting a pseudo-protector like Charles Manson. It's not surprising that Manson is able to assemble a tribe of willing waifs.

I'm already nostalgic for the good times at the inception of the counterculture. Earlier in the decade, it was easy to tell someone's politics and intent simply from how they dressed or spoke. That's no longer the case. Foregone is the sense of playful camaraderie inherent in the early platforms of the Merry Pranksters and activists like Abby Hoffman and Ben Levin. Guys like Tom Haydn and Dave Dellinger, the brains—the intellectuals—of the counterculture movement for peace and social justice, are being increasingly marginalized.

Manson is at the southern locus of the Hippie Highway, but my take is that things in the Bay Area are also going terribly awry, especially when formerly friendly Berkeley locals begin resonating to a bumper sticker that states, "If you think cops are pigs, next time you're in trouble, call a hippie."

The 1967 summer of our discontent sows the seeds of confrontation and chaos that bloom into Altamont, Kent State, the Democratic National Convention in Chicago, the Hearst kidnapping, and the assassinations of Martin Luther King and Robert Kennedy. Death and murder, exemplified by the Manson massacre, hover like a pall over so many good intentions.

It seems that across America the flowers have lost their power and we're marching to the drums and guns of the Tet Offensive: the war is very much with us.

48

SOME PERSONAL NEWS from the home front in New Jersey is equally laden with lunacy.

Everyone in my family knew about the gun: in Collier it had been a particular object of contention between Mama and Daddy. When he parked his truck along the road during his brief stays in Kentucky, Daddy insisted on bringing the handgun into the house, because he feared it would be stolen. When we moved to New Jersey, he contended that all long distance truckers who sleep along the highways and byways at night keep guns for protection. In Sunny Vale, however, Dad parks his truck at a company depot, so he takes to stashing his gun, unloaded but with an accompanying box of ammunition, in the glove compartment of his car.

Luke knew exactly where to find the gun, though why he took it to school was never clear. Was it to show off? To defy authority? Had he actually intended to use it? This was one of those situations in which people invariably ask, "What was he thinking?" and the inevitable answer is, "Not much."

Dodging Prayers and Bullets

Luke stuck to the story that he took the gun to Sunny Vale High School to clean and condition it in metal shop class. He never admitted to intentions beyond that, but his explanation does not account for the bullets.

Piecing together what I can, this is how the incident apparently went down that day: Luke surreptitiously showed the gun to his classmates, and within minutes the word spread and a great brouhaha erupted in the classroom. Obviously, the teacher's attention was caught.

Unfortunately, Mr. Mangino, the shop teacher, is not the sharpest tack in the school supplies closet. Instead of confiscating the gun and admonishing Luke afterwards, he dramatically hefted a chair in front of his body and forced Luke into a corner with the gun.

Luke then gripped the gun like a weapon and started fumbling with the bullets stored in his pocket. In front of a group of highly agitated adolescent boys, some of them banging on shop tables to simulate war drums, some slapping their lips to produce whooping sounds like TV Indians, and others chanting "Ton-to" to cheer Luke on, the shop teacher threatened to call the cops and screamed at Luke, "You're finished. You're expelled. You're going to Reform School—straight up the river. That's it, for you, kid." He dispatched two highly excited boys to inform and fetch the principal, which only aggravated the frenzy.

All the kids at Sunny Vale High School consider the principal the enemy. Nick-named the Rope because he's always hanging around, Principal Joe Montgomery (a formerly active United States Marine) is macho and volatile, endlessly commanding respect rather than earning it. Negotiation is not in his repertoire of responses, so instead of waiting for the cops, who would have recognized Luke as a decent kid from the neighborhood, Mr. Montgomery rushed the metal shop like an old-timey movie sheriff, joining Mr. Mangino in aggressively attempting to collar Luke in the best John Wayne tradition.

The boys in metal shop quieted down in the presence of "the Rope" and were banished to the hallway, where they jousted for good viewing positions. Alone in the room with Mangino and Montgomery, Luke's eyes darted about, wild and unfocused. He had the bullets in his left hand, but he was shaking too much to manage to do anything with them. Noting Luke's confusion and ambivalence, Mr. Montgomery charged.

`Predictably, Luke pointed the still unloaded gun at him and repeatedly clicked the trigger, while shouting, "You stay away from me! I'll blow your fuckin' head off!" Nice, Luke.

The principal knocked the gun out of Luke's right hand; the loose bullets flew from his left hand like lead confetti. A couple of boys in the hall managed to dart in and scoop up souvenir bullets before Mr. Mangino secured the remaining ones. (The bullets will become collector's items as Luke's story is embellished and attains legendary status at Sunny Vale High School.)

Meanwhile, Mr. Montgomery, in Marine reflex, brutally gripped Luke by the neck and shoved him against the wall, denouncing him with, "You little punk. You point a gun at me? You dare bring this to my doorstep?"

`The principal might have killed Luke right then and there, had the cops not arrived in time to intervene. The police officers took Luke, who was limp and sobbing, to the local precinct, where they affectionately teased and comforted him, while making him understand the seriousness of his offense. Most of the officers, after all, are graduates of Sunny Vale High and had at one time also been bullied by "the Rope." The Chief of Police called Dad, who went to the precinct and consulted with Officer Joe Fasano, his friend from our neighborhood. Dad asked Joe to confine Luke in a cell for one night, as a lesson.

Luke was barely sixteen, and William did the legal maneuvering to get him probation without reformatory time. By the time I was informed of all this, Luke had already been suspended from school.

When his period of suspension comes to an end, Luke, despite his elevated status as a heroic renegade among the other kids, announces he's finished with school. I got no information or input on any of this, likely because the intentionally obscured detail was that Luke had obtained the illegal handgun from Daddy's car. (To protect our father, William and the cops concocted a story about Luke finding the gun behind a local tavern.)

I can only imagine the psychic pyrotechnics that ensued between Mother and Dad over the actual particulars. A night in jail was likely a respite for my brother. Poor Luke. And poor Dory, my baby sister, left alone and mystified, having to sort things out on her own regarding the behavior of Luke and our parents.

After that incident, entrenched as I am in Berkeley, I'm not completely shaken when Caitlyn announces her intention to shuffle off to Buffalo with Gene Daniels to await the outcome of his case against the Draft Board. I had always felt guilty I was completing my degree at Berkeley, while Caitlyn was not even enrolled in school. Of course, Caitlyn has written a plethora of poetry and songs since we've been here in the Bay Area, and now her intention is to transfer her North Essex State credits toward an undergraduate degree in creative writing at the University of Buffalo, while Gene works on his Ph.D. in Philosophy. In 1967, the city of Buffalo is an auspice for east coast poets and artists, as well as anti-war activists. Besides, as Caitlyn reminds me, the East Coast has Tuli Kupferberg and the Fugs (a basement band with a scatological bent), and Tim Leary's League for Spiritual Discovery.

Gene and Caitlyn graciously invite me to join them in Buffalo and, even after I defer, they insist upon waiting for me to complete my B.A., so that in early August the three of us can drive back across the country together.

Gabriel, as the best laid plan between us specifies, will make a stopover in New Jersey on his way to Nepal, to join me for William and Mary Ann's wedding at the end of August. The implication is that I will later head back to California to await Gabriel's return from abroad. Beyond that nebulous supposition, however, no discussions or commitments take place between us.

There's no formal graduation ceremony when I complete my degree after summer school, so, intuitively, I pack up all my stuff and ask the University of California at Berkeley to mail my diploma to my parent's address in New Jersey. That will not, however, ever become my actual address again on the East Coast.

Part Four

East Coast

49

AFTER THAT SUMMER of working with her Aunt in Sacramento, Josie Schumacher, the friend Caitlyn and I originally traveled cross-country with to California, had returned to New Jersey. She completed her degree in English at North Essex State College and took a job as a social worker in Paterson, New Jersey. (Anything but teaching high school, my friends had all vowed.)

I know I can't handle staying with my family in Sunny Vale, so I readily accept Josie's enthusiastic offer to live temporarily (she actually said indefinitely) in her apartment in Bloomfield, New Jersey. I determine to go there to build up some resiliency before reporting for wedding duty at my family home in Sunny Vale.

Gene and Caitlyn seem really good together, and our August car trip back to New Jersey from Berkeley was rather subdued and uneventful, unlike the thrilling cross-country adventure that had delivered Caitlyn and me to California. They drop me off in Bloomfield, where it is great to reconnect with Josie. She provides juicy updates on my former classmates and professors at North Essex State.

The most shocking revelation is that, in lieu of being drafted, Tolya has enlisted in the Marines. Supposedly out of consideration for what happened to my brother Gary, Susan Duncan decided not to share this development with me. I'm as flummoxed and saddened by Susan's withholding the information as I am by Tolya's decision to enlist. Josie says that Tolya explained he had done a lot of soul searching (of course he always did) and determined, since his family had emigrated from Russia to the U.S. seeking opportunities afforded by freedom, he had a personal responsibility to protect that freedom.

What any of those lofty ideals have to do with the war in Vietnam escapes me, but, of course, that's why I'm not on Tolya's need-to-know list in the first place.

I stay with Josie almost 2 months before I even contact my family to arrange to visit on the weekend before William's wedding. I know Mother will be a jangle of nerves, but at least the focus will be the wedding, not Gary's demise or Luke's insurrections.

At my request, Josie drops me off in Sunny Vale without coming inside the house.

To welcome me home, Mother prepares a huge Kentucky-style dinner, including chicken and dumplings, beets, biscuits and corn on the cob, all my favorites. Up until the moment Flo-Anna and Lonnie Lee begin their usual fracas at dinner, I actually imagine that things had changed between my parents. Living away from my family has given rise to false hope, allowing me to dwell temporarily in the delusion of a parental reconciliation, or at least their reconstitution as adults. Visiting for a few hours on a Saturday quickly dispels all such fantasies.

I report that I have much to attend to, so I can only spend one overnight in Sunny Vale. While Dory, especially, is disappointed, no one forces the issue or questions my staying with Josie. Denial remains the family's steadfast armor against reality and hurt.

There's no way to explain to my family what my time in Berkeley meant to me. Instead of trying to make myself understood, I choose a different tack. Arranging with Dad to borrow the car on Sunday morning, I invite Mother to go to church. Of course, that means Dory, who has not yet left my side, will go, too. Though I can sense the panic just beneath her determination, Mother rises above her agoraphobia to accompany me that morning. The opportunity to attend church with her daughters prevails over her terror of leaving the house. To minimize the possibility of agitating her, Luke and Dad purposely sleep in that morning. Dory and I stay out of the bathroom as much as possible, so Mother can obsess over getting ready without intrusions. I also make a huge effort to dress "straight, " meaning not "hippie" or counterculture.

As Mother selects a pew near the middle of the Sunny Vale Methodist Church, I'm roiling with emotion about the loss of my brother Gary. Still, I manage to suspend my virulent thoughts about the military and organized religion. This day, I determine, is for Mother. Spotting us and settling in the pew behind us are William and Mary Ann, both church members. Flanked by her family at church, Mother sits up straight and peers about, proud and pleased. She folds her hands in her lap, lowers her head and, I'm sure, prays that Jesus will protect her remaining children. I turn the palms of my hands upward in my lap and meditate on the Universe protecting all sentient beings. Both Mother and I join the rest of the congregation in belting out, "A Mighty Fortress Is Our God." At that moment, we are not, I suppose, so very far apart.

The Methodist Church has a new pastor, whom our mother barely knows, but after the service, she corrals Dory, William, Mary Ann and me and steers us toward the pastor at the Meet and Greet. The minister, who will officiate the wedding ceremony of William and Mary Ann in a few days, knows the two of them well, and he has met Dory on a home visit to Mother.

So, that makes me the object of "show and tell." First indicating the others, Mother says, "Now, you know these ones." Then she takes my arm and thrusts me forward, as she carefully forms her next words. "This here's my eldest daughter, Skyla Fay. They call her Sky around here. She's always been a comfort. Ever since she was a little thang, she took care of the babies. When the Lord took Gary, it hurt her 'bout as much as me."

Whether her platform is anger, sorrow, or, in this case, praise, Mother has a way of cutting right through the bone to reach the marrow. We all stand there bawling in the vestibule of the Sunny Vale Methodist Church.

Dodging Prayers and Bullets

I know I've done the right thing by my mother, but after Sunday dinner I'm overwhelmed and antsy to get back to Josie's place in Bloomfield. William and Mary Ann volunteer to drive me, providing an opportunity for us to catch up on the family and for me to hear the details of the wedding.

I'm missing Gabriel and looking forward to introducing him to my family, even though I'm annoyed at myself for pandering to the notion that having a partner is, indeed, a measure of a woman's worth. But then, even radical Caitlyn took her guy to South Jersey to meet her mother and some of her siblings, before she and Gene "shuffled off" to Buffalo.

So, when the phone call comes in at Josie's, I'm devastated. I don't even know even how to respond, but Josie can tell something bad is up.

Gabe is calling two days before his scheduled arrival to apologize for not being able to make the wedding. His reason, or excuse, is that he's required to attend an extended orientation on Nepal in Washington, D.C. and will not be able to include a stopover in New Jersey in his itinerary.

The worst part is, in order to save face and cling to the hope Gabe is telling me the truth, I must corroborate his story and act disappointed, yet confident, about the future of our relationship. All, no less, in the context of a family wedding! And Gabe doesn't even seem to "get " how depressing and humiliating it is for me that he won't be there. It's the deepest yet of the wounds I have allowed Gabriel Cooper to inflict.

To render this all the worse, I remain deeply (if faux) romantically, in love with him. Over the next year, Gabe writes me a couple of what feel like Dear Sir or Madame letters, and that's it.

Well, at least for the next seven years.

50

RESIGNED TO STAYING on the East Coast after William's wedding and Gabe's departure, I learn that Elaine Agnewski, another friend from North Essex State days, is looking for a roommate to share an apartment. I find a job working with a high school equivalency program for adults in Newark, (at least it's not teaching at a public school), and Elaine and I locate a two-bedroom apartment that we can afford in nearby East Orange.

My adult students help me feel like I'm contributing something to the sorry state of the world, and the grant-supported salary is decent. Regarding my students, I'm astounded to learn that, before the 1960s, despite their completion of high school, the African-American women in the program had been denied diplomas in states like Mississippi. Now in their forties and fifties, they are hungry to learn everything from diagramming sentences to Shakespeare, and are eager to obtain their degrees. I am privileged to get to know and serve them.

Also, living close to Sunny Vale affords me "capped" day visits to my family, where I am more or less doing penance for having abandoned them after Gary's death. I can't do much for Luke, but Dory rejoices that I'm back. She's grateful and thrilled when I bring her to stay with Elaine and me on weekends and sometimes take her into New York to visit museums, see films, or just hang out in the Village. Dory is getting quite good at playing Caitlyn's old guitar.

After Gary's death Mother had burst apart, while Dad had pulled in tight, as if the breath was permanently knocked out of him. At times he sits rigid and disappears deep inside himself, his eyes glazed over and his mouth turned down. There's no way to ask him where he goes, but I can tell it's not a pretty place. Of course, his inaccessibility is nothing new, but the tension between him and Mother begins to take on a deeper, more despairing nature. He seems more sad and defeated than angry; somehow it's easier for me to deflect my mother's verbal assaults than his despondency. I can tell that, these days, Dory and Luke recoil more from Dad's pain than his rage. It's like he is remembering that once, as a young man, he had the hope—and the fortitude—to pursue his dreams, but now he's just marking unkindly time.

I try to spend time with Mother when Dad is asleep or not around, which is most of the time. Sometimes, when I sit sipping iced tea with my mother in her garden, I catch glimpses of a whole person beneath the overlay of paranoia, anger and regret she wears like a shield atop her vulnerable, wounded soul. I remember I once had a "Mama."

Over the years, I perpetually imagined some intervention, some miracle—human, natural, or spiritual—would restore her to the proud vibrancy she once enjoyed in Kentucky. I have come to believe that most children are born capable of evolving beyond their parents; therefore, they can't comprehend and often don't forgive the limitations of their elders. I'm trying.

It's certainly a relief not to sleep in my parents' house, but living in East Orange, New Jersey is doing little for my morale, or career prospects. My roommate Elaine is bemoaning her commute to an ESL job in New York City, and, just as the funding for the GED program I work for in Newark is drying up, I get mugged outside our apartment building.

Elaine and I decide we might as well relocate to New York, where at least getting mugged has some cachet. We take an apartment in Greenwich Village, of course. It was the beginning of the 1970s, so finding apartments was not difficult; people were pretty fluid about moving around from the Village to the Upper West Side to the Lower East Side, wherever. And jobs were plentiful, at least the kind funded by soft money.

I accept a position with the City University of New York, teaching ex-addicts and ex-offenders under a federally funded program that entitles me to free tuition for graduate school. Neither Elaine nor I are dating, so we hang out a lot with friends and host dinner parties where we smoke dope, listen to Cat Stevens music and talk politics.

Though our resistance remains active and strong, the death tolls continue to mount in Vietnam. Horrifically, we also learn that young Fred Hampton, an inspiring and brilliant leader in the Black Panther Party of Chicago, was brutally assassinated in a joint secret operation between the local police and the FBI.

Josie often drops by, usually without her wealthy new boyfriend, Barry Gilbert. We call him "the capitalist" in her presence, and "the capitalist running dog" behind her back. Caitlyn and Gene sometimes drive in from Buffalo and "crash" at our apartment. The East Coast venues for our anti-war activities are Manhattan and Washington, D.C. During one NYC demonstration against the war in Vietnam, Gene got slugged by an ironworker "patriot," when we were in Lower Manhattan near the construction site of the second World Trade Center tower. Obviously, when it comes to the counterculture, New York can be as dicey as San Francisco.

Some incredible news about Tolya and Susan filters down to me through Josie. After enlisting in the Marines, Tolya apparently tried his very best to be a good soldier and citizen, but was simply unable to come to terms with any role he might play in the war against Vietnam. Almost immediately upon his arrival for training, he became disillusioned by his peers in the Marines, who were uniformly uninformed regarding democratic ideology or any personal, social or cultural values in relation to the war. Actually, they seemed to Tolya like unformed children. The introspective Tolya found that the naïve young recruits treated the war like a big-time sporting event or some Hollywood movie they hoped to star in. (I can't help wonder where my brother Gary would have fallen on this victim-to-killer spectrum.) The superior officers, of course, harnessed the unexamined aggression of the young men in the direction of the designated enemy, in the process dehumanizing the recruits as well as the people of Vietnam.

Josie reports the turning point for Tolya came at Parris Island during a training exercise simulating a night attack by the Vietcong. To practice avoiding "friendly fire" incidents, Tolya was supposed to make judgments about when and whom to shoot during the exercise. Instead, he lost control and started shooting (blanks) at anything and everyone around him. He told Susan that, had his own mother popped up in front of him, he would have shot her. Tolya, the sensitive philosopher, was more appalled by the prospect of harming innocent people than by being shot himself. He was not afraid of dying; he was terrified of what the military was trying to turn him into.

I guess it definitely doesn't pay for soldiers to think too deeply about their acts or personal responsibility. My rage over the loss of Gary starts stirring anew.

Susan was the only person with whom Tolya shared the solution he had devised to quell his inner turmoil. When she picked him up for a fully authorized weekend leave, Tolya donned civilian clothes and they drove straight from his base in South Carolina into Canada. Tolya went AWOL from the Marines—he deserted to Canada!

None of us grasped, at the time, that Tolya and Susan would never call the USA "home" again. While splitting for Canada during the Vietnam era was somewhat romanticized (or alternately demonized), it was, in fact, a sobering and far-reaching personal decision. True, there were organizations on both sides of the border to facilitate resisters (deserters were another story), but the majority of Canadians were conservative by nature. While many Canadians opposed America's war in Southeast Asia, this did not mean they generally condoned anti-war activists or welcomed individual fugitives.

When I contemplate how conservative Susan had been in the early 1960s, I'm stunned by her present insurgence. Tolya is now classified a deserter—not a draft resister or a draft dodger or even a conscientious objector; he's a deserter. I know there will never be amnesty for deserters. Susan's acts on behalf of Tolya are far braver and committed than anything Caitlyn, Josie or I will ever do in the face of opposition to the Vietnam War. It seems a little trite to say it, but while we talked the talk, Susan literally walked the walk beside her husband.

In Canada, Tolya and Susan presented themselves as American immigrants seeking teaching positions. They did not identify themselves to their neighbors in any way related to the war. Fortunately, in dress, language and demeanor, neither of them fit the stereotypical profile of an anti-war activist. They chose to settle in a small Canadian suburb, thus attaining anonymity, of sorts, but also eliminating the possibility of a support network. Their Canadian neighbors never suspected that Tolya, a young Russian intellectual, was a deserter from the United States Marines. Tolya could never return to the United States; I wondered whether Susan could safely do so, either. Would her parents ever come to terms with this? And what of Tolya's aging, immigrant parents? I begin to understand that no American hearts or minds would emerge unscathed from the Vietnam War.

51

"A WOMAN WITHOUT A MAN Is Like a Fish Without a Bicycle." This slogan from the arising Women's Movement in America gets me through from the late sixties to almost a decade of my life.

I join the National Organization for Women, poring over the work of French feminist Simone de Beauvoir, avidly consuming the writings of Betty Friedan and Kate Millet, and I adopt Gloria Steinem as my role model. A card-carrying feminist, I subscribe to *MS. Magazine*, and resonate to essays written by women, such as "Why I Want a Wife" and "If Men Could Menstruate." In New York City, in the grand company of Bella Abzug and Florence Kennedy, I attend meetings to hammer out platforms and plan actions in support of the uniquely American take on feminism. We endlessly discuss how to interface an academic and predominantly white feminist theory with emerging Lesbian, African-American and Hispanic constituents. Typically no Lesbians, African-Americans or Spanish speakers are invited to be part of the dialogue.

Dodging Prayers and Bullets

At the time, Civil Rights, the Women's Movement, Gay Liberation and the Anti-War Movement are aligned, though not in a seamless web. We feminists of all stripes have Phyllis Schlafly and Jerry Falwell to hate, so for the most part we manage to put forth a congruent face, even if our back room talk is contentious. Careful not to get bogged down in the mire of what Abby Hoffman labeled "subpoena envy," we support the Chicago Seven while whispering that they are all white males.

In 1969, my friends and I make the trek to Woodstock, because we really do believe in love and peace and the language of music. Still, we are fully cognizant that, along with the great music there is a predominant male energy. Sure, women musicians are present and fabulous at Woodstock: it's just that the females in attendance, many as young as 15, are expected to adopt male-determined (and male biology-serving) norms of "multiple meaningful relationships." (Oh, he wears love beads but fuckin's on his mind.) In other words, the guys are happy because sex is readily available and the women are supposed to be happy that the guys are happy.

As the chant of "NO RAIN!" resounds at Max Yasger's dairy farm, Josie, Elaine and I shake our heads and look at each other. (Gene's motorcycle had broken down en route, so he and Caitlyn never made it to Woodstock.) The women in our small circle of friends understand that the Universe does not respond to negatives, and thus will hear only "Rain."

Woodstock is wet, cold, and laden with people on bad acid trips and narcissistic voyages; fortunately the music and camaraderie somehow manage to prevail. (Nothing before or since is comparable to Joe Cocker contorting to "A Little Help From My Friends"!) Woodstock is definitely, however, one of those events destined to grow in stature and gratification once you have distanced your physical self from the malodorous latrines and your emotional self from an array of delusions.

After Woodstock, I join a women's consciousness-raising group, which is a balm for the separateness I have created while repeatedly dodging hollow prayers and metaphorical bullets. Hearing the poignant stories of other women's loss, assault and abandonment enables me to feel less alone. At last I begin healing from the repressed memories of my childhood abduction and adolescent abuse, and from the senseless loss of my brother Gary during the War on Vietnam.

And, of course, there is Gabriel's desertion. I resign myself to never seeing Gabriel Cooper again, nor ever fully getting over him. I pretty much determine that I'm unlikely ever to marry or have children. Through a mutual friend, I learn that Gabe stayed in Nepal for two years before returning to Stanford to complete his Ph.D. He eventually became a professor of Anthropology at the University of Chicago in Illinois. And, I imagine, he has gone through numerous glamorous girlfriends and relationships; he is likely married, maybe even has children.

Though I have given up hope, I don't really stop thinking about Gabriel. He haunts my night dreams and my day fantasies. I wear out record grooves playing the contradictory messages in Carly Simon's song, "You're So Vain" (get out of my life, please, maybe?) and Cat Stevens' "How Can I Tell You?" (that I love you, when you're not even there). My women's group rolls their eyes whenever I make reference to Gabriel Cooper.

It's like I've put my last dime in a jammed vending machine and keep trying to shake the candy down. Not even I imagine that the proverbial worm will turn once again.

52

ONE DAY in the mid-1970s, along a street in Greenwich Village, I run into Jared Stanton, the young man I dated briefly in high school.

By now I have adopted the persona of a New York City resident—one who bustles along the street without making eye contact or greeting passersby. Still, even when city dwellers are deep in reverie or distraction, their peripheral vision is keenly attuned—they cut their eyes quickly to assess the people and situations around them. Without staring or making eye contact, New Yorkers are able to check out danger or take in an amusing diversion.

Sometimes, there is failure to identify an acquaintance, until, just as the two people are about to pass, the viewing ritual takes place. If there is recognition, both come to a full stop, turn to look at each other, and the mutuality is confirmed. That is exactly how Jared Stanton and I got reacquainted on a street in Greenwich Village, about fifteen years after we had last encountered each other during our adolescence. We cut eyes as we passed, then turned our heads to look back as our bodies glided forward in opposing directions before stopping.

"Jared?" I halt my forward movement, turn, and tentatively lift my eyebrows.

"Sky Jenkins!" he nods and points, since I have confirmed the recognition. We begin jumping up and down and hugging at the pure joy of this coincidental, serendipitous reunion.

I step back to regard Jared, shake my head and smile broadly. "I can't believe it's you! And you still look fabulous!" He has filled out a bit, but still leads with those twinkling blue eyes, the wavy blond hair, and his soft-spoken, gentle manner.

"I never forgot you all these years," he says. "I still feel bad about the way we parted. Eleanor, you know, had way too much influence over me in those days."

"Forget it," I honestly reassure him. "It was an awkward time for everyone. Your mother was a character—I mean—to her credit. Is she still in Sunny Vale?"

"Sadly, no; she had nasty recurring bouts with breast cancer and didn't make it. Just three years ago." Jared smiles fondly. "I'm certain she's up there in heaven, sorting out the riff-raff and writing reviews on all the acts of God."

By now I have figured out that Jared is gay, but I leave it to him to make the acknowledgment. As our chat continues, I clarify my own situation with, "I live with a friend from college, just a roommate, right in this neighborhood."

Jared smiles and contributes, "I live with a friend, too, on the Upper West Side, but he's more than a roommate. We're lovers. I guess you're not surprised. Michael's a gestalt psychologist, and a real patron of the arts. He kept me afloat until I was able to establish myself as a musician—classical. I'm finally doing well enough to earn my keep."

Having forgotten Jared plays the piano, I'm impressed that he has successfully pursued a career in the arts. His mother was proud of that, I'm sure. A cosmopolitan poseur in our backward small town, Eleanor Stanton probably would have even approved of the boyfriend. It was, after all, the "class" thing that had bothered her about me.

I let Jared know that I take his sexual orientation in stride. "I figured you were gay—later on, of course. Who knew anything about any kind of sexual orientation back when we in high school?"

Then I'm stunned, as Jared confesses, "Actually, it was Reverend Hansen, remember the Presbyterian youth minister? He's the one who helped me figure it out. I was getting it on with him, if you can believe that."

"Oh, shit!" I blurt out. "So was I. And Bethany Rogers was, too."

Jared drops his jaw and rolls his eyes, reporting, "And Jimmy Chapin. Remember him? Old Dan—the holy man—must have been making the rounds in those days. You know, Sky, he's the one who instructed me to call you up about coming back to the PYF meetings."

I receive that tidbit like a slap across the face. Jared had not even self-initiated our dating! Obviously, while keeping me literally "intact" for himself, Dan Hansen had schemed for the sexually disoriented young Jared Stanton to take on the public responsibility for me. What a cheap shot at me, and Jared—and the final coup for the Reverend!

Noting my embarrassed consternation, Jared quickly and sincerely adds, "Don't get me wrong. I called you at his prompt, but then I really liked you."

I barely hear the reassurance. "That bastard!" I stammer. "I wonder where he is now. We should go visit him—together."

Jared giggles. "I don't know, Sky, he's pretty rough trade! What he did was unconscionable, for sure, but at least with respect to our dating, he was on your side." I am dismissive, so he adds, "I guess it was complicated, but it was definitely mother who blew the whistle on you and me."

Jared and I decide to duck into a coffee shop, where we sit and review our divergent paths. He apologizes repeatedly for his dearly departed mother's interference in our nascent friendship. With great fervor, we laugh and confess the details of our liaisons with that dissembling sex fiend, the most Reverend Daniel Hansen. It's actually good to talk with another "victim." We speculate about who else might have had their bodies, and first blood, served up to the Presbyterian youth minister. And, we wonder if pathetic Marsha and the poor kids ever managed to escape from him.

Jared and I exchange telephone numbers. Even though classical music is not my "bag," I attend several of his piano recitals, and one weekend visit him and his partner, Michael, at their place in East Hampton. They live well. They seem well suited and committed for the long haul.

The idea of hunting down Dan Hansen stays with me for a long time. One day, Jared and I might have actually teamed up for such a confrontation. Sadly, however, just a few short years after our reunion in Manhattan, beautiful Jared Stanton encountered a force far more deadly than Reverend Dan—he was an early victim of the AIDS epidemic in New York City. Apparently, he and Michael were not a simple dyad.

After Jared's funeral, my women's group encourages me to see a feminist-oriented therapist to address the recurring theme of loss in my life—Kentucky and the mother I knew there, Del Ray, Petey, Gary, Jared, and, of course, Gabriel. I finally go into therapy where I work on some of these issues and, at long last, I let go of Gabriel Cooper.

In 1978, I have a vivid dream in which he appears, ashen, at my door. I look at him and say, "Oh, you're not what I want."

Just after that profound REM sleep assertion, naturally, is when Gabriel turns up in my life again. It starts with the following letter:

Dear Sky,

I guess you're surprised to hear from me. I hope you will hear me out, though I would not blame you if you didn't. I have never forgotten you nor failed to acknowledge, at least to myself, our amazing time together in Berkeley. I felt guilty about leaving for Nepal like that, but I was just not ready for the commitment you deserved and was too messed up at the time to understand that, much less handle it. Don't worry, I'm not writing for forgiveness or even understanding.

I'm contacting you because I recently accepted a position with the Anthropology Department of New York University, and I know you live in Greenwich Village. I did not want to let someone else inform you of this, nor take a chance on bumping into you in your own neighborhood.

Over the years I heard a bit about you from a mutual friend or two, but I honestly have no idea about any specifics, or about how you might feel about the news that I may soon live near you. Maybe it means absolutely nothing to you. I'm enclosing my phone number in case there is anything you want to know or ask me about before I arrive in June. If not, I certainly understand. It is not my intention to invade your turf, so to speak.

He signed it, *Regards, G. Cooper* and left his return address and a phone number in Chicago.

I go into a tailspin and do not mention the note to anyone that day or the next. I pore over the letter obsessively, noting that he gives no indication of whether he is currently seeing anyone in New York or Chicago. For all I know, he's married with several kids. I can't help wondering, is he trying to protect me, or himself?

Of course, when Elaine is not at home, I call Gabe in Chicago. He isn't married, at least now, and no kids are spoken of. We have an awkward, but warm conversation. Whether he is asking or not, I forgive him, and I even invite him to stay with Elaine and me while he's looking for an apartment. (I don't tell that to my women's group, and Gabe is smart enough to decline the offer.) He finds a studio apartment just above the West Village.

I'm really nervous when we agree to meet at an Indian restaurant on the Lower East Side. I still have long hair, but am dressing more upscale, even wearing a little makeup. Gabe has trimmed, though not completely shorn, his locks, and he looks just fine to me in a slim-fitted Italian shirt and dress jeans. I smile to myself when he takes out a pair of reading glasses to scan the menu. His eyes are still striking, but no longer have that hungry look—at least around me. Still, the old mutual attraction is undeniably there. We readily slip into an honest and intimate round of "catch up."

After this first encounter, we see each other casually a few more times, and are soon dating again, exclusively. The Universe must be in cahoots on this one, because within six months, my roommate Elaine decides to move out to live with a new boyfriend. Since I have a pre-war two-bedroom apartment with a fireplace in Greenwich Village, it makes perfect Manhattan sense for Gabriel to move in with me. I insist to skeptical friends that this is more of a commitment to share expenses than to stay together.

Each day it works out surprises me. I always thought love would manifest itself in a Technicolor burst (the way it did with Gabriel and me and everyone else early on in Berkeley) and then would burn on in intensity. Instead, nowadays Gabe and I struggle with our partnership in ordinary black and white, with several shades of gray. Over the years we will manage to add a few sepia tones.

Gabriel and I had been back together almost two years when I went to Washington, DC with my sister and friends for that 1983 Martin Luther King commemoration, and first met up again with Walter "Preacherboy" Perkins. Gabe would have been in DC, as well, had he not been piled over with the work of documenting his academic record for a tenure deadline at NYU.

So, indeed, on the Sunday after the Saturday commemoration where I met up with him, I called Walter to arrange the much-anticipated rendezvous.

53

I SET OUT TO MEET Walter and his friend Reuben for lunch at a Vietnamese restaurant on the Arlington, Virginia side of the Potomac. Walter's partner turns out to be a beautiful black man whose job is to maintain documents related to African-American history and civil rights at the National Archives. No doubt Walter "Preacherboy" Perkins will have quite a tale to tell.

"OK," I beg, after a few preliminaries (mostly concerning my job with City University and my relationship with Gabriel), "I have to hear your story, Walter. Sorry about the bike, by the way!" I proffer, in belated penance.

"I deserved that, and more." Walter shrugs. Then, smiling and pointing at me, "But you *were* a brat! Most folks in Collier blamed Del Ray Minix—we'll get back to him—for your shenanigans, but I knew you two were cut from the same cloth."

"You got me there," I concede, holding up two-fingers in the gesture of peace. "But what about you, not back then, but after that, afterwards, when you left?" Studying his face, I notice that his freckles have faded, but traces of a friendless, abandoned twelve-year-old have left tightened shoulders and a permanent reflection of sadness in his eyes.

"Well," Walter sighs. "You know how my mother, my sole anchor in the world, died suddenly, and that changed everything. Your Aunt Eula and Uncle Earl took me home with them, and what they did was contact my daddy. They knew who he was, because he had been staying with them when he took up with Mother. He was a mission preacher named Lester Jennings out of Tennessee. Have you ever heard of the Highlander Folk School in Monteagle?"

Puzzled, I shrug, and then shake my head. "Never."

"It's about 50 miles Northwest of Chattanooga. An unlikely hotbed of liberalism, so, of course, they were accused of being Communists. Back then, anything that had to do with union organizing or race relations in this country was labeled Communist—you know how that went. Today, if you don't follow the program, they just say you aren't patriotic or you're not a loyal citizen, or something. But, back then, it was: Communist! Anyway, somewhere along the way, Daddy met up with Myles Horton, the one who started the Highlander Folk School. Before that, Lester had been an evangelical minister, which is how he knew Eula. But when Myles befriended him, he eventually left the mission to bring his family to the Highlander community. Early in his transient mission days, of course, he had taken up with my mother at a tent revival meeting in Collier. Apparently, she was a beauty back then, and totally innocent, too. He always felt guilty about abandoning her, and me, but being married with kids and all, he thought the best he could do was send money."

"And gifts, like that bicycle!" I taunt good-naturedly.

Walter grins, "Right! Well, let me tell you, to his credit Lester Jennings and his wife, Marva—my step-mother—welcomed me into their family. They actually told their children I was their brother. You'll have to meet them all; they're good people, Sky. When I first got to the Highlander community, I was terrified, and, at the same time, overcome with grief. My gratitude didn't come 'til later. As you can imagine, I didn't know what to feel or think. But Daddy and Marva—everyone there, really—persisted in love and faith. They only spoke lovingly of my mother. For every verse of nullifying scripture I spouted—you know how I had memorized all the vile stuff—these people substituted something positive and life affirming. I'd puff myself up and declare, *There shall be wailing and gnashing of teeth. The way of the ungodly shall perish, for the wages of sin is death and the eternal burning.* They'd just smile and suggest, *But the fruit of the Spirit is love, joy, peace, patience, kindness, goodness, faithfulness.* It finally got through to me."

"That's amazing!" I spontaneously erupt.

"That's what I always say," Walter grins. "*Amazing Grace*—trite but true. By the way, the Highlander community is still going strong. What shocked me so much back then, of course, was that it's integrated. But the place was so positive, and the people were all just so—loving. There was simply no call for me to be mean-spirited and defensive. I had acquired a real family, with brothers and sisters, and I got to meet all kinds of people, including Dr. King and Stokely Carmichael, and even Rosa Parks. I was accepted, not just by Jesus, but by these beautiful, kind people who sang and danced and practiced Christianity in the light, rather than in the darkness of self-righteousness. It's like I always say, ya wanna talk about *Amazing Grace*? The Highlanders definitely saved a wretch like me!"

"Walter! That's an incredible story! *Amazing* if you will. But, c'mon, now," I protest, "you were smart, and you just needed a chance. Maudie couldn't give it to you; your daddy finally did."

"Right!" enthuses Reuben, who has been listening intently.

I nod, smile at Reuben and add, "You had the right parts, Walter—they just had to be properly assembled."

"OK," concedes Walter Perkins Jennings. "I was no dummy. But it was, in the end, love and faith in God that showed me the way. Don't forget, Eula and Earl Patrick were the ones who 'delivered' me. And I thank Mama, too. She did the best she could to shelter me. When I was born, she was like a child herself, but she made my education the priority, taking me to the bus every morning, so I could go to a better school than that one room place in Collier. No offense to your family! I know Billy Dee did real well with Miss Tackett. Anyway, Mama was just an innocent girl when she got pregnant—that was my daddy's lifelong burden to bear."

"Yes," Reuben interjects. "She and your daddy did right by you, but you have to admit, some good therapy and friendships along the way fortified all that Biblical-based love and faith."

I'm really beginning to like this Reuben.

"That's true," admits Walter. "Therapy, prayers, family, friends—and, of course, you, Reuben. This may sound corny, but I've also come to believe that Mama died in order to save me. You know, they never identified any specific cause of death, and Daddy would never have taken me away from her in her lifetime. It was her passing that set me free. A mother's sacrifice, and the Lord working in mysterious ways—the Holy Ghost is in there somewhere."

Before I'm required to weigh in on the verity of the Holy Ghost and prayer, I inquire of Reuben and Walter, "Where did you two meet?"

They exchange glances, and Walter readily confesses, "Reuben wasn't my first lover."

"Just his best and last!" interjects Reuben.

"That's so," Walter concurs. "Reuben's family is from South Carolina. I met him on a civil rights march in Alabama. He knew Bayard Rustin, the great and controversial—he was openly gay—civil rights leader and thinker."

"Yeah," reports Reuben. "Bayard rejected me, so I was easy pickings for Walter. He had leaped a mighty chasm, and I was stuck in one at the time."

Walter blushes, and we all shake our heads and laugh.

"We've been together almost 20 years," adds Walter., "But what about you, Skyla Fay Jenkins?" he teases. "Tell me about your life in New Jersey and how you ended up in the big bad Apple. And, I want to know about your brothers and—is it just the one?—sister."

I nod and say, "Uh-huh, Dora Lee, the one with me at the Washington Mall."

"And of course, I want to hear all about Flo-Anna and Lonnie Lee. Flona was always kind to me, and your brother Billy Dee's the one that got me through Mama's funeral. Please give him my regards. I should have left him that bike!"

I recount the highlights of my life, including Gary's death and more about meeting Gabriel in Berkeley. I talk about William's success, now that he's a County Prosecutor and a Republican Party official in New Jersey.

"Billy Dee always knew where he was going," I say, "but he remembered to pay homage to where he came from. For a short while after law school, he actually corresponded with Mr. Howard—you know, that attorney in Collier who helped Del Ray—about the possibility of returning to work as a defense counsel, specifically to represent mountain people in their medical and property litigations with the strip-mine companies. His title is William Dean Jenkins, Esquire now, but he still gets a kick out of telling about the days when he accompanied Mr. Howard, riding mules way up into the mountains to reach certain clients. Of course, he finally decided to marry his high school sweetheart and stay in New Jersey. He's settled in with the good life afforded a Republican lawyer in a basically conservative community. We don't talk politics, but he's a good guy and a great brother, the anchor of the family, really."

"I can't help but wish him well," Walter interjects.

"If you want to talk amazing," I go on, "the one who made the real transformation was Lucas, who, of all things, is getting rich in advertising. As a kid, he was involved in a lot of craziness, political and otherwise, but somehow he found a way to get paid for mouthing off! Both Luke and William have kids, and I just adore my nieces and nephews."

I can't talk about my parents without choking up, so Reuben shifts his chair over and drapes his arm around me as I describe my mother's mental deterioration and the discovery of Daddy's lung cancer—compliments of his childhood addiction to Chesterfield cigarettes.

"He's under treatment at the Veteran's hospital in New Jersey," I report. "But they don't hold out much hope with lung cancer. Sadly, Mother doesn't have much to offer in the way of comfort for him. Too much bad blood has passed between them."

"I'm real sorry to hear that," Walter says.

"So, that's it, basically." I shrug, leaving out a multitude of pithy minutia that forms the complex topography of my life. Indicating Reuben, I continue, "Of course, now you two have to visit me in the City to meet Gabriel. And go to New Jersey with me and see Mama and William and Luke, and meet all the kids. And Daddy will want to see you, if he can hang in a while. I'm sure it will perk him up to know you plan to visit. My sister Dory, the one born in New Jersey, would have joined me here to meet you today, except she had planned a get-together with her friends. She came out as Lesbian after college. I don't know if she knew before that. She made a special trip home to tell Mama, who acted like she didn't understand. Later Mama called me up and said Dory shouldn't talk such foolishness.

Dodging Prayers and Bullets

She didn't want to hear the truth from me, either. But then, to their credit, neither she nor Daddy ever gave Dory a hard time. The topic was never raised again, of course. Sadly, the rest of the family never acknowledges Dory's sexual orientation either, but I like to think it's more about their own inhibitions than morality. Dory keeps more distance from them than I do. So, Walter, you bring Reuben along, of course, and identify him however you want. It's your business."

"That all sounds fine," Walter nods. "And what about Del Ray Minix? And Collier? Have you been back?" he inquires, and answers for himself, "I was tempted to go back after I was ordained, but it seemed like there were too many ghosts, too much negative energy, and I would have had too much explaining to do. Can you imagine?"

"I know what you mean," I say. "We were lucky to get out. I'd-a-probably had four kids before I was eighteen."

"And I'd be sticking my hand in snake boxes at the pulpit and heaping condemnations on the likes of you!" says Walter, pointing a finger toward Reuben and then toward me.

We all laugh, in recognition and relief. Walter insists on picking up the lunch tab, and he and I agree to stay in touch.

"You both need to take a trip to Collier," Reuben concludes. "I'll go with you. It'll be a hoot. I'd like to see that place and meet some of the characters I've heard about over the years—that is, if they're still alive."

I find culling up memories of Collier as painful as thinking about my parents. My stomach clutches, as I call off the names. "Let's see, there's Eula and Earl, they're doing OK, and Eula's still doing mission work. But, as you know, their son Petey drowned back before we lost Gary. I think one of Eula's daughters—remember the twins?—lives in or near Collier with her family. And, of course, there's Del Ray, who's in bad shape, so I hear. How could he not be, with all that drinking and jail time? Hard livin', Mother used to call it. But Clytie's still hanging on. I can't think who else right now. Do you think Collier is ready for us, Walter?"

Reuben intrudes, "Of course, the real question for both of you is: Are you ready for Collier?"

54

LESS THAN nine months later, it's like Walter Jennings is expecting my call. When I tell him Aunt Eula called Mother to report that Del Ray Minix is hospitalized with advanced liver cancer, Walter volunteers to drive to Collier with me.

"Get a train to DC tomorrow," he says. "We'll leave after I take care of some things the next morning. Reuben will come along to help with the driving and give us some moral support."

When we set out, Reuben insists on sitting in the back seat of the car. As soon as we hit the road, I experience a rush of exhilaration and anxiety. I know it's better to go back to Collier with Walter rather than Gabriel this first time, since the Kentucky kin don't "cotton to strangers," and trying to explain my common-law relationship with Gabriel will be awkward. Besides, for Gabe, a trip to Collier will be about anthropology; for me, it's about family.

As for Reuben—he's Walter's problem. I admire their courage in taking on the "folks" of Collier. And I agree with Walter that Reuben can help us maintain a little psychic distance on this momentous journey. I also appreciate that Reuben brings out a playful side of Walter—helps the reverend in him drop back a bit. Effortlessly, the three of us fall into an easy intimacy of singing spirituals, joking, and talking "hillbilly." I call Walter "Preach" and he refers to me as Skyla Fay." Reuben jokes, "Just don't think up any Southern nicknames for me."

We had started off a bit late, so as we pull into Wheeling, West Virginia for the night, we rejoice that we have arrived--the real South. By tomorrow we could easily make Collier, Kentucky. Setting out from Wheeling the next morning, we are confounded first by rain, then sleet and snow. In April? It feels as if we're already off script. Following the Ohio River past town after little town, we're aghast at the levels of poverty and pollution.

By late afternoon, we cross the state line into Kentucky. The sun isn't exactly shining "bright on my old Kentucky home" as the song promises, but at least the precipitation has let up. Immediately, I'm let down. Instead of the rolling hills and lush tobacco fields I recall from my childhood, there's the clamor of large industrial vehicles, and, everywhere, the detritus of strip mining. Mama used to complain about "strangers from the mines comin' in and ruinin' ever'thang." Now I can understand exactly what she feared. The spontaneous fires dotting the huge mounds of black coal cast an eerie, desolate, almost unearthly feeling. I'm relieved we're not yet in the vicinity of Collier.

It's toward sunset when we finally approach Crockett County. My anxiety definitely mounts the first time I see the name "Collier" on a road sign. I wonder if Walter is as unsettled as I, but both of us have retreated into contemplative silence. At least the terrain here is more palatable—everything is up on the hillside, the road apparently carved right through the mountain. It's easy enough to make small talk about the obvious changes on the outskirts of town, where new construction is underway at numerous sites. Then, we spot motels: two of them! That's definitely different. Since none of us travelers feel ready to descend upon the relatives, some of whom still live in shacks without plumbing or heat, we select the Appalachian Motel for our first night's accommodation.

Now it's Reuben's turn to grapple with anxiety. The motel owners are obviously not used to seeing black people, especially in the company of white people. And the way the owners divert their eyes whenever we address them reflects their uneasiness about the business of "these three Yankee strangers" and what their relationship to each other might be. (It's obviously predetermined our alliance is unholy, whatever the configuration.)

Intentionally displaying his driver's license that identifies him as clergy, Walter registers for two rooms without indicating who will stay where. After quickly unpacking a few items, I knock on the door of the two men and beg to take a quick drive through Collier before dark.

Walter has some inner radar that directs him from the motel into town. As we cruise along, I'm shocked at how small Collier is—barely two streets that intersect to form a T. When I was a child, the town seemed daunting and far from our house. I try to explain to Reuben and Walter what I'm experiencing. "It's like, I'm seeing this place for the first time … yet, there is something familiar, like from another lifetime or something."

"I figured you'd be some kind of Buddhist," Walter teases, and I appreciate the levity.

Actually, what I'm resonating to is a recall of *this* life—a life of bare feet and second-hand clothes; of slop jars and outhouses and baths in a big tin washtub; of buttered biscuits with molasses and greens cooked in fatback; of eggs still soft and warm in the roost, and pails of frothy raw milk. Feeling a bit overwhelmed with memories and wonder, and noticing Reuben's discomfort at the icy stares we're receiving from a handful of men on the street, I suggest that we head back to the motel.

A plastic-adorned, ill-constructed anathema to contemporary life and traditional values, the Appalachian Motel does not auger well for the future of Crockett County. When I go to the lobby to look for a local newspaper, the plain, middle-aged woman behind the desk inquires about where I'm from.

"New York City," I announce, with pride.

The woman's eyes widen, "Gol-lee! What's it like up thar?"

"It's like always livin' in a party," I quip cleverly.

As the woman looks down and retreats disapprovingly, I note the religious artifacts and salvation literature in the lobby: the Bible belt. So much for that conversation. The next morning, however, I redeem myself at the front desk by mentioning to the woman that the preacher and I were born in Collier, and I still have family in this region. That makes us "folks" instead of "strangers," so there are smiles and howdies all around, even for Reuben, when he inquires whereabouts we can get some good grits and gravy for breakfast.

After breakfast, with the clouds rapidly surrendering to an intense sun, Collier seems sadder, but far less intimidating. We discover that the beautiful old Gothic courthouse, formerly the pride of Collier and where Mama worked for Papaw and later Mr. Howard, had fallen into disrepair and was torn down and replaced by an unappealing modern box. I shake my head in disillusion.

Hoping to cheer me up, Walter points out that Clayton Whitt's General Store is still standing. I smile and ask him to pull over several yards away and let me out of the car ahead of him and Reuben. "Give me a few minutes," I instruct, "then you come in. If Clayton's there, I want to see if he remembers me."

"All right," says Walter, indulgently. "Just don't steal anything!"

A craggily aged but familiar Clayton Whitt is there, and when I nod hello, he calls for his wife Mazie to come in from out back to see who's here. I'm astonished they recognize me, even before I inquire, "So, you know who I am?"

"Why, honey, you're the spittin' image of yer mama. I'd know you anywhere," declares Mazie, as Clayton nods in agreement. I motion for Walter and Reuben to come in.

"I know that-un, too," says Clayton, nodding at Walter.

He pretends not to notice Reuben, but chokes out a "Welcome" when Walter introduces Reuben as our friend. Walter and I continue to be astounded as we encounter old friends and relatives in Collier. We have not told anyone we're coming, because we understand that they would start cooking and insisting that we stay with them. We even have to beg off hospitality from Clayton and Mazie, though I do accept a pack of Teaberry gum and some molasses pull candy.

As he hands over the treats, Clayton winks and teases, "I allus tole ya you could have it!"

Stopping in at the general store turns out to be a serendipitous move, because, as in the old days, the store is a revolving portal of neighbors and passers-by. Clayton introduces me as a Reece, and the locals oblige by recalling some amusing or endearing story about Papaw or Mama. People are impressed that Wally is a real preacher now, but all of them treat Reuben like he's either invisible or must be a driver Wally and Skyla Fay have hired for the day.

A handsome young man named Travis Ray Jeffers comes into the store. He's the son of Arlo Jeffers, one of my former playmates. Arlo is now the successful head of a local construction business. I say to the boy, "Tell your daddy Skyla Fay Jenkins says that building all those lean-tos apparently paid off!" Travis grins and reports that his Uncle Juddy now lives in California, where he's trying to make it as an actor. That boggles my mind.

Suddenly there's a ruckus in the main square of town, so we all pour out of the general store to see what's going on.

Though Crockett County votes dry every year, the majority of the local men are alcoholics, and today there's an unmistakable whiff of alcohol adrift in the breeze. In front of the Courthouse, we get to observe a truly preposterous, yet apparently not uncommon, occurrence in Collier. The townspeople are crowded around a pickup truck, while an assortment of zealous citizens, including women and children, are pouring individual cans of beer into the street. The liquid froths toward the gutter, amid whoops of "Amen" from the virtuous and sighs of abject dismay from the indulgent.

Walter queries the bystanders, to discover some bootleggers have been apprehended with this truckload of illicit spirits. Lest others be tempted toward such transgression, the Sheriff is orchestrating a public ritual of castigation and cleansing.

Clayton Whitt shakes his head and snorts, "Shoot, that there's jist fer show—he's jist tryin' to skere off the competition. The Sheriff, he keeps the good stuff for hisself. He'll be a-sellin' it hisself tonight."

Walter and I are astounded, but the locals seem to take the goings-on in stride. I conclude this must be one of those cognitive dissonance things the South is so famous for. Since there is little employment of any type available in the county, the "dry vote" provides work in the trade for bootleggers and keeps the others occupied chasing or preaching at them and their customers.

Clayton motions us back into his store. He and Mazie have a direct feed into the local news and gossip, that being the major preoccupation of their lives. Old Harley Rudd, senile and helpless, has finally been placed in a nursing home by the county; Stella Adams is dead; my cousin Alma Sue Dunn, as I may have heard but had forgotten, is seriously ill with diabetes, living up the holler with a house full of young-uns and a perpetually besotted husband.

Referring back to young Travis, Clayton discloses that, in fact, his uncle, Juddy Jeffers, ran off to Los Angeles and became "one o' them porno stars." Mazie giggles and throws up her arms at that one.

I ask about Earl and Eula and learn that they have just returned from Eula's mission work in Ohio. Their daughter Sarah, one of the Patrick twins, has recently built a new house just outside of town with her husband, Chad.

Clayton hesitates, then adds, "I reckon ya know your runnin' partner is purdy bad off." He means Del Ray Minix, of course.

"Yes," I admit. "That's one of the reasons we're here. We plan to visit him at the hospital."

"First I figured he was jist dryin' out agin," Clayton continues in his slow southern drawl. "A man cain't set much store by all that hard livin'. Del Ray's followed his daddy's footsteps in that regard. He'll be right glad you all come to see him. And I reckon he cain't do ya much damage in his present condition."

The remarks transport me right back to my childhood; I resent this denigration of Del as much now as I did then. Still, I take a deep breath, invoke the bodhisattva of compassion, and simply smile. As we're leaving, I thank the Whitts profusely for the various introductions and updates, and of course, for the candy.

Heading toward the car with Walter and Reuben, Clayton calls after me, "One more thang ya oughtta know, if'n ya don't. Yer Aunt Vertie is back in Collier. She stays in that old ramshackle house—more like a shed—near the New Baptist Church, the one just outsida town, not the Freewill. That's where she lives—when she stays put, that is. She's a rambler, that one!"

I'm stunned by that tidbit. In the car, I tell Reuben and Walter of my lifelong curiosity about the mysterious Aunt Vertie. Of course, like most family secrets, it takes only the right poke to discover the gossamer it's made of.

"Why, that's no secret," shrugs Walter. "Don't you know her story?" He can tell by my widened eyes and dropped mouth that I don't know, so he continues. "You probably only know about the shock treatments—that's all people ever talked about. But the story is, Vertie got married young to a drunk—a womanizer to boot—you know, like most of the available fellers around Collier. He used to get surly and beat up on her pretty bad. I believe his name was Prater, yes, Preston Prater. Anyway, this Preston got himself killed in a car accident, and the Prater family came forward to claim the two kids. They tried to make out like Vertie was crazy and had driven Preston to drink and what not. When it seemed like the in-laws might get custody of the children, Vertie truly went off the deep end. Now here's the worst part. She killed her own babies—drowned both of 'em, right in Churning River. They shipped her right off to the State hospital at Lexington. Then came the shock treatments and the rest."

"Jesus!" I exclaim.

"Not really," Walter responds. "People. And poverty and deprivation. As a matter o' fact, I thank Jesus *ever' day* for delivering me from this place."

"Sorry," I correct myself. "I'm really not angry at God, and I got nuthin' against Jesus. I'm just blown away by that story. Especially after all these years of wondering, and here you knew all along."

"You never asked me," says Walter. "Probably a good thing, back then. I mighta up and taunted you about it. Anyway, if you wanna see Vertie, we'll make a point of it. And I'm not offended by your Jesus expletives! It just shows you're still thinking about Him!"

There it is again: Christianity, the shadow that has tagged along after me all my life. I never found Jesus in any church, and I certainly won't confess to Walter or Aunt Eula my disinterest in the concepts of salvation and surrender to God. And, while the Christian tenet of "you are accepted" seems like a good one, I wonder how Walter justifies the fact that homosexuals aren't accepted in most Christian communities. In Collier, neither are Jews, Poles, Arabs, or even Wasps accepted. Black and Latino people don't even exist.

But, of course, the likes of Reverend Dan in Sunny Vale and Brother Lester Jennings, the roving evangelist who begat Walter, are protected by the fold. From time to time, I glimpse the Christian goodness in people, or maybe certain good people just happen to be Christian. But the notion of Jesus as the son of a God who immaculately impregnated a young virgin? I find that an entertaining conceit, at best. I guess that's why they call the practice of religion 'faith.' Which is not to say I don't find life itself awe-inspiring. The idea of God is a powerful, maybe even necessary, construct. It just took me nearly a generation of losses, wars, and introspection to appreciate the difference between being a religious person and being a spiritual one.

I grin and lift my eyebrows, and quickly divert the conversation toward Reuben, "How ya doin' there, Reuben?"

"Around these parts? You bet I'm thinking 'bout Jesus, and praying, too!" he answers.

"Let's head on up to Sow Holler to see Eula and Earl," Walter suggests. "You'll be welcome there, Reuben. Eula will be more concerned with your soul than your skin color, so you'll fit right in."

"And I'll behave," I promise Walter.

When I catch sight of the Patrick farm, my mood lifts. As we emerge from the car, Aunt Eula calls out, "Praise the Lord!" Uncle Earl, in his overalls and work boots, looks just as I remember him, except when he smiles—his crooked teeth have been replaced by dentures, which no doubt improved his health but, in my opinion, diminished his features. Aunt Eula, big-boned and droopy-bosomed, wears black-rimmed glasses now and her graying hair is pulled back in a tight bun. Still, her face is open and smiling.

If either she or Earl is shocked at the sight of Reuben, neither one lets on. (I think, *at last, Christians willing to take in the proverbial wayfaring stranger*!) Of course, Eula is used to Black preachers and is accustomed to visiting the ill and retrieving lost souls in surrounding (always segregated) minority communities.

Earl and Eula gladly shepherd the three of us into their home, and in no time set a great spread of food before us. The lengthy prayer before the meal informs me that God (and the devil) are still very present in Collier, Kentucky.

Like everyone else in Collier, Aunt Eula and Uncle Earl never ask why Walter and I have come back. After the meal, without prompting, Eula scrambles to fetch her entire photo collection. She does not reference anything by age or date; time is marked by recalling incidents, especially, those related to death, births or illness: "When you had the whooping cough …" "When Ila Sue was born …" "That time when Papaw's house caught afire …" There's a yellowed photograph of Papaw Reece and all his children that must have been taken shortly after Mamaw Reece had died. Eula carefully identifies each child, and I squint to see if I can recognize any of myself in the image of my mama.

Eula has many stories to share. I cleave especially to those about my mother. Walter and I don't need to initiate or direct any of the conversation. Memory after memory pours forth from my elderly Aunt. As with other kin we will meet, there's no mention of the future; scant attention is paid to the present (Are y'all OK?); and, there's a pervasive preoccupation with the past, but just one generation back. (Whenever I ask older family members where our ancestors are from, they invariably answer, "From Kentucky, always from Kentucky.")

Eula shows us a photo taken of my mother posing with her sister Clytie and Walter's mother, Maudie, at the homeplace. All about eleven or twelve years old, the trio is perched on the stone ledge in front of Papaw's house with their legs crossed and their arms interlocked; their faces are innocent and hopeful, like they will be friends forever and there will always be happy endings. I can tell Walter is as moved by the photo as I, and Aunt Eula graciously honors my request to borrow the snapshot so that I can have copies made.

Then Aunt Eula smiles at me. "Yer mother was somethin'—so proud, ya know. Flona went to work before she even finished high school. Lawd, she didn't wanna be dependent on nobody. We allus said Flo-Anna don't skere easy. When yer daddy run off up North, she worked to pay off all the debts and raise you up in that little ole shack. Why, ever'body knew Flo-Anna Reece Jenkins, here in town and back up in the hills. She was allus dressed so fine and was smart as a whip. She 'minded ever'body o' Bette Davis, ya know. After he got ta drinkin', Papaw wouldn't a-held that County Clerk job fer a day without Flona ta back 'im up."

Can that be my mother that Aunt Eula is extolling? My mother, who in New Jersey doesn't have a friend outside the family? My mother, an agoraphobic who lives among the children and ventures out only to her vegetable patch? My mother, whom I envision in house dresses purchased from mail order catalogs? Torn between pride in the past and loss in the present, there's not a word I can utter.

Aunt Eula also talks about my daddy. "Lonnie Lee was so much smarter than them other fellas that hung around. He could fix most anything, and he drove that truck with pride. I reckon ya know about him ridin' that bicycle backwards 'round town. Why, I ain't never seen nuthin' like it afore nor since. And Law', he courted Flona like them other fella wouldn't know how. Yer mother, she was proud—she wouldn't take jist anybody, y'know."

Such a different perspective on my father! To me, he's a simple, sad, usually bad-tempered truck driver—not even an eighth grade education, and always poor. "No account" is what Mama labels him. (She has forgotten to value his wit and ingenuity.)

Yet, in his youth Lonnie Lee had impressed Mama by informing her of his personal vows never to take to the bottle, nor to go to prison, nor to desert his family. I guess you could say Daddy was successful with the first promise, walked the line on the second, and succeeded, on a technicality, on the third—that is, he left numerous times, but eventually always came back. Over the years, whatever money Daddy managed to lay hands on, he spent quickly; if we happened to be around when the money crossed his palm, he shared it freely with Mama and us kids. If he regrets his liaison with Flo-Anna Reece, he never gives voice to it. At the end of his life, Lonnie Lee has little to show for his hard work or good intentions, but considering where he came from, I reckon my daddy did the best he could. Mama, she's not so forgiving of him.

Aunt Eula has offered up a primal affirmation of family, and I'm left to mourn the lost children inside my parents and the parents lost to me. By the time Eula starts recalling Maudie, I'm so overcome by regret and pride that I can barely pay attention. I know Walter is hanging on every word, though.

Uncle Earl picks up on our deepening sorrow and provides a digression. Rambling on about the crooked sheriff and his deputies, Earl is a caricature of a slow-talking hillbilly man. He reports Papaw held the deed to some mineral rights on the property of a man named Grub Darnell. A coal company found the deed and, according to Earl, is "skulkin' 'roun' tryin' t'git the family to sell out." He explains strip mining to us, emphasizing the negligence with which the land is divested of its resources—and not for the benefit of those with the entitlements.

I recall my mother saying, "Money has a way o' stickin' to money." I explain to Eula that we plan to visit Del at the hospital in Stony. She's pleased by that, and is also glad to know we intend to head up into Coon Holler to see Clytie, who, Eula reports, is in a bad way.

Walter knows that the house where he once lived with his mother has long been razed and replaced with a restaurant, but Earl assures us that we can at least take a look at the land where the old Reece homeplace used to stand. He says the property has not yet been developed, though the house burned down a decade or so ago.

When I bring up the idea of seeking out Aunt Vertie, Eula turns somber, shakes her head, and says, "I wish ya luck findin' that one at home, let alone gittin' anything outta her."

Earl gives us directions to the hospital in Stony, but trying to get directions to Clytie's place, "back up the holler," is more of a challenge. There are no street signs, traffic lights or landmarks. Places are "over yonder" or "up the lane" or "past one yella house, then two white houses, then one ole broke-down barn." With a grin, Earl suggests, "Y'all kin try askin' when ya git right close. O' course, bear in mind, mountain folks figure, if'n ya belong thar ya know where thangs are; otherwise, maybe it ain't in anybody's interest to enlighten ya."

Earl also discreetly offers Reuben an alternative to the dubious notion of meandering about the holler. "If'n ya don't mind lendin' a hand here and there, I kin show ya 'round the farm and tell ya a bit about the mountains." Reuben, who was raised on a farm in South Carolina, gratefully accepts Earl's offer, while Walter and I set out first for Sow Holler, then for Coon Holler in search of Clytie. The last stop will be a visit with Del Ray at the hospital in Stony.

I don't ask for directions to Sow Holler because I have such vivid memories of hiking up the lane to the homeplace I'm sure I can find it on my own. Walter parks the car at the edge of town and we begin our ascent. There are no sidewalks or well-manicured lawns to ramble along—just weeds and mud and gutted pathways and old ramshackle houses. We quickly ascertain there's an unnatural hush and a dearth of faces, as if bad news is about to be delivered and might bypass those who lay low. A couple of old mangy dogs lurk in the dust and a coonhound howls in the distance.

We understand what such stillness signifies: strangers afoot. We can sense eyes peering from behind crooked window frames and ragged curtains, but no voices call out or faces appear. I attempt to assume a polite and friendly posture to indicate Walter and I are neither dangerous nor lewd. Mountain people, I know, are not unfriendly—just extremely shy and cautious.

Eventually, we wander toward an area of new construction, but I know it can't be the homeplace land, since Earl assured us Papaw's property has not been reclaimed. I'm convinced this is the vicinity, however, so Walter and I work our way through some nearby weeds and brambles, forging anew what might have once been a path. I try to picture where things would have been—the house itself, the smokehouse, the cornfield, the outhouse. The layout looks about right, but how can I be certain?

My eyes dart about for some vestige of assurance, until, suddenly, I gasp, "The wall! Walter, the wall!"

He helps me brush aside some foliage and dirt to expose a slab of stone about 3 feet by 4 feet. I have literally unearthed my verification! That stone ledge stood in front of Papaw's house and served as a prop in almost every family photo taken at the homeplace. Everyone has posed in front of it or on top of it. As a child, Billy Dee once broke his arm when he toppled from it.

Walter recognizes it as well as I. We feel like the Howard Carter expedition stumbling upon the marker for King Tut's tomb. Walter steps back a bit so that I can stand in meditation, solemnly paying homage to Papaw and the refuge that was long ago known as the homeplace.

We walk back to the main road, both of us deep in contemplation. It's time to drive into Coon Hollow to seek out Clytie Minix. Right off, we have trouble finding the unmarked turn. Feeling frustrated, we finally park the car along a ridge and start hiking again. Once more the local inhabitants make themselves scarce, while keeping us on their radar. I felt intuitive about finding the homeplace, but it will take more than divining rods to guide me to Clytie. I take a deep breath and regard the scenery.

Almost in defiance of the detritus created by the human inhabitants of the area, the hills are green and lush, the blossoming wild flowers elegant and delicate. We peer into the yards and porches that, sadly, look exactly the way old photos and movie sets depict such abject poverty: broken bottles and discarded rags; rusted machine parts; gutted and abandoned cars; tin wash tubs, washboards and broken-down wringer-style washing machines; rain-bloated mattresses and sofas with the springs and stuffing bursting and spilling over like exploded seed pods.

The debris of despondency is how it registers in my mind. I recall a line from the Robert Frost poem, *Death of the Hired Man*: *Nothing to look backward to with pride, nothing to look forward to with hope.* Eventually, we spot a weathered man and worn-out looking woman with four grimy, skinny little towheaded children on the porch. A shotgun is propped against the doorframe.

Walter calls out, "Howdy" and the man nods. Encouraged, we scoot partially down the embankment to try to talk to them. I gladly let Walter take the lead and do the talking. He announces, "We got family in these parts. Use-ta live in Collier ourselves. We're tryin' to find Clytie Minix—I believe her cabin is somewhere around here. Can you maybe direct us?"

The kids gather in a tight silent knot around the woman, who keeps her head down and eyes averted. The man stares at us for an uncomfortable, interminable 15 seconds, then responds, "I reckon if'n y'all use-ta live here, ya knows where ta find yer kin." All I keep thinking is, Reuben made the right decision to stay with Uncle Earl.

Walter smiles and tries, "It was a mighty long time ago, and lots has changed."

"Maybe fer y'all," the man counters, but then, thankfully, grins. I guess we have passed the test. He points up the mountain. "Go on up 'round that next ridge and likely you'll find it."

"Thank ya all kindly," Walter chimes, as we nod simultaneously like Tweedle Dee and Tweedle Dum.

We scramble back toward the road while the family remains rigid and staring on the porch, bringing to mind, despite the century, a museum diorama I once saw documenting early American pioneer life. Heading further up the mountain on foot, I feel as if I'm in some lawless, uncharted wilderness; anything can happen and we might never be heard from again. I start to worry about the car, but decide not to mention it.

Finally, some houses, old barns and overgrown fields come into view. Thanks to Walter's residual memories, we're able to locate Clytie's shack, where it's perched along the edge of a steep cliff. We notice that there are no windowpanes or curtains, only sheets of plastic taped over the window openings. The front door has been partially repaired with cardboard. It's 1983, so Clytie has some electricity, but no heat, and no hot water or indoor plumbing.

As we draw close, my anxiety mounts; I start calling out, "Aunt Clytie, it's me, Skyla Fay."

She is seated on the porch in a rocking chair with a shotgun propped diagonally across the chair arms over her lap, the gun aimed in our direction and her hand hovering above the trigger. As soon as she recognizes us, Clytie sets the shotgun aside and begins nodding and smiling, lifting her arms and praising the Lord. We climb the broken stairs and stand back respectfully while she deftly uses two stick canes to pull herself up. She wants to feed us, of course, and to put us up for the night.

When I mention we intend to see Del Ray, she starts weeping. "I reckin' y'all will git to see him; he cain't run off now. I figured he was at the hospital takin' a cure, but the pastor says he's a-fixin' ta die." Clytie's eyes begin to dart about and she spews forth a venomous diatribe against *They*. "Ever since Del Ray's been gone, *They* been skulkin' round here at night. Me and my chile has surely been forsaken. *They* beat out my windows. And I know *They* is controllin' Del Ray's mind."

I already know about *They* from my own mother; the identity of *They* depends upon who is perceived as the enemy at the moment— the devil, the in-laws, the neighbors, the Catholics, even the law.

"Doesn't Del have a wife and some kids?" I inquire.

Clytie grunts and responds, "Sech as it is. Her low-down brothers been a-robbin' Del Ray's house, gittin' at 'im while he's down. They took all his thangs, and stole his paintings, too. It cain't be hepped. The sheriff, he won't do nuthin' fer the likes of us."

I'm devastated, and can only mumble, "I'm so sorry." Walter graciously offers to pray for Del and Clytie.

"I 'preciate that." Clytie nods. "I reads the Bible and prays ever day. I allus done good as far as I know how. That's my only salvation. Delford Ray, it seems like fer most of his life, he's been forsaken. But he talks to Jesus now. Done a lot a back-slidin' in his time, but that boy had a hard life. I ain't a-sayin' old Rufus deserved to die thataway, but, fact o' the matter, he warn't much of a daddy. And no husband a'tall. The drink claimed him, jist like my boy."

Then Clytie, in the true spirit of the mountain woman, pulls herself together. She begins apologizing for the "state" of her house and her health.

"I cain't git out no more," she informs us, "an I don't allow jist ever'body to visit."

She looks and sounds so much like my mother that that I'm a bit unnerved. On the other hand, I know how to deal with her—just drink the proffered tea and focus on the family. Soon Clytie is jabbering away about kinfolk and old times, momentarily engaging in rational conversation. I notice that her home is filled with religious books and drawings, some done by Del Ray. (All I can think is, all that potential come to naught.) From among the dust and mouse droppings, Clytie pulls out her photo albums, wipes them off with a rag and invites us to look. Sure enough, in numerous photos people are posed right there at the rock ledge in front of Papaw's house. She begins recollecting that I was "a feisty little thang with that odd eye."

When Clytie calls off Vertie's name in one of the photos, I shamelessly probe, "How d'ya think she's doin'?"

Clytie shakes her head. "Vertie, she waren't no criminal. Them takin' her away in handcuffs thataway, that's the disgrace. Why, she was nacherly distraught over them Praters a-tryin to take them young-uns away. They shoulda jist let her be. It's upta God to judge her deeds. Afore that business, Vertie was real smart. Problem was, she didn't know how to control her powers." Then Clytie whispers, just the way my mother does, "They gives her shock treatments!"

Apparently, the righteous indignation that seethed within the hellfire and brimstone foundation of Collier had spewed to the surface over the drowning of Vertie's children. People called for a murder trial, scurrilous editorials were written in the local papers, the entire Reece family was shamed and harassed. For the kin, it was a blessing when Vertie was taken away. Unfortunately, because no one in the family will talk about what happened, the psychic memory lingers all the more venomously within the Reece collective unconscious. The elders, it seems, unanimously determined it better to deny and repress than try to soothe that much anguish and raw humanity. A generation of children likely suffer disaffection from that determination.

Examining the rickety old piano still standing in Clytie's shack, Walter requests that she play. She humbly agrees and sings us some sad hymns about the suffering of Jesus. Before taking our leave, we lug up a good supply of water for Clytie from the well down the lane. Apparently, there are neighbors and church people who generally look in on her and keep her in supplies, especially now that Del Ray is incapacitated. Clytie is grateful that we are headed to the hospital in Stony to see him. We offer to bring her along, but back off when we see panic in her face at the suggestion of her leaving the house.

Walter and I leave knowing we have treated Clytie lovingly, and that she has courageously given to us of her life, in its direct simplicity and complex insanity.

55

HE'S ALONE and asleep when I peek into the hospital room. His face is pale and puffy, and I can see his dark curls are starting to grow out a bit. I stand at the foot of the bed and tentatively whisper, "Do you know me?"

His eyes are dull and glazed, but they still reproach me for having to ask. "Skyla Fay Jenkins," Del Ray responds hoarsely. "I loved you all my good-for-nuthin' life."

I shift forward and place my hand upon his cheek, sounding my lament. "I feel troubled seeing you like this."

I can tell it's an effort for him to project his voice, but he persists, "Gal, you ain't got nothing' to feel low about. I ain't a-painin'. And I'm mighty pleased you come to see me." Looking past me toward the door to the hallway, he inquires, "Have ya got you a husband out there with you?"

"No, Del. I never did marry." Then, adding quickly, defensively, "But that was by choice. I got me a man, though. Up there in New York City."

Dodging Prayers and Bullets

I find myself falling into his speech pattern. It's confounding how, when northerners go south, they immediately imitate the southern dialect, but the opposite does not seem to hold true. No matter how long a southerner lives up north, the telltale trace of a southern accent will linger.

I want Del to know about me, but feel guilty about my good fortune. Worse, and shamefully, I don't want to feel his emotional pain. I sense his neediness—a great abyss of loneliness and despair I dare not broach. Finally, I shake off my narcissistic anguish and rely upon a buffer, "You'll be real surprised about who I came down here with. You know him as Wally Perkins."

Del cocks his head and inquires incredulously, "Preacherboy?" Then he catches himself. "Oh, I better hush up 'bout that. Waell, bring him on in. Tell him I ain't a-totin' no gun!"

We both laugh and I feel like I should do some explaining. "He's a real preacher now, and I believe a good one, too." I roll my eyes. "No more of that hellfire stuff. Goes by the name of Walter now." I lean in close and confide, "Got hisself a boyfriend, too—a real nice feller." I don't mention that Reuben is a Black man and has accompanied us on the trip.

Del Ray halfway grins through a grimace. "Well, I kin believe 'at. I never did know what to make o' that un. But if'n you say he's all right, I reckon that's good enough fer me."

A nurse enters the room with a pushcart, announcing it's time for Del's medication. I step out into the hall, figuring it's the right time to retrieve Walter, who has retreated to the hospital lounge. I shake my head and rotate my extended hand to indicate the visit is hard and Del is faring poorly. I assure Walter Del wants to see him.

As the nurse is leaving, she pauses to inform us that Del will likely fall asleep soon. Walter enters the room, goes straight up to Del, and takes his hand, saying, "It's been a long time Del. I'm praying for ya."

"I'll take it," Del replies, looking worn out and dispirited after the blood work and injection. "Don't seem like much else is a-workin'." He sighs and looks toward me, adding, "I been runnin' against the wind muh whole sorry life. Allus a-fixin'-to, never a-doin', if'n ya know what I mean. I reckin' I waren't meant fer this here world. Worst of it is, after what I done, I ain't even sure 'bout the next un."

Not prepared for the directness and intimacy with which Del addresses me, I protest, "You just never had any real chances, that's all."

I know Del is bright and intuitive, and even had some formal education in prison. But I can tell he's been broken in a way that good intentions can't fix.

Walter is also moved by seeing Del so deep in the valley of affliction. He tries, "There's always room in the House of the Lord; I can assure you of that, Del. You acknowledged your mistakes and you've paid heavy for them. I heard you always looked after your mama, too. That's somethin'. And I understand you've got some young-uns yourself."

"I had me a wife," Del laments, "but she done run off. Folks allus said she waren't much good, no ways. Still, I reckon I got to dependin' on her too much. I'm use-ta her sleepin' up against my back and now it feels so cold there." He slowly shakes his head, and then adds, "She ain't even called me here at the hospital. She was jist fourteen and already had one chile when I married her. Now she got five chillern she says are mine, but I don't claim but two of em."

I can't help knitting my brow at the sadness of hearing Del talk like his daddy, Rufus.

It's like he reads my mind when he remarks, "Maybe when I git ta feelin' better, we can all hike up into the holler—up thar whar Rufus use-ta hide his still. You allus was curious about that, Skyla Fay."

"Yup, we'll surely have to do that!" I lie, knowing I will never see Delford Ray Minix again, alive or dead. But then, if the truth be told, I had left him for dead a long time ago.

Del, never one to let bullshit fester, summons his strength and looks directly into me, "You're the own-liest person I ever loved, and I ain't ashamed to say it." Then, he gracefully includes Walter with a side glance. "I'm grateful to y'all fer a-comin' here. I wisht I coulda followed either one o' ya off."

The words sting. I understand that "getting out of Collier" meant more for Walter and me than the simple act of leaving. Both of us were afforded the opportunity to reach out for a new way of being in the world.

Walter takes each of our hands, and asks, "D'ya mind if I say a few words?"

Del manages to wink at me in little boy awkwardness and tease, "Skyla Fay ain't much about prayin'. I know that much."

"OK, I'll meditate, Del Ray Minix! It's the same thing." The levity is a relief, and I form a circle by taking his other hand.

I'm surprised Del has more in him. "I done made my peace with Jesus, ya know. Aunt Eula saw to that. I cain't say God has spoken ta me, but I talk to Him ever' day. I won't ask ya ta pray fer my soul, Skyla Fay, but I do ask ya ta remember me."

I'm choked up and can barely eke out, "I love you, Del. You were the best part of my childhood." As Walter "Preacherboy" Perkins Jennings bows his head and gently petitions the Lord on behalf of all us Collier kids, I am awash in constant sorrow and eternal hope.

Del is sound asleep when Walter finishes the blessing and gently releases our hands. I'm grateful, as there are no more promises to make or keep. I drop Del's hand and lean down to kiss him on the forehead before Walter and I slip out of the hospital room.

I'm ready to leave Crockett County, and I know Reuben is more than prepared to make tracks out of the entire territory. On the way back to the Patrick farm to pick up Reuben, Walter doesn't utter a word about God.

56

WE KNOW Del will not hang on much longer, but despite Eula and Earl's invitation to stay with them to await the passing, we determine to head out. We've caused enough of a ruckus in Collier by just showing up to visit. Del will certainly understand our decision to skip the religious trappings of a southern funeral. It's time for us to go.

"I'll surely be a-prayin' for y'all," Aunt Eula assures us. She's not about to let me get away, however, without posing The Big Question. "Skyla Fay, honey, have you been saved?"

I take a deep breath and respond, "No, Aunt Eula, but I been rescued more than once, and I believe there's some grace in that."

Aunt Eula smiles and takes my hand. "I don't doubt it a bit. Bless you, chile," she says. I'm 38 years old but still feel like a 10-year-old taking succor from a kindly elder.

Walter steps forward and requests that once again we join in a circle of prayer. There, on Eula's front porch, we bow our heads and raise our interlocked hands straight up above our heads, calling upon

Dodging Prayers and Bullets

God—or the Universe, whatever—to sustain us in our travels and intentions.

As we pull away from the Patrick farm, I am drained and done, but Walter insists we take care of a bit more business. "You've entered the house of resolution, so ya might as well look behind all the doors," he insists.

We head back toward Collier to seek out Aunt Vertie's residence. We wonder if Clayton Whitt was right about where to look for her. Reuben waits in the car, while Walter and I examine what appears to be an abandoned shed near the New Baptist Church. There's no answer when we knock at the door and call out, and the place seems pretty forlorn. Walter checks the beat-up mailbox and finds some official-looking mail with the name Vertrice Prater on it. We look about for more clues. Noticing an elderly man keeping an eye on us from his front porch across the road, we walk over and introduce ourselves.

The man speculates, "Vertie, she's likely out a-rambling. No tellin' when she'll turn up." Then he considers us a bit. "Or maybe she got word that y'all was comin' 'round and done hid out. She ain't real sociable, that un." He considers us again and tags on, "Unless'n she's appealin' to yer charity." Apparently, these days Vertie is Collier's version of the shopping bag lady. "Y'all kin leave her a note in that thar mailbox, and she might ta pick it up," the neighbor suggests. Then he addresses me, "I kin see youz a relation. You Reece gals all favors one 'nuther."

I'm unable to stifle my contamination by genetics anxiety. Could "favoring" imply that my generation will inevitably become religious fanatics or social degenerates suffering from borderline personality disorders? I'm ashamed of thinking that way, so I quickly divert the conversation toward my grandfather. The neighbor accommodates.

"Lacy Reece? I surely knowed the man. Thar warn't nobody could beat him in a election. He won the County Clerk seat ever' time he run. Lacy, he tipped the bottle a bit, ya know, but he was jist too good fer his own good. Give away all his money, ya know. He never could collect debts from them poor people. He'd give 'em his own money, right outta his pocket."

That perks me up, so I write a note including my address in New York and leave it in the mailbox for Vertie. I want to leave her some money, but decide it might be better to mail her something later. Feeling stirred up and unsettled from coming up empty on Vertie, I suggest to Walter that we head over to the Freewill Baptist near Churning River and the Jackson Bridge, so I can forge my goodbye to Collier standing upon the little piece of land behind the church that once served as my playground and home.

The Jackson Bridge still looks like it's made from an erector set, though it's been bolstered up in more than a few spots. I can picture Del Ray pitching that bicycle into the briars on the lower bank of the river near the bridge. Churning River is flowing steady and clear, once again beckoning me to dip my feet and skip a few stones. We park in front of the Freewill Baptist Church, which stands exactly as I remember it—I half-expect the caretaker, Harley Rudd, to amble on out, broom in hand, to greet me. Walking around behind the church, we see a bulldozer parked beside piles of dirt and a heap of garbage—evidence a construction project is about to get underway where our shack, topped by Stella's Second Hand Store, once stood.

I realize this will be my last opportunity to stand in reminiscence at this spot before some arbitrary contemporary structure obliterates my childhood landscape. Reuben and Walter hang back and turn toward the river to afford me a bit of time for contemplation. My childhood flashes before me. Not all the memories are sweet—the floods, the "disgrace," a rusty nail in my foot, taunts from "Preacherboy." Mostly, though, I recall me 'n' Del 'n' Gary romping, giggling and scrapping, our bellies full of green apples and black walnuts. We had bare feet and hand-me-down clothes, and sometimes Santa didn't find us. But we also had imagination and freedom and the out-of-doors, and no such thing as kindergarten or adult authority to cramp our style. I didn't know that, in some books, it didn't constitute a proper upbringing.

Taking a final survey of the Baptist Church, Churning River and the Jackson Bridge, I begin to understand that the purpose of my journey was beyond seeing Del Ray Minix for the last time. I needed to review my story, to revisit my childhood, to return to Collier, the place of my birth, not in shame, but in humility. I needed to experience the people and the hills from my adult self. I needed to honor the spirit, if not the religion, of the place. My mother had very carefully planted the mountain roots inside me, but I had not nourished them, had not allowed their flowers to bloom in the sunlight.

I returned not to say "hello-goodbye" to my old Kentucky home, but to say "welcome" and to depart while its people and ways are at rest within me. "Y'all come back," they say.

I did, and I'm glad.

About the Author

One of seven surviving children, Karen Beatty anchored her early childhood in a shack near the Licking River in Eastern Kentucky. Her academic education began when her father uprooted the family from Appalachia to Bound Brook, New Jersey, just off an outlet of the Raritan River. In the late 1960s, Karen served as a Peace Corps Volunteer in Thailand.

She then settled in New York City, where she got schooled in life, attained a Ph.D. in Counseling Psychology and raised an amazing daughter. Her life has been defined by travel and activism on behalf of women's rights and international peace and justice. At John Jay College of the City University of New York, Karen trained human service professionals and served as a trauma-informed counselor for police officers, fire fighters, veterans, and immigrants.

Karen likes her music gritty and soulful (think Melissa Etheridge or Tom Waits), and there is always a song in her head and a pen in her hand, whether she is delivering medical supplies to Cuba or trekking the mountain jungles of Laos to converse with Buddhist monks in training. She loves exploring New York neighborhoods and, during summers, enjoys body surfing down the Jersey shore.

You Might Also Enjoy

CARNIVAL FARM
by Lisa Jacob

When a local veterinarian decides to take over a traveling carnival's petting zoo, she doesn't realize the insanity behind the scenes.

STILL LIFE
by Paul Skenazy

When his wife, Edie, dies, Will Moran abandons all he used to be, and do, to paint still life canvases of rocks and driftwood on the walls of his house.

SMITH: AN UNAUTHORIZED FICTOGRAPHY
by Jory Post

In this kaleidoscopic, episodic joy ride, Jory Post treats us to thirty interviews that may or may not be real, with an array of "ordinary" people who turn out to be anything but.

Available from Paper Angel Press in
hardcover, trade paperback, digital, and audio editions
paperangelpress.com

Printed in the USA
CPSIA information can be obtained
at www.ICGtesting.com
LVHW091457271023
762201LV00012B/1439

9 781957 146546